PENGUIN BOOKS

MODERN IRISH STORIES

Ben Forkner is professor of English and American literature at the University of Angers in France. A graduate of Stetson University in Florida, he received his Ph.D. from the University of North Carolina at Chapel Hill. He has published essays on writers from Ireland and from the American South and has edited another anthology of Irish short stories, *A New Book of Dubliners*. He has also edited a pair of companion anthologies, *Louisiana Stories* and *Georgia Stories,* devoted to the two major historical sources of the modern Southern short story, and with Patrick Samway, S.J., he has co-edited four anthologies of Southern literature: *Stories of the Old South* (Penguin), *Stories of the Modern South* (Penguin), *A Modern Southern Reader,* and *A New Reader of the Old South*. Recently, he has written the text for *Cajun,* an album featuring the photography of Fonville Winans. Forkner's two-volume French edition of John James Audubon's journals and essays, *Journaux et Récits*, appeared in 1992.

D0063301

Modern Irish Short Stories

Edited by Ben Forkner
Preface by Anthony Burgess

Penguin Books

PENGUIN BOOKS
Published by the Penguin Group
Penguin Books USA Inc., 375 Hudson Street,
New York, New York 10014, U.S.A.
Penguin Books Ltd, 27 Wrights Lane,
London W8 5TZ, England
Penguin Books Australia Ltd, Ringwood, Victoria, Australia
Penguin Books Canada Ltd, 10 Alcorn Avenue,
Toronto, Ontario, Canada M4V 3B2
Penguin Books (N.Z.) Ltd, 182–190 Wairau Road,
Auckland 10, New Zealand

Penguin Books Ltd, Registered Offices:
Harmondsworth, Middlesex, England

First published in simultaneous hardcover and paperback editions by
Viking Penguin Inc. and Penguin Books 1980
This edition published in Penguin Books 1995

5   7   9   10   8   6   4

Pages 11–14 constitute an extension of this copyright page.

LIBRARY OF CONGRESS CATALOGING IN PUBLICATION DATA
Main entry under title:
Modern Irish short stories.
I. Short Stories, English—Irish authors.
1. Forkner, Ben.
(PZ1.M71944   1980b)   (PR8875)   823´.01´08   80–19292
ISBN 0 14 02.4699 1

Printed in the United States of America
Set in CRT Garamond

TO WELDON THORNTON

Contents

Acknowledgments

Three people in particular have generously helped with the making of this collection: Anthony Burgess, whose lively Preface was a magnificent gift to his Breton-American godson, Benjamin Sands Yves; Weldon Thornton, whose teaching and friendship will remain two of the great fortunes of my Chapel Hill days; and Patricia Mulcahy, my editor at Penguin, whose sensitive advice and cheerful telephone calls have improved the book and made its final preparation a pleasure.

Grateful acknowledgment is made for permission to reprint the following copyrighted works:

George Moore: "Home Sickness" from *The Untilled Field.* Copyright 1903 by George Moore. Reprinted by permission of J. C. Medley and Colin Smythe Ltd.

E. OE. Somerville and Martin Ross: "Poisson d'Avril" from *Further Experiences of an Irish R.M.* First published in 1908. Reprinted by permission of John Farquharson Ltd.

W. B. Yeats: "The Twisting of the Rope" from *The Stories of Red Hanrahan.* Copyright 1914 by Macmillan Publishing Co., Inc. Copyright 1942 by Bertha Georgie Yeats. Reprinted by permission of Macmillan Publishing Co., Inc., and A. P. Watt.

J. M. Synge: "An Autumn Night in the Hills" from *Collected Works, Vol. 2, Prose,* edited by Alan Price, 1966. Reprinted by permission of Oxford University Press.

Daniel Corkery: "Rock-of-the-Mass" from *The Wager and Other Stories.* Copyright 1950 by the Devin-Adair Company. Copyright renewed © 1978. Reprinted by permission of The Devin-Adair Co., Inc., Old Greenwich, Connecticut 06870.

Seumas O'Kelly: "The Weaver's Grave" from *The Golden*

by Chatto & Windus Ltd. Reprinted by permission of Grove Press, Inc., and John Calder (Publishers) Ltd. All rights reserved.

Michael McLaverty: "Six Weeks on and Two Ashore" from *Collected Short Stories*. Copyright © Michael McLaverty, 1978. Reprinted by permission of Poolbeg Press.

Bryan MacMahon: "Exile's Return" from *The Red Petticoat and Other Stories*. Copyright 1955 by Bryan MacMahon. Reprinted by permission of E. P. Dutton and A. P. Watt.

Flann O'Brien (Brian O'Nolan): "The Martyr's Crown" from *Stories and Plays*. Copyright 1950 by Brian O'Nolan. Copyright © Evelyn O'Nolan, 1973. Reprinted by permission of Viking Penguin Inc. and Granada Publishing Ltd.

Mary Lavin: "Happiness" from *Happiness*. Copyright © Mary Lavin, 1969. Reprinted by permission of Houghton Mifflin Company, Constable & Co. Ltd., and the author.

Benedict Kiely: "A Ball of Malt & Madame Butterfly" from *The State of Ireland*. Copyright © Benedict Kiely, 1970, 1980. Reprinted by permission of David R. Godine Publisher, Inc., and A. P. Watt.

James Plunkett: "A Walk Through the Summer" from *The Trusting and the Maimed*. Copyright © James Plunkett, 1959. Published in England by Hutchinson Publishing Group. Reprinted by permission of A. D. Peters & Co. Ltd.

Aidan Higgins: "Killachter Meadow" from *Asylum and Other Stories*. Published by John Calder (Publishers) Ltd., London, and Riverrun Press, Inc., New York. Reprinted by permission of John Calder (Publishers) Ltd.

William Trevor: "The Ballroom of Romance" from *The Ballroom of Romance*. Copyright © William Trevor, 1971. Reprinted by permission of Viking Penguin Inc. and John Johnson, authors' agents.

Edna O'Brien: "The Creature" from *A Scandalous Woman and Other Stories*. Copyright © Edna O'Brien, 1973. Reprinted by permission of Harcourt Brace Jovanovich, Inc., and Wei-

Preface

Any man, whatever his nationality, has a right to admire and to propagandize for Irish literature, but it helps if he possesses Irish blood or a mad capacity for empathizing with Ireland. Although I call myself an Englishman, my grandmother was a Mary Ann Finnegan from Tipperary and I was brought up in Manchester (like Liverpool, a kind of outpost of Ireland) by priests from Maynooth. Professor Forkner is an American from the South, and what Irish blood he may have is perhaps less important than an upbringing in an environment agricultural, traditional, and imbrued with a sense of historical wrong.

Both Professor Forkner and myself discovered our Irish inheritance through reading James Joyce, a typical Irish writer in his refusal to work in Ireland and an equal refusal to write about anything but Ireland. (It is perhaps noteworthy that I am penning this preface in the South of France, where I live, having married into Italy, and Professor Forkner has put together his anthology in the North of France, having married into France. The exilic condition comes naturally to a certain kind of Irishman.) As the other Forkner, who spells his name Faulkner, opened up the meaning of the South to several generations of American Southerners—including such an uncompromising black writer as Ralph Ellison—so Joyce has provided a way into the whole of Irish culture, and, as an incidental bonus, the whole of European culture as well.

Irish writers excel in brief forms, lyrical or dramatic. The English stage was moribund when Goldsmith and Sheridan came along; moribund again when Shaw and Wilde arrived; moribund once more when Synge and Yeats and O'Casey showed that the stage needed poetry as well as wit. The two greatest poets of the last hundred years have been Yeats, a Dublin Protestant, and Hopkins, an English Jesuit who died while a professor at University College, Dublin, both scions of a culture of the ear which the Anglo-Saxons, who pride themselves on sharpness of the eye and quickness of the trigger finger, began to neglect when Cromwell put his curse on the Commonwealth. Because Irish literature depends so much on the ear, it seems to follow that it does best in the poem and the short story. The short story is a form you may listen to, and its length conforms to the span of attention that a listener may give to an oral narrator. Edgar Allan Poe said that a piece of literature should be like a piece of music, brief enough for the single uninterrupted session. He did not write novels, and the Irish do not write them either.

That assertion seems demented, or, if you like, Irish. How about *Ulysses,* the greatest novel of the age? *Ulysses,* alas, is not a novel, it is a grossly expanded short story and began its life as a possible component of *Dubliners.* Joyce greatly admired the Book of Kells and acknowledged its influence on *Finnegans Wake,* another non-novel: you take a simple statement, like *Tunc,* and embroider it to the limit. *At Swim-Two-Birds* is not a novel either. If a novel is a long work whose length is justified by the presentation of characters capable of moral or temperamental change, then the Irish, who have a very idiosyncratic notion of human character, are not greatly given to the form. George Moore? Moore was a Frenchman. Maria Edgeworth? You perhaps have me there.

Whatever harebrained theory I may have about the aptitude of the Irish for the composition of short stories, there is no doubt that, as this selection demonstrates, the brief narrative is the form in which they excel. A character is revealed, not in the imposition upon him of a large number of vicissitudes, which is the way of the novel, but in some single incident. Joyce used to talk of the *epiphany* ("He got some Greek out of his Latin lessons," Gogarty sourly said), meaning the showing forth of some great truth in the presentation of the ordinary. The Magi came to worship the Saviour of the World and found him wrapped in dirty blankets in a derelict stable. Brightness does not fall from the air but suddenly flashes out of the filthy Liffey or the remark of a prostitute pinning up her hair for the evening's trade. The truth about human nature is revealed in an instant, when the epiphanic character responds to the fumes of the tenth whiskey or a chance word about his sister Kate.

It is the poetical element in the Irish which enables their writers to set up atmosphere in a few words; they do not need the laborious constructive apparatus of a Balzac. Any of these stories you are about to read establishes place, season, historical moment with the minimum of words. Then we proceed steadily, with the only economy which the Irish people seem able to manage well, to revelation of character and, very frequently, to an implied revelation of what is known as the Irish character. Nobody really knows what the Irish character is. Any attempt to define it results in the recounting of anecdotes, so we may as well eschew definition, tell the story, and have done with it. Sigmund Freud said that the Irish were the only race which could not profit from psychoanalysis. One of his followers split up human psychology into two categories—Irish and non-Irish. The Irish, like the Neapolitans, are not sure what truth is, and they have a system of logic which defies logic. They have something in common with Chekhov's Russians, and it is no accident that many of the stories here will seem Chekhovian. I was taking a bath in a Leningrad hotel when the floor concierge yelled that she had a cable for me. "Put it under the door," I cried. "I can't," she shouted, "it's on a tray." There is a deep logic, or epistemology, there which is far from absurd. The Irish and the Russians have one way of looking at entities (the entity in this instance was a cable-on-a-tray) and the rest of the world another. There is another aspect of the Russo-Irish

character which is too profound to pursue here—the disconti-
nuity, the lack of a bundle of binding attributes. The hero of
the biggest work of Irish fiction is a Hungarian Jew (really a
Triestine one): he has a unity, a solidity of identity which his
fellow citizens do not have. He holds together, by his very for-
eignness, the personages of another *Dubliners.*

The Irish have always something to write about. Present-day
Northern Ireland recapitulates the struggles of the past and is
producing, chiefly in the work of citizens of the Free State, a
new literature of bitter violence. I spent two years recently as
fiction critic for the *Irish Press* and was overwhelmed with volumes of short stories, mainly published in Dublin, which were
rich in the age-old themes: the paradox of a green land dedicated to powerful faith and rural tranquillity being torn by
urban struggles; the thrust of bigotry and the unexpected revelation of charity; the sense of a turbulent history as old as the
papal bull *Laudabilitur* present in every moment of violent en-
actment; the baffling refusal of the "Irish character" to con-
form to exotic parameters. What is always most notable is the
presence of a kind of grace—a moral elegance that frames all
sorts of wretchedness.

But the themes, and the styles, of the stories you have here
defy generalization. What they all have in common is, I suppose, an awareness of verbal tradition. When a word is used it
carries not only its present meaning but a haze of harmonics
derived from the long sounding of that word in the literature
of the past. Such modern American novelists as Thomas Pyn-
chon have attempted to free literature from its literary associations, to make the allusions derive from comic strip, television
soap opera, *Time* magazine, anything but books. The Irish, tied
to their past, are tied also to the literature of the past. Not even
Joxer in *Juno and the Paycock,* seedy quoter of cracker mottoes
and tenth-rate melodramas, can divest himself of culture. Irish
writers try to add to the literature they already know. They are
serious craftsmen aware of the devotion to craft of their own

predecessors, right back to the bards. That is why you will keep this book and read parts of it again and again. You will take it on journeys or keep it by the bed. Each time you enter it you will be in the presence of Ireland, the most fantastic country in the world and perhaps the only country that can be regarded as a custodian of unchanging human truth.

Anthony Burgess

Introduction

In the twentieth century, Irish writers have been dominant forces in all the major forms of literature: Yeats in poetry, Joyce in the novel, Synge and O'Casey in drama. But the Irish achievement in the short story has been so rich, various, and consistent, and has expressed so fully the details of Irish society, that it should probably be claimed as one of Ireland's natural resources.

Certainly in no other country in Europe in this century have so many writers excelled in the genre. In Ireland there are major writers for whom a collection of stories is not merely a diversion from novel writing, but a measure of artistic development. Writers such as Frank O'Connor, Sean O'Faolain, and Mary Lavin have all written novels, but their careers, even when considered by the writers themselves, are defined primarily by volume after volume of stories. Just before leaving for the United States for a writer-in-residence post at Hollins College, Benedict Kiely remembers walking along the Grand Canal in Dublin with Frank O'Connor and talking about literary reputations. Though Kiely already had several fine novels to his credit, these were not, according to O'Connor, what distinguished his career and gave hope for the future. As he wished Kiely a safe journey to the States, O'Connor remarked, "Another book of stories like *A Journey to the Seven Streams* and you'll be an international figure." And Mary Lavin, author of two novels herself, has written in her preface to *Selected Stories,* "I . . . wish that I could break up the two long novels I have published into the few short stories they ought to have been."

The modern Irish short story began early in the century with the meeting of two powerful forces: the search for native themes and styles that had been one of the active impulses of the Literary Revival, and the arrival from the Continent of literary realism, with its emphasis on ordinary lives embodied in an appropriate form and diction. The fusion of these two forces can be dated exactly with the publication in 1903 of George Moore's *The Untilled Field,* the first wholly modern collection of Irish stories. The following year the twenty-two-year-old James Joyce began publishing in *The Irish Homestead* the first of the stories in *Dubliners,* a collection that remains a landmark not only in the Irish story, but in the history of modern letters.

If Moore and Joyce can rightly be credited with transforming the Irish story into a modern art, it has continued to flourish because it is firmly rooted in a land where a high premium has traditionally been placed on the spoken word, especially in the form of the story or tale. The earliest stories we have of the Irish Celts—the mythological cycle concerning the local Irish gods, the Tuatha Dé Danaan; the great Red Branch or Ulster cycle of tales centering on the adventures of Cuchulain; and the stories dealing with the legendary Finn MacCumaill and his son Oisín—all stem from a culture where the poet-storyteller was a sacred figure. He preserved the identity of the race by composing, memorizing, and passing down from generation to generation the mythology, legend, and history of his people.

Even centuries later, after the Gaelic language and society began to decline during the seventeenth century when English control became permanent, the tradition of formal storytelling remained strong. As late as the nineteenth century, and in scattered, isolated pockets in the twentieth, there were Gaelic storytellers whose art was publicly prized and encouraged. These storytellers were of two kinds. The most remarkable were the *sgéalaí,* who told long and intricate folktales usually dealing with legendary heroes and their adventures. They were told in the third person and resemble in form and plot the marvel-filled folktales of other countries, notably the early *conte* in France and the *Märchen* in Germany. The second type of Gaelic storyteller was the *seanchaí*, who specialized in shorter stories based on local associations. Though they usually contain supernatural and faery lore, they also portray familiar places and families in the *seanchaí's* own region. The *seanchaí's* stories were usually told in the first person, as if actually witnessed, and they bring us close to the popular delight in almost any individual act of speech, from formal oratory to marketplace anecdote to pubroom polemics, that characterizes Ireland's vigorous oral culture.

There are several reasons why special values are placed on speech and story in Ireland. It has always been a predominantly rural society, where oral traditions are strongest. Its rural isolation is heightened by Ireland's location, an island on the outermost edge of Europe—the Irish have always known the islander's eagerness for news from abroad. Added to this, Ireland has had an unstable and precarious history—of invasion, occupation, and oppression—where very often the spoken word was the only means of preserving anything resembling a national identity. Sean O'Faolain, in his excellent little cultural history *The Irish,* makes the point that the Irish are surrounded on all sides by reminders of their own impermanence: "Because of colonization and wars and persecutions, there is no physical continuity in Ireland like to the physical continuity in Britain, i.e. no ancient villages, with 'mossed cottage-trees,' old inns, timbered houses, cropped greens; and handcrafts survive only in the simplest needs—turf-baskets, churns, farming implements, a few kitchen utensils. We have, that is, an unfurnished countryside." As O'Faolain observes, what Ireland does have to preserve and unite is its memory of a Celtic past—in this respect the physical reminders, mostly ruins, are plentiful—and its capacity to express in word and song its character and history. Given Ireland's past of colonization and the resultant native Irish poverty—widespread and rock-bottom—the act of speech remained the only index of personal value and collective

power; language, with its potential wealth of vocabulary, metaphor, image, and music, became a way of affirming spiritual
claims in the midst of material misery.

In terms of Ireland's success in modern fiction, however,
perhaps the most important reason behind a special sense of
language lies in the country's dual linguistic heritage: the
coexistence of the Gaelic language, an old, rich tongue fallen
into disuse, a "banished language" as Denis Donoghue has described it, almost extinct in the mid-nineteenth century, and an
English, mother tongue for the majority of Irish, too keenly
associated with centuries of oppression.

The question of language tended to become a national problem especially as the struggle for Irish independence intensified
in the late nineteenth century. Though it proved unrealistic to
think that Gaelic could ever replace English, the very possibility of separate nationhood seemed to require some sort of
choice. It finally took the success of the Abbey Theatre to fully
bring home the fact that the English spoken in the Irish
countryside, with its direct borrowings of syntax, rhythm, and
metaphor from Gaelic, was as distinctive an expression of Ireland as its music.

In this context, it is not surprising that so many works of
Irish fiction have centered on language not only as medium,
but as theme. The fantastic boasts of Synge's *Playboy,* the futile
garrulity of O'Casey's characters, Yeats's constant, almost mys-
tical belief in the relationship between style and personality,
and Joyce's lifelong explorations of language and perception,
all place a particularly Irish stress on the power of the word.

In Joyce's *Portrait of the Artist,* Stephen Dedalus, growing up
at a time when questions of nationality and language were at
their most intense, is asked to explain to an English dean what
the word *tundish* means. Though Stephen later confirms that it
is a perfectly good "English" word, the fact that Irish English
has retained it longer than British English leads him to the following meditation: "The language we are speaking is his before

it is mine. How different are the words *home, Christ, ale, master,* on his lips and on mine! I cannot speak or write these words without unrest of spirit. His language, so familiar and so foreign, will always be for me an acquired speech. I have not made or accepted its words. My voice holds them at bay. My soul frets in the shadow of his language." The important distinction is between the words *acquired* and *made and accepted.* Though Stephen at this stage feels in a kind of foster relationship to his language, Joyce and all the other major Irish writers of his generation came to exult in the possibilities of making and accepting their own "English." Joyce in particular saw the problem as one he could exploit, and spent his career drawing on the strengths of both traditions: the rich written tradition of English literature, and the equally rich oral tradition of Irish English, especially its Dublin variant.

It took some time for Ireland's multiple linguistic heritage to be fully realized in literature, but even at the beginning of the Literary Revival the question of a native Irish idiom in English had been a central impulse. Two of the stories in this collection, Yeats's "The Twisting of the Rope" and Synge's "An Autumn Night in the Hills," stem directly from this impulse and are worth looking at before turning to George Moore. The history of Yeats's story is particularly illustrative of the period's attitudes.

Yeats was always fascinated with the Irish oral tradition, especially its easy mingling of the natural and the supernatural, and he remembered all his life tales he had heard as a boy in Sligo. During the early years of his career he edited several volumes of Irish stories and folktales. His most important collection was *The Celtic Twilight,* published in 1893. These are his literary versions of tales he had heard himself—many, he explains in the preface, from Paddy Flynn, "a little bright-eyed old man, who lived in a leaky and one-roomed cabin in the village of Ballisodore." In writing down the stories of ghosts, faeries, and legendary figures that make up *The Celtic Twilight,*

Yeats tried to do justice to the simple yet expressive Irish English speech he had heard; but it was only when he wrote his own Irish stories, and in particular the ones dealing with the wandering poet Red Hanrahan, that he began to realize the possibilities of using that speech as a narrative medium.

Dialects of English in Ireland had been used before, but almost exclusively for comic dialogue. Even a nineteenth-century writer as knowledgeable of the Irish oral tradition as William Carleton all too often spoils the tone of his tales by surrounding his accurate dialogue with the stiff, artificial English of nineteenth-century journalese. Yeats, on the other hand, after several false starts, eventually sought to inform even the narrative part of his folk stories with the natural rhythms of country speech.

In working on his stories, Yeats was inspired by the translations of Douglas Hyde, founder of the Gaelic League, and one of Ireland's best Gaelic scholars. In his book *Beside the Fire,* published in 1890, Hyde had translated into a quiet but powerful Irish English stories he had heard from Gaelic storytellers; his translations were the first to demonstrate the deep resources of Irish peasant speech in forging a distinctly Irish narrative prose. Yeats first published his Hanrahan stories in 1897, but as he himself complains, they were corrupted by an inappropriate, artificial style. He was fortunate in rewriting the stories to have the advice and the example of Lady Gregory, who shared with Hyde a gift for recreating the speech she heard. Yeats has explained how Lady Gregory helped him revise the Hanrahan stories from "that artificial, elaborate English so many of us played with in the 'nineties' [into] that simple English she had learned from her Galway countrymen."

Of course by the time the Hanrahan stories were rewritten in their final form (1904, 1907), the Abbey Theatre and the early plays of Synge were bringing a new dimension to the literary uses of Irish English, informing it with a much greater sweep and depth of expression than previous writers had commanded; but the impulse behind Yeats' revisions does mark a turning point in the history of Irish prose fiction. "The Twisting of the Rope" is the best, most self-contained of the revised Hanrahan stories, though it does help to know that Hanrahan has previously been enthralled by a vision of the faery world. It is a type of modern literary folktale of which Seumas O'Kelly's "The Weaver's Grave" is the great Irish masterpiece, and, perhaps more important, it is written in a straightforward, vigorous Irish English based on the spoken word that has become one of the distinguishing features of the modern Irish short story.

J. M. Synge's "An Autumn Night in the Hills" shows the same concern for lively dialogue and dramatic structure he was to master in his Abbey plays. It was published in 1903, the same year his first play, *In the Shadow of the Glen,* was performed, and the same year George Moore's *The Untilled Field* appeared. Synge had a much better knowledge of Gaelic and a more direct contact with Irish English dialects than Yeats, but he too admitted a debt to Hyde and Lady Gregory. When in 1902 Lady Gregory published her book *Cuchulain of Muirthemne,* a version of the Cuchulain stories written in the dialect she had heard from the native Irish in her own region, Synge wrote to her that her *"Cuchulain* is part of my daily bread." Synge published "An Autumn Night in the Hills" as a sort of autobiographical essay, but its tightly controlled dramatic action places it squarely within the realistic art of the modern story. As Synge's nephew and biographer, E. M. Stephens, has written: "He wrote his articles by collecting notes of kindred experiences into groups to which he could give titles. In doing this he did not interfere with the spontaneous quality of his first impressions, but combined recollections so as to make each article an artistic whole, internally balanced like a musical composition."

When George Moore moved to Dublin in 1901 to offer his services to the Literary Revival, the first phase of the Revival, with its Celtic Twilight emphasis on Irish myth, legend, and supernatural beliefs, had begun to shift to a more realistic expression of Irish culture as it existed in the present. Since Irish culture, especially the native Irish culture of the west, conserved many archaic features of Gaelic manners and customs, the shift was not so much a reaction against Ireland's ancient past as it was a fresh interest in how much of that past still remained. With the arrival of Moore, however, a more abrupt shift occurred. Moore had already made a reputation for himself as a novelist and man of letters on the Continent, where he had been strongly influenced by the literary movements of realism and naturalism, particularly as they were defined in French fiction. During his sojourn in Dublin—he left Ireland for good after nine years—he contributed several important works to modern Irish literature, including the eccentric but brilliant autobiography *Hail and Farewell.* By far his most influential book, however, was the collection of short stories he entitled *The Untilled Field* as an appreciative bow to Turgenev.

Moore claimed he wrote the stories "in the hope of furnishing the young Irish of the future with models," and the thirteen stories in the first edition do demonstrate an impressive display of narrative styles and Irish themes. Several of the stories had appeared in a Gaelic translation in 1902. But Moore, knowing no Gaelic himself, though enthusiastic about the Gaelic language movement, was disappointed in the translation's reception, and published the rest of the stories in English. The stories are realistic portrayals of ordinary Irish men and women usually in the throes of some typically Irish frustration or obsession, often religious, that finally overpowers them. They are especially critical of the strong grip of Irish Catholic puritanism, which Moore, like the young Joyce, felt thwarted all impulse toward a creative culture. In terms of modern literature, the stories are not innovative in style or structure. What does stamp them as original in the history of the Irish short story is their willingness to dismiss the romantic idealization of Irish rural society and dramatize instead the poverty, fear, frustration, and provincialism that clearly did exist, despite all the nationalists' claims to the contrary. Many of the stories are strained and overly didactic, but "Home Sickness," Frank O'Connor's favorite story by Moore, represents his realistic, ironic art at its best. Narrated in the third person, but from the perspective of the protagonist, James Bryden, and in the quiet, natural tones of his own speech, "Home Sickness" concentrates in Bryden's dilemma most of the themes of *The Untilled Field:* exile, barren land, religious domination and interference, and provincial boredom and despair. And in Bryden's inability to make a choice, to decide between Ireland and the outside world, Moore not only cuts through to one of the typical burdens of the modern Irishman; he dramatizes as well the unresolved conflicts in his own mind.

James Joyce began writing his *Dubliners* in 1904, the year after the publication of *The Untilled Field.* Joyce's stories have often been described as a sort of urban counterpart to Moore's rural Ireland, and there are obvious similarities in their realistic exposures of Irish society. Joyce's stories, however, are not only far superior in stylistic precision and symbolic design; they also reflect a bitter reaction to the dullness and despair that the twenty-two-year-old Joyce felt seeping into his own literary life. When George Russell generously invited Joyce to publish a few "simple stories" for the magazine *The Irish Homestead,* Joyce saw an opportunity to offer his own candid antidote to the romantic excesses of the Literary Revival, and to justify at the same time the necessity for exile. As Richard Ellmann explains: Joyce's "short stories, with their grim exactitude and submerged lyricism, had broken away from the Irish literary movement in which, though he denied the fact, his poems fitted pretty well. As the author of these stories, he was free to attack his literary compatriots for dealing in milk and water which tasted no better for being Irish and spiritual."

Joyce published "The Sisters," his first story, in *The Irish*

Homestead during the summer of 1904. Two other stories followed soon after, "Eveline" and "After the Race." By the time the latter story appeared, Joyce had made the decisive step of his career: he had left Ireland for a lifelong exile, accompanied by Nora Barnacle, several unfinished manuscripts, and the hope of a job in Zurich that proved, like so many of his hopes, a delusion. By December 1905 he had completed twelve stories, and he sent them off to Grant Richards, a publisher in London. They were first accepted, then refused, and Joyce was subjected to nine bitter years of unreasonable demands, broken contracts, and futile correspondence before they were finally published in 1914.

In one of his many letters to Richards, Joyce clearly explained the motives behind the form and theme he had chosen: "My intention was to write a chapter of the moral history of my country and I chose Dublin for the scene because that city seemed to me the centre of paralysis. I have tried to present it to the indifferent public under four of its aspects: childhood, adolescence, maturity, and public life. I have written it for the most part in a style of scrupulous meanness." Most of the stories, from "The Sisters" to "Grace," are brilliant performances of symbolic naturalism, describing in a precise, ironic prose the futility of escape or change in a Dublin society paralyzed by debased dreams, blinding religious authority, and monotonous social conventions. It cannot be overemphasized how Irish these stories are. Joyce's large and exact memory for local idioms, allusions, and places is evident in each story, and a familiar knowledge of Irish religion, Irish politics, and Irish English is as essential to a full understanding of *Dubliners* as it is to Joyce's other works.

The final story in *Dubliners*, "The Dead," differs from the others in a number of ways. Though in a sense it does reverberate back to all the failed lives of the other stories, its central character, Gabriel Conroy, is a much more complex figure. "The Dead" was written in 1907, two years after the other stories, and three years after the beginning of Joyce's European exile. Richard Ellmann has suggested that three years of struggle on the Continent caused Joyce to look with more sympathetic eyes toward Ireland; but whatever the reason, "The Dead" does mark a distinct shift in his literary concerns and methods. Unlike the other adult characters in *Dubliners,* Gabriel Conroy is seen from within, and unlike the other characters, he does manage to redeem himself through at least a partial self-discovery.

The basic conflict of "The Dead" lies in the confrontation between Gabriel, a teacher, journalist and sophisticated Anglo-Irishman with his eye on the Continent, and the more primitive, vital Irish culture represented by the Irish nationalist, Miss Ivors, but more importantly by Gabriel's wife, Gretta, who comes from the west of Ireland. Perhaps the feature that best identifies the hand of the mature Joyce is the way the language of the narrative is made to reflect the gradual movement of the story into Gabriel's inner thoughts. The easygoing, expectant, colloquial tones of the opening paragraphs, as the two Miss Morkans welcome their guests, progressively give way, especially after the false notes of Gabriel's dinner tribute, to the artificial, bookish vocabulary of Gabriel's inner speech, a late-Victorian romantic English as lifeless and insubstantial as the conventional exchanges in the Morkans' music room.

Joyce's characterization of Gabriel's failure is masterly, and "The Dead" remains one of the great stories in the modern tradition. If Moore's stories in *The Untilled Field* were the first to adapt the methods of literary realism to specific Irish themes, Joyce's *Dubliners* gave the Irish short story a standard of artistic perfection that went far beyond national boundaries. With the stories of Moore and Joyce, it is not going too far to claim that the directions of the modern Irish short story were largely set. It was to be generally realistic and uncompromising, and it was to derive its dramatic form and ironic energies from the spoken word. Moore, the middle-aged convert, and

Joyce, the rebellious exile, in different ways and from different motives, proved together that the matter of Ireland was as distinctive and as varied as its speech, a discovery that the rich, individual voices of their successors have confirmed in story after story.

In stating that the modern Irish story is predominantly a realistic genre, it is best to remember that "realism" in Ireland comprises a broader range of experience than modern conventional standards would ordinarily accept. The archaic Celtic belief in the local gods that fascinated Yeats in the folkways of the Irish peasant, and the easy coexistence of pagan and Christian worlds that Synge dramatized in his plays, to some extent represent permanent features of Ireland's collective memory. If modern Irish writers have been quick to disdain the quaint surface details of faery superstition—details that the caricatures of the commercial markets have now stripped of their natural surroundings—they continue to remain close to a world whose invisible powers are nonetheless real, for all their strangeness.

Certainly several of the stories written early in the century still reflect a world in which the natural and the supernatural are two halves of a single reality. In Yeats's "The Twisting of the Rope," for example, the poet Red Hanrahan conducts himself the way he does out of bondage to the *Leanhaun sidhe*, the Gaelic muse. In addition, the action of the story centers on the old Gaelic respect for the power of the poet's word. As "poet of the Gael," Hanrahan's curse is considered a physical act, capable of withering the corn in the fields and of drying up the cows' milk. "The Twisting of the Rope" is the only story in this collection not set in modern times, but Synge's more modern "An Autumn Night in the Hills" shows an equal respect for unseen forces. When the old woman fearfully gives her account of the lake spirit, her story, the will and loyalty of the wounded dog, and the life and death of Mary Kinsella all seem bound together in a single unknowable mystery. Even Joyce's "The Dead," solidly set in the cultivated world of the modern drawing room, is a story of ghosts—ghosts with more life than the living.

In two stories, Seumas O'Kelly's literary folktale "The Weaver's Grave" and Daniel Corkery's "Rock-of-the-Mass," the special boundaries of Irish realism in the early twentieth century are particularly striking. O'Kelly and Corkery shared a direct, lifelong contact with rural, peasant Ireland that set them apart from their contemporaries Moore and Joyce. O'Kelly was brought up in East Galway, and Corkery, whose influence was to assert itself so strongly in the early careers of Frank O'Connor and Sean O'Faolain, possessed an intimate knowledge of the desolate West Cork hillsides and farms. Both depict the physical details of the Irish landscape and record the accents of Irish country speech with unerring accuracy, but both accept too the strange words and passionate gestures of a world where visionary experience is not limited to what Coleridge called the "despotism of the eye."

As the subtitle of O'Kelly's story states, "The Weaver's Grave" is a story of old men. It is also a story of communal memory and the power of ritual taken to nearly grotesque extremes. The four men who dominate the story from the beginning—the dead weaver and his ancient contemporaries, the stone-breaker, the nailer, and the cooper—defy the modern world as fiercely as they defy each other. As the long search progresses, however, the weaver's stubborn hold on the living is gradually forced to give way. His widow, nameless and obscured by the spell of memory and age at the beginning of the story, slowly awakens to mysteries of her own individual youth as powerful as the old men's mysteries of their communal past. Finally, she combines wake and resurrection by choosing one of the gravediggers along with the site of her husband's grave.

There is less exaggeration and broad humor in Corkery's more realistic story "Rock-of-the-Mass," but the grip of an invisible force asserts its presence just as strongly. Corkery's story, like so many Irish stories, eventually takes the form of a retrospective monologue, though in his case there is a sympathetic audience present. An old farmer, Michael Hodnett, looks back on a life shaped by a single choice he made between his old rocky farm in the hills and the new showplace farm in the lowlands he has struggled, at great pains, to make prosper. He has lost three sons in the process; but the loss he regrets most is the holy place on his old farm, a pile of rock where Mass had been said in the days of the penal laws. It is a compassionate portrait of a tragic conflict between spiritual and worldly realities, a conflict whose losses are made to cut even more deeply with the story's final ironic thrust.

Corkery, like O'Kelly, affords us a good example of the continuity of the Irish story, its filial links with old Gaelic Ireland. In many of his stories the spirit of declining native ways broods over his characters' lives as insistently as the abandoned rock pile broods over Michael Hodnett. But more to our immediate purpose, Corkery, with his long career of teaching and writing the short story, provides a sort of natural bridge between first- and second-generation writers of the modern tradition. In his early volumes, he was responsible for introducing some of the major themes of the Irish story; and through his decision to devote an entire career to perfecting the art of the story, he helped determine the attitudes and aims of his two famous students, Frank O'Connor and Sean O'Faolain.

By the 1920s the first generation of Irish short story writers could look back on an impressive achievement. If George Moore and James Joyce stand out as the most original, the first to successfully wed native themes with modern forms, their contemporaries Somerville and Ross, Stephens, O'Kelly, and Corkery each made permanent contributions to the genre. Even with these bright beginnings, though, if one period were to be singled out as the golden age of the modern Irish story it would have to be that of the second generation, dominated by three names: Liam O'Flaherty, Frank O'Connor, and Sean O'Faolain. Much of their best work was written in the late

1920s (O'Flaherty) and the decades before and during World War II. There were other good writers, of course, but these three did more than anyone else to establish the Irish short story as an independent art form, a form as various and as demanding as the novel or the play. Unlike the period of Moore and Joyce, it was not a time of great experimentation or sudden new departures, but rather a deliberate ripening of the established realist tradition.

With the exception of Corkery, the first-generation writers did not think of their stories as the chief aim of their literary lives. Joyce, for example, wrote his last story when he was twenty-five. For the writers after Corkery, however, the art of the short story was one of conscious specialization. O'Connor and O'Faolain did make a few infrequent forays in the novel, but they considered themselves first and foremost professional craftsmen of the story. Both were willing to judge their own work against the best stories of Russia, France, and the United States, and they both measured their artistic development in terms of each successive collection.

It is difficult to speak convincingly in general or collective terms when considering the main figures of the second generation. The individual voices of O'Flaherty, O'Connor, and O'Faolain, as their stories never fail to demonstrate, are indelibly their own. But for all their differences, they do share certain Irish realities of a specific time, reflected, however diversely, in their work. Like the majority of Irishmen raised in the first decades of the twentieth century, they all had firsthand experience of poverty, the Catholic Church, and nationalist fervor. They were young men at the time of Ireland's struggles for independence, and they all fought briefly for the defeated Republican forces. Most importantly, at least in terms of their art, they all suffered at the very outset of their careers from a society that tended to choke and suffocate its best creative energies. This was nothing new, of course, but the memory of war made the entrenchment of established authority even deeper.

And in trying in various ways to budge the fixed lines of official thought, all three had stormy relations with Irish church and state. As Richard Fallis reminds us in his fine survey *The Irish Renaissance,* "The Irish Free State was the creation of men who had hated *The Playboy* fifteen years before, and the attitudes of those who found *The Playboy* unpatriotic, *The Countess Cathleen* irreligious, and *Ulysses* irredeemably obscene were the dominant tastes in the Ireland of the 1920's and 1930's."

These dates could easily be extended, for even in the 1960s almost ten thousand books, including most of the major writers of the century, had been officially forbidden. Such was the great extent of censorship power and hostility that both O'Connor and O'Faolain at different times became focal points of national campaigns against their work. It is probably not so surprising then that in so many of their stories, and in the stories of O'Flaherty also, the drama centers on an individual in conflict with a social or religious order, or in rebellion against official codes. If they reacted publicly as men of letters against cultural stagnation, censorship, and general authoritarianism, in their art they identified closely with the common man and all his frustrations and humors. O'Connor and O'Faolain may have dealt chiefly with the low- and middle-class provincial Irish Catholic, and O'Flaherty with the more isolated figure of the western peasant or the mountainy farmer, but all three sided with the individual little man, however pigheaded, up against the inhospitable powers of the world.

The sheer wealth of stories written by the main figures of the second generation made any choice of a "best story" a treacherous if not impossible task. Actually, they have each written a half-dozen stories worthy of any collection. The ones I finally chose are not only among their best; they are also uniquely representative of each author. O'Connor's "In the Train," O'Flaherty's "The Pedlar's Revenge," and O'Faolain's "Falling Rocks, Narrowing Road, Cul-de-Sac, Stop," show these writers in full control of distinctive, original, and compelling voices.

Frank O'Connor's story "In the Train," from his second collection, *Bones of Contention,* demonstrates a mastery of Irish dialogue he often equalled but never surpassed. O'Connor was concerned perhaps more than any other writer of his generation with the rhythms of speech and the various ways the spoken word reveals character. He once observed that he wrote about Ireland because he knew to a syllable how everything in Ireland could be said, and the great diversity of individual speech in his stories fully proves his claim. "In the Train" is remarkable for the skill in which excerpts of dialogue, as the speakers shift from one theme to another and from one group to another, gradually fill in the story's background, exposing the characters' past and future in a few swift dramatic exchanges. "In the Train" is remarkable, too, as a portrait of a small Irish community, tightly bound together in a collective refusal to inform on one of their own in the Dublin courts, but at the same time meting out a punishment in their private speech and behavior as severe and as cruel as any big-city judge. O'Connor thus combines two of his favorite subjects: public rebellion of native Irish values against the official system, and the private rebellion of the outcast individual.

Liam O'Flaherty writes of fiercer, more isolated passions than either O'Connor or O'Faolain. Born on the Aran Islands, he once wrote: "I was born on a storm-swept rock and hate the soft growth of sunbaked lands where there is no frost in men's bones. Swift thoughts, and the swift flight of ravenous birds, and the squeal of terror of hunted animals are to me a reality." O'Flaherty has often been described as the most "naturalistic" of the Irish realists, but his brand of naturalism has very little in common with the self-satisfied certitudes of continental writers. Always there prevails a deep sense of mystery in the face of uncontrollable passions, an attitude mindful of the primitive notion that the passions are the voices of the gods. O'Flaherty has also been described as a writer who writes more for the eye than the ear. This may be an accurate enough account of the luminous visual power of some of his animal stories, but it misrepresents his keen ear for Irish dialogue in such stories as "The Post Office," "Lovers," and "The Pedlar's Revenge." "The Pedlar's Revenge" is one of O'Flaherty's most successful stories, fuller and less melodramatic than many of his early "naturalistic" portraits. The harsh, shrewd voice of the pedlar is a variation on what is now almost a standard Irish subject, the wild old man. In this collection it looks back toward the fierce, defiant old men of O'Kelly's "The Weaver's Grave" and forward to the sour-spoken blind man in Plunkett's "A Walk Through the Summer."

Sean O'Faolain's "Falling Rocks, Narrowing Road, Cul-de-Sac, Stop" comes from his latest collection of stories, *Foreign Affairs,* and represents his alert, sophisticated prose at its liveliest. Unlike many of his contemporaries who have generally chosen to have their characters narrate their own stories, O'Faolain has experimented again and again with a single authorial voice. He has often been contrasted with O'Connor as a short story writer who observes rather than embodies his characters, but such a comparison does an injustice to the wide range of tones his narrative voice can cover. Moreover, from the very beginning of his career, with the volume *Midsummer Night Madness,* he has written about a greater diversity of Irish characters than any other writer of his generation. *Foreign Affairs,* for example, includes some of the few successful treatments of those strange breeds, the Irish professional, doctor or diplomat, and the Irish intellectual. It is true, however, that O'Faolain's stories are most convincing when the narrator's powers of invention most fully correspond to those of O'Faolain himself, and when the literary rhythms give way to the conversational. In "Falling Rocks, Narrowing Road, Cul-de-Sac, Stop," his narrative voice is completely confident and at ease, taking as much delight in the act of spinning out the tale as in the tale itself. The comic asides, the unembarrassed digressions, the ample description, the counterthrusts of learned allusion and earthy dialogue—this is the work of a master musician effortlessly showing off, enjoying impromptu runs and brilliant variations, but all the time making sure the melody rings out clear and true.

O'Faolain's story gives us a good example of another distinctly Irish form of modern story, the literary yarn. It goes back to Somerville and Ross's hilarious stories of an Irish resident magistrate, Major Yeates, a bewildered Englishman cast afloat in provincial Ireland. The plots of these anecdotal stories, such as the one in "Poisson d'Avril," are often slight, but the comic thrusts of Irish speech and the shrewd insights into the Irish mind are as exact today as they were at the beginning of the century. With O'Faolain, though, the two most accomplished writers of the literary yarn are Flann O'Brien and Benedict Kiely. O'Brien equals Joyce in his mastery of Dublin wit and Dublin speech, and though his best work was done in such novels as *At Swim-Two-Birds, The Third Policeman,* and *The Dalkey Archive,* his story "The Martyr's Crown" shows his brilliant powers of Irish farce at full strength. Kiely, like O'Brien, came to Dublin out of the north, but he has made Dublin as much his literary province as his native Tyrone. "A Ball of Malt and Madame Butterfly" is one of his masterpieces, a genial Dublin yarn which, typically enough, turns out to be a tragicomic urban pastoral *and* a pubroom joke.

However conspicuously O'Flaherty, O'Connor, and O'Faolain stand out during the middle years of the Irish short story, the depth and diversity of the period may best be appreciated by reading the stories of their Irish contemporaries. Many of them are less well known in the history of the Irish story simply because they wrote fewer stories.

Samuel Beckett, for example, though not especially recognized as a writer of stories, or as a writer who draws on the particularities of Irish place and Irish speech, succeeds in both in his brilliant satire "Dante and the Lobster," a story whose last line is as polemically Irish as the setting down of a glass of stout. Elizabeth Bowen sets many of her stories in England, and is best known for her novels; but in her troubling evocation of neutral Ireland during World War II, "Summer Night," she has made a classic probe into the claustrophobic blind alleys of a certain Irish conscience. And Bryan MacMahon and Michael McLaverty, in "Exile's Return" and "Six Weeks on and Two Ashore," have both written strong, ironic dramas of those typical Irish experiences, a return and a departure.

Mary Lavin deserves to be treated separately, but in the same breath as the three masters, since she is well on her way to becoming the fourth. She continues to publish a major collection every two years or so, and she has long proved herself to be one of the surest and most original stylists of the subjective narrative. Her great themes are those intense states of anticipation or retrospection which frame the histories of intimate relationships. Her characters always seem on the threshold or the back steps of a definitive experience. In "Happiness," both states are brilliantly merged as a grown-up daughter lovingly looks back on her mother's insistent struggle to assure three daughters— and herself—that "happiness" is possible.

In turning to the contemporary state of the Irish story, and the final group of stories in the collection, it is obviously misleading to speak too abruptly of a new generation. Certainly there is no lack of young writers and young presses to publish them; but much of the best work is still being done by writers such as Benedict Kiely, Mary Lavin, and James Plunkett, whose careers stretch back to the 1940s. Even the old masters O'Connor and O'Faolain can justifiably be called contemporary figures. O'Connor wrote some of his best stories in the early sixties, and Sean O'Faolain continued to open up new directions in *Foreign Affairs,* a collection containing some of the freshest, most tonic stories of the last decade.

Still, there are several younger writers who deserve to be included in any standard edition of the modern Irish story. Even
though most of them began publishing in the 1960s, they have
already established themselves firmly, perhaps permanently, in
the modern Irish tradition. In the stories of William Trevor,
John McGahern, Edna O'Brien, and Eugene McCabe, for example, the special virtues of the Irish story announced by
Moore and Joyce—strong characterization and vivid, dramatic
dialogue—still predominate. If anything, the realism is more
stringent, and closer to the subject. This new harshness obviously owes much to the daily jolts of violence and horror in
Northern Ireland, but it may also owe something to the sudden transformations Ireland shares with other traditional socie-
ties compelled to adapt pell-mell to the contemporary world.
As the Dublin suburbs grow indistinguishable from their English counterparts, and as rural, provincial Ireland understand-
ably yearns for those same suburbs' comfortable securities,
there seems little to choose from between Ireland's past and
Ireland's future. Certainly there is something fateful and final
in the empty rural lives William Trevor and John McGahern
describe in "A Ballroom of Romance" and "All Sorts of Impossible Things."

But even amid the convulsions and changes of contemporary
Ireland, there is something affirmative and life-giving in the
very process and presence of successful art. Patrick Boyle's satire in "Pastorale" may bark *and* bite, and that is a good thing
in all satire; but when the judgment is made, it is made with
humor and with a delight in ripe country speech. Even in
Aidan Higgins's more acid portraits in "Killachter Meadow,"
the brilliant, dense, damning prose is full of a rich wit that I
find heartening even though it is inscribed on a tombstone.
What is perhaps most remarkable about these writers is their
capacity to affirm voices all their own, and yet all unmistakably
Irish, and to bring new vitality and intelligence to a tradition
that already loomed large, even before they began to make

their own contributions, as one of the triumphant achieve-
ments of a national art in modern times.

Ben Forkner
Nantes, France

Modern Irish
Short Stories

George Moore (1852–1933)

George Moore was born at Moore Hall, County Mayo, in 1852. His family were Catholic landowners, and he was educated at Oscott, a Roman Catholic boarding school in England. He first wanted to paint, and after inheriting his father's estate he left for Paris in 1873. He soon abandoned his dreams of a career as a professional artist and turned to literature. During the next twenty-five years, dividing his time between Paris and London, he gradually acquired a reputation as one of the major English writers of his time. Among his books during these years are A Drama in Muslin *(1886),* Confessions of a Young Man *(1888),* Impressions and Opinions *(1891),* Modern Painting *(1893), and the famous novel* Esther Waters *(1894). It came as a surprise, therefore, to many of his contemporaries when he left the sophisticated world of literature and art on the Continent, and returned to Ireland to take an active role in the Literary Revival. In 1898 he helped W. B. Yeats, Edward Martyn, and Lady Gregory found the Irish Literary Theatre, the forerunner of the Abbey, and in 1901 he moved to Dublin, remaining there nine years. During this period Moore brought to the Revival a familiarity with European literature and art and a lively, ironic temperament. He also brought a mind that tended to change suddenly, and absolutely, from one enthusiasm to another, and he could never reconcile his love of Ireland, especially its pagan past, with his hate of Ireland's religious superstition and social convention. Finally, considering himself as a sort of failed and rebuffed cultural messiah, he left Ireland and settled in London. He did contribute several major works to modern Irish literature, however, beginning with the seminal collection of short stories* The Untilled Field, *published in English in 1903. Several of these stories*

*had appeared in an Irish translation in 1902. "Home Sickness"
from* The Untilled Field *was Frank O'Connor's favorite story by
Moore. Moore later wrote a collection of historical and legendary
stories,* A Story-Teller's Holiday *(1918); but his best books are
his novel* The Lake *(1905) and his masterpiece, the three-volume
autobiography* Hail and Farewell *(1911–1914), an eccentric, bi-
ased, and fully entertaining account of the Literary Revival.*

Home Sickness

He told the doctor he was due in the barroom at eight o'clock
in the morning; the barroom was in a slum in the Bowery; and
he had only been able to keep himself in health by getting up
at five o'clock and going for long walks in the Central Park.

"A sea voyage is what you want," said the doctor. "Why not
go to Ireland for two or three months? You will come back a
new man."

"I'd like to see Ireland again."

And he began to wonder how the people at home were getting on. The doctor was right. He thanked him, and three
weeks after he landed in Cork.

As he sat in the railway carriage he recalled his native village,
built among the rocks of the large headland stretching out into
the winding lake. He could see the houses and the streets, and
the fields of the tenants, and the Georgian mansion and the
owners of it; he and they had been boys together before he
went to America. He remembered the villagers going every
morning to the big house to work in the stables, in the garden,
in the fields—mowing, reaping, digging, and Michael Malia
building a wall; it was all as clear as if it were yesterday, yet he
had been thirteen years in America; and when the train stopped

at the station the first thing he did was to look round for any changes that might have come into it. It was the same blue limestone station as it was thirteen years ago, with the same five long miles between it and Duncannon. He had once walked these miles gaily, in little over an hour, carrying a heavy bundle on a stick, but he did not feel strong enough for the walk today, though the evening tempted him to try it. A car was waiting at the station, and the boy, discerning from his accent and his dress that Bryden had come from America, plied him with questions, which Bryden answered rapidly, for he wanted to hear who were still living in the village, and if there was a house in which he could get a clean lodging. The best house in the village, he was told, was Mike Scully's, who had been away in a situation for many years, as a coachman in the King's County, but had come back and built a fine house with a concrete floor. The boy could recommend the loft, he had slept in it himself, and Mike would be glad to take in a lodger, he had no doubt. Bryden remembered that Mike had been in a situation at the big house. He had intended to be a jockey, but had suddenly shot up into a fine tall man, and had become a coachman instead; and Bryden tried to recall his face, but could only remember a straight nose and a somewhat dusky complexion.

So Mike had come back from King's County, and had built himself a house, had married—there were children for sure running about; while he, Bryden, had gone to America, but he had come back; perhaps he, too, would build a house in Duncannon, and—his reverie was suddenly interrupted by the carman.

"There's Mike Scully," he said, pointing with his whip, and Bryden saw a tall, finely built, middle-aged man coming through the gates, who looked astonished when he was accosted, for he had forgotten Bryden even more completely than Bryden had forgotten him; and many aunts and uncles were mentioned before he began to understand.

"You've grown into a fine man, James," he said, looking at Bryden's great width of chest. "But you're thin in the cheeks, and you're very sallow in the cheeks, too."

"I haven't been very well lately—that is one of the reasons I've come back; but I want to see you all again."

"And thousand welcome you are."

Bryden paid the carman, and wished him Godspeed. They divided the luggage, Mike carrying the bag and Bryden the bundle, and they walked round the lake, for the townland was at the back of the domain; and while walking he remembered the woods thick and well forested; now they were wind worn, the drains were choked, and the bridge leading across the lake inlet was falling away. Their way led between long fields where herds of cattle were grazing, the road was broken—Bryden wondered how the villagers drove their carts over it, and Mike told him that the landlord could not keep it in repair, and he would not allow it to be kept in repair out of the rates, for then it would be a public road, and he did not think there should be a public road through his property.

At the end of many fields they came to the village, and it looked a desolate place, even on this fine evening, and Bryden remarked that the county did not seem to be as much lived in as it used to be. It was at once strange and familiar to see the chickens in the kitchen; and, wishing to reknit himself to the old customs, he begged of Mrs. Scully not to drive them out, saying they reminded him of old times.

"And why wouldn't they?" Mike answered, "he being one of ourselves bred and born in Duncannon, and his father before him."

"Now, is it truth ye are telling me?" and she gave him her hand, after wiping it on her apron, saying he was heartily welcome, only she was afraid he wouldn't care to sleep in a loft.

"Why wouldn't I sleep in a loft, a dry loft! You're thinking a good deal of America over here," he said, "but I reckon it isn't all you think it. Here you work when you like and you sit down when you like; but when you've had a touch of blood-poisoning as I had, and when you have seen young people walking with a stick, you think that there is something to be said for old Ireland."

"You'll take a sup of milk, won't you? You must be dry," said Mrs. Scully.

And when he had drunk the milk Mike asked him if he would like to go inside or if he would like to go for a walk.

"Maybe resting you'd like to be."

And they went into the cabin and started to talk about the wages a man could get in America, and the long hours of work.

And after Bryden had told Mike everything about America that he thought of interest, he asked Mike about Ireland. But Mike did not seem to be able to tell him much. They were all very poor—poorer, perhaps, than when he left them.

"I don't think anyone except myself has a five-pound note to his name."

Bryden hoped he felt sufficiently sorry for Mike. But after all Mike's life and prospects mattered little to him. He had come back in search of health, and he felt better already; the milk had done him good, and the bacon and the cabbage in the pot sent forth a savory odor. The Scullys were very kind, they pressed him to make a good meal; a few weeks of country air and food, they said, would give him back the health he had lost in the Bowery; and when Bryden said he was longing for a smoke, Mike said there was no better sign than that. During his long illness he had never wanted to smoke, and he was a confirmed smoker.

It was comfortable to sit by the mild peat fire watching the smoke of their pipes drifting up the chimney, and all Bryden wanted was to be left alone; he did not want to hear of any-one's misfortunes, but about nine o'clock a number of villagers came in, and Bryden remembered one or two of them—he used to know them very well when he was a boy; their talk was as depressing as their appearance, and he could feel no interest whatever in them. He was not moved when he heard that Higgins the stonemason was dead; he was not affected when he heard that Mary Kelly, who used to go to do the laundry at the Big House, had married; he was only interested when he heard she had gone to America. No, he had not met her there; America is a big place. Then one of the peasants asked him if he remembered Patsy Carabine, who used to do the gardening at the Big House. Yes, he remembered Patsy well. He had not been able to do any work on account of his arm; his house had fallen in; he had given up his holding and gone into the poorhouse. All this was very sad, and to avoid hearing any further unpleasantness, Bryden began to tell them about America. And they sat round listening to him; but all the talking was on his side; he wearied of it; and looking round the group he recognized a ragged hunchback with grey hair; twenty years ago he was a young hunchback and, turning to him, Bryden asked him if he were doing well with his five acres.

"Ah, not much. This has been a poor season. The potatoes failed; they were watery—there is no diet in them."

These peasants were all agreed that they could make nothing out of their farms. Their regret was that they had not gone to America when they were young; and after striving to take an interest in the fact that O'Connor had lost a mare and a foal worth forty pounds, Bryden began to wish himself back in the slum. And when they left the house he wondered if every evening would be like the present one. Mike piled fresh sods on the fire, and he hoped it would show enough light in the loft for Bryden to undress himself by.

The cackling of some geese in the street kept him awake, and he seemed to realize suddenly how lonely the country was, and he foresaw mile after mile of scanty fields stretching all round the lake with one little town in the far corner. A dog howled in the distance, and the fields and the boreens between him and the dog appeared as in a crystal. He could hear Michael breathing by his wife's side in the kitchen, and he could barely resist the impulse to run out of the house, and he might have yielded to it, but he wasn't sure that he mightn't awaken Mike as he came down the ladder. His terror increased, and he drew the blanket over his head. He fell asleep and awoke and fell asleep again, and lying on his back he dreamed of the men he had seen sitting round the fireside that evening, like specters they seemed to him in his dream. He seemed to have been asleep only a few minutes when he heard Mike calling him. He had come halfway up the ladder, and was telling him that breakfast was ready.

"What kind of a breakfast will he give me?" Bryden asked himself as he pulled on his clothes. There were tea and hot griddle cakes for breakfast, and there were fresh eggs; there was sunlight in the kitchen, and he liked to hear Mike tell of the work he was going to be at in the farm—one of about fifteen acres, at least ten of it was grass; he grew an acre of potatoes, and some corn, and some turnips for his sheep. He had a nice bit of meadow, and he took down his scythe, and as he put the whetstone in his belt Bryden noticed a second scythe, and he asked Mike if he should go down with him and help him to finish the field.

"It's a long time since you've done any mowing, and it's heavier work than you think for. You'd better go for a walk by the lake." Seeing that Bryden looked a little disappointed he added, "if you like you can come up in the afternoon and help me to turn the grass over." Bryden said he would, and the morning passed pleasantly by the lakeshore—a delicious breeze rustled in the trees, and the reeds were talking together, and the ducks were talking in the reeds; a cloud blotted out the sunlight, and the cloud passed and the sun shone, and the reed cast its shadow again in the still water; there was a lapping always about the shingle; the magic of returning health was sufficient distraction for the convalescent; he lay with his eyes fixed upon the castles, dreaming of the men that had manned the battlements; whenever a peasant driving a cart or an ass or an old woman with a bundle of sticks on her back went by, Bryden kept them in chat, and he soon knew the village by heart. One day the landlord from the Georgian mansion set on the pleasant green hill came along, his retriever at his heels, and stopped surprised at finding somebody whom he didn't know on his property. "What, James Bryden!" he said. And the story was told again how ill health had overtaken him at last, and he had come home to Duncannon to recover. The two walked as far as the pinewood, talking of the county, what it had been, the ruin it was slipping into, and as they parted Bryden asked for the loan of a boat.

"Of course, of course!" the landlord answered, and Bryden rowed about the islands every morning; and resting upon his oars looked at the old castles, remembering the prehistoric raiders that the landlord had told him about. He came across the stones to which the lake dwellers had tied their boats, and these signs of ancient Ireland were pleasing to Bryden in his present mood.

As well as the great lake there was a smaller lake in the bog where the villagers cut their turf. This lake was famous for its pike, and the landlord allowed Bryden to fish there, and one evening when he was looking for a frog with which to bait his line he met Margaret Dirken driving home the cows for the milking. Margaret was the herdsman's daughter, and lived in a cottage near the Big House; but she came up to the village whenever there was a dance, and Bryden had found himself opposite to her in the reels. But until this evening he had had little opportunity of speaking to her, and he was glad to speak to someone, for the evening was lonely, and they stood talking together.

"You're getting your health again," she said, "and will be leaving us soon."

"I'm in no hurry."

"You're grand people over there; I hear a man is paid four dollars a day for his work."

"And how much," said James, "has he to pay for his food and for his clothes?"

Her cheeks were bright and her teeth small, white, and beautifully even; and a woman's soul looked at Bryden out of her soft Irish eyes. He was troubled and turned aside, and catching sight of a frog looking at him out of a tuft of grass, he said:

"I have been looking for a frog to put upon my pike line."

The frog jumped right and left, and nearly escaped in some bushes, but he caught it and returned with it in his hand.

"It is just the kind of frog a pike will like," he said. "Look at its great white belly and its bright yellow back."

And without more ado he pushed the wire to which the hook was fastened through the frog's fresh body, and dragging it through the mouth he passed the hooks through the hind legs and tied the line to the end of the wire.

"I think," said Margaret, "I must be looking after my cows; it's time I got them home."

"Won't you come down to the lake while I set my line?"

She thought for a moment and said:

"No, I'll see you from here."

He went down to the reedy tarn, and at his approach several snipe got up, and they flew above his head uttering sharp cries. His fishing rod was a long hazel stick, and he threw the frog as far as he could in the lake. In doing this he roused some wild ducks; a mallard and two ducks got up, and they flew towards the larger lake in a line with an old castle; and they had not disappeared from view when Bryden came towards her, and he and she drove the cows home together that evening.

They had not met very often when she said: "James, you had better not come here so often calling to me."

"Don't you wish me to come?"

"Yes, I wish you to come well enough, but keeping company isn't the custom of the country, and I don't want to be talked about."

"Are you afraid the priest would speak against us from the altar?"

"He has spoken against keeping company, but it is not so much what the priest says, for there is no harm in talking."

"But if you're going to be married there is no harm in walking out together."

"Well, not so much, but marriages are made differently in these parts; there isn't much courting here."

And next day it was known in the village that James was going to marry Margaret Dirken.

His desire to excel the boys in dancing had caused a stir of gaiety in the parish, and for some time past there had been dancing in every house where there was a floor fit to dance upon; and if the cottager had no money to pay for a barrel of beer, James Bryden, who had money, sent him a barrel, so that Margaret might get her dance. She told him that they sometimes crossed over into another parish where the priest was not so averse to dancing, and James wondered. And next morning at Mass he wondered at their simple fervor. Some of them held their hands above their head as they prayed, and all this was very new and very old to James Bryden. But the obedience of these people to their priest surprised him. When he was a lad they had not been so obedient, or he had forgotten their obedience; and he listened in mixed anger and wonderment to the priest, who was scolding his parishioners, speaking to them by name, saying that he had heard there was dancing going on in their homes. Worse than that, he said he had seen boys and girls loitering about the road, and the talk that went on was of one kind—love. He said that newspapers containing love stories were finding their way into the people's houses, stories about love, in which there was nothing elevating or ennobling. The people listened, accepting the priest's opinion without question. And their pathetic submission was the submission of a primitive people clinging to religious authority, and Bryden contrasted the weakness and incompetence of the people about him with the modern restlessness and cold energy of the people he left behind him.

One evening, as they were dancing, a knock came to the door, and the piper stopped playing, and the dancers whispered:

"Someone has told on us: it is the priest."

And the awestricken villagers crowded round the cottage fire, afraid to open the door. But the priest said that if they didn't open the door he would put his shoulder to it and force it open. Bryden went towards the door, saying he would allow no one to threaten him, priest or no priest, but Margaret caught his arm and told him that if he said anything to the priest, the priest would speak against them from the altar, and they would be shunned by the neighbors.

"I've heard of your goings-on," he said—"of your beer drinking and dancing. I'll not have it in my parish. If you want that sort of thing you had better go to America."

"If that is intended for me, sir, I'll go back tomorrow. Margaret can follow."

"It isn't the dancing, it's the drinking I'm opposed to," said the priest, turning to Bryden.

"Well, no one has drunk too much, sir," said Bryden.

"But you'll sit here drinking all night," and the priest's eyes went to the corner where the women had gathered, and Bryden felt that the priest looked on the women as more dangerous than the porter. "It's after midnight," he said, taking out his watch.

By Bryden's watch it was only half past eleven, and while they were arguing about the time, Mrs. Scully offered Bryden's umbrella to the priest, for in his hurry to stop the dancing the priest had gone out without his; and, as if to show Bryden that he bore him no ill will, the priest accepted the loan of the umbrella, for he was thinking of the big marriage fee that Bryden would pay him.

"I shall be badly off for the umbrella tomorrow," Bryden said, as soon as the priest was out of the house. He was going with his father-in-law to a fair. His father-in-law was learning him how to buy and sell cattle. The country was mending, and a man might become rich in Ireland if he only had a little capital. Margaret had an uncle on the other side of the lake who would give twenty pounds, and her father would give another twenty pounds. Bryden had saved two hundred pounds. Never in the village of Duncannon had a young couple begun life with so much prospect of success, and some time after Christmas was spoken of as the best time for the marriage; James Bryden said that he would not be able to get his money out of America before the spring. The delay seemed to vex him, and he seemed anxious to be married, until one day he received a letter from America, from a man who had served in the bar with him. This friend wrote to ask Bryden if he were coming back. The letter was no more than a passing wish to see Bryden again. Yet Bryden stood looking at it, and everyone wondered what could be in the letter. It seemed momentous, and they hardly believed him when he said it was from a friend who wanted to know if his health were better. He tried to forget the letter, and he looked at the worn fields, divided by walls of loose stones, and a great longing came upon him.

The smell of the Bowery slum had come across the Atlantic, and had found him out in his western headland; and one night he awoke from a dream in which he was hurling some drunken customer through the open doors into the darkness. He had seen his friend in his white duck jacket throwing drink from glass into glass amid the din of voices and strange accents; he had heard the clang of money as it was swept into the till, and his sense sickened for the barroom. But how should he tell Margaret Dirken that he could not marry her? She had built her life upon this marriage. He could not tell her that he would not marry her ... yet he must go. He felt as if he were being hunted; the thought that he must tell Margaret that he could not marry her hunted him day after day as a weasel hunts a rabbit. Again and again he went to meet her with the intention of telling her that he did not love her, that their lives were not for one another, that it had all been a mistake, and that happily he had found out it was a mistake soon enough. But Margaret, as if she guessed what he was about to speak of, threw her arms about him and begged him to say he loved her, and that they would be married at once. He agreed that he loved her, and that they would be married at once. But he had not left her many minutes before the feeling came upon him that he could not marry her—that he must go away. The smell of the barroom hunted him down. Was it for the sake of the money that he might make there that he wished to go back? No, it was not the money. What then? His eyes fell on the bleak country, on the little fields divided by bleak walls; he remembered the pathetic ignorance of the people, and it was these things that he could not endure. It was the priest who came to forbid the dancing. Yes, it was the priest. As he stood looking at the line of the hills the barroom seemed by him. He heard the politicians, and the excitement of politics was in his blood again. He must go away from this place—he must get back to the barroom. Looking up, he saw the scanty orchard, and he hated the spare road that led to the village, and he hated the little hill at the top of which the village began, and he hated more than all other places the house where he was to live with Margaret Dirken—if he married her. He could see it from where he stood—by the edge of the lake, with twenty acres of pasture land about it, for the landlord had given up part of his demesne land to them.

He caught sight of Margaret, and he called her to come through the stile.

"I have just had a letter from America."

"About the money?"

"Yes, about the money. But I shall have to go over there."

He stood looking at her, wondering what to say; and she guessed that he would tell her that he must go to America before they were married.

"Do you mean, James, you will have to go at once?"

"Yes," he said, "at once. But I shall come back in time to be married in August. It will only mean delaying our marriage a month."

They walked on a little way talking, and every step he took James felt that he was a step nearer the Bowery slum. And when they came to the gate Bryden said:

"I must walk on or I shall miss the train."

"But," she said, "you are not going now—you are not going today?"

"Yes, this morning. It is seven miles. I shall have to hurry not to miss the train."

And then she asked him if he would ever come back.

"Yes," he said, "I am coming back."

"If you are coming back, James, why don't you let me go with you?"

"You couldn't walk fast enough. We should miss the train."

"One moment, James. Don't make me suffer; tell me the truth. You are not coming back. Your clothes—where shall I send them?"

He hurried away, hoping he would come back. He tried to think that he liked the country he was leaving, that it would be better to have a farmhouse and live there with Margaret Dirken than to serve drinks behind a counter in the Bowery. He did not think he was telling her a lie when he said he was coming back. Her offer to forward his clothes touched his heart, and at the end of the road he stood and asked himself if he should go back to her. He would miss the train if he waited another minute, and he ran on. And he would have missed the train if he had not met a car. Once he was on the car he felt himself safe—the country was already behind him. The train and the boat at Cork were mere formulae; he was already in America.

And when the tall skyscraper stuck up beyond the harbor he felt the thrill of home that he had not found in his native village and wondered how it was that the smell of the bar seemed more natural than the smell of fields, and the roar of crowds more welcome than the silence of the lake's edge. He entered into negotiations for the purchase of the barroom. He took a wife, she bore him sons and daughters, the barroom prospered, property came and went; he grew old, his wife died, he retired from business, and reached the age when a man begins to feel there are not many years in front of him, and that all he has had to do in life has been done. His children married, lonesomeness began to creep about him in the evening, and when he looked into the firelight, a vague tender reverie floated up, and Margaret's soft eyes and name vivified the dusk. His wife and children passed out of mind, and it seemed to him that a memory was the only real thing he possessed, and the desire to see Margaret again grew intense. But she was an old woman, she had married, maybe she was dead. Well, he would like to be buried in the village where he was born.

There is an unchanging, silent life within every man that none knows but himself, and his unchanging silent life was his memory of Margaret Dirken. The barroom was forgotten and all that concerned it, and the things he saw most clearly were the green hillside, and the bog lake and the rushes about it, and the greater lake in the distance, and behind it the blue line of wandering hills.

E. OE. Somerville (1858–1949)
Martin Ross (1862–1915)

Edith Somerville was born in Corfu in 1858, and Martin Ross (Violet Florence Martin) in Ross, County Galway, in 1862. They were second cousins from well-established Anglo-Irish Ascendancy stock, and much of their best work humorously contrasts native Irish culture with the often bewildered Anglo-Irish gentry. They began collaborating in 1886, and published their first book, An Irish Cousin, *in 1889. Their best novel,* The Real Charlotte, *a realistic portrait of Ascendancy society, was published in 1894. In 1899 appeared* Some Experiences of an Irish R.M., *the first of a three-volume series of stories treating the Irish adventures of the Englishman Major Sinclair Yeates, a resident magistrate (R.M.) in the West of Ireland. "Poisson d'Avril" is taken from the second volume,* Further Experiences of an Irish R.M., *published in 1908. Though Somerville and Ross do owe much to the nineteenth-century comic anecdotal story, their knowledge of Irish folkways and their keen, appreciative ear for different forms of Irish English place them firmly within the modern Irish literary tradition. The third volume of R.M. stories,* In Mr. Knox's Country, *was published in 1915, the year Martin Ross died.*

Poisson d'Avril

The atmosphere of the waiting room set at naught at a single glance the theory that there can be no smoke without fire. The stationmaster, when remonstrated with, stated, as an incontrovertible fact, that any chimney in the world would smoke in a southeasterly wind, and further, said there wasn't a poker, and that if you poked the fire the grate would fall out. He was, however, sympathetic, and went on his knees before the smoldering mound of slack, endeavoring to charm it to a smile by subtle proddings with the handle of the ticket punch. Finally, he took me to his own kitchen fire and talked politics and salmon fishing, the former with judicious attention to my presumed point of view, and careful suppression of his own, the latter with no less tactful regard for my admission that for three days I had not caught a fish, while the steam rose from my wet boots, in witness of the ten miles of rain through which an outside car had carried me.

Before the train was signaled I realized for the hundredth time the magnificent superiority of the Irish mind to the trammels of officialdom, and the inveterate supremacy in Ireland of the personal element.

"You might get a foot warmer at Carrig Junction," said a species of lay porter in a knitted jersey, ramming my suitcase upside down under the seat. "Sometimes they're in it, and more times they're not."

The train dragged itself rheumatically from the station, and a cold spring rain—the time was the middle of a most inclement April—smote it in flank as it came into the open. I pulled up both windows and began to smoke; there is, at least, a semblance of warmth in a thoroughly vitiated atmosphere.

It is my wife's habit to assert that I do not read her letters, and being now on my way to join her and my family in Gloucestershire, it seemed a sound thing to study again her latest letter of instructions.

"I am starting today, as Alice wrote to say we must be there two days before the wedding, so as to have a rehearsal for the pages. Their dresses have come, and they look too delicious in them—"

(I here omit profuse particulars not pertinent to this tale.)
"—It is sickening for you to have had such bad sport. If the worst comes to the worst couldn't you buy one?—"

I smote my hand upon my knee. I had forgotten the infernal salmon! What a score for Philippa! If these *contretemps* would only teach her that I was not to be relied upon, they would have their uses, but experience is wasted upon her; I have no objection to being called an idiot, but, that being so, I ought to be allowed the privileges and exemptions proper to idiots. Philippa had, no doubt, written to Alice Hervey, and assured her that Sinclair would be only too delighted to bring her a salmon, and Alice Hervey, who was rich enough to find much enjoyment in saving money, would reckon upon it, to its final fin in mayonnaise.

Plunged in morose meditations, I progressed through a country parceled out by shaky and crooked walls into a patch-wood of hazel scrub and rocky fields, veiled in rain. About every six miles there was a station, wet and windswept; at one the sole occurrence was the presentation of a newspaper to the guard by the stationmaster; at the next the guard read aloud some choice excerpts from the same to the porter. The Personal Element was potent on this branch of the Munster and Connaught Railway. Routine, abhorrent to all artistic minds, was sheathed in conversation; even the engine driver, a functionary ordinarily as aloof as the Mikado, alleviated his enforced isolation by sociable shrieks to every level crossing, while the long row of public houses that formed, as far as I could judge, the town of Carrig, received a special and, as it seemed, humorous salutation.

The timetable decreed that we were to spend ten minutes at Carrig Junction; it was fifteen before the crowd of market people on the platform had been assimilated; finally, the window of a neighboring carriage was flung open, and a wrathful English voice asked how much longer the train was going to wait. The stationmaster, who was at the moment engrossed in con-

versation with the guard and a man who was carrying a long
parcel wrapped in newspaper, looked round, and said gravely:
"Well now, that's a mystery!"

The man with the parcel turned away, and convulsively studied a poster. The guard put his hand over his mouth.

The voice, still more wrathfully, demanded the earliest hour
at which its owner could get to Belfast.

"Ye'll be asking me next when I take me breakfast," replied
the stationmaster, without haste or palpable annoyance.

The window went up again with a bang, the man with the
parcel dug the guard in the ribs with his elbow, and the parcel
slipped from under his arm and fell on the platform.

"Oh my! oh my! Me fish!" exclaimed the man, solicitously
picking up a remarkably good-looking salmon that had slipped
from its wrapping of newspaper.

Inspiration came to me, and I, in my turn, opened my window and summoned the stationmaster.

Would his friend sell me the salmon? The stationmaster entered upon the mission with ardor, but without success.

No; the gentleman was only just after running down to the
town for it in the delay, but why wouldn't I run down and get
one for myself? There was half a dozen more of them below at
Coffey's, selling cheap; there would be time enough, the mail
wasn't signaled yet.

I jumped from the carriage and doubled out of the station at
top speed, followed by an assurance from the guard that he
would not forget me.

Congratulating myself on the ascendancy of the personal element, I sped through the soapy limestone mud towards the
public houses. En route I met a heated man carrying yet another salmon, who, without preamble, informed me that there
were three or four more good fish in it, and that he was after
running down from the train himself.

"Ye have whips o' time!" he called after me. "It's the first
house that's not a public house. Ye'll see boots in the win-

dow—she'll give them for tenpence a pound if ye're stiff with her!"

I ran past the public houses.

"Tenpence a pound!" I exclaimed inwardly, "at this time of year! That's good enough."

Here I perceived the house with boots in the window, and dived into its dark doorway.

A cobbler was at work behind a low counter. He mumbled something about Herself, through lengths of waxed thread that hung across his mouth, a fat woman appeared at an inner door, and at that moment I heard, appallingly near, the whistle of the incoming mail. The fat woman grasped the situation in an instant, and with what appeared but one movement, snatched a large fish from the floor of the room behind her and flung a newspaper round it.

"Eight pound weight!" she said swiftly. "Ten shillings!"

A convulsive effort of mental arithmetic assured me that this was more than tenpence a pound, but it was not the moment for stiffness. I shoved a half-sovereign into her fishy hand, clasped my salmon in my arms, and ran.

Needless to say it was uphill, and at the steepest gradient another whistle stabbed me like a spur; above the station roof successive and advancing puffs of steam warned me that the worst had probably happened, but still I ran. When I gained the platform my train was already clear of it, but the personal element held good. Every soul in the station, or so it seemed to me, lifted up his voice and yelled. The stationmaster put his fingers in his mouth and sent after the departing train an unearthly whistle, with a high trajectory and a serrated edge. It took effect; the train slackened, I plunged from the platform and followed it up the rails, and every window in both trains blossomed with the heads of deeply interested spectators. The guard met me on the line, very apologetic and primed with an explanation that the gentleman going for the boat train wouldn't let him wait any longer, while from our rear came an exultant cry from the stationmaster.

"Ye *told* him ye wouldn't forget him!"

"There's a few countrywomen in your carriage, sir," said the guard, ignoring the taunt, as he shoved me and my salmon up the side of the train, "but they'll be getting out in a couple of stations. There wasn't another seat in the train for them!"

My sensational return to my carriage was viewed with the utmost sympathy by no less than seven shawled and cloaked countrywomen. In order to make room for me one of them seated herself on the floor with her basket in her lap, another, on the seat opposite to me, squeezed herself under the central elbow flap that had been turned up to make room. The aromas of wet cloaks, turf smoke, and salt fish formed a potent blend. I was excessively hot, and the eyes of the seven women were fastened upon me with intense and unwearying interest.

"Move west a small piece, Mary Jack, if you please," said a voluminous matron in the corner, "I declare we're as throng as three in a bed this minute!"

"Why then, Julia Casey, there's little throubling yourself," grumbled the woman under the flap. "Look at the way meself is! I wonder is it to be putting humps on themselves the gentry has them things down on top o' them! I'd sooner be carrying a basket of turnips on me back than to be scrooged this way!"

The woman on the floor at my feet rolled up at me a glance of compassionate amusement at this rustic ignorance, and tactfully changed the conversation by supposing that it was at Coffey's I got the salmon.

I said it was.

There was a silence, during which it was obvious that one question burnt in every heart.

"I'll go bail she axed him tinpence!" said the woman under the flap, as one who touches the limits of absurdity.

"It's a beautiful fish!" I said defiantly. "Eight pounds weight. I gave her ten shillings for it."

What is described in newspapers as "sensation in court" greeted this confession.

"Look!" said the woman under the flap, darting her head out of the hood of her cloak, like a tortoise, " 'tis what it is, ye haven't as much roguery in your heart as 'd make ye a match for her!"

"Divil blow the ha'penny Eliza Coffey paid for that fish!" burst out the fat woman in the corner. "Thim lads o' her's had a creel full o' thim snatched this morning before it was making day!"

"How would the gentleman be a match for her!" shouted the woman on the floor through a long-drawn whistle that told of a coming station. "Sure a Turk itself wouldn't be a match for her! That one has a tongue that'd clip a hedge!"

At the station they clambered out laboriously, and with groaning. I handed down to them their monster baskets, laden, apparently, with ingots of lead; they told me in return that I was a fine *grauver* man, and it was a pity there weren't more like me; they wished, finally, that my journey might well thrive with me, and passed from my ken, bequeathing to me, after the agreeable manner of their kind, a certain comfortable mental sleekness that reason cannot immediately dispel. They also left me in possession of the fact that I was about to present the irreproachable Alice Hervey with a contraband salmon.

The afternoon passed cheerlessly into evening, and my journey did not conspicuously thrive with me. Somewhere in the dripping twilight I changed trains, and again later on, and at each change the salmon moulted some more of its damp raiment of newspaper, and I debated seriously the idea of interring it, regardless of consequences, in my portmanteau. A lamp was banged into the roof of my carriage, half an inch of orange flame, poised in a large glass globe, like a goldfish, and of about as much use as an illuminant. Here also was handed in the dinner basket that I had wired for, and its contents, arid though they were, enabled me to achieve at least some measure of mechanical distension, followed by a dreary lethargy that was not far from drowsiness.

At the next station we paused long; nothing whatever occurred, and the rain drummed patiently upon the roof. Two nuns and some schoolgirls were in the carriage next door, and their voices came plaintively and in snatches through the partition; after a long period of apparent collapse, during which I closed my eyes to evade the cold gaze of the salmon through the netting, a voice in the next carriage said resourcefully:

"Oh, girls, I'll tell you what we'll do! We'll say the Rosary!"

"Oh, that will be lovely!" said another voice; "well, who'll give it out? Theresa Condon, you'll give it out."

Theresa Condon gave it out, in a not unmelodious monotone, interspersed with the responses, always in a lower cadence; the words were indistinguishable, but the rise and fall of the western voices was lulling as the hum of bees. I feel asleep.

I awoke in total darkness; the train was motionless, and complete and profound silence reigned. We were at a station, that much I discerned by the light of a dim lamp at the far end of a platform glistening with wet. I struck a match and ascertained that it was eleven o'clock, precisely the hour at which I was to board the mail train. I jumped out and ran down the platform; there was no one in the train; there was no one even on the engine, which was forlornly hissing to itself in the silence. There was not a human being anywhere. Every door was closed, and all was dark. The nameboard of the station was faintly visible; with a lighted match I went along it letter by letter. It seemed as if the whole alphabet were in it, and by the time I had got to the end I had forgotten the beginning. One fact I had, however, mastered, that it was not the junction at which I was to catch the mail.

I was undoubtedly awake, but for a moment I was inclined to entertain the idea that there had been an accident, and that I had entered upon existence in another world. Once more I assailed the station house and the appurtenances thereof, the ticket office, the waiting room, finally, and at some distance, the goods store, outside which the single lamp of the station commented feebly on the drizzle and the darkness. As I approached it a crack of light under the door became perceptible, and a voice was suddenly uplifted within.

"Your best now agin that! Throw down your jack!"

I opened the door with pardonable violence, and found the guard, the stationmaster, the driver, and the stoker seated on barrels round a packing case, on which they were playing a game of cards.

To have too egregiously the best of a situation is not, to a generous mind, a source of strength. In the perfection of their overthrow I permitted the driver and stoker to wither from their places, and to fade away into the outer darkness without any suitable send-off; with the guard and the stationmaster I dealt more faithfully, but the pleasure of throwing water on drowned rats is not a lasting one. I accepted the statements that they thought there wasn't a Christian in the train, that a few minutes here or there wouldn't signify, that they would have me at the junction in twenty minutes, and it was often the mail was late.

Fired by this hope I hurried back to my carriage, preceded at an emulous gallop by the officials. The guard thrust in with me the lantern from the card table, and fled to his van.

"Mind the Goods, Tim!" shouted the stationmaster, as he slammed my door, "she might be coming any time now!"

The answer traveled magnificently back from the engine.

"Let her come! She'll meet her match!" A war whoop upon the steam whistle fittingly closed the speech, and the train sprang into action.

We had about fifteen miles to go, and we banged and bucketed over it in what was, I should imagine, record time. The carriage felt as if it were galloping on four wooden legs, my teeth chattered in my head, and the salmon slowly churned its way forth from its newspaper, and moved along the netting with dreadful stealth.

All was of no avail.

"Well," said the guard, as I stepped forth on to the deserted platform of Loughranny, "that owld Limited Mail's th'unpunctualest thrain in Ireland! If you're a minute late she's gone from you, and maybe if you were early you might be half an hour waiting for her!"

On the whole the guard was a gentleman. He said he would show me the best hotel in the town, though he feared I would be hard set to get a bed anywhere because of the "Feis" (a Feis, I should explain, is a festival, devoted to competitions in Irish songs and dances). He shouldered my portmanteau, he even grappled successfully with the salmon, and, as we traversed the empty streets, he explained to me how easily I could catch the morning boat from Rosslare, and how it was, as a matter of fact, quite the act of providence that my original scheme had been frustrated.

All was dark at the uninviting portals of the hotel favored by the guard. For a full five minutes we waited at them, ringing hard: I suggested that we should try elsewhere.

"He'll come," said the guard, with the confidence of the Pied Piper of Hamelin, retaining an implacable thumb upon the button of the electric bell. "He'll come. Sure it rings in his room!"

The victim came, half awake, half dressed, and with an inch of dripping candle in his fingers. There was not a bed there, he said, nor in the town neither.

I said I would sit in the dining room till the time for the early train.

"Sure there's five beds in the dining room," replied the boots, "and there's mostly two in every bed."

His voice was firm, but there was a wavering look in his eye.

"What about the billiard room, Mike?" said the guard, in wooing tones.

"Ah, God bless you! we have a mattress on the table this minute!" answered the boots, wearily, "and the fellow that got the First Prize for Reels asleep on top of it!"

"Well, and can't ye put the palliasse on the floor under it, ye omadhawn?" said the guard, dumping my luggage and the salmon in the hall, "sure there's no snugger place in the house! I must run away home now, before Herself thinks I'm dead altogether!"

His retreating footsteps went lightly away down the empty street.

"Annything don't throuble *him*!" said the boots bitterly.

As for me, nothing save the Personal Element stood between me and destitution.

It was in the dark of the early morning that I woke again to life and its troubles. A voice, dropping, as it were, over the edge of some smothering overworld, had awakened me. It was the voice of the First Prize for Reels, descending through a pocket of the billiard table.

"I beg your pardon, sir, are ye going on the 5 to Cork?"

I grunted a negative.

"Well, if ye were, ye'd be late," said the voice.

I received this useful information in indignant silence, and endeavored to wrap myself again in the vanishing skirts of a dream.

"I'm going on the 6:30 meself," proceeded the voice, "and it's unknown to me how I'll put on me boots. Me feet is swelled the size o' three-pound loaves with the dint of the little dancing shoes I had on me in the competition last night. Me feet's delicate that way, and I'm a great epicure about me boots."

I snored aggressively, but the dream was gone. So, for all practical purposes was the night.

The First Prize for Reels arose, presenting an astonishing spectacle of grass-green breeches, a white shirt, and pearl-grey stockings, and accomplished a toilet that consisted of removing these and putting on ordinary garments, completed by the apparently excruciating act of getting into his boots. At any other hour of the day I might have been sorry for him. He then removed himself and his belongings to the hall, and there entered upon a resounding conversation with the boots, while I crawled forth from my lair to renew the strife with circumstances and to endeavor to compose a telegram to Alice Hervey of explanation and apology that should cost less than seven and sixpence. There was also the salmon to be dealt with.

Here the boots intervened, opportunely, with a cup of tea, and the intelligence that he had already done up the salmon in straw bottle covers and brown paper, and that I could travel Europe with it if I liked. He further informed me that he would run up to the station with the luggage now, and that maybe I wouldn't mind carrying the fish myself; it was on the table in the hall.

My train went at 6:15. The boots had secured for me one of many empty carriages, and lingered conversationally till the train started; he regretted politely my bad night at the hotel, and assured me that only for Jimmy Durkan having a little drink taken—Jimmy Durkan was the First Prize for Reels—he would have turned him off the billiard table for my benefit. He finally confided to me that Mr. Durkan was engaged to his sister, and was a rising baker in the town of Limerick; "indeed," he said, "any girl might be glad to get him. He dances like whalebone, and he makes grand bread!"

Here the train started.

It was late that night when, stiff, dirty, with tired eyes blinking in the dazzle of electric lights, I was conducted by the Herveys' beautiful footman into the Herveys' baronial hall, and was told by the Herveys' imperial butler that dinner was over, and the gentlemen had just gone into the drawing room. I was in the act of hastily declining to join them there, when a voice cried:

"Here he is!"

And Philippa, rustling and radiant, came forth into the hall, followed in shimmers of satin, and flutterings of lace, by Alice Hervey, by the bride elect, and by the usual festive rout of exhilarated relatives, male and female, whose mission it is to keep things lively before a wedding.

"Is this a wedding present for me, Uncle Sinclair?" cried the bride elect, through a deluge of questions and commiserations, and snatched from under my arm the brown paper parcel that had remained there from force of direful habit.

"I advise you not to open it!" I exclaimed; "it's a salmon!"

The bride elect, with a shriek of disgust, and without an instant of hesitation, hurled it at her nearest neighbor, the head bridesmaid. The head bridesmaid, with an answering shriek, sprang to one side, and the parcel that I had cherished with a mother's care across two countries and a stormy Channel fell, with a crash, on the flagged floor.

Why did it crash?

"A salmon!" screamed Philippa, gazing at the parcel, round which a pool was already forming, "why, that's whiskey! Can't you smell it?"

The footman here respectfully interposed, and kneeling down, cautiously extracted from folds of brown paper a straw bottle cover full of broken glass and dripping with whiskey.

"I'm afraid the other things are rather spoiled, sir," he said seriously, and drew forth, successively, a very large pair of high-low shoes, two long grey worsted stockings, and a pair of grass-green breeches.

They brought the house down, in a manner doubtless famil-

iar to them when they shared the triumphs of Mr. Jimmy Durkan, but they left Alice Hervey distinctly cold.

"You know, darling," she said to Philippa afterwards, "I
don't think it was very clever of dear Sinclair to take the wrong
parcel. I *had* counted on that salmon."

W. B. Yeats (1865–1939)

William Butler Yeats was born in Sandymount, near Dublin, in 1865. His father was J. B. Yeats, an artist and a brilliant conversationalist, and his mother was Susan Pollexfen, whose family were merchants in W. B. Yeats's favorite place, the small coastal town of Sligo. Yeats's position as one of the greatest modern poets in the English language is even more secure now than when he was awarded the Nobel Prize for literature in 1923. From the very beginning of his literary career—his first volume of poetry, The Wandering of Oisin and Other Poems, *appeared in 1889—he was the central, driving force behind the Irish Literary Revival. He helped organize the Irish dramatic movement, including the founding of the Abbey Theatre in 1904; he encouraged other Irish authors to create a national literature by searching out distinctively Irish themes and styles; and he generated, year after year, through his own poetry, drama, essays, and speeches, international interest in Ireland's new literature. Perhaps because he dominated the literary movement so completely, and through so many phases of its growth, from an early fascination with Celtic legend and myth and on through Ireland's bitter struggles for independence and political stability, his life and work seem to embody modern Ireland itself. His* Collected Poems *and* Collected Plays *are both modern classics, but his prose, perhaps less well known, is rich and abundant. It includes stories, essays, literary criticism, a philosophical treatise, biographies, autobiographies, political speeches, letters, diaries, and an unfinished novel. His short stories belong to the first part of his literary career and stem from two lasting enthusiasms: occult symbolism and native Irish folklore. His early stories were published in the 1890s and are now collected in the volume* Mythologies. *Though his occult stories are skillful and elaborate works of art—"Tables of the Law" and "The Adoration of the Magi" were favorites of the young James Joyce—his literary folk tales are much closer to the sources of the modern Irish short story.* The Stories of Red Hanrahan *were first published in 1897 in the volume* The Secret Rose, *but they were later revised (1904) with Lady Gregory's help and republished. "The Twisting of the Rope" (1907 version) is not only the best and most self-contained of the Hanrahan stories; it is important because it provided the basis for the first modern Gaelic play, Douglas Hyde's* Casadh an tSugain, *performed in Dublin in 1901.*

The Twisting of the Rope

Hanrahan was walking the roads one time near Kinvara at the fall of day, and he heard the sound of a fiddle from a house a little way off the roadside. He turned up the path to it, for he never had the habit of passing by any place where there was music or dancing or good company, without going in. The man of the house was standing at the door, and when Hanrahan came near he knew him and he said, "A welcome before you, Hanrahan, you have been lost to us this long time." But the woman of the house came to the door and she said to her husband, "I would be as well pleased for Hanrahan not to come in tonight, for he has no good name now among the priests, or with women that mind themselves, and I wouldn't wonder from his walk if he has a drop of drink taken." But the man said, "I will never turn away Hanrahan of the poets from my door," and with that he bade him enter.

There were a good many neighbors gathered in the house, and some of them remembered Hanrahan; but some of the little lads that were in the corners had only heard of him, and they stood up to have a view of him, and one of them said, "Is not that Hanrahan that had the school, and that was brought away by Them?" But his mother put her hand over his mouth and bade him be quiet, and not be saying things like that. "For Hanrahan is apt to grow wicked," she said, "if he hears talk of that story, or if anyone goes questioning him." One or another called out then, asking him for a song, but the man of the house said it was no time to ask him for a song, before he had rested himself; and he gave him whiskey in a glass, and Hanrahan thanked him and wished him good health and drank it off.

The fiddler was tuning his fiddle for another dance, and the man of the house said to the young men, they would all know what dancing was like when they saw Hanrahan dance, for the like of it had never been seen since he was there before. Hanrahan said he would not dance, he had better use for his feet now, traveling as he was through the four provinces of Ireland. Just as he said that, there came in at the half door Oona, the daughter of the house, having a few bits of bog deal from Connemara in her arms for the fire. She threw them on the hearth, and the flame rose up and showed her to be very comely and smiling, and two or three of the young men rose up and asked for a dance. But Hanrahan crossed the floor and brushed the others away, and said it was with him she must dance, after the long road he had traveled before he came to her. And it is likely he said some soft word in her ear, for she said nothing against it, and stood out with him, and there were little blushes in her cheeks. Then other couples stood up, but when the dance was going to begin, Hanrahan chanced to look down, and he took notice of his boots that were worn and broken, and the ragged grey socks showing through them; and he said angrily it was a bad floor, and the music no great thing, and he sat down in the dark place beside the hearth. But if he did, the girl sat down there with him.

The dancing went on, and when that dance was over another was called for, and no one took much notice of Oona and Red

Hanrahan for a while, in the corner where they were. But the mother grew to be uneasy, and she called to Oona to come and help her to set the table in the inner room. But Oona that had never refused her before said she would come soon, but not yet, for she was listening to whatever he was saying in her ear. The mother grew yet more uneasy then, and she would come nearer them, and let on to be stirring the fire or sweeping the hearth, and she would listen for a minute to hear what the poet was saying to her child. And one time she heard him telling about white-handed Deirdre, and how she brought the sons of Usna to their death; and how the blush in her cheeks was not so red as the blood of kings' sons that was shed for her, and her sorrows had never gone out of mind; and he said it was maybe the memory of her that made the cry of the plover on the bog as sorrowful in the ear of the poets as the keening of young men for a comrade. And there would never have been that memory of her, he said, if it was not for the poets that had put her beauty in their songs. And the next time she did not well understand what he was saying, but as far as she could hear, it had the sound of poetry though it was not rhymed, and this is what she heard him say: "The sun and the moon are the man and the girl, they are my life and your life, they are traveling and ever traveling through the skies as if under the one hood. It was God made them for one another. He made your life and my life before the beginning of the world, He made them that they might go through the world, up and down, like the two best dancers that go on with the dance up and down the long floor of the barn, fresh and laughing, when all the rest are tired out and leaning against the wall."

The old woman went then to where her husband was playing cards, but he would take no notice of her, and then she went to a woman of the neighbors and said, "Is there no way we can get them from one another?" and without waiting for an answer she said to some young men that were talking together, "What good are you when you cannot make the best girl in the house come out and dance with you? And go now the whole of you," she said, "and see can you bring her away from the poet's talk." But Oona would not listen to any of them, but only moved her hand as if to send them away. Then they called to Hanrahan and said he had best dance with the girl himself, or let her dance with one of them. When Hanrahan heard what they were saying he said, "That is so, I will dance with her; there is no man in the house must dance with her but myself."

He stood up with her then, and led her out by the hand, and some of the young men were vexed, and some began mocking at his ragged coat and his broken boots. But he took no notice, and Oona took no notice, but they looked at one another as if all the world belonged to themselves alone. But another couple that had been sitting together like lovers stood out on the floor at the same time, holding one another's hands and moving their feet to keep time with the music. But Hanrahan turned his back on them as if angry, and in place of dancing he began to sing, and as he sang he held her hand, and his voice grew louder, and the mocking of the young men stopped, and the fiddle stopped, and there was nothing heard but his voice that had in it the sound of the wind. And what he sang was a song he had heard or had made one time in his wanderings on Slieve Echtge, and the words of it as they can be put into English were like this:

> O Death's old bony finger
> Will never find us there
> In the high hollow townland
> Where love's to give and to spare;
> Where boughs have fruit and blossom
> At all times of the year;
> Where rivers are running over
> With red beer and brown beer.

> An old man plays the bagpipes
> In a golden and silver wood;
> Queens, their eyes blue like the ice,
> Are dancing in a crowd.

And while he was singing it Oona moved nearer to him, and the color had gone from her cheek, and her eyes were not blue now, but grey with the tears that were in them, and anyone that saw her would have thought she was ready to follow him there and then from the west to the east of the world.

But one of the young men called out, "Where is that country he is singing about? Mind yourself, Oona, it is a long way off, you might be a long time on the road before you would reach to it." And another said, "It is not to the Country of the Young you will be going if you go with him, but to Mayo of the bogs." Oona looked at him then as if she would question him, but he raised her hand in his hand, and called out between singing and shouting, "It is very near us that country is, it is on every side; it may be on the bare hill behind it is, or it may be in the heart of the wood." And he said out very loud and clear, "In the heart of the wood; O, Death will never find us in the heart of the wood. And will you come with me there, Oona?" he said.

But while he was saying this the two old women had gone outside the door, and Oona's mother was crying, and she said, "He has put an enchantment on Oona. Can we not get the men to put him out of the house?"

"That is a thing you cannot do," said the other woman, "for he is a poet of the Gael, and you know well if you would put a poet of the Gael out of the house, he would put a curse on you that would wither the corn in the fields and dry up the milk of the cows, if it had to hang in the air seven years."

"God help us," said the mother, "and why did I ever let him into the house at all, and the wild name he has!"

"It would have been no harm at all to have kept him out-side, but there would great harm come upon you if you put him out by force. But listen to the plan I have to get him out of the house by his own doing, without any one putting him from it at all."

It was not long after that the two women came in again, each of them having a bundle of hay in her apron. Hanrahan was not singing now, but he was talking to Oona very fast and soft, and he was saying, "The house is narrow, but the world is wide, and there is no true lover that need be afraid of night or morning or sun or stars or shadows of evening, or any earthly thing." "Hanrahan," said the mother then, striking him on the shoulder, "will you give me a hand here for a minute?" "Do that, Hanrahan," said the woman of the neighbors, "and help us to make this hay into a rope, for you are ready with your hands, and a blast of wind has loosened the thatch on the haystack."

"I will do that for you," said he, and he took the little stick in his hands, and the mother began giving out the hay, and he twisting it, but he was hurrying to have done with it, and to be free again. The women went on talking and giving out the hay, and encouraging him, and saying what a good twister of a rope he was, better than their own neighbors or than anyone they had ever seen. And Hanrahan saw that Oona was watch-ing him, and he began to twist very quick and with his head high, and to boast of the readiness of his hands, and the learn-ing he had in his head, and the strength in his arms. And as he was boasting, he went backward, twisting the rope always till he came to the door that was open behind him, and without thinking he passed the threshold and was out on the road. And no sooner was he there than the mother made a sudden rush, and threw out the rope after him, and she shut the door and the half door and put a bolt upon them.

She was well pleased when she had done that, and laughed

out loud, and the neighbors laughed and praised her. But they heard him beating at the door, and saying words of cursing outside it, and the mother had but time to stop Oona that had her hand upon the bolt to open it. She made a sign to the fiddler then, and he began a reel, and one of the young men asked no leave but caught hold of Oona and brought her into the thick of the dance. And when it was over and the fiddle had stopped, there was no sound at all of anything outside, but the road was as quiet as before.

As to Hanrahan, when he knew he was shut out and that there was neither shelter nor drink nor a girl's ear for him that night, the anger and the courage went out of him, and he went on to where the waves were beating on the strand.

He sat down on a big stone, and he began swinging his right arm and singing slowly to himself, the way he did always to hearten himself when every other thing failed him. And whether it was that time or another time he made the song that is called to this day "The Twisting of the Rope," and that begins, "What was the dead cat that put me in this place," is not known.

But after he had been singing awhile, mist and shadows seemed to gather about him, sometimes coming out of the sea, and sometimes moving upon it. It seemed to him that one of the shadows was the queen-woman he had seen in her sleep at Slieve Echtge; not in her sleep now, but mocking, and calling out to them that were behind her, "He was weak, he was weak, he had no courage." And he felt the strands of the rope in his hand yet, and went on twisting it, but it seemed to him as he twisted that it had all the sorrows of the world in it. And then it seemed to him as if the rope had changed in his dream into a great water worm that came out of the sea, and that twisted itself about him, and held him closer and closer. And then he got free of it, and went on, shaking and unsteady, along the edge of the strand, and the gray shapes were flying here and there around him. And this is what they were saying: "It is a pity for him that refuses the call of the daughters of the Sidhe, for he will find no comfort in the love of the women of the earth to the end of life and time, and the cold of the grave is in his heart for ever. It is death he has chosen; let him die, let him die, let him die."

J. M. Synge (1871–1909)

John Millington Synge was born in Rathfarnham, near Dublin, in 1871. He was descended from Protestant landowners, including, among his ancestors, five bishops. He attended Trinity College, Dublin, where he learned Gaelic, but he left for Europe after his graduation in 1892, traveling in Germany and France. He first aimed at a career as a concert violinist, but turned to literature in 1894 when he settled in Paris to write literary criticism. The turning point in his literary career, and in his life, came in 1896 when he met W. B. Yeats in Paris. Yeats had just visited the Aran Islands where his "imagination was full of those grey islands where men must reap with knives because of the stones." Yeats advised Synge to go there and immerse himself in the native Irish culture and language: "Give up Paris. You will never create anything by reading Racine, and Arthur Symons will always be a better critic of French literature. Go to the Aran Islands. Live there as if you were one of the people themselves; express a life that has never found expression." Synge visited the islands for the first time in 1898, and there began gathering the images and forging the strange, spirited Irish English that inform his plays. As a consequence, three of his plays, Riders to the Sea (1904), The Well of the Saints (1905), and The Playboy of the Western World (1907), *gave the Abbey Theatre its first masterpieces. Synge's prose, especially* The Aran Islands (1907), *was also instrumental in attracting attention to the hard but richly imaginative life of the Irish peasantry. "An Autumn Night in the Hills" first appeared in 1903 in* The Gael. *Though published as a sort of autobiographical essay, its dramatic structure and tightly organized action place it in the mainstream of the modern realistic short story.*

An Autumn Night in the Hills

A few years ago a pointer dog of my acquaintance was wounded by accident in a wild glen on the western slope of County Wicklow. He was left at the cottage of an underkeeper or bailiff—the last cottage on the edge of two ranges of mountains that stretch on the north and west to the plain of Kildare—and a few weeks later I made my way there to bring him down to his master.

It was an afternoon of September, and some heavy rain of the night before had made the road which led up to the cottage through the middle of the glen as smooth as a fine beach, while the clearness of the air gave the granite that ran up on either side of the way a peculiar tinge that was nearly luminous against the shadow of the hills. Every cottage that I passed had a group of rowan trees beside it covered with scarlet berries that gave brilliant points of color of curious effect.

Just as I came to the cottage the road turned across a swollen river which I had to cross on a range of slippery stones. Then, when I had gone a few yards further, I heard a bark of welcome, and the dog ran down to meet me. The noise he made brought two women to the door of the cottage, one a finely made girl, with an exquisitely open and graceful manner, the other a very old woman. A sudden shower had come up without any warning over the rim of the valley, so I went into the cottage and sat down on a sort of bench in the chimney corner, at the end of a long low room with open rafters.

"You've come on a bad day," said the old woman, "for you won't see any of the lads or men about the place."

"I suppose they went out to cut their oats," I said, "this morning while the weather was fine."

"They did not," she answered, "but they're after going down to Aughrim for the body of Mary Kinsella, that is to be brought this night from the station. There will be a wake then at the last cottage you're after passing, where you saw all them trees with the red berries on them."

She stopped for a moment while the girl gave me a drink of milk.

"I'm afraid it's a lot of trouble I'm giving you," I said as I took it, "and you busy, with no men in the place."

"No trouble at all in the world," said the girl, "and if it was itself, wouldn't anyone be glad of it in the lonesome place we're in?"

The old woman began talking again:

"You saw no sign or trace on the road of the people coming with the body?"

"No sign," I said, "and who was she at all?"

"She was a fine young woman with two children," she went on, "and a year and a half ago she went wrong in her head, and they had to send her away. And then up there in the Richmond asylum maybe they thought the sooner they were shut of her the better, for she died two days ago this morning, and now they're bringing her up to have a wake, and they'll bury her beyond at the churches, far as it is, for it's there are all the people of the two families."

While we talked I had been examining a wound in the dog's side near the end of his lung.

"He'll do rightly now," said the girl who had come in again and was putting tea-things on the table. "He'll do rightly now. You wouldn't know he'd been hurted at all only for a kind of a cough he'll give now and again. Did they ever tell you the way he was hit?" she added, going down on her knees in the chimney corner with some dry twigs in her hand and making a little fire on the flagstone a few inches from the turf.

I told her I had heard nothing but the fact of his wound.

"Well," she said, "a great darkness and storm came down that night and they all out on the hill. The rivers rose, and they were there groping along by the turf track not minding the dogs. Then an old rabbit got up and run before them, and a man put up his gun and shot across it. When he fired that dog run out from behind a rock, and one grain of the shot cut the scruff off his nose, and another went in there where you were looking, at the butt of his ribs. He dropped down bleeding and howling, and they thought he was killed. The night was falling and they had no way they could carry him, so they made a kind of a shelter for him with sticks and turf, and they left him while they would be going for a sack."

She stopped for a moment to knead some dough and put down a dozen hot cakes—cut out with the mouth of a tumbler—in a frying pan on the little fire she had made with the twigs. While she was doing so the old woman took up the talk.

"Ah," she said, "there do be queer things them nights out on the mountains and in the lakes among them. I was reared beyond in the valley where the mines used to be, in the valley of the Lough Nahanagan, and it's many a queer story I've heard of the spirit does be in that lake."

"I have sometimes been there fishing till it was dark," I said when she paused, "and heard strange noises in the cliff."

"There was an uncle of mine," she continued, "and he was there the same way as yourself, fishing with a big fly in the darkness of the night, and the spirit came down out of the clouds and rifted the waters asunder. He was afeared then and he run down to the houses trembling and shaking. There was another time," she went on, "a man came round to this county who was after swimming through the water of every lake in Ireland. He went up to swim in that lake, and a brother of my own went up along with him. The gentleman had heard tell of the spirit but not a bit would he believe in it. He went down on the bank, and he had a big black dog with him, and he took off his clothes.

" 'For the love of God,' said my brother, 'put that dog in before you go in yourself, the way you'll see if he ever comes out of it.' The gentleman said he would do that and they threw in a stick or a stone and the dog leapt in and swam out to it. Then he turned round again and he swam and he swam, and not a bit nearer did he come.

"'He's a long time swimming back," said the gentleman.

"'I'm thinking your honor'll have a grey beard before he comes back,' said my brother, and before the word was out of his mouth the dog went down out of their sight, and the inside out of him came up on the top of the water."

By this time the cakes were ready and the girl put them on a plate for me at the table, and poured out a cup of tea from the teapot, putting the milk and sugar herself into my cup as is the custom with the cottage people of Wicklow. Then she put the teapot down in the embers of the turf and sat down in the place I had left.

"Well," she said, "I was telling you the story of that night. When they got back here they sent up two lads for the dog, with a sack to carry him on if he was alive and a spade to bury him if he was dead. When they came to the turf where they left him they saw him near twenty yards down the path. The crathur thought they were after leaving him there to die, and he got that lonesome he dragged himself along like a Christian till he got too weak with the bleeding. James, the big lad, walked up again him first with the spade in his hand. When he seen the spade he let a kind of a groan out of him.

"That dog's as wise as a child, and he knew right well it was to bury him they brought the spade. Then Mike went up and laid down the sack on the ground, and the minute he seen it he jumped up and tumbled in on it himself. Then they carried him down, and the crathur getting his death with the cold and the great rain was falling. When they brought him in here you'd have thought he was dead. We put up a settle bed before the fire, and we put him into it. The heat roused him a bit, and he stretched out his legs and gave two groans out of him like an old man. Mike thought he'd drink some milk so we heated a cup of it over the fire. When he put down his tongue into it he began to cough and bleed, then he turned himself over in the settle bed and looked up at me like an old man. I sat up with him that night and it raining and blowing. At four in the morning I gave him a sup more of the milk and he was able to drink it.

"The next day he was stronger, and we gave him a little new milk every now and again. We couldn't keep him near the fire. So we put him in the little room beyond by the door and an armful of hay in along with him. In the afternoon the boys were out on the mountain and the old woman was gone somewhere else, and I was chopping sticks in the lane. I heard a sort of a noise and there he was with his head out through the window looking out on me in the lane. I was afraid he was lonesome in there all by himself, so I put in one of our old dogs to keep him company. Then I stuffed an old hat into the window and I thought they'd be quiet together.

"But what did they do but begin to fight in there all in the dark as they were. I opened the door and out runs that lad before I could stop him. Not a bit would he go in again, so I had to leave him running about beside me. He's that loyal to me now you wouldn't believe it. When I go for the cow he comes along with me, and when I go to make up a bit of hay on the hill he'll come and make a sort of bed for himself under a haycock, and not a bit of him will look at Mike or the boys."

"Ah," said the old woman, as the girl got up to pour me out another cup from the teapot, "it's herself will be lonesome when that dog is gone, he's never out of her sight, and you'd do right to send her down a little dog all for herself."

"You would so," said the girl, "but maybe he wouldn't be loyal to me, and I wouldn't give a thraneen for a dog as wasn't loyal."

"Would you believe it," said the old woman again, "when the gentleman wrote down about that dog Mike went out to where she was in the haggard, and says, 'They're after sending me the prescription for that dog,' says he, 'to put on his tomb-stone.' And she went down quite simple, and told the boys below in the bog, and it wasn't till they began making game of her that she seen the way she'd been humbugged."

"That's the truth," said the girl, "I went down quite simple, and indeed it's a small wonder, that dog's as fit for a decent burial as many that gets it."

Meanwhile the shower had turned to a dense torrent of mountain rain, and although the evening was hardly coming on, it was so dark that the girl lighted a lamp and hung it at the corner of the chimney. The kitchen was longer than most that I have met with and had a skeleton staircase at the far end that looked vague and shadowy in the dim light. The old woman wore one of the old-fashioned caps with a white frill round the face, and entered with great fitness into the general scheme of the kitchen. I did not like leaving them to go into the raw night for a long walk on the mountains, and I sat down and talked to them for a long time, till the old woman thought I would be benighted.

"Go out now," she said at last to the girl, "go out now and see what water is coming over the fall above, for with this rain the water'll rise fast, and maybe he'll have to walk down to the bridge, a rough walk when the night is coming on."

The girl came back in a moment.

"It's riz already," she said. "He'll want to go down to the bridge." Then turning to me: "If you'll come now I'll show you the way you have to go, and I'll wait below for the boys; it won't be long now till they come with the body of Mary Kin-sella."

We went out at once and she walked quickly before me through a maze of small fields and pieces of bog, where I would have soon lost the track if I had been alone.

The bridge, when we reached it, was a narrow wooden struc-ture fastened up on iron bars which pierced large boulders in the bed of the river. An immense gray flood was struggling among the stones, looking dangerous and desolate in the half-light of the evening, while the wind was so great that the bridge wailed and quivered and whistled under our feet. A few paces further on we came to a cottage where the girl wished me a good journey and went in to wait for her brothers.

The daylight still lingered but the heavy rain and a thick white cloud that had come down made everything unreal and dismal to an extraordinary degree. I went up a road where on one side I could see the trunks of beech trees reaching up wet and motionless—with odd sighs and movements when a gust caught the valley—into a grayness overhead, where nothing could be distinguished. Between them there were masses of shadow, and masses of half-luminous fog with black branches across them. On the other side of the road flocks of sheep I could not see coughed and choked with sad guttural noises in the shelter of the hedge, or rushed away through a gap when they felt the dog was near them. Above everything my ears were haunted by the dead heavy swish of the rain. When I came near the first village I heard a loud noise and commotion. Many cars and gigs were collected at the door of the public house, and the bar was filled with men who were drinking and making a noise. Everything was dark and confused yet on one car I was able to make out the shadow of a coffin, strapped in the rain, with the body of Mary Kinsella.

Daniel Corkery (1878–1964)

Daniel Corkery was born in Cork in 1878 and remained there his entire life. He was a remarkable teacher—Frank O'Connor and Sean O'Faolain were two of his students—and taught at almost every level of education, beginning as an elementary school teacher in 1898 and ending his career as a professor of English at University College, Cork, from 1931 to 1947. He was a member of the Gaelic League, a teacher of Gaelic, and an ardent nationalist during the most active years of Ireland's struggle for independence. In 1909 he founded the Cork Dramatic Society and began a lifelong career as writer, critic, and propagandist of native Irish culture. He wrote important works in a number of different genres. Three of his plays, The Labour Leader *(1919),* The Yellow Bittern *(1920), and* Fohnam the Sculpter *(1939), were performed by the Abbey Theatre. His novel* The Threshold of Quiet, *a realistic portrait of early modern Ireland, appeared in 1917. His two books of literary criticism,* The Hidden Ireland *(1925) and especially* Syngc and Anglo-Irish Literature *(1931) have been attacked for their nationalistic bias and their lack of scholarship, but they both contain valuable insights into Irish culture. Corkery is best known, however, for his short stories, many of which take place in the desolate mountains and rocky hillsides of West Cork. He published four volumes of stories,* A Munster Twilight *(1916),* The Hounds of Banba *(1920),* The Stormy Hills *(1929), and* Earth Out of Earth *(1939). His stories are uneven in quality, but several rank with the best in modern Irish fiction. "Rock-of-the-Mass," arguably his masterpiece, and his most ambitious story, comes from* The Stormy Hills.*

Rock-of-the-Mass

I

Dunerling East was its name, the model farm in all that countryside. Only after many years it had come to be so; and Michael Hodnett, the farmer who had made it so, lay fast asleep in
his armchair on the right-hand side of the front door. As of its
own weight his big strong-looking head had sunk itself deep
into his deep chest. The sunshine of the October afternoon was
depositing itself lavishly upon him, thickening upon him, it
seemed, while slumber bound him there, so huge and lumpish,
so inert, so old and fallen. Dunerling East just now was looking more model-like than ever before. The house itself had had
all its sashes, its doors, its timber work painted afresh; its blinds
and curtains had been renewed; its ivy growths trimmed; and
the whole farm, even its farthest fields and screening thickets,
spoke of the same well-being, the same skillful management.
The sleeper might lawfully take his rest, his spirit had so indis-
putably established itself everywhere within the far-flung mear-
ings. Even were he to pass away in his sleep, and stranger folk,
as reckless as might be, to come into possession of the land,
many years must needs go by before Dunerling East became
hail-fellow-well-met with the farms round about it, shaggy and
scraggy as they were, waterlogged in the bottoms and bleached
or perished on the uplands, unsheltered by larch or beech.

All this cleaning up had been done in preparation for the
first coming together, after many years, of all or nearly all that
were left of the family. The arrival of Stephen Hodnett, the
third youngest son, from the States had been the occasion. He
had brought with him his young wife, and, as well, an elder
sister of hers, a young widow, for whose distraction indeed the
voyage had been undertaken. Of all the sons of the house this
son, Stephen, perhaps had done best: he was now manager of a
large bakery store in New York. But the brother next to him
in years, Finnbarr, had done well too. He was come, also ac-

companied by his wife, from Kerry, where he managed a very successful creamery. The son to whom the care of the farm had fallen, to whom indeed the farm now legally belonged, Nicholas by name, had maintained it in the condition to which his father, this old man asleep in the chair, had brought it; perhaps he had even bettered it, but, of course, the land had been got into good heart long before it fell to his turn to till it. Nicholas, though older than Stephen or Finnbarr, had never married: he would wait until his father's death. The only other son of the house was up in Dublin—Father Philip Hodnett, a curate in Saint Multose's parish. He was the one living member who was not at present in Dunerling East. Within the house lurked somewhere the eldest living of all the old man's family, Ellen, the second child born to him. She looked old enough to be the mother of those mentioned, even of Nicholas, the eldest of them. She was sixty and looked more. Her cheeks were thin and haggard, colorless, her hair grey, and her eyes stared blankly at the life moving before them as if it were but an insipid and shadowy thing when compared with what moved restlessly, perhaps even disastrously, within the labyrinths of her own brain. On her the mothering of the whole family had fallen when Michael Hodnett buried his wife in Inchigeela.

From the feet of the sleeping figure the ground fell away downwards to a bracken-covered stream. Beyond the bracken it rose again; much more suddenly however, so suddenly indeed that the red earth showed in patches through the tangled greenery. Those reddish patches looked like corbels supporting the cornice-like ledge of the upward-sloping grazing grounds above. Just now, along that sun-drenched ledge, a procession of shapely deep-uddered cattle was moving from left to right, the beasts in single file or in pairs or groups, deliberately pacing. Thirty-one milkers were to pass like that, making for the unseen bridgeway across the stream in the hollow. Presently they would dip from sight and again be discovered in the tree-covered passage trailing up towards the milking sheds, the rich sunshine catching their deep-colored flanks and slipping swiftly and suddenly from their horns and moving limbs. Anyone who had ever come to know how deeply the sight of that afternoon ritual used to thrill the old man, now so sunken in his sleep, could hardly forbear from waking him to witness it.

Behind the cattle sauntered Nicholas. His head was bent, and in his right hand a sliver from a sally tree lazily switched the cattle along. Although a working day, he was dressed in his Sunday clothes. His gaiters were new, rich brown in color, and had straps about them; his boots also were new and brown. All day since morning his visitors, his brothers Stephen and Finnbarr and their people, had been away motoring in the hills towards the west—around Keimaneigh and Gougane Barra—and he had found the idle day as long as a week. "Stay where you are," he had said to one of the laborers who were digging out potatoes in the fields behind the house; "stay where you are, and I'll bring them in," and he was glad of the chance to go through the fields one after another until he was come to where the impatient cattle were gathered, anxious and crying, about the fastened gate. Their time for milking was overdue, and they needed no urging towards the sheds. When they were safe across the bridge he left them to themselves: by that time the first of them were already head-bound in the stalls. Closing a gate behind them he made diagonally up the sloping field. At his approach his father suddenly raised his head.

" 'Tisn't Sunday?" he said, and then, recollecting himself: "They haven't come back yet?"

"Any moment now," Nicholas answered. He then turned his back on him and gazed across the countryside where a couple of roads could be picked out. The weather had been very fine for some weeks and little clouds of sunny dust wavered above them.

"Are the cows in?"

"I'm after bringing them across."

"Is Finn after looking at them?"

"Yes, he'd get rid of the Kerry, he said."

"Didn't I tell you! Didn't I tell you!"

He had filled up with passionate life. As he blurted out the words, he raised his heavy stick in his blob of a hand. Nicholas glanced away from him, and again searched the countryside with his eyes:

"They won't be long now: 'tis as good for us to be going in!"

He put his arm beneath his father's. He lifted him. The old man's right foot trailed uselessly along the ground. But his thoughts were on the cows:

" 'Tis often I do be thinking on the two beasts we had and we coming hither from Carrig-an-afrinn. Scraggy animals, scraggy, splintery things."

II

Mrs. Muntleberry, the young American widow, and her sister, Stephen's wife, were both thoughtful gentle women; it was plain in their quiet eyes, their quiet faces. After the meal, homely in its way, but good, they now sat bent forward earnestly staring at the old man who was keeping himself so alert and upright in their midst, ruling the roomful with word, gesture, glance. Of his power of work, of his downrightness, they had, of course, often heard from Stephen: in Stephen himself they had found something of the same character: until today, however, they had not realized how timid in him were the strong traits of his father's character. They had been motoring in a world of rock-strewn hillsides; they had swung into glens that struck them cold, so bleak they were, so stern-looking even in the softest tide of the year. Carrig-an-afrinn they had not actually passed through: it would have meant threading slowly up many twisting narrow hillside bohereens in which their car could scarcely turn: perhaps also Stephen had not cared to have them actually come upon the bedraggled home-stead—little else than a hut—from which the Hodnetts had risen. They had, however, gone as close to it as the main road allowed them, had seen, and felt almost in their bones, the niggardliness of life among those hillsides of tumultuously tumbled rocks. That wayfaring in bleak places had brought them to understand Stephen's father; even if he were no different this evening, had remained as he had been ever since their arrival—drowsing between sleep and waking, mumbling old songs, sometimes losing count of who they were—they would nevertheless because of this day's excursioning have more deeply understood the tough timber that was in him. But all the evening he had been quite different. The names of old places, of old families, had been in the air about him. He grew young to hear them, to bethink himself of them. They had aroused him. Stephen had forgotten many of them. He would say, " 'Tis north from Inchimore," and his father had enough to catch at: " 'Tis the Sweeneys were north of Inchimore. 'Tis Keimcorravoola you're thinking of." And of itself either the place name or the family name was enough to spur the old man's brain to all manner of recollections. So it had been with him all the evening, alert as they had never seen him, a new man, and not a bit modest about his powers when young, whether at fighting or hurley or farming. His stick was in the air about their heads: and once without warning he had brought it down on the table, making them all leap to their feet and grab at the dancing tea-things—down with all his force lest they should not clearly understand how final had been the stroke with which he had felled a Twomey man in a faction fight at Ballyvourney. And when in speaking of some other ancient wrestling bout he referred to his adversary's trunk, how he had clasped it and could not be shaken off, the two women looked at himself, alert yet lumpish before them, noted his body's girth and depth, and felt that "trunk" was indeed the right word to use of such bodies.

Finn's wife, the Kerry woman, was enjoying it heartily. Her Kerry eyes, deep hazel in color, were dancing to watch the old man's antics, grotesque and unashamed, were dancing also to note the quiet, still, well-schooled Americans opening the doors of their minds to comprehend adequately this rough-hewn chunk of peasant humankind. The expression coming and going on the faces of the three sons, she also enjoyed. She watched to see how they took every gross countryside word and phrase that would unconcernedly break from the old man's lips. Her own Finn she held for the cleverest of them because he had the gift of slipping in some contrary word that would excite his father to still more energetic gestures or more emphatic expletives.

In time old Hodnett had exhausted the tale of the great deeds of his prime: a gentler mood descended on him: "Like you'd shut that door, or like you'd tear a page out of a book and throw it from you, I put an end to all that folly and wildness. Listen now, let ye listen now, this is what happened and I coming over here from Carrig-an-afrinn."

III

He told them how on that day which of all the days of his long life stood most clearly before his mind, he had made swiftly home from the fair at Macroom. Michael, his eldest son, a boy of about sixteen years at the time, had hastened down from the potato field on hearing the jolting of the returning cart. As usual with him he examined his father's face. He was at first relieved and then puzzled to discover from it that his father had scarcely taken any drink during that long day of absence from home, of boon companionship in the town. More than that, his father was going about in a sort of constraint, as if he had had something happen to him while away, or had come upon some tidings which now must be dwelt upon within himself. Yet he did not seem gloomy or rough, and he could be gloomy enough and rough enough when the fit was on him. Often and often after a long day in Macroom, he had turned in from the road, flung the reins on the horse's back, and without preface begun to heap malediction on the head of the villain pig buyers from Cork with whom he had been trafficking. Today he was different:

"Is Johnny above?" he questioned his son as he loosed the horse from the shafts. The boy nodded.

"Up with you then. Up with you while there's light in it."

The boy, climbing up to where he had left old Johnny, who was helping them to dig out the potatoes, was still wondering over the mood his father had returned in.

"What is he after getting?" the laborer asked him.

"Four ten."

"He'd get more in Dunmanway last Friday."

"He's satisfied. He says he is."

Before long they saw himself coming through the gap. "What way are they up along there?" he asked them, nodding his head towards the sloping ridges they had been digging.

"Small enough then," his son answered.

The father stooped and picked up one of the potatoes. He began to rub it between his finger and thumb.

"They'll be different in Dunerling East," his son said, complacently tossing his head.

As if that were the last thing he had expected to come from the boy's lips his father looked sharply at him.

Dunerling East was the farm he had been for several weeks negotiating the purchase of. It was ten miles away towards the east, ten miles farther from the hardness of the mountains, the cold rains, the winds, the mists. In those ten miles the barren hills that separate Cork from Kerry had space to stretch themselves out, to die away into gentle curves, to become soft and kind. So curiously his father had looked at him the boy wondered if something had not happened to upset the purchase. He was not surprised when his father, peering at him under his brows, spoke to him in a cold voice:

"The potatoes might be better. The grass too. And the cattle. Only the Hodnetts might be worse."

Michael glanced at the laborer, then back at his father. He found him still skinning the potato with his hard thumb. But he could also see, young and all as he was, that his thought was not on the potato, big or little. The laborer had once more bent to his digging; and Michael, withdrawing his eyes slowly from his father's face, spat on his hands and gripped the spade: yet he could not resist saying:

"They're poor return for a man's labor."

He scornfully touched the potatoes hither and thither with the tip of his spade, freeing them from the turfy earth, black and fibrous. They were indeed small.

The father seemed careless of their size. He stood there, a solid piece of humankind, huge, big-faced, with small round eyes, shrewd-looking, not unhumorous. He said: "If I hadn't that fifty pound paid on it, I'd put Dunerling East out of my mind."

He turned from them and made for the gap through which he had come. They questioned each other with their eyes and then stared after the earnest figure until the broken hillside swallowed it up.

It was a soft, still evening. Here and there a yellow leaf fell from the few scattered birch trees growing among the rocks which, on every side, surrounded the little patch of tilled earth. A robin was singing quietly, patiently—the robin's way. The air was moist; and because a break in the weather seemed near, they worked on, the two of them, until they could no longer see the potatoes. Then Johnny straightened his back, lit his bit of a pipe and shouldered his spade. Together both of them, taking long slow strides, made down towards the house. Suddenly the boy said:

"Look at himself!"

They saw him standing upright on one of the numerous ledges of rock which broke up through the surface of their stubble field. He had his back towards them. He was staring downwards, overlooking his own land, towards the straggling road, staring intently, although little except the general shape of the countryside could now be distinguished.

"Is it? Is it him at all, do you think?" old Johnny asked.

" 'Tis sure," Michael answered. Then he cried out, sending the vowels traveling:

"Ho-o! Ho-o!"

His father turned and after a pause began to make towards them. Awkwardly they awaited him; they did not know what to say. He said:

" 'Tis at Carrig-an-afrinn I was looking."

Carrig-an-afrinn was the name of the whole farm, a large district, mostly a hillside of rock and heather; they were standing in Carrig-an-afrinn: but they understood that what he had been looking at was Carrig-an-afrinn itself—the Rock of the Mass, the isolated pile of rock by the roadside from which the plowland had got its name.

They walked beside him then.

"I'm after hearing a thing this day I never knew before," he said, and then stopping up and examining their faces he added:

" 'Tis what I heard: In any place where a Mass was ever celebrated an angel is set on guard for ever and ever."

" 'Twould be a likely thing," the old laborer said.

"I never heard tell of it," Michael said.

"Myself never heard tell of it," his father snapped out.

" 'Twould be a likely thing," old Johnny said again, "remembering the nature of the Mass."

"Who was it told you?"

"One who was well able!"

The three of them turned and looked downwards towards the rough altar-like pile of rock where Mass used to be said secretly for the people in the penal days when it was felony to celebrate Mass in public. Only the pile of rock was visible, and that not distinctly, so thick the light had become.

"You know very well that Mass was said there hundreds and hundreds of times."

The father spoke to his son almost as if he had been contra-
dicting him. He received no reply. Then he added in a suddenly
deepened voice:

"Likely that place is thick with angels."

The laborer uncovered his head without a word.

In stillness they stood there on the lonely hillside; and in the
darkening rocks and fields there was no sound, except of small
things stirring at their feet. After a few seconds, the farmer
faced again for the house. Without thought, it seemed, he
avoided the rocky patches. Indeed even at midnight he could
have walked unperplexed through those rock-strewn fields. The
others heard his voice coming to them in the dusk over his
shoulder:

" 'Tis a strange thing that I never heard of that wonder until
I'm just leaving the place for good and all. A strange thing;
and it frightens me."

When they found themselves free of the fields and in the
poirse, or laneway, that led up to their yard, he said again with
sudden passion:

" 'Tis a small thing would make me break the bargain."

The boy flared up:

"A queer thing you'd do then."

"Queer!"

"It may be years and years before we have the chance of buying a place like Dunerling East."

He spoke the name as if that of itself were worth the purchase money.

"Carrig-an-afrinn is not a bad farm at all."

At this Michael burst out:

"Johnny, do you hear him? And he raging and swearing at
them rocks as long as I remember—raging and swearing at
them as if they were living men and they against him! And he
praying to God to take us out of it before his eyes were blinded
with the years. And now he'd stay in it!"

Of that incident and of the night that followed it, the old

man, forty-four years after, remembered every detail—every word spoken and every thought that disturbed his rest.

IV

Having given them to understand all that has been here set down, he went on: "I tell ye, I didn't shut an eye that night, only thinking and thinking and I twisting and turning in my bed. When I looked back through the years and thought of what a poor place Carrig-an-afrinn was—there was scarcely a poorer—'twas little less than a miracle to have me able to buy out a big place like this—a place that had been in the grip of the gentry for hundreds and hundreds of years. And up to that I always thought that I had no one to thank for it but my-self—the strength of my own four bones, but after what I was told in Macroom that day, how did I know but that maybe it was in Carrig-an-afrinn itself the luck was? and that good for-tune would follow whoever lived in it like good Christians, and that maybe secret friends would help them, and they at the plowing or waiting up in the nights for a calf to come, or a young foal or a litter of bonhams itself? Who knows? Who knows? And what puzzled me entirely was that I should be ignorant of all that until the very day, as you may say, I was set-tled on leaving it. It frightened me. While we were in Carrig-an-afrinn no great sickness befell us or misfortune, except a horse to break his leg or a cow to miscarry or a thing like that; and I thought of all the strong farmers I was after seeing in my time, and they having to sell off their places and scatter away with themselves into Cork or Dublin, or maybe to America it-self. Sure this place itself, if ye saw it when we came hither, the dirty state 'twas in, the land gone back, exhausted, and the house and sheds broken, everything in wrack and ruin—'tisn't with a light heart ye'd undertake it. But of course only for that I couldn't have bought it all at all. So I said to myself, and I listening to the clock ticking at the foot of the bed, I'm under-taking that big place, and maybe 'twon't thrive with me. And if it fails me, where am I? That's what I said. If it fails me, where am I? I tell ye, I was broken with thinking on it. And all the time, and this is the queerest thing of all, I heard someone saying, 'Carrig-an-afrinn, Carrig-an-afrinn. Carrig-an-afrinn, Carrig-an-afrinn.' And not once or twice or three times, but all the night long, and I thinking and thinking. Of course, there was no one saying it at all, only maybe the beating of my own heart to be like a tune. But I was afraid. I thought maybe music might come rising up to me out of the *cummer*, and it thronged with angels, or a great light come striking in at the window. And sure enough at last I started up and I cried out, 'There it is! There it is!' But 'twas no unnatural light at all, only the dawn of day breaking in on top of me. 'Tis how I was after dozing off for a little while unknown to myself, and I woke up suddenly in confusion and dread.

"That morning and I rising up my limbs were like wisps of straw. I was terrified of the long day before me, and that's the worst way a man can be. But when I came out and stood in the broad sun, and 'twas a morning of white frost, I drew in the air to myself, and I took courage to see my poor animals grazing so peacefully on the hill, just like what you see in a picture. If the big farms broke the men that were born to softness and luxury, Dunerling East wouldn't break me, and I reared hard and tough! That's what I said, with great daring in my breast.

"Not long after that we moved our handful of stock east to this place. I laughed to picture the two scraggy beasts, and all the deep feeding of Dunerling East to themselves. And that same evening myself and Michael, Michael that's dead, God rest him, went over and hither and in and out through the length and breadth of this estate and round by the boundary ditch; and 'tis a thing I will not forget till my dying day what he said to me, my son Michael, that same evening, and we killed from the exertion. He stopped and looked up at me before he spoke:

" 'Look,' he said, 'why have you your hands like that?'

"My two hands, clenched, and stiff, *stiff,* like you'd have them in a fight, watching your opponent, watching to catch him off his guard, or for fear he'd spring on you. That's how I had my hands. And 'twas natural for me to have my hands like that, for what I was saying to myself was: I'll break it! I'll break it! And I was saying that because if I didn't break it I was sport for the world. Like a bully at a fair I was, going about my own land the first day I walked it!"

In recalling the labors of his prime he had become a new man. When they looked at him they saw not the stricken old creature whose days were now spent in the drowsy sun, but the indomitable peasant who had wrung enough from the rocks of Carrig-an-afrinn to buy out Dunerling East from the broken gentry, and who then had reclaimed Dunerling East from its hundred years of neglect. When he could not find words to fit his thought his left eye would close tight, and one big tooth, that he still retained in his upper gum, would dig itself into his lower lip, until the struggling words came to him. And they noticed that his two hands had clenched themselves long before he needed them clenched to illustrate how it was he had tackled the reclamation of the sluggish marshlands of Dunerling East. His own sons quailed before him. The two Americans had drawn together, shoulder touching shoulder: they watched him across the table with wide eyes, their faces drawn. The creamery manager from Kerry dared no longer to put in his jocose word. He wished rather to be able to draw off the old man's mind from this renewal of the unrelenting warfare of his manhood. But no such word could he find: his father was abroad in a passion of fictitious energy: it would indeed be a potent word that could stay or hinder him. Every now and then the timbers of the heavy chair groaned beneath the movement of his awkward carcass. He was unconscious of it. It meant as little to him as his own exposing of the shifts, the meanness, the overreaching, the unintentional tyranny he had practiced while he worked out his dream.

"My poor boy, Michael," he went on, "was the first to go. He was great for the work. For a boy that was slight and tender I never saw the equal of him. 'Twas how he had great spirit. A word was worse to him than a whip. When we'd be cutting the deep grass in the inches, half a dozen of us all in a line, and he'd fall behind, being young and soft, I'd say to him, 'Ah, Michael,' I'd say, 'God be with the little fields of Carrig-an-afrinn, you could cut them with a scissors'; that would bring him into line I tell ye. The poor boy. 'Twas pleurisy he got first; and we thought nothing of it: maybe we didn't take it in time. But what chance was there to be taking him into Macroom to the doctor, or from one holy well to another? The time he died too, it could not be a worse time. Herself was after bringing little Stephen into the world—and before she was rightly fit the harvest was upon us; and 'twas the first real good harvest we got out of Dunerling East. When I looked at it standing I said: ' 'Tis my doing and my boy's doing, and my boy is dead!' But herself was better than any man in a harvest field. Maybe she overworked herself. She wasn't the one to give in. The day she was laid in Inchigeela 'tis well if I didn't curse the day I came hither from Carrig-an-afrinn. Father O'Herlihy was standing by. 'The Lord giveth and the Lord taketh away,' he said, and his hand on my shoulder, and 'twas all I could do to say 'Amen' to that. There I was with a houseful of them about me and only herself, that poor thing inside, only herself to do a ha'porth for them. I don't blame her for being as she is—knitting, knitting, knitting, or looking into the fire and thinking—I don't blame her at all. What she went through after that, pulling and hauling and slashing and digging, 'twould kill half a parish. Up at four in the morning getting the pigs' food ready, or the mash for the calves; and milking the cows, and keeping the children from mischief. The only other girl I had, she was second after Nicholas there, I lost her just when she was rising to be of use to me. 'Twas a fever she got from drinking bad water. And the two boys I lost after that, one of

them was the terror of the countryside. He turned against herself inside; he was wild and fiery. Mind you, he dared me to my
face. He said what no son of mine ever said to me. I won't repeat it. I won't repeat it. The eyes were blazing in his head. The
delicacy was showing in him. The brains of that kind is a terror. He went off with himself and left me in the lurch. And
then he came back—one twelvemonth after—and 'tis like herself inside he was. Only bitter, and the health wasted. The same
as any laboring boy he walked in to me. Not a shirt to his back,
or what you would call a shirt. He shamed me, the way he was.
And he dying on his feet. 'Twas a dead man was patrolling the
fields for months before he took to the bed entirely. And I
daren't say a word to him because he had a tongue would raise
blisters on a withered skull. The other poor boy, his name was
Laurence, was a handsome boy. Everybody used to say he'd
make a handsome priest. But sure at that time I couldn't dream
of such a thing. It takes a power of money to make a priest. He
died of pneumonia, and not a thing to happen to him only a
bit of a pain in his side. Only for that I hadn't time to be
thinking on it I'd be saying there was a curse on top of us; but
no, because year after year the produce was getting better and
better; and in spite of all the sickness and deaths and funerals—and funerals are the greatest robbers of all—the money
began to rise up on me, and I could get in the help when I
wanted it—'tis often I had a score of men at the harvesting,
besides what neighbors would come of themselves. Those there
(he nodded at his three sons, all of them sitting with bowed
heads, with pipes in their mouths, not daring to break across
his speech)—those there, they only knew the end of the story.
Ah boys, ah boys, the softness comes out of the hard, like the
apple from the old twisted bough, and 'tis only the softness ye
knew of. And then in the end of it all, the great change in the
laws came about and I bought out the land and 'twas my own,
as you may say. The day I signed for it, a sort of lowness came

over me, and I remembered my poor dead boy saying, and he my firstborn. 'Look how you're holding your hands!' Let ye listen to me now; I cried down my eyes to my own self that night because herself was in the clay. That poor soul inside, you might as well be talking to a cock of last year's hay, dull with the weather and the sun, you'd only get yes and no for an answer. And the rest—those here—were too young. What I did was to send over for old Johnny, old Johnny I would have helping me an odd time in Carrig-an-afrinn, to come over to me, that I wanted him. God knows all I wanted him for was to keep me in talk against that terrible fit of darkness and loneliness would fall on me again. He came over and together we walked the land, every perch of it. He knew what sort it was when we came hither, and 'tis he was the man could tell the difference. What he said was, now, let ye listen, let ye listen to what he said, and he only a poor ignorant man: 'After all, 'twas only a rush in your hand!' Now that was what a wrestler would say of another in the old times, 'He was only a rush in my hands,' meaning by that that he had no trouble in breaking him. That was great praise and yet it couldn't rouse me for I was after walking the land field after field; and one field I found was the same as another. That's a strange thing to say. Maybe 'tis how I was old and I coming hither. 'Twas in Carrig-an-afrinn I grew up. There was never a man drove a handful of cattle of his own rearing to a fair that hadn't some favorite among them; and he sees the dealers come round them and strike them and push them, and knock them about, and he knows that they are all the same to him, that he sees no difference between one and the other, except one to be riper than another, or a thing like that. And 'twas so with me. I walked my fields and one was the same as another. There was no corner of them that I could make for when the darkness would fall on me. I knew 'twould be different in Carrig-an-afrinn. And that's what I was thinking of when old Johnny said to me that after all Dunerling East was like a rush in my hands. I opened my heart to him. I told him I felt like the steward of the place, and not like the owner of it. He said 'twasn't right for me to be saying a thing like that, that 'tis down on my two knees I should be and I thanking God, but that the heart of man was only a sieve. The very next day and I still going about like that, counting up the great improvements I was after making since I came in, and arguing with myself, and yet dissatisfied with myself, I wandered up the hillside opposite, and whatever turn I gave or however the sun was shining, 'twas about four o'clock in the evening, I saw Doughill and Douse rising up in the west and snug away down at the foot of Doughill I saw a little shoulder of a hill, and 'Honor of God,' I said, 'if that isn't Carrig-an-afrinn itself!' Let ye listen to me, I fell down on my knees in thanksgiving like a pagan would be praying to the sun! And from that day forward I had a spot of land to turn to when the black fit would fall on me. Mind you, 'twas a good time I found it, for while I was breaking the place and wrestling with it I didn't think of anything else, only to be going ahead and going ahead. But 'twas different when I could pay for the help, and I had time to look around, and the rent wasn't half what it used to be. Ah, the soft comes out of the hard, and the little lambs from the hailstones. If Dunerling East is a good property now 'twas many the hot sweat fell into the sods of its ridges. But sure them that could witness to that, they're all dead, except that poor thing inside, God help her; and 'tis she took the burden as well as the next."

V

His voice fell and the glow of exaltation vanished from his features.

"They're all dead?" Mrs. Muntleberry said, quietly.

"Dead!" the old man answered her, and having said it, his head kept on moving slightly up and down to some pulse in his brain.

"Then these," she said again, and indicated the three sons with her eyes, "these are a second crop."

"A second crop," he said, "except that poor creature inside."

They found it hard to break the silence that had fallen on them. Earlier in the evening both Stephen and Finnbarr had been, as one might say, themselves—Stephen, the bakery manager, a hustler, and Finn, the creamery manager, not unable to hustle also. But as the story went on, and, though they had heard it all in a fragmentary way before, they had scattered from the homestead without ever having made themselves one clear unified picture of what coming hither from Carrig-an-afrinn had meant for their father. They had never seen him clearly as one who would not be beaten, no matter who by his side fell worsted in the struggle. Only the oldest of them, Nicholas, the farmer, could recall any of the dead, and he was a soft quiet creature, strong of body, but inactive of brain. The one mood, however, had come upon all three; they were not much different from what they had been before they had scattered, from what they had been when Ellen would still them by whispering the one word: "Himself."

It was Finn who first rose. He went and lightly beat the inverted bowl of his pipe against the bars of the fire grate. Then drawing with his strong lips through the empty stem, head in the air, he took a few steps towards the window and drew back one of the heavy curtains. The color, the glow had gone from the day. Instead there were now everywhere filmy veils of mist. Beyond the sunken stream the hillside looked near and the screens of trees, ash and beech, seemed tall and unsubstantial: in the twilight softness the homely features of farming and cattle trafficking were hidden away. The scene was gracious and tender. They all stared through the window.

"It looks fine, so it does," Finn said.

"It does; it looks fine," his wife added, letting the words die away.

The old man was listening.

" 'Tis what a traveler said, and he a man that had recourse to all the places in the world, 'tis what he said: that it had the appearance of a gentleman's place out and out."

Mrs. Muntleberry turned and let her eyes rest softly on his face:

"Still you liked Carrig-an-afrinn too?"

He lifted his head; such words he had not expected: "Ah, ma'am, ah, ma'am," he said, making an effort to move his trunk so that he might face her directly, "Carrig-an-afrinn, Carrig-an-afrinn, the very name of it, the very name of it!" And he stared at her with a fixity of expression that frightened her, stared at her in blank hopelessness of saying even the first word of all the words that rioted within him. He recovered. He swept his hand across his brow, toying with his hair. "They tell me Pat Leary, who's there ever since we came hither—there's only the one year between us—they tell me he sits in the *cummer* an odd hour at the foot of the rock where the Chalice used to stand. His work is done. He'll catch hold of plow nor snaffle no more, same as myself. 'Tis a great comfort to him to sit there."

She was sorry she had brought Carrig-an-afrinn back to his thoughts.

"The heart is a sieve," she said, watching him to see how he'd take old Johnny's word. But he was not so easily moved from mood to mood.

"You saw it today?" he questioned earnestly, "You saw it today?"

"We went quite close to it. Did we see the Rock itself? Did we, Stephen?"

Stephen said as boldly as he could:

"Oh yes, we went quite close to it."

"Ah, ma'am, Nicholas there, some day he's going to pack me into the motor car; and over with us to see it. It can't be long I have to stay."

Before he had finished, almost indeed at the first word, Nicholas had risen and quietly taken down a shabby-looking old violin from the top of a heavy cupboard that stood in the corner. While they all looked at him he tuned it without a word, and to him tuning was no easy task. Then he stretched his two long legs out from the chair and began to play.

The instrument was almost toneless, and the player almost without skill. He played the old songs of the countryside, going straight from one to another, from a *caoine* to a reel, from a love song to a lively rattle about cattle dealing or horse racing. Nerveless, toneless, yet the playing was quiet; and it was the music itself, and not the instrument or musician was in the fiddler's mind. After a while this the Americans noticed. Then the scratching, the imperfect intonation, the incongruous transition from melody to melody disturbed them but little. He played on and on; and they were all thankful to him. The room darkened, but the sky was still bright. At last he lowered the fiddle, a string needed to be tightened. The others at once broke into talk. Mrs. Muntleberry was nearest to Nicholas. She had her eyes on the instrument. He noticed how at the word "Carrig-an-afrinn" which was again on the lips of the old man, her head had raised itself. He whispered to her, without taking his eyes off his task:

"He'll never see Carrig-an-afrinn again."

"No?" she whispered back, with a little gasp of surprise.

"Nor nobody else," he went on; "they're after blasting it away to make the road wider: 'tis how two lorries couldn't pass on it. I'm in dread of my life he'll find it out. 'Twould be terrible."

She turned her eyes on the old man's face. The music had restored him again to confidence. His eyes were glowing. He had reestablished his mastery. "Let ye listen, let ye listen to me," he was saying.

Seumas O'Kelly (1881–1918)

Seumas O'Kelly was born in Loughrea, County Galway, in 1881. He was educated at Saint Brendan's College, a Catholic secondary school, and he began his literary career as a journalist and editor. He was a member of the Gaelic League and a founding member of Arthur Griffith's nationalistic organization, Sinn Fein. O'Kelly was the editor of the Leinster Leader *in 1918 when Arthur Griffith was imprisoned in Dublin. Though in ill health, O'Kelly immediately left for Dublin, where he replaced Griffith as editor of the Sinn Fein newspaper,* Nationality. *He died of a heart attack soon after when a group of British soldiers staged a riot and vandalized the* Nationality *offices. In his own time perhaps best known as a playwright, O'Kelly had four plays performed by the Abbey Theatre,* The Shuiler's Child *(1910),* The Bribe *(1913),* The Parnellite *(1917), and* Meadowsweet *(1919). He also wrote two novels,* The Lady of Deerpark *(1917) and* Wet Clay *(1922), an inferior work unfortunately published after his death. Though O'Kelly's first book of stories,* By the Stream of Killmeen *(1906), showed little promise and was criticized by the young James Joyce, then living in Europe, he later wrote several excellent stories. The best are found in three volumes,* Waysiders *(1917),* The Golden Barque and The Weaver's Grave *(1919), and* Hillsiders *(1921). "The Weaver's Grave" is his masterpiece, and one of the great literary folktales of the twentieth century.*

* * *

The Weaver's Grave
A Story of Old Men

I

Mortimer Hehir, the weaver, had died, and they had come in search of his grave to Cloon na Morav, the Meadow of the Dead. Meehaul Lynskey, the nail maker, was first across the stile. There was excitement in his face. His long warped body moved in a shuffle over the ground. Following him came Cahir Bowes, the stone breaker, who was so beaten down from the hips forward that his back was horizontal as the back of an animal. His right hand held a stick which propped him up in front, his left hand clutched his coat behind, just above the small of the back. By these devices he kept himself from toppling head over heels as he walked. Mother earth was the brow of Cahir Bowes by magnetic force, and Cahir Bowes was resisting her fatal kiss to the last. And just now there was animation in the face he raised from its customary contemplation of the ground. Both old men had the air of those who had been unexpectedly let loose. For a long time they had lurked somewhere in the shadows of life, the world having no business for them, and now, suddenly, they had been remembered and called forth to perform an office which nobody else on earth could perform. The excitement in their faces as they crossed over the stile into Cloon na Morav expressed a vehemence in their belated usefulness. Hot on their heels came two dark, handsome, stoutly built men, alike even to the cord that tied their corduroy trousers under their knees, and, being gravediggers, they carried flashing spades. Last of all, and after a little delay, a firm white hand was laid on the stile, a dark figure followed, the figure of a woman whose palely sad face was picturesquely, almost dramatically, framed in a black shawl which hung from the crown of the head. She was the widow of Mortimer Hehir, the weaver, and she followed the others into Cloon na Morav, the Meadow of the Dead.

To glance at Cloon na Morav as you went by on the hilly
road was to get an impression of a very old burial ground; to
pause on the road and look at Cloon na Morav was to become
conscious of its quiet situation, of winds singing down from
the hills in a chant for the dead; to walk over to the wall and
look at the mounds inside was to provoke quotations from
Gray's "Elegy"; to make the sign of the cross, lean over the
wall, observe the gloomy lichened background of the wall opposite, and mark the things that seemed to stray about, like
yellow snakes in the grass, was to think of Hamlet moralizing
at the graveside of Ophelia, and hear him establish the identity
of Yorrick. To get over the stile and stumble about inside was
to forget all these things and to know Cloon na Morav for itself. Who could tell the age of Cloon na Morav? The mind
could only swoon away into mythology, paddle about in the
dotage of paganism, the toothless infancy of Christianity. How
many generations, how many septs, how many clans, how
many families, how many people, had gone into Cloon na
Morav? The mind could only take wing on the romances of
mathematics. The ground was billowy, grotesque. Several partially suppressed insurrections—a great thirsting, worming,
pushing, and shouldering under the sod—had given it character. A long tough growth of grass wired it from end to end,
Nature, by this effort, endeavoring to control the strivings of
the more daring of the insurgents of Cloon na Morav. No path
here; no plan or map or register existed; if there ever had been
one or the other it had been lost. Invasions and wars and fam-
ines and feuds had swept the ground and left it. All claims to
interment had been based on powerful traditional rights. These
rights had years ago come to an end—all save in a few outstanding cases, the rounding up of a spent generation. The
overflow from Cloon na Morav had already set a new cemetery
on its legs a mile away, a cemetery in which limestone headstones and Celtic crosses were springing up like mushrooms,
advertising the triviality of a civilization of men and women,

who, according to their own epitaphs, had done exactly the two things they could not very well avoid doing: they had all, their obituary notices said, been born and they had all died. Obscure quotations from Scripture were sometimes added by way of apology. There was an almost unanimous expression of forgiveness to the Lord for what had happened to the deceased. None of this lack of humor in Cloon na Morav. Its monuments were comparatively few, and such of them as it had not swallowed were well within the general atmosphere. No obituary notice in the place was complete; all were either wholly or partially eaten up by the teeth of time. The monuments that had made a stout battle for existence were pathetic in their futility. The vanity of the fashionable of dim ages made one weep. Who on earth could have brought in the white marble slab to Cloon na Morav? It had grown green with shame. Perhaps the lettering, once readable upon it, had been conscientiously picked out in gold. The shrieking winds and the fierce rains of the hills alone could tell. Plain heavy stones, their shoulders rounded with a chisel, presumably to give them some off-handed resemblance to humanity, now swooned at fantastic angles from their settings, as if the people to whose memory they had been dedicated had shouldered them away as an impertinence. Other slabs lay in fragments on the ground, filling the mind with thoughts of Moses descending from Mount Sinai and, waxing angry at sight of his followers dancing about false gods, casting the stone tables containing the Commandments to the ground, breaking them in pieces—the most tragic destruction of a first edition that the world has known. Still other heavy square dark slabs, surely creatures of a pagan imagination, were laid flat down on numerous short legs, looking sometimes like representations of monstrous black cockroaches, and again like tables at which the guests of Cloon na Morav might sit down, goblin-like, in the moonlight, when nobody was looking. Most of the legs had given way and the tables lay overturned, as if there had been a quarrel at cards the night before. Those that had kept their legs exhibited great cracks or fissures across their backs, like slabs of dark ice breaking up. Over by the wall, draped in its pattern of dark green lichen, certain families of dim ages had made an effort to keep up the traditions of the Eastern sepulchers. They had showed an aristocratic reluctance to take to the common clay in Cloon na Morav. They had built low casket-shaped houses against the gloomy wall, putting an enormously heavy iron door with ponderous iron rings—like the rings on a pier by the sea at one end, a tremendous lock—one wondered what Goliath kept the key—finally cementing the whole thing up and surrounding it with spiked iron railings. In these contraptions very aristocratic families locked up their dead as if they were dangerous wild animals. But these ancient vanities only heightened the general democracy of the ground. To prove a traditional right to a place in its community was to have the bond of your pedigree sealed. The act of burial in Cloon na Morav was in itself an epitaph. And it was amazing to think that there were two people still over the sod who had such a right—one Mortimer Hehir, the weaver, just passed away, the other Malachi Roohan, a cooper, still breathing. When these two survivors of a great generation got tucked under the sward of Cloon na Morav its terrific history would, for all practical purposes, have ended.

II

Meehaul Lynskey, the nailer, hitched forward his bony shoulders and cast his eyes over the ground—eyes that were small and sharp, but unaccustomed to range over wide spaces. The width and the wealth of Cloon na Morav were baffling to him. He had spent his long life on the lookout for one small object so that he might hit it. The color that he loved was the golden glowing end of a stick of burning iron; wherever he saw that he seized it in a small sconce at the end of a long handle, wrenched it off by a twitch of the wrist, hit it with a flat hammer several deft taps, dropped it into a vessel of water, out of which it came a cool and perfect nail. To do this thing several hundred times six days in the week, and pull the chain of a bellows at short intervals, Meehaul Lynskey had developed an extraordinary dexterity of sight and touch, a swiftness of business that no mortal man could exceed, and so long as he had been pitted against nail makers of flesh and blood he had more than held his own; he had, indeed, even put up a tremendous but an unequal struggle against the competition of nail-making machinery. Accustomed as he was to concentrate on a single, glowing, definite object, the complexity and disorder of Cloon na Morav unnerved him. But he was not going to betray any of these professional defects to Cahir Bowes, the stone breaker. He had been sent there as an ambassador by the caretaker of Cloon na Morav, picked out for his great age, his local knowledge, and his good character, and it was his business to point out to the twin gravediggers, sons of the caretaker, the weaver's grave, so that it might be opened to receive him. Meehaul Lynskey had a knowledge of the place, and was quite certain as to a great number of grave sites, while the caretaker, being an official without records, had a profound ignorance of the whole place.

Cahir Bowes followed the drifting figure of the nail maker over the ground, his face hitched up between his shoulders, his eyes keen and grey, glint-like as the mountains of stones he had in his day broken up as road material. Cahir, no less than Meehaul, had his knowledge of Cloon na Morav, and some of his own people were buried here. His sharp, clear eyes took in the various mounds with the eye of a prospector. He, too, had been sent there as an ambassador, and as between himself and Meehaul Lynskey he did not think there could be any two opinions; his knowledge was superior to the knowledge of the nailer. Whenever Cahir Bowes met a loose stone on the grass quite instinctively he turned it over with his stick, his sharp old eyes judging its grain with a professional swiftness, then cracking at it with his stick. If the stick were a hammer the stone, attacked on its most vulnerable spot, would fall to pieces like glass. In stones Cahir Bowes saw not sermons but seams. Even the headstones he tapped significantly with the ferrule of his stick, for Cahir Bowes had an artist's passion for his art, though his art was far from creative. He was one of the great destroyers, the reducers, the makers of chaos, a powerful and remorseless critic of the Stone Age.

The two old men wandered about Cloon na Morav, in no hurry whatever to get through with their business. After all they had been a long time pensioned off, forgotten, neglected, by the world. The renewed sensation of usefulness was precious to them. They knew that when this business was over they were not likely to be in request for anything in this world again. They were ready to oblige the world, but the world would have to allow them their own time. The world, made up of the two gravediggers and the widow of the weaver, gathered all this without any vocal proclamation. Slowly, mechanically as it were, they followed the two ancients about Cloon na Morav. And the two ancients wandered about with the labor of age and the hearts of children. They separated, wandered about silently as if they were picking up old acquaintants, stumbling upon forgotten things, gathering up the threads of days that were over, reviving their memories, and then drew together, beginning to talk slowly, almost casually, and all their talk was of the dead, of the people who lay in the ground about them. They warmed to it, airing their knowledge, calling up names and complications of family relationships, telling stories, reviving all virtues, whispering at past vices, past vices that did not sound like vices at all, for the long years are great mitigators and run in splendid harness with the coyest of all the virtues, Charity. The whispered scandals of Cloon na Morav were seen by the twin gravediggers and the widow of the weaver through such a haze of antiquity that they were no longer scandals but

romances. The rake and the drab, seen a good way down the
avenue, merely look picturesque. The gravediggers rested their
spades in the ground, leaning on the handles in exactly the
same graveyard pose, and the pale widow stood in the background, silent, apart, patient, and, like all dark, tragic-looking
women, a little mysterious.

The stone breaker pointed with his quivering stick at the
graves of the people whom he spoke about. Every time he
raised that forward support one instinctively looked, anxious
and fearful, to see if the clutch were secure on the small of the
back. Cahir Bowes had the sort of shape that made one eter-
nally fearful for his equilibrium. The nailer, who, like his friend
the stone breaker, wheezed a good deal, made short, sharp gestures, and always with the right hand; the fingers were hooked
in such a way, and he shot out the arm in such a manner, that
they gave the illusion that he held a hammer and that it was
struck out over a very hot fire. Every time Meehaul Lynskey
made this gesture one expected to see sparks flying.

"Where are we to bury the weaver?" one of the gravediggers
asked at last.

Both old men labored around to see where the interruption,
the impertinence, had come from. They looked from one twin
to the other, with gravity, indeed anxiety, for they were not
sure which was which, or if there was not some illusion in the
resemblance, some trick of youth to baffle age.

"Where are we to bury the weaver?" the other twin repeated, and the strained look on the old men's faces deepened.
They were trying to fix in their minds which of the twins had
interrupted first and which last. The eyes of Meehaul Lynskey
fixed on one twin with the instinct of his trade, while Cahir
Bowes ranged both and eventually wandered to the figure of
the widow in the background, silently accusing her of impatience in a matter which it would be indelicate for her to show
haste.

"We can't stay here forever," said the first twin.

It was the twin upon whom Meehaul Lynskey had fastened his small eyes, and, sure of his man this time, Meehaul Lynskey hit him.

"There's many a better man than you," said Meehaul Lynskey, "that will stay here forever." He swept Cloon na Morav with the hooked fingers.

"Them that stays in Cloon na Morav forever," said Cahir Bowes with a wheezing energy, "have nothing to be ashamed of—nothing to be ashamed of. Remember that, young fellow."

Meehaul Lynskey did not seem to like the intervention, the help, of Cahir Bowes. It was a sort of implication that he had not—*he*, mind you—had not hit the nail properly on the head.

"Well, where are we to bury him, anyway?" said the twin, hoping to profit by the chagrin of the nailer—the nailer who, by implication, had failed to nail.

"You'll bury him," said Meehaul Lynskey, "where all belonging to him is buried."

"We come," said the other twin, "with some sort of intention of that kind." He drawled out the words, in imitation of the old men. The skin relaxed on his handsome dark face and then bunched in puckers of humor about the eyes; Meehaul Lynskey's gaze, wandering for once, went to the handsome dark face of the other twin and the skin relaxed and then bunched in puckers of humor about *his* eyes, so that Meehaul Lynskey had an unnerving sensation that these young gravediggers were purposely confusing him.

"You'll bury him—" he began with some vehemence, and was amazed to again find Cahir Bowes taking the words out of his mouth, snatching the hammer out of his hand, so to speak.

"—where you're told to bury him," Cahir Bowes finished for him.

Meehaul Lynskey was so hurt that his long slanting figure moved away down the graveyard, then stopped suddenly. He had determined to do a dreadful thing. He had determined to do a thing that was worse than kicking a crutch from under a cripple's shoulder; that was like stealing the holy water out of a room where a man lay dying. He had determined to ruin the last day's amusement on this earth for Cahir Bowes and himself by prematurely and basely disclosing the weaver's grave!

"Here," called back Meehaul Lynskey, "is the weaver's grave, and here you will bury him."

All moved down to the spot, Cahir Bowes going with extraordinary spirit, the ferrule of his terrible stick cracking on the stones he met on the way.

"Between these two mounds," said Meehaul Lynskey, and already the twins raised their twin spades in a sinister movement, like swords of lancers flashing at a drill.

"Between these two mounds," said Meehaul Lynskey, "is the grave of Mortimer Hehir."

"Hold on!" cried Cahir Bowes. He was so eager, so excited, that he struck one of the gravediggers a whack of his stick on the back. Both gravediggers swung about to him as if both had been hurt by the one blow.

"Easy there," said the first twin.

"Easy there," said the second twin.

"Easy yourselves," cried Cahir Bowes. He wheeled about his now quivering face on Meehaul Lynskey.

"What is it you're saying about the spot between the mounds?" he demanded.

"I'm saying," said Meehaul Lynskey vehemently, "that it's the weaver's grave."

"What weaver?" asked Cahir Bowes.

"Mortimer Hehir," replied Meehaul Lynskey. "There's no other weaver in it."

"Was Julia Rafferty a weaver?"

"What Julia Rafferty?"

"The midwife, God rest her."

"How could she be a weaver if she was a midwife?"

"Not a one of me knows. But I'll tell you what I do know and know rightly: that it's Julia Rafferty is in that place and no weaver at all."

"Amn't I telling you it's the weaver's grave?"

"And amn't I telling you it's not?"

"That I may be as dead as my father but the weaver was buried there."

"A bone of a weaver was never sunk in it as long as weavers was weavers. Full of Raffertys it is."

"Alive with weavers it is."

"Heavenlyful Father, was the like ever heard: to say that a grave was alive with dead weavers."

"It's full of them—full as a tick."

"And the clean grave that Mortimer Hehir was never done boasting about—dry and sweet and deep and no way bulging at all. Did you see the burial of his father ever?"

"I did, in troth, see the burial of his father—forty year ago if it's a day."

"Forty year ago—it's fifty-one year come the sixteenth of May. It's well I remember it and it's well I have occasion to re-member it, for it was the day after that again that myself ran away to join the soldiers, my aunt hotfoot after me, she to be buying me out the week after, I a high-spirited fellow morebe-token."

"Leave the soldiers out of it and leave your aunt out of it and stick to the weaver's grave. Here in this place was the last weaver buried, and I'll tell you what's more. In a straight line with it is the grave of—"

"A straight line, indeed! Who but yourself, Meehaul Lyn-skey, ever heard of a straight line in Cloon na Morav? No such thing was ever wanted or ever allowed in it."

"In a straight direct line, measured with a rule—"

"Measured with crooked, stumbling feet, maybe feet half reeling in drink."

"Can't you listen to me now?"

"I was always a bad warrant to listen to anything except sense. Yourself ought to be the last man in the world to talk about straight lines, you with the sight scattered in your head, with the divil of sparks flying under your eyes."

"Don't mind me sparks now, nor me sight neither, for in a straight measured line with the weaver's grave was the grave of the Cassidys."

"What Cassidys?"

"The Cassidys that herded for the O'Sheas."

"Which O'Sheas?"

"O'Shea Ruadh of Cappakelly. Don't you know any one at all, or is it gone entirely your memory is?"

"Cappakelly *inagh!* And who cares a whistle about O'Shea Ruadh, he or his seed, breed, and generations? It's a rotten lot of land-grabbers they were."

"Me hand to you on that. Striving ever they were to put their red paws on this bit of grass and that perch of meadow."

"Hungry in themselves even for the cutaway bog."

"And Mortimer Hehir a decent weaver, respecting every man's wool."

"His forehead pallid with honesty over the yarn and the loom."

"If a bit broad-spoken when he came to the door for a smoke of the pipe."

"Well, there won't be a mouthful of clay between himself and O'Shea Ruadh now."

"In the end what did O'Shea Ruadh get after all his striving?"

"I'll tell you that. He got what land suits a blind fiddler."

"Enough to pad the crown of the head and tap the sole of the foot! Now you're talking."

"And the devil a word out of him now no more than any one else in Cloon na Morav."

"It's easy talking to us all about land when we're packed up in our timber boxes."

"As the weaver was when he got sprinkled with the holy water in that place."

"As Julia Rafferty was when they read the prayers over her in that place, she a fine, buxom, cheerful woman in her day, with great skill in her business."

"Skill or no skill, I'm telling you she's not there, wherever she is."

"I suppose you want me to take her up in my arms and show her to you?"

"Well then, indeed, Cahir, I do not. 'Tisn't a very handsome pair you would make at all, you not able to stand much more hardship than Julia herself."

From this there developed a slow, labored, aged dispute between the two authorities. They moved from grave to grave, pitting memory against memory, story against story, knocking down reminiscence with reminiscence, arguing in a powerful intimate obscurity that no outsider could hope to follow, blasting knowledge with knowledge, until the whole place seemed strewn with the corpses of their arguments. The two gravediggers followed them about in a grim silence; impatience in their movements, their glances; the widow keeping track of the grand tour with a miserable feeling, a feeling, as site after site was rejected, that the tremendous exclusiveness of Cloon na Morav would altogether push her dead man, the weaver, out of his privilege. The dispute ended, like all epics, where it began. Nothing was established, nothing settled. But the two old men were quite exhausted, Meehaul Lynskey sitting down on the back of one of the monstrous cockroaches, Cahir Bowes leaning against a tombstone that was half-submerged, its end up like the stern of a derelict at sea. Here they sat glaring at each other like a pair of grim vultures.

The two gravediggers grew restive. Their business had to be done. The weaver would have to be buried. Time pressed. They held a consultation apart. It broke up after a brief exchange of views, a little laughter.

"Meehaul Lynskey is right," said one of the twins. Meehaul Lynskey's face lit up. Cahir Bowes looked as if he had been slapped on the cheeks. He moved out from his tombstone.

"Meehaul Lynskey is right," repeated the other twin. They had decided to break up the dispute by taking sides. They raised their spades and moved to the site which Meehaul Lynskey had urged upon them.

"Don't touch that place," Cahir Bowes cried, raising his stick. He was measuring the back of the gravedigger again when the man spun round upon him, menace in his handsome dark face.

"Touch me with that stick," he cried, "and I'll—"

Some movement in the background, some agitation in the widow's shawl, caused the gravedigger's menace to dissolve, the words to die in his mouth, a swift flush mounting the man's face. A faint smile of gratitude swept the widow's face like a flash. It was as if she had cried out, "Ah, don't touch the poor old, cranky fellow! you might hurt him." And it was as if the gravedigger had cried back: "He has annoyed me greatly, but I don't intend to hurt him. And since you say so with your eyes I won't even threaten him."

Under pressure of the half threat, Cahir Bowes shuffled back a little way, striking an attitude of feeble dignity, leaning out on his stick while the gravediggers got to work.

"It's the weaver's grave, surely," said Meehaul Lynskey.

"If it is," said Cahir Bowes, "remember his father was buried down seven feet. You gave in to that this morning."

"There was no giving in about it," said Meehaul Lynskey. "We all know that one of the wonders of Cloon na Morav was the burial of the last weaver seven feet, he having left it as an injunction on his family. The world knows he went down the seven feet."

"And remember this," said Cahir Bowes, "that Julia Rafferty was buried no seven feet. If she is down three feet it's as much as she went."

Sure enough, the gravediggers had not dug down more than three feet of ground when one of the spades struck hollowly on unhealthy timber. The sound was unmistakable and ominous. There was silence for a moment. Then Cahir Bowes made a sudden short spurt up a mound beside him, as if he were some sort of mechanical animal wound up, his horizontal back quivering. On the mound he made a superhuman effort to straighten himself. He got his ears and his blunt nose into a considerable elevation. He had not been so upright for twenty years. And raising his weird countenance, he broke into a cackle that was certainly meant to be a crow. He glared at Meehaul Lynskey, his emotion so great that his eyes swam in a watery triumph.

Meehaul Lynskey had his eyes, as was his custom, upon one thing, and that thing was the grave, and especially the spot on the grave where the spade had struck the coffin. He looked stunned and fearful. His eyes slowly withdrew their gimlet-like scrutiny from the spot, and sought the triumphant crowing figure of Cahir Bowes on the mound.

Meehaul Lynskey looked as if he would like to say something, but no words came. Instead he ambled away, retired from the battle, and standing apart, rubbed one leg against the other, above the back of the ankles, like some great insect. His hooked fingers at the same time stroked the bridge of his nose. He was beaten.

"I suppose it's not the weaver's grave," said one of the gravediggers. Both of them looked at Cahir Bowes.

"Well, you know it's not," said the stone breaker. "It's Julia Rafferty you struck. She helped many a one into the world in her day, and it's poor recompense to her to say she can't be at rest when she left it." He turned to the remote figure of Meehaul Lynskey and cried: "Ah-ha, well you may rub your ignorant legs. And I'm hoping Julia will forgive you this day's ugly work."

In silence, quickly, with reverence, the twins scooped back

the clay over the spot. The widow looked on with the same quiet, patient, mysterious silence. One of the gravediggers turned on Cahir Bowes.

"I suppose you know where the weaver's grave is?" he asked.

Cahir Bowes looked at him with an ancient tartness, then said:

"You suppose!"

"Of course, you know where it is."

Cahir Bowes looked as if he knew where the gates of heaven were, and that he might—or might not—enlighten an ignorant world. It all depended! His eyes wandered knowingly out over the meadows beyond the graveyard. He said:

"I do know where the weaver's grave is."

"We'll be very much obliged to you if you show it to us."

"Very much obliged," endorsed the other twin.

The stone breaker, thus flattered, led the way to a new site, one nearer to the wall, where were the plagiarisms of the Eastern sepulchers. Cahir Bowes made little journeys about, measuring so many steps from one place to another, mumbling strange and unintelligible information to himself, going through an extraordinary geometrical emotion, striking the ground hard taps with his stick.

"Glory be to the Lord," cried Meehaul Lynskey, "he's like the man they had driving the water for the well in the quarry field, he whacking the ground with his magic hazel wand."

Cahir Bowes made no reply. He was too absorbed in his own emotion. A little steam was beginning to ascend from his brow. He was moving about the ground like some grotesque spider weaving an invisible web.

"I suppose now," said Meehaul Lynskey, addressing the marble monument, "that as soon as Cahir hits the right spot one of the weavers will turn about below. Or maybe he expects one of them to whistle up at him out of the ground. That's it; devil a other! When we hear the whistle we'll all know for certain where to bury the weaver."

Cahir Bowes was contracting his movements, so that he was now circling about the one spot, like a dog going to lie down.

Meehaul Lynskey drew a little closer, watching eagerly, his grim yellow face, seared with yellow marks from the fires of his workshop, tightened up in a sceptical pucker. His half-muttered words were bitter with an aged sarcasm. He cried:

"Say nothing; he'll get it yet, will the man of knowledge, the know-all, Cahir Bowes! Give him time. Give him until this day twelvemonth. Look at that for a right-about-turn on the left heel. Isn't the nimbleness of that young fellow a treat to see? Are they whistling to you from below, Cahir? Is it dancing to the weaver's music you are? That's it, devil a other."

Cahir Bowes was mapping out a space on the grass with his stick. Gradually it took, more or less, the outline of a grave site. He took his hat and mopped his steaming brow with a red handkerchief, saying:

"There is the weaver's grave."

"God in Heaven," cried Meehaul Lynskey, "will you look at what he calls the weaver's grave? I'll say nothing at all. I'll hold my tongue. I'll shut up. Not one word will I say about Alick Finlay, the mildest man that ever lived, a man full of religion, never at the end of his prayers! But, sure, it's the saints of God that get the worst of it in this world, and if Alick escaped during life, faith he's in for it now, with the pirates and the body snatchers of Cloon na Morav on top of him."

A corncrake began to sing in the nearby meadow, and his rasping notes sounded like a queer accompaniment to the words of Meehaul Lynskey. The gravediggers, who had gone to work on the Cahir Bowes site, laughed a little, one of them looking for a moment at Meehaul Lynskey, saying:

"Listen to that damned old corncrake in the meadow! I'd like to put a sod in his mouth."

The man's eye went to the widow. She showed no emotion one way or the other, and the gravedigger got back to his work. Meehaul Lynskey, however, wore the cap. He said:

"To be sure! I'm to sing dumb. I'm not to have a word out of me at all. Others can rattle away as they like in this place, as if they owned it. The ancient good old stock is to be nowhere and the scruff of the hills let rampage as they will. That's it, devil a other. Castles falling and dunghills rising! Well, God be with the good old times and the good old mannerly people that used to be in it, and God be with Alick Finlay, the holiest—"

A sod of earth came through the air from the direction of the grave, and, skimming Meehaul Lynskey's head, dropped somewhere behind. The corncrake stopped his notes in the meadow, and Meehaul Lynskey stood statuesque in a mute protest, and silence reigned in the place while the clay sang up in a swinging rhythm from the grave.

Cahir Bowes, watching the operations with intensity, said:

"It was nearly going astray on me."

Meehaul Lynskey gave a little snort. He asked:

"What was?"

"The weaver's grave."

"Remember this: the last weaver is down seven feet. And remember this: Alick Finlay is down less than Julia Rafferty."

He had no sooner spoken when a fearful thing happened. Suddenly out of the soft cutting of the earth a spade sounded harsh on tinware, there was a crash, less harsh, but painfully distinct, as if rotten boards were falling together, then a distinct subsidence of the earth. The work stopped at once. A moment's fearful silence followed. It was broken by a short, dry laugh from Meehaul Lynskey. He said:

"God be merciful to us all! That's the latter end of Alick Finlay."

The two gravediggers looked at each other. The shawl of the widow in the background was agitated. One twin said to the other:

"This can't be the weaver's grave."

The other agreed. They all turned their eyes upon Cahir

Bowes. He was hanging forward in a pained strain, his head quaking, his fingers twitching on his stick. Meehaul Lynskey turned to the marble monument and said with venom:

"If I was guilty I'd go down on my knees and beg God's pardon. If I didn't I'd know the ghost of Alick Finlay, saint as he was, would leap upon me and guzzle me—for what right would I have to set anybody at him with driving spades when he was long years in his grave?"

Cahir Bowes took no notice. He was looking at the ground, searching about, and slowly, painfully, began his web-spinning again. The gravediggers covered in the ground without a word. Cahir Bowes appeared to get lost in some fearful maze of his own making. A little whimper broke from him now and again. The steam from his brow thickened in the air, and eventually he settled down on the end of a headstone, having got the worst of it. Meehaul Lynskey sat on another stone facing him, and they glared, sinister and grotesque, at each other.

"Cahir Bowes," said Meehaul Lynskey, "I'll tell you what you are, and then you can tell me what I am."

"Have it whatever way you like," said Cahir Bowes. "What is it that I am?"

"You're a gentleman, a grand oul' stone-breaking gentleman. That's what you are, devil a other!"

The wrinkles on the withered face of Cahir Bowes contracted, his eyes stared across at Meehaul Lynskey, and two yellow teeth showed between his lips. He wheezed:

"And do you know what you are?"

"I don't."

"You're a nailer, that's what you are, a damned nailer."

They glared at each other in a quaking, grim silence.

And it was at this moment of collapse, of deadlock, that the widow spoke for the first time. At the first sound of her voice one of the twins perked his head, his eyes going to her face. She said in a tone as quiet as her whole behavior:

"Maybe I ought to go up to the Tunnel Road and ask Malachi Roohan where the grave is."

They had all forgotten the oldest man of them all, Malachi
Roohan. He would be the last mortal man to enter Cloon na
Morav. He had been the great friend of Mortimer Hehir, the
weaver, in the days that were over, and the whole world knew
that Mortimer Hehir's knowledge of Cloon na Morav was perfect. Maybe Malachi Roohan would have learned a great deal
from him. And Malachi Roohan, the cooper, was so long bed-
ridden that those who remembered him at all thought of him
as a man who had died a long time ago.

"There's nothing else for it," said one of the twins, leaving
down his spade, and immediately the other twin laid his spade
beside it.

The two ancients on the headstones said nothing. Not even
they could raise a voice against the possibilities of Malachi
Roohan, the cooper. By their terrible aged silence they gave
consent, and the widow turned to walk out of Cloon na
Morav. One of the gravediggers took out his pipe. The eyes of
the other followed the widow, he hesitated, then walked after
her. She became conscious of the man's step behind her as she
got upon the stile, and turned her palely sad face upon him. He
stood awkwardly, his eyes wandering, then said:

"Ask Malachi Roohan where the grave is, the exact place."

It was to do this the widow was leaving Cloon na Morav; she
had just announced that she was going to ask Malachi Roohan
where the grave was. Yet the man's tone was that of one who
was giving her extraordinarily acute advice. There was a little
half-embarrassed note of confidence in his tone. In a dim way
the widow thought that, maybe, he had accompanied her to
the stile in a little awkward impulse of sympathy. Men were
very curious in their ways sometimes. The widow was a very
well-mannered woman, and she tried to look as if she had received a very valuable direction. She said:

"I will. I'll put that question to Malachi Roohan."
And then she passed out over the stile.

III

The widow went up the road, and beyond it struck the first
of the houses of the nearby town. She passed through faded
streets in her quiet gait, moderately grief-stricken at the death
of her weaver. She had been his fourth wife, and the widowhoods of fourth wives have not the rich abandon, the great
emotional cataclysm, of first, or even second, widowhoods. It is
a little chastened in its poignancy. The widow had a nice feeling that it would be out of place to give way to any of the characteristic manifestations of normal widowhood. She shrank
from drawing attention to the fact that she had been a fourth
wife. People's memories become so extraordinarily acute to
family history in times of death! The widow did not care to
come in as a sort of dramatic surprise in the gossip of the
people about the weaver's life. She had heard snatches of such
gossip at the wake the night before. She was beginning to understand why people love wakes and the intimate personalities
of wakehouses. People listen to, remember, and believe what
they hear at wakes. It is more precious to them than anything
they ever hear in school, church, or playhouse. It is hardly because they get certain entertainment at the wake. It is more because the wake is a grand review of family ghosts. There one
hears all the stories, the little flattering touches, the little un-
flattering bitternesses, the traditions, the astonishing records,
of the clans. The woman with a memory speaking to the company from a chair beside a laid-out corpse carries more authority than the bishop allocuting from his chair. The wake is
realism. The widow had heard a great deal at the wake about
the clan of the weavers, and noted, without expressing any
emotion, that she had come into the story not like other
women, for anything personal to her own womanhood—for
beauty, or high spirit, or temper, or faithfulness, or unfaithful-

ness—but simply because she was a fourth wife, a kind of curiosity, the backwash of Mortimer Hehir's romances. The widow felt a remote sense of injustice in all this. She had said to herself that widows who had been fourth wives deserved more sympathy than widows who had been first wives, for the simple reason that fourth widows had never been, and could never be, first wives! The thought confused her a little, and she did not pursue it, instinctively feeling that if she did accept the conventional view of her condition she would only crystallize her widowhood into a grievance that nobody would try to understand, and which would, accordingly, be merely useless. And what was the good of it, anyhow? The widow smoothed her dark hair on each side of her head under her shawl.

She had no bitter and no sweet memories of the weaver. There was nothing that was even vivid in their marriage. She had no complaints to make of Mortimer Hehir. He had not come to her in any fiery love impulse. It was the marriage of an old man with a woman years younger. She had recognized him as an old man from first to last, a man who had already been thrice through a wedded experience, and her temperament, naturally calm, had met his half-stormy, half-petulant character, without suffering any sort of shock. The weaver had tried to keep up to the illusion of a perennial youth by dyeing his hair, and marrying one wife as soon as possible after another. The fourth wife had come to him late in life. She had a placid understanding that she was a mere flattery to the weaver's truculent egoism.

These thoughts, in some shape or other, occupied, without agitating, the mind of the widow as she passed, a dark shadowy figure, through streets that were clamorous in their quietudes, painful in their lack of all the purposes for which streets have ever been created. Her only emotion was one which she knew to be quite creditable to her situation: a sincere desire to see the weaver buried in the grave to which the respectability of his family and the claims of his ancient house fully and fairly entitled him to. The proceedings in Cloon na Morav had been painful, even tragical, to the widow. The weavers had always been great authorities and zealous guardians of the ancient burial place. This function had been traditional and voluntary with them. This was especially true of the last of them, Mortimer Hehir. He had been the greatest of all authorities on the burial places of the local clans. His knowledge was scientific. He had been the grand savant of Cloon na Morav. He had policed the place. Nay, he had been its tyrant. He had over and over again prevented terrible mistakes, complications that would have appalled those concerned if they were not beyond all such concerns. The widow of the weaver had often thought that in his day Mortimer Hehir had made his solicitation for the place a passion, unreasonable, almost violent. They said that all this had sprung from a fear that had come to him in his early youth that through some blunder an alien, an inferior, even an enemy, might come to find his way into the family burial place of the weavers. This fear had made him what he was. And in his later years his pride in the family burial place became a worship. His trade had gone down, and his pride had gone up. The burial ground in Cloon na Morav was the grand proof of his aristocracy. That was the coat-of-arms, the estate, the mark of high breeding, in the weavers. And now the man who had minded everybody's grave had not been able to mind his own. The widow thought that it was one of those injustices which blacken the reputation of the whole earth. She had felt, indeed, that she had been herself slack not to have learned long ago the lie of this precious grave from the weaver himself; and that he himself had been slack in not properly instructing her. But that was the way in this miserable world! In his passion for classifying the rights of others, the weaver had obscured his own. In his long and entirely successful battle in keeping alien corpses out of his own aristocratic pit he had made his own corpse alien to every pit in the place. The living high priest was the dead pariah of Cloon na Morav. Nobody could now tell except, perhaps, Malachi Roohan, the precise spot which he had defended against the blunders and confusions of the entire community, a dead-forgetting, indifferent, slack lot!

The widow tried to recall all she had ever heard the weaver say about his grave, in the hope of getting some clue, something that might be better than the scandalous scatterbrained efforts of Meehaul Lynskey and Cahir Bowes. She remembered various detached things that the weaver, a talkative man, had said about his grave. Fifty years ago since that grave had been last opened, and it had then been opened to receive the remains of his father. It had been thirty years previous to that since it had taken in his father, that is, the newly dead weaver's father's father. The weavers were a long-lived lot, and there were not many males of them; one son was as much as any one of them begot to pass to the succession of the loom; if there were daughters they scattered, and their graves were continents apart. The three wives of the late weaver were buried in the new cemetery. The widow remembered that the weaver seldom spoke of them, and took no interest in their resting place. His heart was in Cloon na Morav and the sweet, dry, deep, aristocratic bed he had there in reserve for himself. But all his talk had been generalization. He had never, that the widow could recall, said anything about the site, about the signs and measurements by which it could be identified. No doubt, it had been well known to many people, but they had all died. The weaver had never realized what their slipping away might mean to himself. The position of the grave was so intimate to his own mind that it never occurred to him that it could be obscure to the minds of others. Mortimer Hehir had passed away like some learned and solitary astronomer who had discovered a new star, hugging its beauty, its exclusiveness, its possession to his heart, secretly rejoicing how its name would travel with his own through heavenly space for all time—and forgetting to mark its place among the known stars grouped upon his charts. Meehaul Lynskey and Cahir Bowes might now be two seasoned

astronomers of venal knowledge looking for the star which the
weaver, in his love for it, had let slip upon the mighty complexity of the skies.

The thing that is clearest to the mind of a man is often the
thing that is most opaque to the intelligence of his bosom
companion. A saint may walk the earth in the simple belief
that all the world beholds his glowing halo; but all the world
does not; if it did the saint would be stoned. And Mortimer
Hehir had been as innocently proud of his grave as a saint
might be ecstatic of his halo. He believed that when the time
came he would get a royal funeral—a funeral fitting to the last
of the line of great Cloon na Morav weavers. Instead of that
they had no more idea of where to bury him than if he had
been a wild tinker of the roads.

The widow, thinking of these things in her own mind, was
about to sigh when, behind a windowpane, she heard the sudden bubble of a roller canary's song. She had reached, half absentmindedly, the home of Malachi Roohan, the cooper.

IV

The widow of the weaver approached the door of Malachi
Roohan's house with an apologetic step, pawing the threshold
a little in the manner of peasant women—a mannerism picked
up from shy animals—before she stooped her head and made
her entrance.

Malachi Roohan's daughter withdrew from the fire a face
which reflected the passionate soul of a cook. The face cooled
as the widow disclosed her business.

"I wouldn't put it a-past my father to have knowledge of the
grave," said the daughter of the house, adding, "The Lord a
mercy on the weaver."

She led the widow into the presence of the cooper.

The room was small and low and stuffy, indifferently served
with light by an unopenable window. There was the smell of
old age, of decay, in the room. It brought almost a sense of

faintness to the widow. She had the feeling that God had made her to move in the ways of old men—passionate, cantankerous, egoistic old men, old men for whom she was always doing something, always remembering things, from missing buttons to lost graves.

Her eyes sought the bed of Malachi Roohan with an un-emotional, quietly sceptical gaze. But she did not see anything of the cooper. The daughter leaned over the bed, listened attentively, and then very deftly turned down the clothes, revealing the bust of Malachi Roohan. The widow saw a weird face, not in the least pale or lined, but ruddy, with a mahogany bald head, a head upon which the leathery skin—for there did not seem any flesh—hardly concealed the stark outlines of the skull. From the chin there strayed a grey beard, the most shaken and whipped-looking beard that the widow had ever seen; it was, in truth, a very miracle of a beard, for one wondered how it had come there, and having come there, how it continued to hang on, for there did not seem anything to which it could claim natural allegiance. The widow was as much astonished at this beard as if she saw a plant growing in a pot without soil. Through its gaps she could see the leather of the skin, the bones of a neck, which was indeed a neck. Over this head and shoulders the cooper's daughter bent and shouted into a crumpled ear. A little spasm of life stirred in the mummy. A low, mumbling sound came from the bed. The widow was already beginning to feel that perhaps she had done wrong in remembering that the cooper was still extant. But what else could she have done? If the weaver was buried in a wrong grave she did not believe that his soul would ever rest in peace. And what could be more dreadful than a soul wandering on the howling winds of the earth? The weaver would grieve, even in heaven, for his grave, grieve, maybe, as bitterly as a saint might grieve who had lost his halo. He was a passionate old man, such an old man as would have a turbulent spirit. He would surely—. The widow stifled the thoughts that flashed into her mind. She was no more superstitious than the rest of us, but—. These vague and terrible fears, and her moderately decent sorrow, were alike banished from her mind by what followed. The mummy on the bed came to life. And, what was more, he did it himself. His daughter looked on with the air of one whose sensibilities had become blunted by a long familiarity with the various stages of his resurrections. The widow gathered that the daughter had been well drilled; she had been taught how to keep her place. She did not tender the slightest help to her father as he drew himself together on the bed. He turned over on his side, then on his back, and stealthily began to insinuate his shoulder blades on the pillow, pushing up his weird head to the streak of light from the little window. The widow had been so long accustomed to assist the aged that she made some involuntary movement of succor. Some half-seen gesture by the daughter, a sudden lifting of the eyelids on the face of the patient, disclosing a pair of blue eyes, gave the widow instinctive pause. She remained where she was, aloof like the daughter of the house. And as she caught the blue of Malachi Roohan's eyes it broke upon the widow that here in the essence of the cooper there lived a spirit of extraordinary independence. Here, surely, was a man who had been accustomed to look out for himself, who resented the attentions, even in these days of his flickering consciousness. Up he wormed his shoulder blades, his mahogany skull, his leathery skin, his sensational eyes, his miraculous beard, to the light and to the full view of the visitor. At a certain stage of the resurrection—when the cooper had drawn two long, stringy arms from under the clothes—his daughter made a drilled movement forward, seeking something in the bed. The widow saw her discover the end of a rope, and this she placed in the hands of her indomitable father. The other end of the rope was fastened to the iron rail of the foot of the bed. The sinews of the patient's hands clutched the rope, and slowly, wonderfully, magically, as it seemed to the widow, the cooper raised himself to a sitting

posture in the bed. There was dead silence in the room except
for the labored breathing of the performer. The eyes of the
widow blinked. Yes, there was that ghost of a man hoisting
himself up from the dead on a length of rope reversing the
usual procedure. By that length of rope did the cooper hang on
to life, and the effort of life. It represented his connection with
the world, the world which had forgotten him, which marched
past his window outside without knowing the stupendous
thing that went on in his room. There he was, sitting up in the
bed, restored to view by his own unaided efforts, holding his
grip on life to the last. It cost him something to do it, but he
did it. It would take him longer and longer every day to grip
along that length of rope; he would fail ell by ell, sinking back
to the last helplessness on his rope, descending into eternity as
a vessel is lowered on a rope into a dark, deep well. But there
he was now, still able for his work, unbeholding to all, self-
dependent and alive, looking a little vaguely with his blue eyes
at the widow of the weaver. His daughter swiftly and quietly
propped pillows at his back, and she did it with the air of one
who was allowed a special privilege.

"Nan!" called the old man to his daughter.

The widow, cool-tempered as she was, almost jumped on her
feet. The voice was amazingly powerful. It was like a shout,
filling the little room with vibrations. For four things did
the widow ever after remember Malachi Roohan—for his rope,
his blue eyes, his powerful voice, and his magic beard. They
were thrown on the background of his skeleton in powerful
relief.

"Yes, Father," his daughter replied, shouting into his ear. He
was apparently very deaf. This infirmity came upon the widow
with a shock. The cooper was full of physical surprises.

"Who's this one?" the cooper shouted, looking at the
widow. He had the belief that he was delivering an aside.

"Mrs. Hehir."

"Mrs. Hehir—what Hehir would she be?"

"The weaver's wife."

"The weaver? Is it Mortimer Hehir?"

"Yes, Father."

"In troth I know her. She's Delia Morrissey, that married the weaver; Delia Morrissey that he followed to Munster, a raving lunatic with the dint of love."

A hot wave of embarrassment swept the widow. For a moment she thought the mind of the cooper was wandering. Then she remembered that the maiden name of the weaver's first wife was, indeed, Delia Morrissey. She had heard it, by chance, once or twice.

"Isn't it Delia Morrissey herself we have in it?" the old man asked.

The widow whispered to the daughter:

"Leave it so."

She shrank from a difficult discussion with the specter on the bed on the family history of the weaver. A sense of shame came to her that she could be the wife to a contemporary of this astonishing old man holding on to the life rope.

"I'm out!" shouted Malachi Roohan, his blue eyes lighting suddenly. "Delia Morrissey died. She was one day eating her dinner and a bone stuck in her throat. The weaver clapped her on the back, but it was all to no good. She choked to death before his eyes on the floor. I remember that. And the weaver himself near died of grief after. But he married secondly. Who's this he married secondly, Nan?"

Nan did not know. She turned to the widow for enlightenment. The widow moistened her lips. She had to concentrate her thoughts on a subject which, for her own peace of mind, she had habitually avoided. She hated genealogy. She said a little nervously:

"Sara MacCabe."

The cooper's daughter shouted the name into his ear.

"So you're Sally MacCabe, from Looscaun, the one Mortimer took off the blacksmith? Well, well, that was a great business surely, the pair of them hot-tempered men, and your own beauty going to their heads like strong drink."

He looked at the widow, a half-sceptical, half-admiring expression flickering across the leathery face. It was such a look as he might have given to Dergorvilla of Leinster, Deirdre of Uladh, or Helen of Troy.

The widow was not the notorious Sara MacCabe from Looscaun; that lady had been the second wife of the weaver. It was said they had led a stormy life, made up of passionate quarrels and partings, and still more passionate reconciliations, Sara MacCabe from Looscaun not having quite forgotten or wholly neglected the blacksmith after her marriage to the weaver. But the widow again only whispered to the cooper's daughter:

"Leave it so."

"What way is Mortimer keeping?" asked the old man.

"He's dead," replied the daughter.

The fingers of the old man quivered on the rope.

"Dead? Mortimer Hehir dead?" he cried. "What in the name of God happened him?"

Nan did not know what happened him. She knew that the widow would not mind, so, without waiting for a prompt, she replied:

"A weakness came over him, a sudden weakness."

"To think of a man being whipped off all of a sudden like that!" cried the cooper. "When that's the way it was with Mortimer Hehir what one of us can be sure at all? Nan, none of us is sure! To think of the weaver, with his heart as strong as a bull, going off in a little weakness! It's the treacherous world we live in, the treacherous world, surely. Never another yard of tweed will he put up on his old loom! Morty, Morty, you were a good companion, a great warrant to walk the hills, whistling the tunes, pleasant in your conversation and as broad-spoken as the Bible."

"Did you know the weaver well, Father?" the daughter asked.

"Who better?" he replied. "Who drank more pints with him than what myself did? And indeed it's to his wake I'd be setting out, and it's under his coffin my shoulder would be going, if I wasn't confined to my rope."

He bowed his head for a few moments. The two women exchanged a quick, sympathetic glance.

The breathing of the old man was the breathing of one who slept. The head sank lower.

The widow said:

"You ought to make him lie down. He's tired."

The daughter made some movement of dissent; she was afraid to interfere. Maybe the cooper could be very violent if roused. After a time he raised his head again. He looked in a new mood. He was fresher, more wide-awake. His beard hung in wisps to the bedclothes.

"Ask him about the grave," the widow said.

The daughter hesitated a moment, and in that moment the cooper looked up as if he had heard, or partially heard. He said:

"If you wait a minute now I'll tell you what the weaver was." He stared for some seconds at the little window.

"Oh, we'll wait," said the daughter, and turning to the widow, added, "won't we, Mrs. Hehir?"

"Indeed we will wait," said the widow.

"The weaver," said the old man suddenly, "was a dream."

He turned his head to the women to see how they had taken it.

"Maybe," said the daughter, with a little touch of laughter, "maybe Mrs. Hehir would not give in to that."

The widow moved her hands uneasily under her shawl. She stared a little fearfully at the cooper. His blue eyes were clear as lake water over white sand.

"Whether she gives in to it, or whether she doesn't give in to it," said Malachi Roohan, "it's a dream Mortimer Hehir was. And his loom, and his shuttles, and his warping bars, and his bobbin, and the threads that he put upon the shifting racks, were all a dream. And the only thing he ever wove upon his loom was a dream."

The old man smacked his lips, his hard gums whacking. His daughter looked at him with her head a little to one side.

"And what's more," said the cooper, "every woman that ever came into his head, and every wife he married, was a dream. I'm telling you that, Nan, and I'm telling it to you of the weaver. His life was a dream, and his death is a dream. And his widow there is a dream. And all the world is a dream. Do you hear me, Nan, this world is all a dream?"

"I hear you very well, Father," the daughter sang in a piercing voice.

The cooper raised his head with a jerk, and his beard swept forward, giving him an appearance of vivid energy. He spoke in a voice like a trumpet blast:

"And I'm a dream!"

He turned his blue eyes on the widow. An unnerving sensation came to her. The cooper was the most dreadful old man she had ever seen, and what he was saying sounded the most terrible thing she had ever listened to. He cried:

"The idiot laughing in the street, the king looking at his crown, the woman turning her head to the sound of a man's step, the bells ringing in the belfry, the man walking his land, the weaver at his loom, the cooper handling his barrel, the Pope stooping for his red slippers—they're all a dream. And I'll tell you why they're a dream: because this world was meant to be a dream."

"Father," said the daughter, "you're talking too much. You'll overreach yourself."

The old man gave himself a little pull on the rope. It was his gesture of energy, a demonstration of the fine fettle he was in. He said:

"You're saying that because you don't understand me."

"I understand you very well."

"You only think you do. Listen to me now, Nan. I want you to do something for me. You won't refuse me?"

"I will not refuse you, Father; you know very well I won't."

"You're a good daughter to me, surely, Nan. And do what I tell you now. Shut close your eyes. Shut them fast and tight. No fluttering of the lids now."

"Very well, Father."

The daughter closed her eyes, throwing up her face in the attitude of one blind. The widow was conscious of the woman's strong, rough features, something good-natured in the line of the large mouth. The old man watched the face of his daughter with excitement. He asked:

"What is it that you see now, Nan?"

"Nothing at all, Father."

"In troth you do. Keep them closed tight and you'll see it."

"I see nothing only—"

"Only what? Why don't you say it?"

"Only darkness, Father."

"And isn't that something to see? Isn't it easier to see darkness than to see light? Now, Nan, look into the darkness."

"I'm looking, Father."

"And think of something—anything at all—the stool before the kitchen fire outside."

"I'm thinking of it."

"And do you remember it?"

"I do well."

"And when you remember it what do you want to do—sit on it, maybe?"

"No, Father."

"And why wouldn't you want to sit on it?"

"Because—because I'd like to see it first, to make sure."

The old man gave a little crow of delight. He cried:

"There it is! You want to make sure that it is there, although you remember it well. And that is the way with everything in this world. People close their eyes and they are not sure of anything. They want to see it again before they believe. There is Nan, now, and she does not believe in the stool before the fire, the little stool she's looking at all her life, that her mother used to seat her on before the fire when she was a small child. She closes her eyes, and it is gone! And listen to me now, Nan—if you had a man of your own and you closed your eyes you wouldn't be too sure he was the man you remembered, and you'd want to open your eyes and look at him to make sure he was the man you knew before the lids dropped on your eyes. And if you had children about you and you turned your back and closed your eyes and tried to remember them you'd want to look at them to make sure. You'd be no more sure of them than you are now of the stool in the kitchen. One flash of the eyelids and everything in this world is gone."

"I'm telling you, Father, you're talking too much."

"I'm not talking half enough. Aren't we all uneasy about the world, the things in the world that we can only believe in while we're looking at them? From one season of our life to another haven't we a kind of belief that some time we'll waken up and find everything different? Didn't you ever feel that, Nan? Didn't you think things would change, that the world would be a new place altogether, and that all that was going on around us was only a business that was doing us out of something else? We put up with it while the little hankering is nibbling at the butt of our hearts for the something else! All the men there be who believe that some day The Thing will happen, that they'll turn round the corner and waken up in the new great Street!"

"And sure," said the daughter, "maybe they are right, and maybe they will waken up."

The old man's body was shaken with a queer spasm of laughter. It began under the clothes on the bed, worked up his trunk, ran along his stringy arms, out into the rope, and the iron foot of the bed rattled. A look of extraordinarily malicious humor lit up the vivid face of the cooper. The widow beheld him with fascination, a growing sense of alarm. He might say anything. He might do anything. He might begin to sing some fearful song. He might leap out of bed.

"Nan," he said, "do you believe you'll swing round the corner and waken up?"

"Well," said Nan, hesitating a little, "I do."

The cooper gave a sort of peacock crow again. He cried:

"Och! Nan Roohan believes she'll waken up! Waken up from what? From a sleep and from a dream, from this world! Well, if you believe that, Nan Roohan, it shows you know what's what. You know what the thing around you, called the world, is. And it's only dreamers who can hope to waken up— do you hear me, Nan; it's only dreamers who can hope to waken up."

"I hear you," said Nan.

"The world is only a dream, and a dream is nothing at all! We all want to waken up out of the great nothingness of this world."

"And, please God, we will," said Nan.

"You can tell all the world from me," said the cooper, "that it won't."

"And why won't we, Father?"

"Because," said the old man, "we ourselves are the dream. When we're over the dream is over with us. That's why."

"Father," said the daughter, her head again a little to one side, "you know a great deal."

"I know enough," said the cooper shortly.

"And maybe you could tell us something about the weaver's grave. Mrs. Hehir wants to know."

"And amn't I after telling you all about the weaver's grave? Amn't I telling you it is all a dream?"

"You never said that, Father. Indeed you never did."

"I said everything in this world is a dream, and the weaver's grave is in this world, below in Cloon na Morav."

"Where in Cloon na Morav? What part of it, Father? That is what Mrs. Hehir wants to know. Can you tell her?"

"I can tell her," said Malachi Roohan. "I was at his father's burial. I remember it above all burials, because that was the day the handsome girl, Honor Costello, fell over a grave and fainted. The sweat broke out on young Donohoe when he saw Honor Costello tumbling over the grave. Not a marry would he marry her after that, and he sworn to it by the kiss of her lips. 'I'll marry no woman that fell on a grave,' says Donohoe. 'She'd maybe have a child by me with turned-in eyes or a twisted limb.' So he married a farmer's daughter, and the same morning Honor Costello married a cattle drover. Very well, then. Donohoe's wife had no child at all. She was a barren woman. Do you hear me, Nan? A barren woman she was. And such childer as Honor Costello had by the drover! Yellow hair they had, heavy as seaweed, the skin of them clear as the wind, and limbs as clean as a whistle! It was said the drover was of the blood of the Danes, and it broke out in Honor Costello's family!"

"Maybe," said the daughter, "they were Vikings."

"What are you saying?" cried the old man testily. "Ain't I telling you it's Danes they were. Did any one ever hear a greater miracle?"

"No one ever did," said the daughter, and both women clicked their tongues to express sympathetic wonder at the tale.

"And I'll tell you what saved Honor Costello," said the cooper. "When she fell in Cloon na Morav she turned her cloak inside out."

"What about the weaver's grave, Father? Mrs. Hehir wants to know."

The old man looked at the widow; his blue eyes searched her face and her figure; the expression of satirical admiration flashed over his features. The nostrils of the nose twitched. He said:

"So that's the end of the story! Sally MacCabe, the blacksmith's favorite, wants to know where she'll sink the weaver out of sight! Great battles were fought in Looscaun over Sally MacCabe! The weaver thought his heart would burst, and the blacksmith damned his soul for the sake of Sally MacCabe's idle hours."

"Father," said the daughter of the house, "let the dead rest."

"Ay," said Malachi Roohan, "let the foolish dead rest. The dream of Looscaun is over. And now the pale woman is looking for the black weaver's grave. Well, good luck to her!"

The cooper was taken with another spasm of grotesque laughter. The only difference was that this time it began by the rattling of the rail of the bed, traveled along the rope, down his stringy arms dying out somewhere in his legs in the bed. He smacked his lips, a peculiar harsh sound, as if there was not much meat to it.

"Do I know where Mortimer Hehir's grave is?" he said ruminatingly. "Do I know where me rope is?"

"Where is it, then?" his daughter asked. Her patience was great.

"I'll tell you that," said the cooper. "It's under the elm tree of Cloon na Morav. That's where it is surely. There was never a weaver yet that did not find rest under the elm tree of Cloon na Morav. There they all went as surely as the buds came on the branches. Let Sally MacCabe put poor Morty there; let her give him a tear or two in memory of the days that his heart was ready to burst for her, and believe you me no ghost will ever haunt her. No dead man ever yet came back to look upon a woman!"

A furtive sigh escaped the widow. With her handkerchief she wiped a little perspiration from both sides of her nose. The old man wagged his head sympathetically. He thought she was the long dead Sally MacCabe lamenting the weaver! The widow's emotion arose from relief that the mystery of the grave had at last been cleared up. Yet her dealings with old men had taught her caution. Quite suddenly the memory of the handsome dark face of the gravedigger who had followed her to the stile came back to her. She remembered that he said something about "the exact position of the grave." The widow prompted yet another question:

"What position under the elm tree?"

The old man listened to the question; a strained look came into his face.

"Position of what?" he asked.

"Of the grave."

"Of what grave?"

"The weaver's grave."

Another spasm seized the old frame, but this time it came from no aged merriment. It gripped his skeleton and shook it. It was as if some invisible powerful hand had suddenly taken him by the back of the neck and shaken him. His knuckles rattled on the rope. They had an appalling sound. A horrible feeling came to the widow that the cooper would fall to pieces like a bag of bones. He turned his face to his daughter. Great tears had welled into the blue eyes, giving them an appearance of childish petulance, then of acute suffering.

"What are you talking to me of graves for?" he asked, and the powerful voice broke. "Why will you be tormenting me like this? It's not going to die I am, is it? Is it going to die I am, Nan?"

The daughter bent over him as she might bend over a child. She said:

"Indeed, there's great fear of you. Lie down and rest yourself. Fatigued out and out you are."

The grip slowly slackened on the rope. He sank back, quite helpless, a little whimper breaking from him. The daughter stooped lower, reaching for a pillow that had fallen in by the wall. A sudden sharp snarl sounded from the bed, and it dropped from her hand.

"Don't touch me!" the cooper cried. The voice was again restored, powerful in its command. And to the amazement of the widow she saw him again grip along the rope and rise in the bed.

"Amn't I tired telling you not to touch me?" he cried. "Have I any business talking to you at all? Is it gone my authority is in this house?"

He glared at his daughter, his eyes red with anger, like a dog crouching in his kennel, and the daughter stepped back, a wry smile on her large mouth. The widow stepped back with her, and for a moment he held the women with their backs to the wall by his angry red eyes. Another growl and the cooper sank back inch by inch on the rope. In all her experience of old men the widow had never seen anything like this old man; his resurrections and his collapse. When he was quite down the daughter gingerly put the clothes over his shoulders and then beckoned the widow out of the room.

The widow left the house of Malachi Roohan, the cooper, with the feeling that she had discovered the grave of an old man by almost killing another.

V

The widow walked along the streets, outwardly calm, inwardly confused. Her first thought was "the day is going on me!" There were many things still to be done at home; she remembered the weaver lying there, quiet at last, the candles lighting about him, the brown habit over him, a crucifix in his hands— everything as it should be. It seemed ages to the widow since he had really fallen ill. He was very exacting and peevish all that time. His death agony had been protracted, almost melodramatically violent. A few times the widow had nearly run out of the house, leaving the weaver to fight the death battle alone. But her common sense, her good nerves, and her religious convictions had stood to her, and when she put the pennies on the weaver's eyes she was glad she had done her duty to the last. She was glad now that she had taken the search for the grave out of the hands of Meehaul Lynskey and Cahir Bowes;

Malachi Roohan had been a sight, and she would never forget
him, but he had known what nobody else knew. The widow, as
she ascended a little upward sweep of the road to Cloon na
Morav, noted that the sky beyond it was more vivid, a red band
of light having struck across the gray-blue, just on the horizon.
Up against this red background was the dark outline of landscape, and especially Cloon na Morav. She kept her eyes upon it
as she drew nearer. Objects that were vague on the landscape
began to bulk up with more distinction.

She noted the back wall of Cloon na Morav, its green lichen
more vivid under the red patch of the skyline. And presently,
above the green wall, black against the vivid sky, she saw ele-
vated the bulk of one of the black cockroaches. On it were
perched two drab figures, so grotesque, so still, that they
seemed part of the thing itself. One figure was sloping out
from the end of the tombstone so curiously that for a moment
the widow thought it was a man who had reached down from
the table to see what was under it. At the other end of the table
was a slender warped figure, and as the widow gazed upon it
she saw a sign of animation. The head and face, bleak in their
outlines, were raised up in a gesture of despair. The face was
turned flush against the sky, so much so that the widow's eyes
instinctively sought the sky too. Above the slash of red, in the
west, was a single star, flashing so briskly and so freshly that it
might have never shone before. For all the widow knew, it
might have been a young star frolicking in the heavens with all
the joy of youth. Was that, she wondered, at what the old
man, Meehaul Lynskey, was gazing. He was very, very old, and
the star was very, very young! Was there some protest in the
gesture of the head he raised to that thing in the sky; was there
some mockery in the sparkle of the thing of the sky for the face
of the man? Why should a star be always young, a man aged so
soon? Should not a man be greater than a star? Was it this
Meehaul Lynskey was thinking? The widow could not say, but
something in the thing awed her. She had the sensation of one

who surprises a man in some act that lifts him above the commonplaces of existence. It was as if Meehaul Lynskey were discovered prostrate before some altar, in the throes of a religious agony. Old men were, the widow felt, very, very strange, and she did not know that she would ever understand them. As she looked at the bleak head of Meehaul Lynskey up against the vivid patch of the sky, she wondered if there could really be something in that head which would make him as great as a star, immortal as a star? Suddenly Meehaul Lynskey made a movement. The widow saw it quite distinctly. She saw the arm raised, the hand go out, with its crooked fingers, in one, two, three quick, short taps in the direction of the star. The widow stood to watch, and the gesture was so familiar, so homely, so personal, that it was quite understandable to her. She knew then that Meehaul Lynskey was not thinking of any great things at all. He was only a nailer! And seeing the Evening Star sparkle in the sky he had only thought of his workshop, of the bellows, the irons, the fire, the sparks, and the glowing iron which might be made into a nail while it was hot! He had in imagination seized a hammer and made a blow across interstellar space at Venus! All the beauty and youth of the star frolicking on the pale sky above the slash of vivid redness had only suggested to him the making of yet another nail! If Meehaul Lynskey could push up his scarred yellow face among the stars of the sky he would only see in them the sparks of his little smithy.

Cahir Bowes was, the widow thought, looking down at the earth, from the other end of the tombstone, to see if there were any hard things there which he could smash up. The old men had their backs turned upon each other. Very likely they had had another discussion since, which ended in this attitude of mutual contempt. The widow was conscious again of the unreasonableness of old men, but not much resentful of it. She was too long accustomed to them to have any great sense of revolt. Her emotion, if it could be called an emotion, was a settled, dull toleration of all their little bigotries.

She put her hand on the stile for the second time that day, and again raised her palely sad face over the graveyard of Cloon na Morav. As she did so she had the most extraordinary experience of the whole day's sensations. It was such a sensation as gave her at once a wonderful sense of the reality and the unreality of life. She paused on the stile, and had a clear insight into something that had up to this moment been obscure. And no sooner had the thing become definite and clear than a sense of the wonder of life came to her. It was all very like the dream Malachi Roohan had talked about.

In the pale grass, under the vivid colors of the sky, the two gravediggers were lying on their backs, staring silently up at the heavens. The widow looked at them as she paused on the stile. Her thoughts of these men had been indifferent, subconscious, up to this instant. They were handsome young men. Perhaps if there had been only one of them the widow would have been more attentive. The dark handsomeness did not seem the same thing when repeated. Their beauty, if one could call it beauty, had been collective, the beauty of flowers, of dark, velvety pansies, the distinctive marks of one faithfully duplicated on the other. The good looks of one had, to the mind of the widow, somehow nullified the good looks of the other. There was too much borrowing of Peter to pay Paul in their well-favored features. The first gravedigger spoiled the illusion of individuality in the second gravedigger. The widow had not thought so, but she would have agreed if anybody whispered to her that a good-looking man who wanted to win favor with a woman should never have so complete a twin brother. It would be possible for a woman to part tenderly with a man, and, if she met his image and likeness around the corner, knock him down. There is nothing more powerful, but nothing more delicate in life than the valves of individuality.

To create the impression that humanity was a thing which could be turned out like a coinage would be to ruin the whole illusion of life. The twin gravediggers had created some sort of such impression, vague, and not very insistent, in the mind of the widow, and it had made her lose any special interest in them. Now, however, as she hesitated on the stile, all this was swept from her mind at a stroke. That most subtle and powerful of all things, personality, sprang silently from the twins and made them, to the mind of the widow, things as far apart as the poles. The two men lay at length, and exactly the same length and bulk, in the long, gray grass. But, as the widow looked upon them, one twin seemed conscious of her presence, while the other continued his absorption in the heavens above. The supreme twin turned his head, and his soft, velvety brown eyes met the eyes of the widow. There was welcome in the man's eyes. The widow read that welcome as plainly as if he had spoken his thoughts. The next moment he had sprung to his feet, smiling. He took a few steps forward, then, self-conscious, pulled up. If he had only jumped up and smiled the widow would have understood. But those few eager steps forward and then that stock stillness! The other twin rose reluctantly, and as he did so the widow was conscious of even physical differences in the brothers. The eyes were not the same. No such velvety soft lights were in the eyes of the second one. He was more sheepish. He was more phlegmatic. He was only a plagiarism of the original man! The widow wondered how she had not seen all this before. The resemblance between the twins was only skin deep. The two old men, at the moment the second twin rose, detached themselves slowly, almost painfully, from their tombstone, and all moved forward to meet the widow. The widow, collecting her thoughts, piloted her skirts modestly about her legs as she got down from the narrow stonework of the stile and stumbled into the contrariness of Cloon na Morav. A wild sense of satisfaction swept her that she had come back the bearer of useful information.

"Well," said Meehaul Lynskey, "did you see Malachi Roo-han?" The widow looked at his scorched, sceptical, yellow face, and said:

"I did."

"Had he any word for us?"

"He had. He remembers the place of the weaver's grave." The widow looked a little vaguely about Cloon na Morav.

"What does he say?"

"He says it's under the elm tree."

There was silence. The stone breaker swung about on his legs, his head making a semicircular movement over the ground, and his sharp eyes were turned upward, as if he were searching the heavens for an elm tree. The nailer dropped his underjaw and stared tensely across the ground, blankly, pa-tiently, like a fisherman on the edge of the shore gazing over an empty sea. The gravedigger turned his head away shyly, like a boy, as if he did not want to see the confusion of the widow; the man was full of the most delicate mannerisms. The other gravedigger settled into a stolid attitude, then the skin bunched up about his brown eyes in puckers of humor. A mis-erable feeling swept the widow. She had the feeling that she stood on the verge of some collapse.

"Under the elm tree," mumbled the stone breaker.

"That's what he said," added the widow. "Under the elm tree of Cloon na Morav."

"Well," said Cahir Bowes, "when you find the elm tree you'll find the grave."

The widow did not know what an elm tree was. Nothing had ever happened in life as she knew it to render any special knowledge of trees profitable, and therefore desirable. Trees were good; they made nice firing when chopped up; timber, and all that was fashioned out of timber, came from trees. This knowledge the widow had accepted as she had accepted all the other remote phenomena of the world into which she had been born. But that trees should have distinctive names, that they should have family relationships, seemed to the mind of the widow only an unnecessary complication of the affairs of the universe. What good was it? She could understand calling fruit trees fruit trees and all other kinds simply trees. But that one should be an elm and another an ash, that there should be name after name, species after species, giving them peculiarities and personalities, was one of the things that the widow did not like. And at this moment, when the elm tree of Malachi Roohan had raised a fresh problem in Cloon na Morav, the likeness of old men to old trees—their crankiness, their complexity, their angles, their very barks, bulges, gnarled twistiness, and kinks—was very close, and brought a sense of oppression to the sorely tried brain of the widow.

"Under the elm tree," repeated Meehaul Lynskey. "The elm tree of Cloon na Morav." He broke into an aged cackle of a laugh. "If I was any good at all at making a rhyme I'd make one about that elm tree, devil a other but I would."

The widow looked around Cloon na Morav, and her eyes, for the first time in her life, were consciously searching for trees. If there were numerous trees there she could understand how easy it might be for Malachi Roohan to make a mistake. He might have mistaken some other sort of tree for an elm—the widow felt that there must be plenty of other trees very like an elm. In fact, she reasoned that other trees, do their best, could not help looking like an elm. There must be thousands and millions of people like herself in the world who pass through life in the belief that a certain kind of tree was an elm when, in reality, it may be an ash or an oak or a chestnut or a beech, or even a poplar, a birch or a yew. Malachi Roohan was never likely to allow anybody to amend his knowledge of an elm tree. He would let go his rope in the belief that there was an elm tree in Cloon na Morav, and that under it was the weaver's grave—that is, if Malachi Roohan had not, in some ghastly aged kink, invented the thing. The widow, not sharply, but

still with an appreciation of the thing, grasped that a dispute
about trees would be the very sort of dispute in which Meehaul
Lynskey and Cahir Bowes would, like the very old men that
they were, have reveled. Under the impulse of the message she
had brought from the cooper they would have launched out
into another powerful struggle from tree to tree in Cloon na
Morav; they would again have strewn the place with the
corpses of slain arguments, and in the net result they would
not have been able to establish anything either about elm trees
or about the weaver's grave. The slow, sad gaze of the widow
for trees in Cloon na Morav brought to her, in these circumstances, both pain and relief. It was a relief that Meehaul Lynskey and Cahir Bowes could not challenge each other to a
battle of trees; it was a pain that the tree of Malachi Roohan
was nowhere in sight. The widow could see for herself that
there was not any sort of a tree in Cloon na Morav. The
ground was enclosed upon three sides by walls, on the fourth
by a hedge of quicks. Not even old men could transform a
hedge into an elm tree. Neither could they make the few
struggling briars clinging about the railings of the sepulchers
into anything except briars. The elm tree of Malachi Roohan
was now nonexistent. Nobody would ever know whether it
had or had not ever existed. The widow would as soon give the
soul of the weaver to the howling winds of the world as go
back and interview the cooper again on the subject.

"Old Malachi Roohan," said Cahir Bowes with tolerant decision, "is doting."

"The nearest elm tree I know," said Meehaul Lynskey, "is
half a mile away."

"The one above at Carragh?" questioned Cahir Bowes.

"Ay, beside the mill."

No more was to be said. The riddle of the weaver's grave was
still the riddle of the weaver's grave. Cloon na Morav kept its
secret. But, nevertheless, the weaver would have to be buried.

He could not be housed indefinitely. Taking courage from all the harrowing aspects of the deadlock, Meehaul Lynskey went back, plump and courageously, to his original allegiance.

"The grave of the weaver is there," he said, and he struck out his hooked fingers in the direction of the disturbance of the sod which the gravediggers had made under pressure of his earlier enthusiasm.

Cahir Bowes turned on him with a withering, quavering glance.

"Aren't you afraid that God would strike you where you stand?" he demanded.

"I'm not—not a bit afraid," said Meehaul Lynskey. "It's the weaver's grave."

"You say that," cried Cahir Bowes, "after what we all saw and what we all heard?"

"I do," said Meehaul Lynskey, stoutly. He wiped his lips with the palm of his hand, and launched out into one of his arguments, arguments, as usual, packed with particulars.

"I saw the weaver's father lowered in that place. And I'll tell you, what's more, it was Father Owen MacCarthy that read over him, he a young red-haired curate in this place at the time, long before ever he became parish priest of Benelog. There was I, standing in this exact spot, a young man, too, with a light mustache, holding me hat in me hand, and there one side of me—maybe five yards from the marble stone of the Keernahans—was Patsy Curtin that drank himself to death after, and on the other side of me was Honor Costello, that fell on the grave and married the cattle drover, a big, loose-shouldered Dane."

Patiently, half absentmindedly, listening to the renewal of the dispute, the widow remembered the words of Malachi Roohan, and his story of Honor Costello, who fell on the grave over fifty years ago. What memories these old men had! How unreliable they were, and yet flashing out astounding corroborations of each other. Maybe there was something in what Meehaul Lynskey was saying. Maybe—but the widow checked her thoughts. What was the use of it all? This grave could not be the weaver's grave; it had been grimly demonstrated to them all that it was full of stout coffins. The widow, with a gesture of agitation, smoothed her hair down the gentle slope of her head under the shawl. As she did so her eyes caught the eyes of the gravedigger; he was looking at her! He withdrew his eyes at once, and began to twitch the ends of his dark mustache with his fingers.

"If," said Cahir Bowes, "this be the grave of the weaver, what's Julia Rafferty doing in it? Answer me that, Meehaul Lynskey."

"I don't know what's she doing in it, and what's more, I don't care. And believe you my word, many a queer thing happened in Cloon na Morav that had no right to happen in it. Julia Rafferty, maybe, isn't the only one that is where she had no right to be."

"Maybe she isn't," said Cahir Bowes, "but it's there she is, anyhow, and I'm thinking it's there she's likely to stay."

"If she's in the weaver's grave," cried Meehaul Lynskey, "what I say is, out with her!"

"Very well, then, Meehaul Lynskey. Let you yourself be the powerful man to deal with Julia Rafferty. But remember this, and remember it's my word, that touch one bone in this place and you touch all."

"No fear at all have I to right a wrong. I'm no backslider when it comes to justice, and justice I'll see done among the living and the dead."

"Go ahead, then, me hearty fellow. If Julia herself is in the wrong place somebody else must be in her own place, and you'll be following one rightment with another wrongment until in the end you'll go mad with the tangle of dead men's wrongs. That's the end that's in store for you, Meehaul Lynskey."

Meehaul Lynskey spat on his fist and struck out with the hooked fingers. His blood was up.

"That I may be as dead as my father!" he began in a traditional oath, and at that Cahir Bowes gave a little cry and raised his stick with a battle flourish. They went up and down the dips of the ground, rising and falling on the waves of their anger, and the widow stood where she was, miserable and downhearted, her feet growing stone cold from the chilly dampness of the ground. The twin who did not now count took out his pipe and lit it, looking at the old men with a stolid gaze. The twin who now counted walked uneasily away, bit an end off a chunk of tobacco, and came to stand in the ground in a line with the widow, looking on with her several feet away; but again the widow was conscious of the man's growing sympathy.

"They're a nice pair of boyos, them two old lads," he remarked to the widow. He turned his head to her. He was very handsome.

"Do you think they will find it?" she asked. Her voice was a little nervous, and the man shifted on his feet, nervously responsive.

"It's hard to say," he said. "You'd never know what to think. Two old lads, the like of them, do be very tricky."

"God grant they'll get it," said the widow.

"God grant," said the gravedigger.

But they didn't. They only got exhausted as before, wheezing and coughing, and glaring at each other as they sat down on two mounds.

The gravedigger turned to the widow.

She was aware of the nice warmth of his brown eyes.

"Are you waking the weaver again tonight?" he asked.

"I am," said the widow.

"Well, maybe some person—some old man or woman from the country—may turn up and be able to tell where the grave is. You could make inquiries."

"Yes," said the widow, but without any enthusiasm, "I could make inquiries."

The gravedigger hesitated for a moment, and said more sympathetically, "We could all, maybe, make inquiries." There was a softer personal note, a note of adventure, in the voice.

The widow turned her head to the man and smiled at him quite frankly.

"I'm beholding to you," she said and then added with a little wounded sigh, "Everyone is very good to me."

The gravedigger twirled the ends of his mustache.

Cahir Bowes, who had heard, rose from his mound and said briskly, "I'll agree to leave it at that." His air was that of one who had made an extraordinary personal sacrifice. What he was really thinking was that he would have another great day of it with Meehaul Lynskcy in Cloon na Morav tomorrow. He'd show that oul' fellow, Lynskey, what stuff Boweses were made of.

"And I'm not against it," said Meehaul Lynskey. He took the tone of one who was never to be outdone in magnanimity. He was also thinking of another day of effort tomorrow, a day that would, please God, show the Boweses what the Lynskeys were like.

With that the party came straggling out of Cloon na Morav, the two old men first, the widow next, the gravediggers waiting to put on their coats and light their pipes.

There was a little upward slope on the road to the town, and as the two old men took it the widow thought they looked very spent after their day. She wondered if Cahir Bowes would ever be able for that hill. She would give him a glass of whiskey at home, if there was any left in the bottle. Of the two, and as limp and slack as his body looked, Meehaul Lynskey appeared the better able for the hill. They walked together, that is to say, abreast, but they kept almost the width of the road between each other, as if this gulf expressed the breach of friendship between them on the head of the dispute about the weaver's grave. They had been making liars of each other all day, and they would, please God, make liars of each other all day to-morrow. The widow, understanding the meaning of this hostil-ity, had a faint sense of amusement at the contrariness of old men. How could she tell what was passing in the head which Cahir Bowes hung, like a fuchsia drop, over the road? How could she know of the strange rise and fall of the thoughts, the little frets, the tempers, the faint humors, which chased each other there? Nobody—not even Cahir Bowes himself—could account for them. All the widow knew was that Cahir Bowes stood suddenly on the road. Something had happened in his brain, some old memory cell long dormant had become nas-cent, had a stir, a pulse, a flicker of warmth, of activity, and swiftly as a flash of lightning in the sky, a glow of lucidity lit up his memory. It was as if a searchlight had suddenly flooded the dark corners of his brain. The immediate physical effect on Cahir Bowes was to cause him to stand stark still on the road, Meehaul Lynskey going ahead without him. The widow saw Cahir Bowes pivot on his heels, his head, at the end of the horizontal body, swinging round like the movement of a hand on a runaway clock. Instead of pointing up the hill homeward the head pointed down the hill and back to Cloon na Morav. There followed the most extraordinary movements—shuf-flings, gyrations—that the widow had ever seen. Cahir Bowes wanted to run like mad away down the road. That was plain. And Cahir Bowes believed that he was running like mad away down the road. That was also evident. But what he actually did was to make little jumps on his feet, his stick rattling the ground in front, and each jump did not bring him an inch of ground. He would have gone more rapidly in his normal shuf-fle. His efforts were like a terrible parody on the springs of a kangaroo. And Cahir Bowes, in a voice that was now more a scream than a cackle, was calling out unintelligible things. The widow, looking at him, paused in wonder, then over her face there came a relaxation, a color, her eyes warmed, her expression lost its settled pensiveness, and all her body was shaken with uncontrollable laughter. Cahir Bowes passed her on the road in his fantastic leaps, his abortive buck-jumps, screaming and cracking his stick on the ground, his left hand still gripped tightly on the small of his back behind, a powerful brake on the small of his back.

Meehaul Lynskey turned back and his face was shaken with an aged emotion as he looked after the stone breaker. Then he removed his hat and blessed himself.

"The cross of Christ between us and harm," he exclaimed. "Old Cahir Bowes has gone off his head at last. I thought there was something up with him all day. It was easily known there was something ugly working in his mind."

The widow controlled her laughter and checked herself, making the sign of the cross on her forehead, too. She said:

"God forgive me for laughing and the weaver with the habit but fresh upon him."

The gravedigger who counted was coming out somewhat eagerly over the stile, but Cahir Bowes, flourishing his stick, beat him back again and then himself reentered Cloon na Morav. He stumbled over the grass, now rising on a mound, now disappearing altogether in a dip of the ground, traveling in a giddy course like a hooker in a storm; again, for a long time, he remained submerged, showing, however, the eternal stick, his periscope, his indication to the world that he was about his business. In a level piece of ground, marked by stones with large mottled white marks upon them, he settled and cried out to all, and calling God to witness, that this surely was the weaver's grave. There was scepticism, hesitation, on the part of the gravediggers, but after some parley, and because Cahir Bowes was so passionate, vehement, crying and shouting, dribbling water from the mouth, showing his yellow teeth, pouring sweat on his forehead, quivering on his legs, they began to dig carefully in the spot. The widow, at this, rearranged the shawl on her head and entered Cloon na Morav, conscious, as she shuffled over the stile, that a pair of warm brown eyes were, for a moment, upon her movements and then withdrawn. She stood a little way back from the digging and waited the result with a slightly more accelerated beating of the heart. The twins looked as if they were ready to strike something unexpected at any moment, digging carefully, and Cahir Bowes hung over the place, cackling and crowing, urging the men to swifter work. The earth sang up out of the ground, dark and rich in color, gleaming like gold, in the deepening twilight in the place. Two feet, three feet, four feet of earth came up, the spades pushing through the earth in regular and powerful pushes, and still the coast was clear. Cahir Bowes trembled with excitement on his stick. Five feet of a pit yawned in the ancient ground. The spade work ceased. One of the gravediggers looked up at Cahir Bowes and said:

"You hit the weaver's grave this time right enough. Not another grave in the place could be as free as this."

The widow sighed a quick little sigh and looked at the face of the other gravedigger, hesitated, then allowed a remote smile of thankfulness to flit across her palely sad face. The eyes of the man wandered away over the darkening spaces of Cloon na Morav.

"I got the weaver's grave surely," cried Cahir Bowes, his old face full of a weird animation. If he had found the Philosopher's Stone he would only have broken it. But to find the weaver's grave was an accomplishment that would help him into a wisdom before which all his world would bow. He looked around triumphantly and said:

"Where is Meehaul Lynskey now; what will the people be saying at all about his attack on Julia Rafferty's grave? Julia will haunt him, and I'd sooner have any one at all haunting me than the ghost of Julia Rafferty. Where is Meehaul Lynskey now? Is it ashamed to show his liary face he is? And what talk had Malachi Roohan about an elm tree? Elm tree, indeed! If it's trees that is troubling him now let him climb up on one of them and hang himself from it with his rope! Where is that old fellow, Meehaul Lynskey, and his rotten head? Where is he, I say? Let him come in here now to Cloon na Morav until I be showing him the weaver's grave, five feet down and not a rib or a knuckle in it, as clean and beautiful as the weaver ever wished it. Come in here, Meehaul Lynskey, until I hear the lies panting again in your yellow throat."

He went in his extraordinary movement over the ground, making for the stile all the while talking.

Meehaul Lynskey had crouched behind the wall outside when Cahir Bowes led the diggers to the new site, his old face twisted in an attentive, almost agonizing emotion. He stood peeping over the wall, saying to himself:

"Whisht, will you! Don't mind that old madman. He hasn't it at all. I'm telling you he hasn't it. Whisht, will you! Let him dig away. They'll hit something in a minute. They'll level him when they find out. His brain has turned. Whisht, now, will you, and I'll have that rambling old lunatic, Cahir Bowes, in a minute. I'll leap in on him. I'll charge him before the world. I'll show him up. I'll take the gab out of him. I'll lacerate him. I'll lambaste him. Whisht, will you!"

But as the digging went on and the terrible cries of triumph arose inside Meehaul Lynskey's knees knocked together. His head bent level to the wall, yellow and grimacing, nerves twitching across it, a little yellow froth gathering at the corners of the mouth. When Cahir Bowes came beating for the stile Meehaul Lynskey rubbed one leg with the other, a little below the calf, and cried brokenly to himself:

"God in Heaven, he has it! He has the weaver's grave."

He turned about and slunk along in the shadow of the wall up the hill, panting and broken. By the time Cahir Bowes had reached the stile Meehaul Lynskey's figure was shadowily dipping down over the crest of the road. A sharp cry from Cahir Bowes caused him to shrink out of sight like a dog at whom a weapon had been thrown.

The eyes of the gravedigger who did not now count followed the figure of Cahir Bowes as he moved to the stile. He laughed a little in amusement, then wiped his brow. He came up out of the grave. He turned to the widow and said:

"We're down five feet. Isn't that enough in which to sink the weaver in? Are you satisfied?"

The man spoke to her without any pretense at fine feeling. He addressed her as a fourth wife should be addressed. The widow was conscious but unresentful of the man's manner. She regarded him calmly and without any resentment. On her part there was no resentment either, no hypocrisy, no make-believe. Her unemotional eyes followed his action as he stuck his spade into the loose mold on the ground. A cry from Cahir Bowes distracted the man, he laughed again, and before the widow could make a reply he said:

"Old Cahir is great value. Come down until we hear him handling the nailer."

He walked away down over the ground.

The widow was left alone with the other gravedigger. He drew himself up out of the pit with a sinuous movement of the body which the widow noted. He stood without a word beside the pile of heaving clay and looked across at the widow. She looked back at him and suddenly the silence became full of unspoken words, of flying, ringing emotions. The widow could see the dark green wall, above it the band of still deepening red, above that the still more pallid gray sky, and directly over the man's head the gay frolicking of the fresh star in the sky. Cloon na Morav was flooded with a deep, vague light. The widow scented the fresh wind about her, the cool fragrance of the earth, and yet a warmth that was strangely beautiful. The light of the man's dark eyes was visible in the shadow which hid his face. The pile of earth beside him was like a vague shape of miniature bronze mountains. He stood with a stillness which was tense and dramatic. The widow thought that the world was strange, the sky extraordinary, the man's head against the red sky a wonder, a poem, above it the sparkle of the great young star. The widow knew that they would be left together like this for one minute, a minute which would be as a flash and as eternity. And she knew now that sooner or later this man would come to her and that she would welcome him. Below at the stile the voice of Cahir Bowes was cackling in its aged notes. Beyond this the stillness was the stillness of heaven and earth. Suddenly a sense of faintness came to the widow. The whole place swooned before her eyes. Never was this world so strange, so like the dream that Malachi Roohan had talked about. A movement in the figure of the man beside the heap of bronze had come to her as a warning, a fear, and a delight. She moved herself a little in response, made a step backward. The next instant she saw the figure of the man spring across the open black mouth of the weaver's grave to her.

A faint sound escaped her and then his breath was hot on her face, his mouth on her lips.

Half a minute later Cahir Bowes came shuffling back, followed by the twin.

"I'll bone him yet," said Cahir Bowes. "Never you fear I'll make that old nailer face me. I'll show him up at the weaver's wake tonight!"

The twin laughed behind him. He shook his head at his brother, who was standing a pace away from the widow. He said:

"Five feet."

He looked into the grave and then looked at the widow, saying:

"Are you satisfied?"

There was silence for a second or two, and when she spoke the widow's voice was low but fresh, like the voice of a young girl. She said:

"I'm satisfied."

James Stephens (1882–1950)

James Stephens was born in Dublin in 1882. Little is known of his origins or his early life, but he obviously had firsthand experience of poverty. He began writing while working as a lawyer's clerk, and by 1907 he was contributing to Arthur Griffith's nationalist weekly, Sinn Fein. *George Russell ("A. E.") recognized his talent and encouraged him. In 1909, Stephens published his first volume of poetry,* Insurrections. *In 1912 appeared the book some still consider his masterpiece,* The Crock of Gold. *Certainly it is his most popular book, and one of the most popular folk fantasies ever written. He wrote in a more realistic mode, however, in his novels* The Charwoman's Daughter (1912) *and* Hunger: A Dublin Story (1918). *But he has written some of his best prose in his short stories, collected in* Here Are Ladies (1913) *and* Etched in Moonlight (1928), *and in his retellings of Irish legends and tales in* Deirdre (1923), Irish Fairy Tales (1920), *and* In the Land of Youth (1924). *Stephens's excellent lyric poems are gathered in* Collected Poems (1954). *"The Blind Man" is taken from Stephens's first book of stories,* Here Are Ladies. *A biographical sketch of Stephens would not be complete without making mention of his remarkable conversation, partly responsible for James Joyce's asking him to finish* Finnegans Wake *should Joyce die before its completion.*

* * *

The Blind Man

He was one who would have passed by the Sphinx without seeing it. He did not believe in the necessity for sphinxes, or in their reality, for that matter—they did not exist for him. Indeed, he was one to whom the Sphinx would not have been visible. He might have eyed it and noted a certain bulk of grotesque stone, but nothing more significant.

He was sex-blind, and, so, peculiarly limited by the fact that he could not appreciate women. If he had been pressed for a theory or metaphysic of womanhood he would have been unable to formulate any. Their presence he admitted, perforce: their utility was quite apparent to him on the surface, but, subterraneously, he doubted both their existence and their utility. He might have said perplexedly—Why cannot they do whatever they have to do without being always in the way? He might have said—Hang it, they are everywhere, and what good are they doing? They bothered him, they destroyed his ease when he was near them, and they spoke a language which he did not understand and did not want to understand. But as his limitations did not press on him neither did they trouble him. He was not sexually deficient, and he did not dislike women; he simply ignored them, and was only really at home with men. All the crudities which we enumerate as masculine delighted him—simple things, for, in the gender of abstract ideas, vice is feminine, brutality is masculine, the female being older, vastly older than the male, much more competent in every way, stronger, even in her physique, than he, and, having little baggage of mental or ethical preoccupations to delay her progress, she is still the guardian of evolution, requiring little more from man than to be stroked and petted for a while.

He could be brutal at times. He liked to get drunk at seasonable periods. He would cheerfully break a head or a window, and would bandage the one damage or pay for the other with equal skill and pleasure. He liked to tramp rugged miles swinging his arms and whistling as he went, and he could sit for hours by the side of a ditch thinking thoughts without words—an easy and a pleasant way of thinking, and one which may lead to something in the long run.

Even his mother was an abstraction to him. He was kind to her so far as doing things went, but he looked over her, or round her, and marched away and forgot her.

Sex-blindness carries with it many other darknesses. We do not know what masculine thing is projected by the feminine consciousness, and civilization, even life itself, must stand at a halt until that has been discovered or created; but art is the female projected by the male: science is the male projected by the male—as yet a poor thing, and to remain so until it has become art; that is, has become fertilized and so more psychological than mechanical. The small part of science which came to his notice (inventions, machinery, etc.) was easily and delightedly comprehended by him. He could do intricate things with a knife and a piece of string, or a hammer and a saw; but a picture, a poem, a statue, a piece of music—these left him as uninterested as they found him: more so, in truth, for they left him bored and dejected.

His mother came to dislike him, and there were many causes and many justifications for her dislike. She was an orderly, busy, competent woman, the counterpart of endless millions of her sex, who liked to understand what she saw or felt, and who had no happiness in reading riddles. To her he was at times an enigma, and at times again a simpleton. In both aspects he displeased and embarrassed her. One has one's sense of property, and in him she could not put her finger on anything that was hers. We demand continuity, logic in other words, but between her son and herself there was a gulf fixed, spanned by no bridge whatever; there was complete isolation; no boat plied between them at all. All the kindly human things which she loved were unintelligible to him, and his coarse pleasures or blunt evasions distressed and bewildered her. When she spoke to him he gaped or yawned; and yet she did not speak on weighty matters, just the necessary small-change of existence— somebody's cold, somebody's dress, somebody's marriage or death. When she addressed him on sterner subjects, the ground, the weather, the crops, he looked at her as if she were a baby, he listened with stubborn resentment, and strode away a confessed boor. There was no contact anywhere between them, and he was a slow exasperation to her—What can we do with that which is ours and not ours? either we own a thing or we do not, and, whichever way it goes, there is some end to it; but certain enigmas are illegitimate and are so hounded from decent cogitation.

She could do nothing but dismiss him, and she could not even do that, for there he was at the required periods, always primed with the wrong reply to any question, the wrong aspiration, the wrong conjecture; a perpetual trampler on mental corns, a person for whom one could do nothing but apologize.

They lived on a small farm, and almost the entire work of the place was done by him. His younger brother assisted, but that assistance could have easily been done without. If the cattle were sick, he cured them almost by instinct. If the horse was lame or wanted a new shoe, he knew precisely what to do in both events. When the time came for plowing, he gripped the handles and drove a furrow which was as straight and as economical as any furrow in the world. He could dig all day long and be happy; he gathered in the harvest as another would gather in a bride; and, in the intervals between these occupations, he fled to the nearest public house and wallowed among his kind.

He did not fly away to drink; he fled to be among men— Then he awakened. His tongue worked with the best of them, and adequately too. He could speak weightily on many things—boxing, wrestling, hunting, fishing, the seasons, the weather, and the chances of this and the other man's crops. He had deep knowledge about brands of tobacco and the peculiar virtues of many different liquors. He knew birds and beetles and worms; how a weasel would behave in extraordinary circumstances; how to train every breed of horse and dog. He recited goats from the cradle to the grave, could tell the name of any tree from its leaf; knew how a bull could be coerced, a cow cut up, and what plasters were good for a broken head. Sometimes, and often enough, the talk would chance on women, and then he laughed as heartily as anyone else, but he was always relieved when the conversation trailed to more interesting things.

His mother died and left the farm to the younger instead of the elder son; an unusual thing to do, but she did detest him. She knew her younger son very well. He was foreign to her in nothing. His temper ran parallel with her own, his tastes were hers, his ideas had been largely derived from her, she could track them at any time and make or demolish him. He would go to a dance or a picnic and be as exhilarated as she was, and would discuss the matter afterwards. He could speak with some cogency on the shape of this and that female person, the hat of such an one, the disagreeableness of tea at this house and the goodness of it at the other. He could even listen to one speaking without going to sleep at the fourth word. In all he was a decent, quiet lad who would become a father the exact replica of his own, and whose daughters would resemble his mother as closely as two peas resemble their green ancestors—So she left him the farm.

Of course, there was no attempt to turn the elder brother out. Indeed, for some years the two men worked quietly together and prospered and were contented; then, as was inevitable, the younger brother got married, and the elder had to look out for a new place to live in, and to work in—things had become difficult.

It is very easy to say that in such and such circumstances a man should do this and that well-pondered thing, but the courts of logic have as yet the most circumscribed jurisdiction. Just as statistics can prove anything and be quite wrong, so reason can sit in its padded chair issuing pronouncements which are seldom within measurable distance of any reality. Everything is true only in relation to its center of thought. Some people think with their heads—their subsequent actions are as logical and unpleasant as are those of the other sort who think only with their blood, and this latter has its irrefutable logic also. He thought in this subterranean fashion, and if he had thought in the other the issue would not have been any different.

Still, it was not an easy problem for him, or for any person lacking initiative—a sexual characteristic. He might have emigrated, but his roots were deeply struck in his own place, so the idea never occurred to him; furthermore, our thoughts are often no deeper than our pockets, and one wants money to move anywhere. For any other life than that of farming he had no training and small desire. He had no money and he was a farmer's son. Without money he could not get a farm; being a farmer's son he could not sink to the degradation of a day laborer; logically he could sink, actually he could not without endangering his own centers and verities—so he also got married.

He married a farm of about ten acres, and the sun began to shine on him once more; but only for a few days. Suddenly the sun went away from the heavens; the moon disappeared from the silent night; the silent night itself fled afar, leaving in its stead a noisy, dirty blackness through which one slept or yawned as one could. There was the farm, of course—one could go there and work; but the freshness went out of the very ground; the crops lost their sweetness and candor; the horses and cows disowned him; the goats ceased to be his friends—It was all up with him. He did not whistle any longer. He did not swing his shoulders as he walked, and, although he continued to smoke, he did not look for a particular green bank whereon he could sit quietly flooded with those slow thoughts that had no words.

For he discovered that he had not married a farm at all. He had married a woman—a thin-jawed, elderly slattern, whose sole beauty was her farm. How her jaws worked! The processions and congregations of words that fell and dribbled and slid out of them! Those jaws were never quiet, and in spite of all he did not say anything. There was not anything to say, but much to do from which he shivered away in terror. He looked at her sometimes through the muscles of his arms, through his big, strong hands, through fogs and fumes and singular, quiet tumults that raged within him. She lessoned him on the things he knew so well, and she was always wrong. She lectured him on those things which she did know, but the unending disquisition, the perpetual repetition, the foolish, empty emphasis, the dragging weightiness of her tongue made him repudiate her knowledge and hate it as much as he did her.

Sometimes, looking at her, he would rub his eyes and yawn with fatigue and wonder—There she was! A something enwrapped about with petticoats. Veritably alive. Active as an insect! Palpable to the touch! And what was she doing to him? Why did she do it? Why didn't she go away? Why didn't she die? What sense was there in the making of such a creature that clothed itself like a bolster, without any freedom or entertainment or shapeliness?

Her eyes were fixed on him and they always seemed to be angry; and her tongue was uttering rubbish about horses, rubbish about cows, rubbish about hay and oats. Nor was this the sum of his weariness. It was not alone that he was married; he was multitudinously, egregiously married. He had married a whole family, and what a family—

Her mother lived with her, her eldest sister lived with her, her youngest sister lived with her—And these were all swathed about with petticoats and shawls. They had no movement.

Their feet were like those of no creature he had ever observed. One could hear the flip-flap of their slippers all over the place, and at all hours. They were down-at-heel, draggle-tailed, and futile. There was no workmanship about them. They were as unfinished, as unsightly as a puddle on a road. They insulted his eyesight, his hearing, and his energy. They had lank hair that slapped about them like wet seaweed, and they were all talking, talking, talking.

The mother was of an incredible age. She was senile with age. Her cracked cackle never ceased for an instant. She talked to the dog and the cat; she talked to the walls of the room; she spoke out through the window to the weather; she shut her eyes in a corner and harangued the circumambient darkness. The eldest sister was as silent as a deep ditch and as ugly. She slid here and there with her head on one side like an inquisitive hen watching one curiously, and was always doing nothing with an air of futile employment. The youngest was a semi-lunatic who prattled and prattled without ceasing, and was always catching one's sleeve, and laughing at one's face. And everywhere those flopping, wriggling petticoats were appearing and disappearing. One saw slack hair whisking by the corner of one's eye. Mysteriously, urgently, they were coming and going and coming again, and never, never being silent.

More and more he went running to the public house. But it was no longer to be among men, it was to get drunk. One might imagine him sitting there thinking those slow thoughts without words. One might predict that the day would come when he would realize very suddenly, very clearly, all that he had been thinking about, and, when this urgent, terrible thought had been translated into its own terms of action, he would be quietly hanged by the neck until he was as dead as he had been before he was alive.

James Joyce (1882–1941)

James Joyce was born in Rathmines, in Dublin, in 1882. His father, John Joyce, was known as a good storyteller and a gregarious wit, but his irresponsible ways gradually led his large family toward financial ruin. Despite his father's improvidence and the steady decline of his parents' resources and social status, James was singled out among his brothers and sisters for an education in some of Ireland's best schools. He attended Clongowes Wood College, a Jesuit school, and after a brief stint at a Christian Brothers' school in Dublin he finished his secondary education at another Jesuit school, Belvedere College. At sixteen he entered University College, Dublin, from which he graduated in 1902. By that time he had already distinguished himself by having an essay on Ibsen published in the English journal The Fortnightly Review *and by attracting the attention of W. B. Yeats and George Russell ("A. E."). He left Dublin with Nora Barnacle in October 1904 and began his lifelong exile from Ireland. From then on, he worked mainly as an English teacher in Paris, Zurich, and Trieste, always in debt, and always on the brink of destitution. His financial troubles were considerably eased in 1919 with a generous gift from Harriet Weaver, the former editor of* The Egoist. *By then Joyce had been recognized by some of the leading critics and writers of his day as one of the most original voices in modern literature, and today his reputation as the major novelist of the twentieth century is secure. Joyce's three novels are* A Portrait of the Artist as a Young Man *(1916),* Ulysses *(1922), and* Finnegans Wake *(1939). His first book was a small collection of lyric poetry,* Chamber Music, *published in 1907. Joyce's first short stories were published in George Russell's journal* The Irish Homestead *in 1904. Though Joyce had finished most of the stories now collected in* Dubliners *(1914) by the end of 1905, a nightmarish series of problems with publishers—including broken contracts and the destruction by Maunsel & Company in Dublin of an edition it had already printed—delayed publication until 1914. "The Dead," written in 1907, is Joyce's most intricate, richest story, and one of the essential stories of the twentieth century.*

The Dead

Lily, the caretaker's daughter, was literally run off her feet. Hardly had she brought one gentleman into the little pantry behind the office on the ground floor and helped him off with his overcoat than the wheezy hall-door bell clanged again and she had to scamper along the bare hallway to let in another guest. It was well for her she had not to attend to the ladies also. But Miss Kate and Miss Julia had thought of that and had converted the bathroom upstairs into a ladies' dressing-room. Miss Kate and Miss Julia were there, gossiping and laughing and fussing, walking after each other to the head of the stairs, peering down over the banisters and calling down to Lily to ask her who had come.

It was always a great affair, the Misses Morkan's annual dance. Everybody who knew them came to it, members of the family, old friends of the family, the members of Julia's choir, any of Kate's pupils that were grown up enough, and even some of Mary Jane's pupils too. Never once had it fallen flat. For years and years it had gone off in splendid style as long as anyone could remember; ever since Kate and Julia, after the death of their brother Pat, had left the house in Stoney Batter and taken Mary Jane, their only niece, to live with them in the dark gaunt house on Usher's Island, the upper part of which they had rented from Mr. Fulham, the corn factor on the ground floor. That was a good thirty years ago if it was a day. Mary Jane, who was then a little girl in short clothes, was now the main prop of the household for she had the organ in Haddington Road. She had been through the Academy and gave a pupils' concert every year in the upper room of the Antient Concert Rooms. Many of her pupils belonged to better-class families on the Kingstown and Dalkey line. Old as they were, her aunts also did their share. Julia, though she was quite grey, was still the leading soprano in Adam and Eve's, and Kate, being too feeble to go about much, gave music lessons to beginners on the old square piano in the back room. Lily, the caretaker's daughter, did housemaid's work for them. Though their life was modest they believed in eating well; the best of everything: diamond-bone sirloins, three-shilling tea, and the best bottled stout. But Lily seldom made a mistake in the orders so that she got on well with her three mistresses. They were fussy, that was all. But the only thing they would not stand was back answers.

Of course they had good reason to be fussy on such a night. And then it was long after ten o'clock and yet there was no sign of Gabriel and his wife. Besides they were dreadfully afraid that Freddy Malins might turn up screwed. They would not wish for worlds that any of Mary Jane's pupils should see him under the influence; and when he was like that it was sometimes very hard to manage him. Freddy Malins always came late but they wondered what could be keeping Gabriel: and that was what brought them every two minutes to the banisters to ask Lily had Gabriel or Freddy come.

—O, Mr. Conroy, said Lily to Gabriel when she opened the door for him, Miss Kate and Miss Julia thought you were never coming. Good-night, Mrs. Conroy.

—I'll engage they did, said Gabriel, but they forget that my wife here takes three mortal hours to dress herself.

He stood on the mat, scraping the snow from his galoshes,

while Lily led his wife to the foot of the stairs and called out:

—Miss Kate, here's Mrs. Conroy.

Kate and Julia came toddling down the dark stairs at once. Both of them kissed Gabriel's wife, said she must be perished alive, and asked was Gabriel with her.

—Here I am as right as the mail, Aunt Kate! Go on up. I'll follow, called out Gabriel from the dark.

He continued scraping his feet vigorously while the three women went upstairs, laughing, to the ladies' dressing-room. A light fringe of snow lay like a cape on the shoulders of his overcoat and like toecaps on the toes of his galoshes; and, as the buttons of his overcoat slipped with a squeaking noise through the snow-stiffened frieze, a cold fragrant air from out-of-doors escaped from crevices and folds.

—Is it snowing again, Mr. Conroy? asked Lily.

She had preceded him into the pantry to help him off with his overcoat. Gabriel smiled at the three syllables she had given his surname and glanced at her. She was a slim, growing girl, pale in complexion and with hay-colored hair. The gas in the pantry made her look still paler. Gabriel had known her when she was a child and used to sit on the lowest step nursing a rag doll.

—Yes, Lily, he answered, and I think we're in for a night of it.

He looked up at the pantry ceiling, which was shaking with the stamping and shuffling of feet on the floor above, listened for a moment to the piano and then glanced at the girl, who was folding his overcoat carefully at the end of a shelf.

—Tell me, Lily, he said in a friendly tone, do you still go to school?

—O no, sir, she answered. I'm done schooling this year and more.

—O, then, said Gabriel gaily, I suppose we'll be going to your wedding one of these fine days with your young man, eh?

The girl glanced back at him over her shoulder and said with great bitterness:

—The men that is now is only all palaver and what they can get out of you.

Gabriel colored as if he felt he had made a mistake and, without looking at her, kicked off his galoshes and flicked actively with his muffler at his patent-leather shoes.

He was a stout tallish young man. The high color of his cheeks pushed upwards even to his forehead where it scattered itself in a few formless patches of pale red; and on his hairless face there scintillated restlessly the polished lenses and the bright gilt rims of the glasses which screened his delicate and restless eyes. His glossy black hair was parted in the middle and brushed in a long curve behind his ears where it curled slightly beneath the groove left by his hat.

When he had flicked luster into his shoes he stood up and pulled his waistcoat down more tightly on his plump body. Then he took a coin rapidly from his pocket.

—O Lily, he said, thrusting it into her hands, it's Christmastime, isn't it? Just ... here's a little. ...

He walked rapidly towards the door.

—O no, sir! cried the girl, following him. Really, sir, I wouldn't take it.

—Christmastime! Christmastime! said Gabriel, almost trotting to the stairs and waving his hand to her in deprecation.

The girl, seeing that he had gained the stairs, called out after him:

—Well, thank you, sir.

He waited outside the drawing-room door until the waltz should finish, listening to the skirts that swept against it and to the shuffling of feet. He was still discomposed by the girl's bitter and sudden retort. It had cast a gloom over him which he tried to dispel by arranging his cuffs and the bows of his tie. Then he took from his waistcoat pocket a little paper and glanced at the headings he had made for his speech. He was undecided about the lines from Robert Browning for he feared they would be above the heads of his hearers. Some quotation that they could recognize from Shakespeare or from the Melodies would be better. The indelicate clacking of the men's heels and the shuffling of their soles reminded him that their grade of culture differed from his. He would only make himself ridiculous by quoting poetry to them which they could not understand. They would think that he was airing his superior education. He would fail with them just as he had failed with the girl in the pantry. He had taken up a wrong tone. His whole speech was a mistake from first to last, an utter failure.

Just then his aunts and his wife came out of the ladies' dressing-room. His aunts were two small plainly dressed old women. Aunt Julia was an inch or so the taller. Her hair, drawn low over the tops of her ears, was grey; and grey also, with darker shadows, was her large flaccid face. Though she was stout in build and stood erect her slow eyes and parted lips gave her the appearance of a woman who did not know where she was or where she was going. Aunt Kate was more vivacious. Her face, healthier than her sister's, was all puckers and creases, like a shrivelled red apple, and her hair, braided in the same old-fashioned way, had not lost its ripe nut color.

They both kissed Gabriel frankly. He was their favorite nephew, the son of their dead elder sister, Ellen, who had married T. J. Conroy of the Port and Docks.

—Gretta tells me you're not going to take a cab back to Monkstown tonight, Gabriel, said Aunt Kate.

—No, said Gabriel, turning to his wife, we had quite enough of that last year, hadn't we. Don't you remember, Aunt Kate, what a cold Gretta got out of it? Cab windows rattling all the way, and the east wind blowing in after we passed Merrion. Very jolly it was. Gretta caught a dreadful cold.

Aunt Kate frowned severely and nodded her head at every word.

—Quite right, Gabriel, quite right, she said. You can't be too careful.

—But as for Gretta there, said Gabriel, she'd walk home in the snow if she were let.

Mrs. Conroy laughed.

—Don't mind him, Aunt Kate, she said. He's really an awful bother, what with green shades for Tom's eyes at night and making him do the dumbbells, and forcing Eva to eat the stirabout. The poor child! And she simply hates the sight of it! ... O, but you'll never guess what he makes me wear now!

She broke out into a peal of laughter and glanced at her husband, whose admiring and happy eyes had been wandering from her dress to her face and hair. The two aunts laughed heartily too, for Gabriel's solicitude was a standing joke with them.

—Galoshes! said Mrs. Conroy. That's the latest. Whenever it's wet underfoot I must put on my galoshes. Tonight even he wanted me to put them on, but I wouldn't. The next thing he'll buy me will be a diving suit.

Gabriel laughed nervously and patted his tie reassuringly while Aunt Kate nearly doubled herself, so heartily did she enjoy the joke. The smile soon faded from Aunt Julia's face and her mirthless eyes were directed towards her nephew's face. After a pause she asked:

—And what are galoshes, Gabriel?

—Galoshes, Julia! exclaimed her sister. Goodness me, don't you know what galoshes are? You wear them over your ... over your boots, Gretta, isn't it?

—Yes, said Mrs. Conroy. Gutta-percha things. We both have a pair now. Gabriel says everyone wears them on the Continent.

—O, on the Continent, murmured Aunt Julia, nodding her head slowly.

Gabriel knitted his brows and said, as if he were slightly angered:

—It's nothing very wonderful but Gretta thinks it very

funny because she says the word reminds her of Christy Min-
strels.

—But tell me, Gabriel, said Aunt Kate, with brisk tact. Of
course, you've seen about the room. Gretta was saying . . .

—O, the room is all right, replied Gabriel. I've taken one in
the Gresham.

—To be sure, said Aunt Kate, by far the best thing to do.
And the children, Gretta, you're not anxious about them?

—O, for one night, said Mrs. Conroy. Besides, Bessie will
look after them.

—To be sure, said Aunt Kate again. What a comfort it is to
have a girl like that, one you can depend on! There's that Lily,
I'm sure I don't know what has come over her lately. She's not
the girl she was at all.

Gabriel was about to ask his aunt some questions on this
point but she broke off suddenly to gaze after her sister who
had wandered down the stairs and was craning her neck over
the banisters.

—Now, I ask you, she said, almost testily, where is Julia
going? Julia! Julia! Where are you going?

Julia, who had gone halfway down one flight, came back and
announced blandly:

—Here's Freddy.

At the same moment a clapping of hands and a final flourish
of the pianist told that the waltz had ended. The drawing-room
door was opened from within and some couples came out.
Aunt Kate drew Gabriel aside hurriedly and whispered into his
ear:

—Slip down, Gabriel, like a good fellow and see if he's all
right, and don't let him up if he's screwed. I'm sure he's
screwed. I'm sure he is.

Gabriel went to the stairs and listened over the banisters. He
could hear two persons talking in the pantry. Then he recognized Freddy Malins' laugh. He went down the stairs noisily.

—It's such a relief, said Aunt Kate to Mrs. Conroy, that Gabriel is here. I always feel easier in my mind when he's here. . . . Julia, there's Miss Daly and Miss Power will take some refreshment. Thanks for your beautiful waltz, Miss Daly. It made lovely time.

A tall wizen-faced man, with a stiff grizzled mustache and swarthy skin, who was passing out with his partner, said:

—And may we have some refreshment, too, Miss Morkan?

—Julia, said Aunt Kate summarily, and here's Mr. Browne and Miss Furlong. Take them in, Julia, with Miss Daly and Miss Power.

—I'm the man for the ladies, said Mr. Browne, pursing his lips until his mustache bristled and smiling in all his wrinkles. You know, Miss Morkan, the reason they are so fond of me is—

He did not finish his sentence, but, seeing that Aunt Kate was out of earshot, at once led the three young ladies into the back room. The middle of the room was occupied by two square tables placed end to end, and on these Aunt Julia and the caretaker were straightening and smoothing a large cloth. On the sideboard were arrayed dishes and plates, and glasses and bundles of knives and forks and spoons. The top of the closed square piano served also as a sideboard for viands and sweets. At a smaller sideboard in one corner two young men were standing, drinking hop-bitters.

Mr. Browne led his charges thither and invited them all, in jest, to some ladies' punch, hot, strong, and sweet. As they said they never took anything strong he opened three bottles of lemonade for them. Then he asked one of the young men to move aside, and, taking hold of the decanter, filled out for himself a goodly measure of whiskey. The young men eyed him respectfully while he took a trial sip.

—God help me, he said, smiling, it's the doctor's orders.

His wizened face broke into a broader smile, and the three young ladies laughed in musical echo to his pleasantry, swaying their bodies to and fro, with nervous jerks of their shoulders. The boldest said:

—O, now, Mr. Browne, I'm sure the doctor never ordered anything of the kind.

Mr. Browne took another sip of his whiskey and said, with sidling mimicry:

—Well, you see, I'm like the famous Mrs. Cassidy, who is reported to have said: *Now, Mary Grimes, if I don't take it, make me take it, for I feel I want it.*

His hot face had leaned forward a little too confidentially and he had assumed a very low Dublin accent so that the young ladies, with one instinct, received his speech in silence. Miss Furlong, who was one of Mary Jane's pupils, asked Miss Daly what was the name of the pretty waltz she had played; and Mr. Browne, seeing that he was ignored, turned promptly to the two young men who were more appreciative.

A red-faced young woman, dressed in pansy, came into the room, excitedly clapping her hands and crying:

—Quadrilles! Quadrilles!

Close on her heels came Aunt Kate, crying:

—Two gentlemen and three ladies, Mary Jane!

—O, here's Mr. Bergin and Mr. Kerrigan, said Mary Jane. Mr. Kerrigan, will you take Miss Power? Miss Furlong, may I get you a partner, Mr. Bergin. O, that'll just do now.

—Three ladies, Mary Jane, said Aunt Kate.

The two young gentlemen asked the ladies if they might have the pleasure, and Mary Jane turned to Miss Daly.

—O, Miss Daly, you're really awfully good, after playing for the last two dances, but really we're so short of ladies tonight.

—I don't mind in the least, Miss Morkan.

—But I've a nice partner for you, Mr. Bartell D'Arcy, the tenor. I'll get him to sing later on. All Dublin is raving about him.

—Lovely voice, lovely voice! said Aunt Kate.

As the piano had twice begun the prelude to the first figure Mary Jane led her recruits quickly from the room. They had hardly gone when Aunt Julia wandered slowly into the room, looking behind her at something.

—What is the matter, Julia? asked Aunt Kate anxiously. Who is it?

Julia, who was carrying in a column of table napkins, turned to her sister and said, simply, as if the question had surprised her:

—It's only Freddy, Kate, and Gabriel with him.

In fact right behind her Gabriel could be seen piloting Freddy Malins across the landing. The latter, a young man of about forty, was of Gabriel's size and build, with very round shoulders. His face was fleshy and pallid, touched with color only at the thick hanging lobes of his ears and at the wide wings of his nose. He had coarse features, a blunt nose, a convex and receding brow, tumid and protruded lips. His heavy-lidded eyes and the disorder of his scanty hair made him look sleepy. He was laughing heartily in a high key at a story which he had been telling Gabriel on the stairs and at the same time rubbing the knuckles of his left fist backwards and forwards into his left eye.

—Good evening, Freddy, said Aunt Julia.

Freddy Malins bade the Misses Morkan good evening in what seemed an off hand fashion by reason of the habitual catch in his voice and then, seeing that Mr. Browne was grinning at him from the sideboard, crossed the room on rather shaky legs and began to repeat in an undertone the story he had just told to Gabriel.

—He's not so bad, is he? said Aunt Kate to Gabriel.

Gabriel's brows were dark but he raised them quickly and answered:

—O no, hardly noticeable.

—Now, isn't he a terrible fellow! she said. And his poor

mother made him take the pledge on New Year's Eve. But come on, Gabriel, into the drawing-room.

Before leaving the room with Gabriel she signaled to Mr. Browne by frowning and shaking her forefinger in warning to and fro. Mr. Browne nodded in answer and, when she had gone, said to Freddy Malins:

—Now, then, Teddy, I'm going to fill you out a good glass of lemonade just to buck you up.

Freddy Malins, who was nearing the climax of his story, waved the offer aside impatiently but Mr. Browne, having first called Freddy Malins' attention to a disarray in his dress, filled out and handed him a full glass of lemonade. Freddy Malins' left hand accepted the glass mechanically, his right hand being engaged in the mechanical readjustment of his dress. Mr. Browne, whose face was once more wrinkling with mirth, poured out for himself a glass of whiskey while Freddy Malins exploded, before he had well reached the climax of his story, in a kink of high-pitched bronchitic laughter and, setting down his untasted and overflowing glass, began to rub the knuckles of his left fist backwards and forwards into his left eye, repeating words of his last phrase as well as his fit of laughter would allow him.

Gabriel could not listen while Mary Jane was playing her Academy piece, full of runs and difficult passages, to the hushed drawing-room. He liked music but the piece she was playing had no melody for him and he doubted whether it had any melody for the other listeners, though they had begged Mary Jane to play something. Four young men, who had come from the refreshment-room to stand in the doorway at the sound of the piano, had gone away quietly in couples after a few minutes. The only persons who seemed to follow the music were Mary Jane herself, her hands racing along the keyboard or lifted from it at the pauses like those of a priestess in momentary imprecation, and Aunt Kate standing at her elbow to turn the page.

Gabriel's eyes, irritated by the floor, which glittered with beeswax under the heavy chandelier, wandered to the wall above the piano. A picture of the balcony scene in *Romeo and Juliet* hung there and beside it was a picture of the two mur-dered princes in the Tower which Aunt Julia had worked in red, blue, and brown wools when she was a girl. Probably in the school they had gone to as girls that kind of work had been taught, for one year his mother had worked for him as a birth-day present a waistcoat of purple tabinet, with little foxes' heads upon it, lined with brown satin and having round mul-berry buttons. It was strange that his mother had had no musi-cal talent though Aunt Kate used to call her the brains carrier of the Morkan family. Both she and Julia had always seemed a little proud of their serious and matronly sister. Her photo-graph stood before the pierglass. She held an open book on her knees and was pointing out something in it to Constantine who, dressed in a man-o'-war suit, lay at her feet. It was she who had chosen the names for her sons for she was very sensi-ble of the dignity of family life. Thanks to her, Constantine was now senior curate in Balbriggan and, thanks to her, Ga-briel himself had taken his degree in the Royal University. A shadow passed over his face as he remembered her sullen oppo-sition to his marriage. Some slighting phrases she had used still rankled in his memory; she had once spoken of Gretta as being country cute and that was not true of Gretta at all. It was Gretta who had nursed her during all her last long illness in their house at Monkstown.

He knew that Mary Jane must be near the end of her piece for she was playing again the opening melody with runs of scales after every bar and while he waited for the end the re-sentment died down in his heart. The piece ended with a trill of octaves in the treble and a final deep octave in the bass. Great applause greeted Mary Jane as, blushing and rolling up her music nervously, she escaped from the room. The most vigorous clapping came from the four young men in the doorway who had gone away to the refreshment-room at the beginning of the piece but had come back when the piano had stopped.

Lancers were arranged. Gabriel found himself partnered with Miss Ivors. She was a frank-mannered talkative young lady, with a freckled face and prominent brown eyes. She did not wear a low-cut bodice and the large brooch which was fixed in the front of her collar bore on it an Irish device.

When they had taken their places she said abruptly:

—I have a crow to pluck with you.

—With me? said Gabriel.

She nodded her head gravely.

—What is it? asked Gabriel, smiling at her solemn manner.

—Who is G. C.? answered Miss Ivors, turning her eyes upon him.

Gabriel colored and was about to knit his brows, as if he did not understand, when she said bluntly:

—O, innocent Amy! I have found out that you write for *The Daily Express*. Now, aren't you ashamed of yourself?

—Why should I be ashamed of myself? asked Gabriel, blinking his eyes and trying to smile.

—Well, I'm ashamed of you, said Miss Ivors frankly. To say you'd write for a rag like that. I didn't think you were a West Briton.

A look of perplexity appeared on Gabriel's face. It was true that he wrote a literary column every Wednesday in *The Daily Express,* for which he was paid fifteen shillings. But that did not make him a West Briton surely. The books he received for review were almost more welcome than the paltry check. He loved to feel the covers and turn over the pages of newly printed books. Nearly every day when his teaching in the college was ended he used to wander down the quays to the secondhand booksellers, to Hickey's on Bachelor's Walk, to Webb's or Massey's on Aston's Quay, or to O'Clohissey's in the bystreet. He did not know how to meet her charge. He wanted to say that literature was above politics. But they were friends of many years' standing and their careers had been parallel, first at the university and then as teachers: he could not risk a grandiose phrase with her. He continued blinking his eyes and trying to smile and murmured lamely that he saw nothing political in writing reviews of books.

When their turn to cross had come he was still perplexed and inattentive. Miss Ivors promptly took his hand in a warm grasp and said in a soft friendly tone:

—Of course, I was only joking. Come, we cross now.

When they were together again she spoke of the University question and Gabriel felt more at ease. A friend of hers had shown her his review of Browning's poems. That was how she had found out the secret: but she liked the review immensely. Then she said suddenly:

—O, Mr. Conroy, will you come for an excursion to the Aran Isles this summer? We're going to stay there a whole month. It will be splendid out in the Atlantic. You ought to come. Mr. Clancy is coming, and Mr. Kilkelly and Kathleen Kearney. It would be splendid for Gretta too if she'd come. She's from Connacht, isn't she?

—Her people are, said Gabriel shortly.

—But you will come, won't you? said Miss Ivors, laying her warm hand eagerly on his arm.

—The fact is, said Gabriel, I have already arranged to go—

—Go where? asked Miss Ivors.

—Well, you know, every year I go for a cycling tour with some fellows and so—

—But where? asked Miss Ivors.

—Well, we usually go to France or Belgium or perhaps Germany, said Gabriel awkwardly.

—And why do you go to France and Belgium, said Miss Ivors, instead of visiting your own land?

—Well, said Gabriel, it's partly to keep in touch with the languages and partly for a change.

—And haven't you your own language to keep in touch with—Irish? asked Miss Ivors.

—Well, said Gabriel, if it comes to that, you know, Irish is not my language.

Their neighbors had turned to listen to the cross-examination. Gabriel glanced right and left nervously and tried to keep his good humor under the ordeal which was making a blush invade his forehead.

—And haven't you your own land to visit, continued Miss Ivors, that you know nothing of, your own people, and your own country?

—O, to tell you the truth, retorted Gabriel suddenly, I'm sick of my own country, sick of it!

—Why? asked Miss Ivors.

Gabriel did not answer for his retort had heated him.

—Why? repeated Miss Ivors.

They had to go visiting together and, as he had not answered her, Miss Ivors said warmly:

—Of course, you've no answer.

Gabriel tried to cover his agitation by taking part in the dance with great energy. He avoided her eyes for he had seen a sour expression on her face. But when they met in the long chain he was surprised to feel his hand firmly pressed. She looked at him from under her brows for a moment quizzically until he smiled. Then, just as the chain was about to start again, she stood on tiptoe and whispered into his ear:

—West Briton!

When the lancers were over Gabriel went away to a remote corner of the room where Freddy Malins' mother was sitting. She was a stout feeble old woman with white hair. Her voice had a catch in it like her son's and she stuttered slightly. She had been told that Freddy had come and that he was nearly all right. Gabriel asked her whether she had had a good crossing. She lived with her married daughter in Glasgow and came to Dublin on a visit once a year. She answered placidly that she had had a beautiful crossing and that the captain had been most attentive to her. She spoke also of the beautiful house her daughter kept in Glasgow, and of all the nice friends they had there. While her tongue rambled on Gabriel tried to banish from his mind all memory of the unpleasant incident with Miss Ivors. Of course the girl or woman, or whatever she was, was an enthusiast but there was a time for all things. Perhaps he ought not to have answered her like that. But she had no right to call him a West Briton before people, even in joke. She had tried to make him ridiculous before people, heckling him and staring at him with her rabbit's eyes.

He saw his wife making her way towards him through the waltzing couples. When she reached him she said into his ear:

—Gabriel, Aunt Kate wants to know won't you carve the goose as usual. Miss Daly will carve the ham and I'll do the pudding.

—All right, said Gabriel.

—She's sending in the younger ones first as soon as this waltz is over so that we'll have the table to ourselves.

—Were you dancing? asked Gabriel.

—Of course I was. Didn't you see me? What words had you with Molly Ivors?

—No words. Why? Did she say so?

—Something like that. I'm trying to get that Mr. D'Arcy to sing. He's full of conceit, I think.

—There were no words, said Gabriel moodily, only she wanted me to go for a trip to the west of Ireland and I said I wouldn't.

His wife clasped her hands excitedly and gave a little jump.

—O, do go, Gabriel, she cried. I'd love to see Galway again.

—You can go if you like, said Gabriel coldly.

She looked at him for a moment, then turned to Mrs. Malins and said:

—There's a nice husband for you, Mrs. Malins.

While she was threading her way back across the room Mrs. Malins, without adverting to the interruption, went on to tell Gabriel what beautiful places there were in Scotland and beautiful scenery. Her son-in-law brought them every year to the lakes and they used to go fishing. Her son-in-law was a splendid fisher. One day he caught a fish, a beautiful big big fish, and the man in the hotel boiled it for their dinner.

Gabriel hardly heard what she said. Now that supper was coming near he began to think again about his speech and about the quotation. When he saw Freddy Malins coming across the room to visit his mother Gabriel left the chair free for him and retired into the embrasure of the window. The room had already cleared and from the back room came the clatter of plates and knives. Those who still remained in the drawing-room seemed tired of dancing and were conversing quietly in little groups. Gabriel's warm trembling fingers tapped the cold pane of the window. How cool it must be outside! How pleasant it would be to walk out alone, first along by the river and then through the park! The snow would be lying on the branches of the trees and forming a bright cap on the top of the Wellington Monument. How much more pleasant it would be there than at the supper-table!

He ran over the headings of his speech: Irish hospitality, sad memories, the Three Graces, Paris, the quotation from Browning. He repeated to himself a phrase he had written in his review: *One feels that one is listening to a thought-tormented music.* Miss Ivors had praised the review. Was she sincere? Had she really any life of her own behind all her propagandism? There had never been any ill-feeling between them until that night. It unnerved him to think that she would be at the supper-table, looking up at him while he spoke with her critical quizzing eyes. Perhaps she would not be sorry to see him fail in his speech. An idea came into his mind and gave him courage. He would say, alluding to Aunt Kate and Aunt Julia: *Ladies and*

Gentlemen, the generation which is now on the wane among us may have had its faults but for my part I think it had certain qualities of hospitality, of humor, of humanity, which the new and very serious and hypereducated generation that is growing up around us seems to me to lack. Very good: that was one for Miss Ivors. What did he care that his aunts were only two ignorant old women?

A murmur in the room attracted his attention. Mr. Browne was advancing from the door, gallantly escorting Aunt Julia, who leaned upon his arm, smiling and hanging her head. An irregular musketry of applause escorted her also as far as the piano and then, as Mary Jane seated herself on the stool, and Aunt Julia, no longer smiling, half turned so as to pitch her voice fairly into the room, gradually ceased. Gabriel recognized the prelude. It was that of an old song of Aunt Julia's—*Arrayed for the Bridal.* Her voice, strong and clear in tone, attacked with great spirit the runs which embellish the air and though she sang very rapidly she did not miss even the smallest of the grace notes. To follow the voice, without looking at the singer's face, was to feel and share the excitement of swift and secure flight. Gabriel applauded loudly with all the others at the close of the song and loud applause was borne in from the invisible supper-table. It sounded so genuine that a little color struggled into Aunt Julia's face as she bent to replace in the music stand the old leather-bound songbook that had her initials on the cover. Freddy Malins, who had listened with his head perched sideways to hear her better, was still applauding when everyone else had ceased and talking animatedly to his mother who nodded her head gravely and slowly in acquiescence. At last, when he could clap no more, he stood up suddenly and hurried across the room to Aunt Julia whose hand he seized and held in both his hands, shaking it when words failed him or the catch in his voice proved too much for him.

—I was just telling my mother, he said, I never heard you sing so well, never. No, I never heard your voice so good as it is tonight. Now! Would you believe that now? That's the truth. Upon my word and honor that's the truth. I never heard your voice sound so fresh and so ... so clear and fresh, never.

Aunt Julia smiled broadly and murmured something about compliments as she released her hand from his grasp. Mr. Browne extended his open hand towards her and said to those who were near him in the manner of a showman introducing a prodigy to an audience:

—Miss Julia Morkan, my latest discovery!

He was laughing very heartily at this himself when Freddy Malins turned to him and said:

—Well, Browne, if you're serious you might make a worse discovery. All I can say is I never heard her sing half so well as long as I am coming here. And that's the honest truth.

—Neither did I, said Mr. Browne. I think her voice has greatly improved.

Aunt Julia shrugged her shoulders and said with meek pride:

—Thirty years ago I hadn't a bad voice as voices go.

—I often told Julia, said Aunt Kate emphatically, that she was simply thrown away in that choir. But she never would be said by me.

She turned as if to appeal to the good sense of the others against a refractory child while Aunt Julia gazed in front of her, a vague smile of reminiscence playing on her face.

—No, continued Aunt Kate, she wouldn't be said or led by anyone, slaving there in that choir night and day, night and day. Six o'clock on Christmas morning! And all for what?

—Well, isn't it for the honor of God, Aunt Kate? asked Mary Jane, twisting round on the piano stool and smiling.

Aunt Kate turned fiercely on her niece and said:

—I know all about the honor of God, Mary Jane, but I think it's not at all honorable for the pope to turn out the women out of the choirs that have slaved there all their lives and put little whippersnappers of boys over their heads. I suppose it is for the good of the Church if the pope does it. But it's not just, Mary Jane, and it's not right.

She had worked herself into a passion and would have continued in defense of her sister for it was a sore subject with her but Mary Jane, seeing that all the dancers had come back, intervened pacifically:

—Now, Aunt Kate, you're giving scandal to Mr. Browne who is of the other persuasion.

Aunt Kate turned to Mr. Browne, who was grinning at this allusion to his religion, and said hastily:

—O, I don't question the pope's being right. I'm only a stupid old woman and I wouldn't presume to do such a thing. But there's such a thing as common everyday politeness and gratitude. And if I were in Julia's place I'd tell that Father Healy straight up to his face . . .

—And besides, Aunt Kate, said Mary Jane, we really are all hungry and when we are hungry we are all very quarrelsome.

—And when we are thirsty we are also quarrelsome, added Mr. Browne.

—So that we had better go to supper, said Mary Jane, and finish the discussion afterwards.

On the landing outside the drawing-room Gabriel found his wife and Mary Jane trying to persuade Miss Ivors to stay for supper. But Miss Ivors, who had put on her hat and was buttoning her cloak, would not stay. She did not feel in the least hungry and she had already overstayed her time.

—But only for ten minutes, Molly, said Mrs. Conroy. That won't delay you.

—To take a pick itself, said Mary Jane, after all your dancing.

—I really couldn't, said Miss Ivors.

—I am afraid you didn't enjoy yourself at all, said Mary Jane hopelessly.

—Ever so much, I assure you, said Miss Ivors, but you really must let me run off now.

—But how can you get home? asked Mrs. Conroy.

—O, it's only two steps up the quay.

Gabriel hesitated a moment and said:

—If you will allow me, Miss Ivors, I'll see you home if you really are obliged to go.

But Miss Ivors broke away from them.

—I won't hear of it, she cried. For goodness sake go in to your suppers and don't mind me. I'm quite well able to take care of myself.

—Well, you're the comical girl, Molly, said Mrs. Conroy frankly.

—*Beannacht libh,* cried Miss Ivors, with a laugh, as she ran down the staircase.

Mary Jane gazed after her, a moody puzzled expression on her face, while Mrs. Conroy leaned over the banisters to listen for the hall door. Gabriel asked himself was he the cause of her abrupt departure. But she did not seem to be in ill humor: she had gone away laughing. He stared blankly down the staircase.

At that moment Aunt Kate came toddling out of the supper-room, almost wringing her hands in despair.

—Where is Gabriel? she cried. Where on earth is Gabriel? There's everyone waiting in there, stage to let, and nobody to carve the goose!

—Here I am, Aunt Kate! cried Gabriel, with sudden animation, ready to carve a flock of geese, if necessary.

A fat brown goose lay at one end of the table and at the other end, on a bed of creased paper strewn with sprigs of parsley, lay a great ham, stripped of its outer skin and peppered over with crust crumbs, a neat paper frill round its shin and beside this was a round of spiced beef. Between these rival ends ran parallel lines of side dishes: two little minsters of jelly, red and yellow; a shallow dish full of blocks of blancmange and red jam, a large green leaf-shaped dish with a stalk-shaped handle, on which lay bunches of purple raisins and peeled almonds, a companion dish on which lay a solid rectangle of Smyrna figs, a dish of custard topped with grated nutmeg, a small bowl full of chocolates and sweets wrapped in gold and silver papers, and a glass vase in which stood some tall celery stalks. In the center of the table there stood, as sentries to a fruit stand which upheld a pyramid of oranges and American apples, two squat old-fashioned decanters of cut glass, one containing port and the other dark sherry. On the closed square piano a pudding in a huge yellow dish lay in waiting and behind it were three squads of bottles of stout and ale and minerals, drawn up according to the colors of their uniforms, the first two black, with brown and red labels, the third and smallest squad white, with transverse green sashes.

Gabriel took his seat boldly at the head of the table and, having looked to the edge of the carver, plunged his fork firmly into the goose. He felt quite at ease now for he was an expert carver and liked nothing better than to find himself at the head of a well-laden table.

—Miss Furlong, what shall I send you? he asked. A wing or a slice of the breast?

—Just a small slice of the breast.

—Miss Higgins, what for you?

—O, anything at all, Mr. Conroy.

While Gabriel and Miss Daly exchanged plates of goose and plates of ham and spiced beef Lily went from guest to guest with a dish of hot floury potatoes wrapped in a white napkin. This was Mary Jane's idea and she had also suggested apple sauce for the goose but Aunt Kate had said that plain roast goose without apple sauce had always been good enough for her and she hoped she might never eat worse. Mary Jane waited on her pupils and saw that they got the best slices and Aunt Kate and Aunt Julia opened and carried across from the piano bottles of stout and ale for the gentlemen and bottles of minerals for the ladies. There was a great deal of confusion and laughter and noise, the noise of orders and counterorders, of knives and forks, of corks and glass stoppers. Gabriel began to carve second helpings as soon as he had finished the first round without serving himself. Everyone protested loudly so that he compromised by taking a long draft of stout for he had found the carving hot work. Mary Jane settled down quietly to her supper but Aunt Kate and Aunt Julia were still toddling round the table, walking on each other's heels, getting in each other's way and giving each other unheeded orders. Mr. Browne begged of them to sit down and eat their suppers and so did Gabriel but they said there was time enough so that, at last, Freddy Malins stood up and, capturing Aunt Kate, plumped her down on her chair amid general laughter.

When everyone had been well served Gabriel said, smiling:

—Now, if anyone wants a little more of what vulgar people call stuffing let him or her speak.

A chorus of voices invited him to begin his own supper and Lily came forward with three potatoes which she had reserved for him.

—Very well, said Gabriel amiably, as he took another preparatory draft, kindly forget my existence, ladies and gentlemen, for a few minutes.

He set to his supper and took no part in the conversation with which the table covered Lily's removal of the plates. The subject of talk was the opera company which was then at the Theatre Royal. Mr. Bartell D'Arcy, the tenor, a dark-complexioned young man with a smart mustache, praised very highly the leading contralto of the company but Miss Furlong thought she had a rather vulgar style of production. Freddy Malins said there was a negro chieftain singing in the second part of the Gaiety pantomime who had one of the finest tenor voices he had ever heard.

—Have you heard him? he asked Mr. Bartell D'Arcy across the table.

—No, answered Mr. Bartell D'Arcy carelessly.

—Because, Freddy Malins explained, now I'd be curious to hear your opinion of him. I think he has a grand voice.

—It takes Teddy to find out the really good things, said Mr. Browne familiarly to the table.

—And why couldn't he have a voice too? asked Freddy Malins sharply. Is it because he's only a black?

Nobody answered this question and Mary Jane led the table back to the legitimate opera. One of her pupils had given her a pass for *Mignon.* Of course it was very fine, she said, but it made her think of poor Georgina Burns. Mr. Browne could go back farther still, to the old Italian companies that used to come to Dublin—Tietjens, Ilma de Murzka, Campanini, the great Trebelli, Giuglini, Ravelli, Aramburo. Those were the days, he said, when there was something like singing to be heard in Dublin. He told too of how the top gallery of the old Royal used to be packed night after night, of how one night an Italian tenor had sung five encores to *Let Me Like a Soldier Fall,* introducing a high C every time, and of how the gallery boys would sometimes in their enthusiasm unyoke the horses from the carriage of some great prima donna and pull her themselves through the streets to her hotel. Why did they never play the grand old operas now, he asked, *Dinorah, Lucrezia Borgia?* Because they could not get the voices to sing them: that was why.

—O, well, said Mr. Bartell D'Arcy, I presume there are as good singers today as there were then.

—Where are they? asked Mr. Browne defiantly.

—In London, Paris, Milan, said Mr. Bartell D'Arcy warmly. I suppose Caruso, for example, is quite as good, if not better than any of the men you have mentioned.

—Maybe so, said Mr. Browne. But I may tell you I doubt it strongly.

—O, I'd give anything to hear Caruso sing, said Mary Jane.

—For me, said Aunt Kate, who had been picking a bone, there was only one tenor. To please me, I mean. But I suppose none of you ever heard of him.

—Who was he, Miss Morkan? asked Mr. Bartell D'Arcy politely.

—His name, said Aunt Kate, was Parkinson. I heàrd him when he was in his prime and I think he had then the purest tenor voice that was ever put into a man's throat.

—Strange, said Mr. Bartell D'Arcy. I never even heard of him.

—Yes, yes, Miss Morkan is right, said Mr. Browne. I remember hearing of old Parkinson but he's too far back for me.

—A beautiful pure sweet mellow English tenor, said Aunt Kate with enthusiasm.

Gabriel having finished, the huge pudding was transferred to the table. The clatter of forks and spoons began again. Gabriel's wife served out spoonfuls of the pudding and passed the plates down the table. Midway down they were held up by Mary Jane, who replenished them with raspberry or orange jelly or with blancmange and jam. The pudding was of Aunt Julia's making and she received praises for it from all quarters. She herself said that it was not quite brown enough.

—Well, I hope, Miss Morkan, said Mr. Browne, that I'm brown enough for you because, you know, I'm all brown.

All the gentlemen, except Gabriel, ate some of the pudding out of compliment to Aunt Julia. As Gabriel never ate sweets the celery had been left for him. Freddy Malins also took a stalk of celery and ate it with his pudding. He had been told that celery was a capital thing for the blood and he was just then under doctor's care. Mrs. Malins, who had been silent all through the supper, said that her son was going down to Mount Melleray in a week or so. The table then spoke of Mount Melleray, how bracing the air was down there, how hospitable the monks were, and how they never asked for a penny-piece from their guests.

—And do you mean to say, asked Mr. Browne incredulously, that a chap can go down there and put up there as if it were a hotel and live on the fat of the land and then come away without paying a farthing?

—O, most people give some donation to the monastery when they leave, said Mary Jane.

—I wish we had an institution like that in our Church, said Mr. Browne candidly.

He was astonished to hear that the monks never spoke, got up at two in the morning, and slept in their coffins. He asked what they did it for.

—That's the rule of the order, said Aunt Kate firmly.

—Yes, but why? asked Mr. Browne.

Aunt Kate repeated that it was the rule, that was all. Mr. Browne still seemed not to understand. Freddy Malins explained to him, as best he could, that the monks were trying to make up for the sins committed by all the sinners in the outside world. The explanation was not very clear for Mr. Browne grinned and said:

—I like that idea very much but wouldn't a comfortable spring bed do them as well as a coffin?

—The coffin, said Mary Jane, is to remind them of their last end.

As the subject had grown lugubrious it was buried in a silence of the table during which Mrs. Malins could be heard saying to her neighbor in an indistinct undertone:

—They are very good men, the monks, very pious men.

The raisins and almonds and figs and apples and oranges and chocolates and sweets were now passed about the table and Aunt Julia invited all the guests to have either port or sherry. At first Mr. Bartell D'Arcy refused to take either but one of his neighbors nudged him and whispered something to him upon which he allowed his glass to be filled. Gradually as the last glasses were being filled the conversation ceased. A pause followed, broken only by the noise of the wine and by unsettlings of chairs. The Misses Morkan, all three, looked down at the tablecloth. Someone coughed once or twice and then a few gentlemen patted the table gently as a signal for silence. The silence came and Gabriel pushed back his chair and stood up.

The patting at once grew louder in encouragement and then ceased altogether. Gabriel leaned his ten trembling fingers on the tablecloth and smiled nervously at the company. Meeting a row of upturned faces he raised his eyes to the chandelier. The piano was playing a waltz tune and he could hear the skirts sweeping against the drawing-room door. People, perhaps, were standing in the snow on the quay outside, gazing up at the lighted windows and listening to the waltz music. The air was pure there. In the distance lay the park where the trees were weighted with snow. The Wellington Monument wore a gleaming cap of snow that flashed westward over the white field of Fifteen Acres.

He began:

—Ladies and Gentlemen.

—It has fallen to my lot this evening, as in years past, to perform a very pleasing task but a task for which I am afraid my poor powers as a speaker are all too inadequate.

—No, no! said Mr. Browne.

—But, however that may be, I can only ask you tonight to take the will for the deed and to lend me your attention for a few moments while I endeavor to express to you in words what my feelings are on this occasion.

—Ladies and Gentlemen. It is not the first time that we have gathered together under this hospitable roof, around this hospitable board. It is not the first time that we have been the recipients—or perhaps, I had better say, the victims—of the hospitality of certain good ladies.

He made a circle in the air with his arm and paused. Everyone laughed or smiled at Aunt Kate and Aunt Julia and Mary Jane who all turned crimson with pleasure. Gabriel went on more boldly:

—I feel more strongly with every recurring year that our country has no tradition which does it so much honor and which it should guard so jealously as that of its hospitality. It is a tradition that is unique as far as my experience goes (and I have visited not a few places abroad) among the modern nations. Some would say, perhaps, that with us it is rather a failing than anything to be boasted of. But granted even that, it is, to my mind, a princely failing, and one that I trust will long be cultivated among us. Of one thing, at least, I am sure. As long as this one roof shelters the good ladies aforesaid—and I wish from my heart it may do so for many and many a long year to come—the tradition of genuine warmhearted courteous Irish hospitality, which our forefathers have handed down to us and which we in turn must hand down to our descendants, is still alive among us.

A hearty murmur of assent ran round the table. It shot through Gabriel's mind that Miss Ivors was not there and that she had gone away discourteously: and he said with confidence in himself:

—Ladies and Gentlemen.

—A new generation is growing up in our midst, a generation actuated by new ideas and new principles. It is serious and enthusiastic for these new ideas and its enthusiasm, even when it is misdirected, is, I believe, in the main sincere. But we are living in a sceptical and, if I may use the phrase, a thought-tormented age: and sometimes I fear that this new generation, educated or hypereducated as it is, will lack those qualities of humanity, of hospitality, of kindly humor which belonged to an older day. Listening tonight to the names of all those great singers of the past it seemed to me, I must confess, that we were living in a less spacious age. Those days might, without exaggeration, be called spacious days: and if they are gone beyond recall let us hope, at least, that in gatherings such as this we shall still speak of them with pride and affection, still cherish in our hearts the memory of those dead and gone great ones whose fame the world will not willingly let die.

—Hear, hear! said Mr. Browne loudly.

—But yet, continued Gabriel, his voice falling into a softer inflection, there are always in gatherings such as this sadder thoughts that will recur to our minds: thoughts of the past, of youth, of changes, of absent faces that we miss here tonight. Our path through life is strewn with many such sad memories: and were we to brood upon them always we could not find the heart to go on bravely with our work among the living. We have all of us living duties and living affections which claim, and rightly claim, our strenuous endeavors.

—Therefore, I will not linger on the past. I will not let any gloomy moralizing intrude upon us here tonight. Here we are gathered together for a brief moment from the bustle and rush of our everyday routine. We are met here as friends, in the spirit of good-fellowship, as colleagues, also to a certain extent, in the true spirit of camaraderie, and as the guests of—what shall I call them?—the Three Graces of the Dublin musical world.

The table burst into applause and laughter at this sally. Aunt Julia vainly asked each of her neighbors in turn to tell her what Gabriel had said.

—He says we are the Three Graces, Aunt Julia, said Mary Jane.

Aunt Julia did not understand but she looked up, smiling, at Gabriel, who continued in the same vein:

—Ladies and Gentlemen.

—I will not attempt to play tonight the part that Paris played on another occasion. I will not attempt to choose between them. The task would be an invidious one and one beyond my poor powers. For when I view them in turn, whether it be our chief hostess herself, whose good heart, whose too good heart, has become a byword with all who know her, or her sister, who seems to be gifted with perennial youth and whose singing must have been a surprise and a revelation to us all tonight, or, last but not least, when I consider our youngest hostess, talented, cheerful, hardworking, and the best of nieces, I confess, Ladies and Gentlemen, that I do not know to which of them I should award the prize.

Gabriel glanced down at his aunts and, seeing the large smile on Aunt Julia's face and the tears which had risen to Aunt Kate's eyes, hastened to his close. He raised his glass of port gallantly, while every member of the company fingered a glass expectantly, and said loudly:

—Let us toast them all three together. Let us drink to their health, wealth, long life, happiness, and prosperity and may they long continue to hold the proud and self-won position which they hold in their profession and the position of honor and affection which they hold in our hearts.

All the guests stood up, glass in hand, and, turning towards the three seated ladies, sang in unison, with Mr. Browne as leader:

> For they are jolly gay fellows,
> For they are jolly gay fellows,
> For they are jolly gay fellows,
> Which nobody can deny.

Aunt Kate was making frank use of her handkerchief and even Aunt Julia seemed moved. Freddy Malins beat time with his pudding fork and the singers turned towards one another, as if in melodious conference, while they sang, with emphasis:

> Unless he tells a lie,
> Unless he tells a lie.

Then, turning once more towards their hostesses, they sang:

> For they are jolly gay fellows,
> For they are jolly gay fellows,
> For they are jolly gay fellows,
> Which nobody can deny.

The acclamation which followed was taken up beyond the door of the supper-room by many of the other guests and re-

newed time after time, Freddy Malins acting as officer with his
fork on high.

The piercing morning air came into the hall where they were
standing so that Aunt Kate said:
—Close the door, somebody. Mrs. Malins will get her death
of cold.
—Browne is out there, Aunt Kate, said Mary Jane.
—Browne is everywhere, said Aunt Kate, lowering her
voice.
Mary Jane laughed at her tone.
—Really, she said archly, he is very attentive.
—He has been laid on here like the gas, said Aunt Kate in
the same tone, all during the Christmas.
She laughed herself this time good-humoredly and then
added quickly:
—But tell him to come in, Mary Jane, and close the door. I
hope to goodness he didn't hear me.
At that moment the hall door was opened and Mr. Browne
came in from the doorstep, laughing as if his heart would
break. He was dressed in a long green overcoat with mock as-
trakhan cuffs and collar and wore on his head an oval fur cap.
He pointed down the snow-covered quay from where the
sound of shrill prolonged whistling was borne in.
—Teddy will have all the cabs in Dublin out, he said.
Gabriel advanced from the little pantry behind the office,
struggling into his overcoat and, looking round the hall, said:
—Gretta not down yet?
—She's getting on her things, Gabriel, said Aunt Kate.
—Who's playing up there? asked Gabriel.
—Nobody. They're all gone.
—O no, Aunt Kate, said Mary Jane. Bartell D'Arcy and Miss
O'Callaghan aren't gone yet.
—Someone is strumming at the piano, anyhow, said Gabriel.

Mary Jane glanced at Gabriel and Mr. Browne and said with a shiver:

—It makes me feel cold to look at you two gentlemen muffled up like that. I wouldn't like to face your journey home at this hour.

—I'd like nothing better this minute, said Mr. Browne stoutly, than a rattling fine walk in the country or a fast drive with a good spanking goer between the shafts.

—We used to have a very good horse and trap at home, said Aunt Julia sadly.

—The never-to-be-forgotten Johnny, said Mary Jane, laughing.

Aunt Kate and Gabriel laughed too.

—Why, what was wonderful about Johnny? asked Mr. Browne.

—The late lamented Patrick Morkan, our grandfather, that is, explained Gabriel, commonly known in his later years as the old gentleman, was a glue-boiler.

—O, now, Gabriel, said Aunt Kate, laughing, he had a starch mill.

—Well, glue or starch, said Gabriel, the old gentleman had a horse by the name of Johnny. And Johnny used to work in the old gentleman's mill, walking round and round in order to drive the mill. That was all very well; but now comes the tragic part about Johnny. One fine day the old gentleman thought he'd like to drive out with the quality to a military review in the park.

—The Lord have mercy on his soul, said Aunt Kate compassionately.

—Amen, said Gabriel. So the old gentleman, as I said, harnessed Johnny and put on his very best tall hat and his very best stock collar and drove out in grand style from his ancestral mansion somewhere near Back Lane, I think.

Everyone laughed, even Mrs. Malins, at Gabriel's manner and Aunt Kate said:

—O now, Gabriel, he didn't live in Back Lane, really. Only the mill was there.

—Out from the mansion of his forefathers, continued Gabriel, he drove with Johnny. And everything went on beautifully until Johnny came in sight of King Billy's statue: and whether he fell in love with the horse King Billy sits on or whether he thought he was back again in the mill, anyhow he began to walk round the statue.

Gabriel paced in a circle round the hall in his galoshes amid the laughter of the others.

—Round and round he went, said Gabriel, and the old gentleman, who was a very pompous old gentleman, was highly indignant. *Go on, sir! What do you mean, sir? Johnny! Johnny! Most extraordinary conduct! Can't understand the horse!*

The peals of laughter which followed Gabriel's imitation of the incident were interrupted by a resounding knock at the hall door. Mary Jane ran to open it and let in Freddy Malins. Freddy Malins, with his hat well back on his head and his shoulders humped with cold, was puffing and steaming after his exertions.

—I could only get one cab, he said.

—O, we'll find another along the quay, said Gabriel.

—Yes, said Aunt Kate. Better not keep Mrs. Malins standing in the draft.

Mrs. Malins was helped down the front steps by her son and Mr. Browne and, after many maneuvers, hoisted into the cab. Freddy Malins clambered in after her and spent a long time settling her on the seat, Mr. Browne helping him with advice. At last she was settled comfortably and Freddy Malins invited Mr. Browne into the cab. There was a good deal of confused talk, and then Mr. Browne got into the cab. The cabman settled his rug over his knees, and bent down for the address. The confusion grew greater and the cabman was directed differently by Freddy Malins and Mr. Browne, each of whom had his head out through a window of the cab. The difficulty was to know where to drop Mr. Browne along the route and Aunt Kate, Aunt Julia, and Mary Jane helped the discussion from the doorstep with cross-directions and contradictions and abundance of laughter. As for Freddy Malins he was speechless with laughter. He popped his head in and out of the window every moment, to the great danger of his hat, and told his mother how the discussion was progressing till at last Mr. Browne shouted to the bewildered cabman above the din of everybody's laughter:

—Do you know Trinity College?

—Yes, sir, said the cabman.

—Well, drive bang up against Trinity College gates, said Mr. Browne, and then we'll tell you where to go. You understand now?

—Yes, sir, said the cabman.

—Make like a bird for Trinity College.

—Right, sir, cried the cabman.

The horse was whipped up and the cab rattled off along the quay amid a chorus of laughter and adieus.

Gabriel had not gone to the door with the others. He was in a dark part of the hall gazing up the staircase. A woman was standing near the top of the first flight, in the shadow also. He could not see her face but he could see the terracotta and salmon-pink panels of her skirt which the shadow made appear black and white. It was his wife. She was leaning on the banisters, listening to something. Gabriel was surprised at her stillness and strained his ear to listen also. But he could hear little save the noise of laughter and dispute on the front steps, a few chords struck on the piano, and a few notes of a man's voice singing.

He stood still in the gloom of the hall, trying to catch the air that the voice was singing and gazing up at his wife. There was grace and mystery in her attitude as if she were a symbol of something. He asked himself what is a woman standing on the stairs in the shadow, listening to distant music, a symbol of. If he were a painter he would paint her in that attitude. Her blue felt hat would show off the bronze of her hair against the darkness and the dark panels of her skirt would show off the light ones. *Distant Music* he would call the picture if he were a painter.

The hall door was closed; and Aunt Kate, Aunt Julia, and Mary Jane came down the hall, still laughing.

—Well, isn't Freddy terrible? said Mary Jane. He's really terrible.

Gabriel said nothing but pointed up the stairs towards where his wife was standing. Now that the hall door was closed the voice and the piano could be heard more clearly. Gabriel held up his hand for them to be silent. The song seemed to be in the old Irish tonality and the singer seemed uncertain both of his words and of his voice. The voice, made plaintive by distance and by the singer's hoarseness, faintly illuminated the cadence of the air with words expressing grief:

> O, the rain falls on my heavy locks
> And the dew wets my skin
> My babe lies cold . . .

—O, exclaimed Mary Jane. It's Bartell D'Arcy singing and he wouldn't sing all the night. O, I'll get him to sing a song before he goes.

—O do, Mary Jane, said Aunt Kate.

Mary Jane brushed past the others and ran to the staircase but before she reached it the singing stopped and the piano was closed abruptly.

—O, what a pity! she cried. Is he coming down, Gretta?

Gabriel heard his wife answer yes and saw her come down towards them. A few steps behind her were Mr. Bartell D'Arcy and Miss O'Callaghan.

—O, Mr. D'Arcy, cried Mary Jane, it's downright mean of you to break off like that when we were all in raptures listening to you.

—I have been at him all the evening, said Miss O'Callaghan, and Mrs. Conroy too and he told us he had a dreadful cold and couldn't sing.

—O, Mr. D'Arcy, said Aunt Kate, now that was a great fib to tell.

—Can't you see that I'm as hoarse as a crow? said Mr. D'Arcy roughly.

He went into the pantry hastily and put on his overcoat. The others, taken aback by his rude speech, could find nothing to say. Aunt Kate wrinkled her brows and made signs to the others to drop the subject. Mr. D'Arcy stood swathing his neck carefully and frowning.

—It's the weather, said Aunt Julia, after a pause.

—Yes, everybody has colds, said Aunt Kate readily, everybody.

—They say, said Mary Jane, we haven't had snow like it for thirty years; and I read this morning in the newspapers that the snow is general all over Ireland.

—I love the look of snow, said Aunt Julia sadly.

—So do I, said Miss O'Callaghan. I think Christmas is never really Christmas unless we have the snow on the ground.

—But poor Mr. D'Arcy doesn't like the snow, said Aunt Kate, smiling.

Mr. D'Arcy came from the pantry, fully swathed and buttoned, and in a repentant tone told them the history of his cold. Everyone gave him advice and said it was a great pity and urged him to be very careful of his throat in the night air. Gabriel watched his wife who did not join in the conversation. She was standing right under the dusty fanlight and the flame of the gas lit up the rich bronze of her hair which he had seen her drying at the fire a few days before. She was in the same attitude and seemed unaware of the talk about her. At last she turned towards them and Gabriel saw that there was color on her cheeks and that her eyes were shining. A sudden tide of joy went leaping out of his heart.

—Mr. D'Arcy, she said, what is the name of that song you were singing?

—It's called *The Lass of Aughrim,* said Mr. D'Arcy, but I couldn't remember it properly. Why? Do you know it?

—*The Lass of Aughrim,* she repeated. I couldn't think of the name.

—It's a very nice air, said Mary Jane. I'm sorry you were not in voice tonight.

—Now, Mary Jane, said Aunt Kate, don't annoy Mr. D'Arcy. I won't have him annoyed.

Seeing that all were ready to start she shepherded them to the door where good-night was said:

—Well, good-night, Aunt Kate, and thanks for the pleasant evening.

—Good-night, Gabriel. Good-night, Gretta!

—Good-night, Aunt Kate, and thanks ever so much. Good-night, Aunt Julia.

—O, good-night, Gretta, I didn't see you.

—Good-night, Mr. D'Arcy. Good-night, Miss O'Callaghan.

—Good-night, Miss Morkan.

—Good-night, again.

—Good-night, all. Safe home.

—Good-night. Good-night.

The morning was still dark. A dull yellow light brooded over the houses and the river; and the sky seemed to be descending. It was slushy underfoot; and only streaks and patches of snow lay on the roofs, on the parapets of the quay, and on the area railings. The lamps were still burning redly in the murky air and, across the river, the palace of the Four Courts stood out menacingly against the heavy sky.

She was walking on before him with Mr. Bartell D'Arcy, her shoes in a brown parcel tucked under one arm and her hands holding her skirt up from the slush. She had no longer any grace of attitude but Gabriel's eyes were still bright with happiness. The blood went bounding along his veins; and the thoughts went rioting through his brain, proud, joyful, tender, valorous.

She was walking on before him so lightly and so erect that he longed to run after her noiselessly, catch her by the shoulders, and say something foolish and affectionate into her ear. She seemed to him so frail that he longed to defend her against something and then to be alone with her. Moments of their secret life together burst like stars upon his memory. A heliotrope envelope was lying beside his breakfast cup and he was caressing it with his hand. Birds were twittering in the ivy and the sunny web of the curtain was shimmering along the floor: he could not eat for happiness. They were standing on the crowded platform and he was placing a ticket inside the warm palm of her glove. He was standing with her in the cold, looking in through a grated window at a man making bottles in a roaring furnace. It was very cold. Her face, fragrant in the cold air, was quite close to his; and suddenly she called out to the man at the furnace:

—Is the fire hot, sir?

But the man could not hear her with the noise of the furnace. It was just as well. He might have answered rudely.

A wave of yet more tender joy escaped from his heart and went coursing in warm flood along his arteries. Like the tender fires of stars moments of their life together, that no one knew of or would ever know of, broke upon and illumined his memory. He longed to recall to her those moments, to make her forget the years of their dull existence together and remember only their moments of ecstasy. For the years, he felt, had not quenched his soul or hers. Their children, his writing, her household cares had not quenched all their souls' tender fire. In one letter that he had written to her then he had said: *Why is it that words like these seem to me so dull and cold? Is it because there is no word tender enough to be your name?*

Like distant music these words that he had written years before were borne towards him from the past. He longed to be alone with her. When the others had gone away, when he and she were in their room in the hotel, then they would be alone together. He would call her softly:

—Gretta!

Perhaps she would not hear at once: she would be undressing. Then something in his voice would strike her. She would turn and look at him. . . .

At the corner of Winetavern Street they met a cab. He was glad of its rattling noise as it saved him from conversation. She was looking out of the window and seemed tired. The others spoke only a few words, pointing out some building or street. The horse galloped along wearily under the murky morning sky, dragging his old rattling box after his heels, and Gabriel was again in a cab with her, galloping to catch the boat, galloping to their honeymoon.

As the cab drove across O'Connell Bridge Miss O'Callaghan said:

—They say you never cross O'Connell Bridge without seeing a white horse.

—I see a white man this time, said Gabriel.

—Where? asked Mr. Bartell D'Arcy.

Gabriel pointed to the statue, on which lay patches of snow. Then he nodded familiarly to it and waved his hand.

—Good-night, Dan, he said gaily.

When the cab drew up before the hotel Gabriel jumped out and, in spite of Mr. Bartell D'Arcy's protest, paid the driver. He gave the man a shilling over his fare. The man saluted and said:

—A prosperous New Year to you, sir.

—The same to you, said Gabriel cordially.

She leaned for a moment on his arm in getting out of the cab and while standing at the curbstone, bidding the others good-night. She leaned lightly on his arm, as lightly as when she had danced with him a few hours before. He had felt proud and happy then, happy that she was his, proud of her grace and wifely carriage. But now, after the kindling again of so many memories, the first touch of her body, musical and strange and perfumed, sent through him a keen pang of lust. Under cover of her silence he pressed her arm closely to his side; and, as they stood at the hotel door, he felt that they had escaped from their lives and duties, escaped from home and friends and run away together with wild and radiant hearts to a new ad-venture.

An old man was dozing in a great hooded chair in the hall. He lit a candle in the office and went before them to the stairs. They followed him in silence, their feet falling in soft thuds on the thickly carpeted stairs. She mounted the stairs behind the porter, her head bowed in the ascent, her frail shoulders curved as with a burden, her skirt girt tightly about her. He could have flung his arms about her hips and held her still for his arms were trembling with desire to seize her and only the stress of his nails against the palms of his hands held the wild im-pulse of his body in check. The porter halted on the stairs to settle his guttering candle. They halted too on the steps below him. In the silence Gabriel could hear the falling of the molten wax into the tray and the thumping of his own heart against his ribs.

The porter led them along a corridor and opened a door. Then he set his unstable candle down on a toilet-table and asked at what hour they were to be called in the morning.

—Eight, said Gabriel.

The porter pointed to the tap of the electric light and began a muttered apology but Gabriel cut him short.

—We don't want any light. We have light enough from the street. And I say, he added, pointing to the candle, you might remove that handsome article, like a good man.

The porter took up his candle again, but slowly for he was surprised by such a novel idea. Then he mumbled good night and went out. Gabriel shot the lock to.

A ghostly light from the streetlamp lay in a long shaft from

one window to the door. Gabriel threw his overcoat and hat on
a couch and crossed the room towards the window. He looked
down into the street in order that his emotion might calm a
little. Then he turned and leaned against a chest of drawers
with his back to the light. She had taken off her hat and cloak
and was standing before a large swinging mirror, unhooking
her waist. Gabriel paused for a few moments, watching her,
and then said:

—Gretta!

She turned away from the mirror slowly and walked along
the shaft of light towards him. Her face looked so serious and
weary that the words would not pass Gabriel's lips. No, it was
not the moment yet.

—You looked tired, he said.

—I am a little, she answered.

—You don't feel ill or weak?

—No, tired: that's all.

She went on to the window and stood there, looking out.
Gabriel waited again and then, fearing that diffidence was
about to conquer him, he said abruptly:

—By the way, Gretta!

—What is it?

—You know that poor fellow Malins? he said quickly.

—Yes. What about him?

—Well, poor fellow, he's a decent sort of chap after all, continued Gabriel in a false voice. He gave me back that sovereign
I lent him and I didn't expect it really. It's a pity he wouldn't
keep away from that Browne, because he's not a bad fellow at
heart.

He was trembling now with annoyance. Why did she seem
so abstracted? He did not know how he could begin. Was she
annoyed, too, about something? If she would only turn to him
or come to him of her own accord! To take her as she was
would be brutal. No, he must see some ardor in her eyes first.
He longed to be master of her strange mood.

—When did you lend him the pound? she asked, after a pause.

Gabriel strove to restrain himself from breaking out into brutal language about the sottish Malins and his pound. He longed to cry to her from his soul, to crush her body against his, to overmaster her. But he said:

—O, at Christmas, when he opened that little Christmas-card shop in Henry Street.

He was in such a fever of rage and desire that he did not hear her come from the window. She stood before him for an instant, looking at him strangely. Then, suddenly raising herself on tiptoe and resting her hands lightly on his shoulders, she kissed him.

—You are a very generous person, Gabriel, she said.

Gabriel, trembling with delight at her sudden kiss and at the quaintness of her phrase, put his hands on her hair and began smoothing it back, scarcely touching it with his fingers. The washing had made it fine and brilliant. His heart was brimming over with happiness. Just when he was wishing for it she had come to him of her own accord. Perhaps her thoughts had been running with his. Perhaps she had felt the impetuous desire that was in him and then the yielding mood had come upon her. Now that she had fallen to him so easily he wondered why he had been so diffident.

He stood, holding her head between his hands. Then, slipping one arm swiftly about her body and drawing her towards him, he said softly:

—Gretta dear, what are you thinking about?

She did not answer nor yield wholly to his arm. He said again, softly:

—Tell me what it is, Gretta. I think I know what is the matter. Do I know?

She did not answer at once. Then she said in an outburst of tears:

—O, I am thinking about that song, *The Lass of Aughrim.*
She broke loose from him and ran to the bed and, throwing
her arms across the bed-rail, hid her face. Gabriel stood stock-
still for a moment in astonishment and then followed her. As
he passed in the way of the cheval-glass he caught sight of
himself in full length, his broad, well-filled shirtfront, the face
whose expression always puzzled him when he saw it in a mirror and his glimmering gilt-rimmed eyeglasses. He halted a few
paces from her and said:

—What about the song? Why does that make you cry?

She raised her head from her arms and dried her eyes with
the back of her hand like a child. A kinder note than he had
intended went into his voice.

—Why, Gretta? he asked.

—I am thinking about a person long ago who used to sing
that song.

—And who was the person long ago? asked Gabriel, smiling.

—It was a person I used to know in Galway when I was living with my grandmother, she said.

The smile passed away from Gabriel's face. A dull anger
began to gather again at the back of his mind and the dull fires
of his lust began to glow angrily in his veins.

—Someone you were in love with? he asked ironically.

—It was a young boy I used to know, she answered, named
Michael Furey. He used to sing that song, *The Lass of Aughrim.*
He was very delicate.

Gabriel was silent. He did not wish her to think that he was
interested in this delicate boy.

—I can see him so plainly, she said after a moment. Such
eyes as he had: big dark eyes! And such an expression in
them—an expression!

—O then, you were in love with him? said Gabriel.

—I used to go out walking with him, she said, when I was
in Galway.

A thought flew across Gabriel's mind.

—Perhaps that was why you wanted to go to Galway with that Ivors girl? he said coldly.

She looked at him and asked in surprise:

—What for?

Her eyes made Gabriel feel awkward. He shrugged his shoulders and said:

—How do I know? To see him perhaps.

She looked away from him along the shaft of light towards the window in silence.

—He is dead, she said at length. He died when he was only seventeen. Isn't it a terrible thing to die so young as that?

—What was he? asked Gabriel, still ironically.

—He was in the gasworks, she said.

Gabriel felt humiliated by the failure of his irony and by the evocation of this figure from the dead, a boy in the gasworks. While he had been full of memories of their secret life together, full of tenderness and joy and desire, she had been comparing him in her mind with another. A shameful consciousness of his own person assailed him. He saw himself as a ludicrous figure, acting as a pennyboy for his aunts, a nervous well-meaning sentimentalist, orating to vulgarians and idealizing his own clownish lusts, the pitiable fatuous fellow he had caught a glimpse of in the mirror. Instinctively he turned his back more to the light lest she might see the shame that burned upon his forehead.

He tried to keep up his tone of cold interrogation but his voice when he spoke was humble and indifferent.

—I suppose you were in love with this Michael Furey, Gretta, he said.

—I was great with him at that time, she said.

Her voice was veiled and sad. Gabriel, feeling now how vain it would be to try to lead her whither he had purposed, caressed one of her hands and said, also sadly:

—And what did he die of so young, Gretta? Consumption, was it?

—I think he died for me, she answered.

A vague terror seized Gabriel at this answer as if, at that hour when he had hoped to triumph, some impalpable and vindictive being was coming against him, gathering forces against him in its vague world. But he shook himself free of it with an effort of reason and continued to caress her hand. He did not question her again for he felt that she would tell him of herself. Her hand was warm and moist: it did not respond to his touch but he continued to caress it just as he had caressed her first letter to him that spring morning.

—It was in the winter, she said, about the beginning of the winter when I was going to leave my grandmother's and come up here to the convent. And he was ill at the time in his lodgings in Galway and wouldn't be let out and his people in Oughterard were written to. He was in decline, they said, or something like that. I never knew rightly.

She paused for a moment and sighed.

—Poor fellow, she said. He was very fond of me and he was such a gentle boy. We used to go out together, walking, you know, Gabriel, like the way they do in the country. He was going to study singing only for his health. He had a very good voice, poor Michael Furey.

—Well; and then? asked Gabriel.

—And then when it came to the time for me to leave Galway and come up to the convent he was much worse and I wouldn't be let see him so I wrote a letter saying I was going up to Dublin and would be back in the summer and hoping he would be better then.

She paused for a moment to get her voice under control and then went on:

—Then the night before I left I was in my grandmother's house in Nuns' Island, packing up, and I heard gravel thrown up against the window. The window was so wet I couldn't see so I ran downstairs as I was and slipped out the back into the garden and there was the poor fellow at the end of the garden, shivering.

—And did you not tell him to go back? asked Gabriel.

—I implored him to go home at once and told him he would get his death in the rain. But he said he did not want to live. I can see his eyes as well as well! He was standing at the end of the wall where there was a tree.

—And did he go home? asked Gabriel.

—Yes, he went home. And when I was only a week in the convent he died and he was buried in Oughterard where his people came from. O, the day I heard that, that he was dead!

She stopped, choking with sobs, and, overcome by emotion, flung herself face downward on the bed, sobbing in the quilt. Gabriel held her hand for a moment longer, irresolutely, and then, shy of intruding on her grief, let it fall gently and walked quietly to the window.

She was fast asleep.

Gabriel, leaning on his elbow, looked for a few moments unresentfully on her tangled hair and half-open mouth, listening to her deep-drawn breath. So she had had that romance in her life: a man had died for her sake. It hardly pained him now to think how poor a part he, her husband, had played in her life. He watched her while she slept as though he and she had never lived together as man and wife. His curious eyes rested long upon her face and on her hair: and, as he thought of what she must have been then, in that time of her first girlish beauty, a strange friendly pity for her entered his soul. He did not like to say even to himself that her face was no longer beautiful but he knew that it was no longer the face for which Michael Furey had braved death.

Perhaps she had not told him all the story. His eyes moved

to the chair over which she had thrown some of her clothes. A petticoat string dangled to the floor. One boot stood upright, its limp upper fallen down: the fellow of it lay upon its side. He wondered at his riot of emotions of an hour before. From what had it proceeded? From his aunt's supper, from his own foolish speech, from the wine and dancing, the merrymaking when saying good-night in the hall, the pleasure of the walk along the river in the snow. Poor Aunt Julia! She, too, would soon be a shade with the shade of Patrick Morkan and his horse. He had caught that haggard look upon her face for a moment when she was singing *Arrayed for the Bridal.* Soon, perhaps, he would be sitting in that same drawing room, dressed in black, his silk hat on his knees. The blinds would be drawn down and Aunt Kate would be sitting beside him, crying and blowing her nose and telling him how Julia had died. He would cast about in his mind for some words that might console her, and would find only lame and useless ones. Yes, yes: that would happen very soon.

The air of the room chilled his shoulders. He stretched himself cautiously along under the sheets and lay down beside his wife. One by one they were all becoming shades. Better pass boldly into that other world, in the full glory of some passion, than fade and wither dismally with age. He thought of how she who lay beside him had locked in her heart for so many years that image of her lover's eyes when he had told her that he did not wish to live.

Generous tears filled Gabriel's eyes. He had never felt like that himself towards any woman but he knew that such a feeling must be love. The tears gathered more thickly in his eyes and in the partial darkness he imagined he saw the form of a young man standing under a dripping tree. Other forms were near. His soul had approached that region where dwell the vast hosts of the dead. He was conscious of, but could not apprehend, their wayward and flickering existence. His own identity was fading out into a grey impalpable world: the solid world itself which these dead had one time reared and lived in was dissolving and dwindling.

A few light taps upon the pane made him turn to the window. It had begun to snow again. He watched sleepily the flakes, silver and dark, falling obliquely against the lamplight. The time had come for him to set out on his journey westward. Yes, the newspapers were right: snow was general all over Ireland. It was falling on every part of the dark central plain, on the treeless hills, falling softly upon the Bog of Allen and, farther westward, softly falling into the dark mutinous Shannon waves. It was falling, too, upon every part of the lonely churchyard on the hill where Michael Furey lay buried. It lay thickly drifted on the crooked crosses and headstones, on the spears of the little gate, on the barren thorns. His soul swooned slowly as he heard the snow falling faintly through the universe and faintly falling, like the descent of their last end, upon all the living and the dead.

Liam O'Flaherty (1896–1984)

Liam O'Flaherty was born in 1896 on the main island of the Aran Islands. The harsh perspectives, immediacy, and power of nature, and the tightly knit, determined island community of his birthplace have strongly marked his life and fiction. He was educated at Catholic schools and was trained for the priesthood until he finally decided against ordination while a student at the Dublin diocesan seminary (Holy Cross College). Soon after, during World War I, he enlisted in the Irish Guards, was shell-shocked in France, and eventually was discharged with a disability pension. During the next several years he traveled widely, worked briefly at a variety of jobs, returned to Ireland during the Civil War, joined the Republican forces, and was finally forced to flee to England. There he wrote his first novel, Thy Neighbor's Wife, *published by Edward Garnett in 1923. Later he returned to Ireland and has since published an impressive quantity of work, including novels, short stories, literary criticism, a tourist guide, a biography of Tim Healy, and several autobiographical pieces. Though he is probably best known for his novel* The Informer *(1925), filmed by John Ford, he is admired primarily for such novels as* The House of Gold *(1929),* Skerret *(1932),* Famine *(1937), and for his short stories.* Spring Sowing *(1924) was his first volume of stories, followed by* Civil War *(1925) and, among others,* The Tent *(1926),* Red Barbara and Other Stories *(1928), and* The Mountain Tavern and Other Stories *(1929). "The Pedlar's Revenge" is taken from* The Pedlar's Revenge and Other Stories *(1976).*

* * *

The Pedlar's Revenge

Old Paddy Moynihan was dead when the police appeared on the scene of the accident. He lay stretched out on his back at the bottom of the deep ravine below the blacksmith's house. His head rested on a smooth round granite stone and his hands were crossed over his enormous stomach. His battered old black hat was tied onto his skull with a piece of twine that passed beneath his chin. Men and boys from the village stood around him in a circle, discussing the manner of his death in subdued tones. Directly overhead, women and girls leaned in a compact group over the low stone wall of the blacksmith's yard. They were all peering down into the shadowy depths of the ravine at the dim shape of the dead man, with their mouths wide open and a fixed look of horror in their eyes.

Sergeant Toomey made a brief inspection of the corpse and then turned to Joe Finnerty, the rate collector.

"Tommy Murtagh told me," he said, "that it was you . . ."

"Yes," said Finnerty. "It was I sent Tommy along to fetch you. I told him to get a priest as well, but no priest came."

"Both the parish priest and the curate are away on sick calls at the moment," said the sergeant.

"In any case," said Finnerty, "there was little that a priest could do for him. The poor old fellow remained unconscious from the moment he fell until he died."

"Did you see him fall?" said the sergeant.

"I did," said Finnerty. "I was coming down the road when I caught sight of him on the blacksmith's wall there above. He was very excited. He kept shouting and brandishing his stick. 'The Pedlar poisoned me,' he said. He kept repeating that statement in a sing-song shout, over and over again, like a whinging child. Then he got to his feet and moved forward, heading for the road. He had taken only half a step, though, when he seemed to get struck by some sort of colic. He dropped his stick, clutched his stomach with both hands and staggered backwards, bent almost double, to sit down again on the wall. The next thing I knew, he was going head over heels into the ravine, backwards, yelling like a stuck pig. Upon my soul! His roaring must have been heard miles away."

"It was a terrific yell, all right," said Peter Lavin, the doctor's servant. "I was mowing down there below in the meadow when I heard it. I raised my head like a shot and saw old Paddy go through the air. Great God! He looked as big as a house. He turned somersault twice before he passed out of my sight, going on away down into the hole. I heard the splash, though, when he struck the ground, like a heavy sack dropped into the sea from a boat's deck."

He pointed towards a deep wide dent in the wet ground to the right and said:

"That was where he landed, sergeant."

The sergeant walked over and looked at the hollow. The whole ground was heavily laden with water that flowed from the mossy face of the cliff. Three little boys had stuck a rolled dock leaf into a crevice and they were drinking in turn at the thin jet of water that came from the bright green funnel.

"Why did he think he was poisoned?" said the sergeant.

"I've no idea," said Finnerty. "It's certain, in any case, that he had swallowed something that didn't agree with him. The poor fellow was in convulsions with pain just before he fell."

The sergeant looked up along the sheer face of the cliff at a thick cluster of ivy that grew just beneath the overarching brow. A clutch of young sparrows were chirping plaintively for food from their nest within the ivy.

"According to him," the sergeant said, as he walked back to the corpse, "The Pedlar was responsible for whatever ailed him."

"That's right," said Finnerty. "He kept repeating that The Pedlar had poisoned him, over and over again. I wouldn't pay much attention to that, though, The Pedlar and himself were deadly enemies. They have accused one another of every crime in the calendar scores of times."

" 'Faith, I saw him coming out of The Pedlar's house a few hours ago," said Anthony Gill. "He didn't look like a poisoned man at that time. He had a broad smile on his face and he was talking to himself, as he came shuffling down along the road towards me. I asked him where he was going in such a great hurry and he told me to mind my own business. I looked back after he had passed and saw him go into Pete Maloney's shop."

"I was there when he came in," said Bartly Timoney. "He was looking for candles."

"Candles?" said the sergeant.

"He bought four candles," Timoney said. "He practically ran out of the shop with them, mumbling to himself and laughing. Begob, like Anthony there said, he seemed to be in great form at the time."

"Candles?" said the sergeant again. "Why should he be in such a great hurry to buy candles?"

"Poor man!" said Finnerty. "He was very old and not quite right in the head. Lord have mercy on him, he's been half mad these last two years, ever since he lost his wife. Ah! The poor old fellow is better off dead than the way he was, living all alone in his little cottage, without anybody to feed him and keep him clean."

The sergeant turned to Peter Lavin and said:

"Did the doctor come back from town yet?"

"He won't be back until this evening," Lavin said.

"He's waiting over for the result of the operation on Tom Kelly's wife."

"All right, lads," the sergeant said. "We might as well see about removing poor old Moynihan."

"That's easier said than done," said Anthony Gill.

"We weighed him a few weeks ago in Quinn's scales against three sacks of flour to settle a bet. Charley Ridge, the lighthouse keeper, bet a pound note that he was heavier than three sacks of flour and Tommy Perkins covered the pound, maintaining that he would fall short of that weight. The lighthouse keeper lost, but it was only by a whisker. I never saw anything go so close. There were only a few ounces in the difference. Well! Three sacks of flour weigh three hundred and thirty-six pounds. How are we going to carry that much dead weight out of this hole?"

"The simplest way, sergeant," said Guard Hynes, "would be to get a rope and haul him straight up to the blacksmith's yard."

Everybody agreed with Hynes.

"I've got a lot of gear belonging to my boat up at the house," said Bartly Timoney. "I'll go and get a strong rope."

He began to clamber up the side of the ravine.

"Bring a couple of slings as well," the sergeant called after him. "They'll keep him steady."

All the younger men followed Timoney, in order to give a hand with the hauling.

"There may be heavier men than old Moynihan," said Finnerty to those that remained below with the corpse, "but he was the tallest and the strongest man seen in this part of the country within living memory. He was six feet ten inches in his bare feet and there was no known limit to his strength. I've seen him toss a full-grown bullock without hardly any effort at all, in the field behind Tom Daly's pub at Gortmor. Then he drank the three gallons of porter that he won for doing it, as quickly as you or I would drink three pints."

"He was a strong man, all right," said Gill. "You could heap a horse's load onto his back and he'd walk away with it, as straight as a rod, calmly smoking his pipe."

"Yet he was as gentle as a child," said Lavin, "in spite of his strength. They say that he never struck anybody in his whole life."

"Many is the day he worked on my land," said Sam Clancy,

"and I'll agree that he was as good as ten men. He could keep going from morning to night without slackening pace. However, it was the devil's own job giving him enough to eat. The side of a pig, or even a whole sheep, would make no more than a good snack for him. The poor fellow told me that he suffered agonies from hunger. He could never get enough to eat. It must have been absolute torture for him, when he got too old to work and had to live on the pension."

Timoney came back and threw down two slings, over the low wall where the women and girls were gathered. Then he let down the end of a stout rope. Sergeant Toomey made one sling fast about Moynihan's upper chest and the other about his knees. Then he passed the end of the rope through the slings and knotted it securely.

"Haul away now," he said to Timoney.

The two old sparrows fluttered back and forth across the ravine, uttering shrill cries, when they saw the corpse drawn up slowly along the face of the cliff. The fledglings remained silent in obedience to these constantly repeated warnings, until old Moynihan's dangling right hand brushed gently against the ivy outside their nest. The light sound being like that made by the bodies of their parents, when entering with food, they broke into a frenzied chatter. Thereupon, the old birds became hysterical with anxiety. The mother dropped a piece of worm from her beak. Then she and her cock hurled themselves at old Moynihan's head, with all their feathers raised. They kept attacking him fiercely, with beak and claw, until he was drawn up over the wall into the yard.

When the corpse was stretched out on the blacksmith's cart, Sergeant Toomey turned to the women that were there and said:

"It would be an act of charity for ye to come and get him ready for burial. He has nobody of his own to wash and shave him."

"In God's name," they said. "We'll do whatever is needed."
They all followed the men that were pushing the cart up the
road towards the dead man's cottage.

"Listen," the sergeant said to Finnerty, as they walked along
side by side. "Didn't The Pedlar bring old Moynihan to court
at one time over the destruction of a shed."

"He did, 'faith," said Finnerty, "and he was awarded dam-
ages, too, by District Justice Roche."

"How long ago was that?" the sergeant said.

"It must be over twenty years," said Finnerty.

"A long time before I came here," said the sergeant. "I never
heard the proper details of the story."

"It was only a ramshackle old shed," said Finnerty, "where
The Pedlar used to keep all the stuff that he collected around
the countryside, rags and old iron and bits of ancient furniture
and all sorts of curiosities that had been washed ashore from
wrecked ships. Moynihan came along one day and saw The
Pedlar's ass tied to the iron staple in the doorjamb of the shed.
Lord have mercy on the dead, he was very fond of playing childish pranks, like all simpleminded big fellows. So he got a turnip and stuck it onto the end of his stick. Then he leaned over
the wall of The Pedlar's backyard and began to torment the ass,
drawing the unfortunate animal on and on after the turnip.
The ass kept straining at its rope until the doorjamb was
dragged out of the wall. Then the wall collapsed and finally the
whole shed came down in a heap. The Pedlar was away at the
time and nobody saw the damage being done except old
Moynihan himself. The poor fellow would have got into no
trouble if he had kept his mouth shut. Instead of doing so, it
was how he ran down into the village and told everybody what
had happened. He nearly split his sides laughing at his own
story. As a result of his confessions, he very naturally didn't
have a foot to stand on when the case came up before the
court."

The dead man's cottage looked very desolate. The little garden in front was overgrown with weeds. There were several large holes in the roof. The door was broken. The windows were covered with sacking. The interior was in a shocking state of filth and disorder.

"He'll have to stay on the cart," said Sergeant Toomey, after he had inspected the two rooms, "until there is a proper place to lay him out like a Christian."

He left Guard Hynes in charge of the body and then set off with Joe Finnerty to The Pedlar's cottage.

"I couldn't find the candles," he said on the way. "Neither could I find out exactly what he had for his last meal. His little pot and his frying pan were on the hearth, having evidently been used to prepare whatever he ate. There was a small piece of potato skin at the bottom of the pot, but the frying pan was licked as clean as a new pin. God only knows what he fried on it."

"Poor old Paddy!" said Finnerty. "He had been half-starved for a long time. He was going around like a dog, scavenging for miserable scraps in shameful places. Yet people gave him sufficient food to satisfy the appetite of any ordinary person, in addition to what he was able to buy with his pension money."

The Pedlar's cottage was only a few yards away from Moynihan's sordid hovel, to which its neatness offered a very striking contrast. It was really very pretty, with its windows painted dark blue and its walls spotlessly white and the bright May sunlight sparkling on its slate roof. The garden was well stocked with fruit trees and vegetables and flowers, all dressed in a manner that bore evidence to the owner's constant diligence and skill. It also contained three hives of honeybees which made a pleasant clamor as they worked among the flowers. The air was charged with a delicious perfume, which was carried up by the gentle breeze from the different plants and flowers.

The Pedlar hailed the two men as they were approaching the

house along a narrow flagged path that ran through the center of the garden.

"Good day," he said to them. "What's goin' on over at Paddy Moynihan's house? I heard a cart and a lot of people arrive there."

He was sitting on a three-legged stool to the right of the open doorway. His palsied hands moved up and down, constantly, along the blackthorn stick that he held erect between his knees. His legs were also palsied. The metaled heels of his boots kept beating a minute and almost inaudible tattoo on the broad smooth flagstone beneath his stool. He was very small and so stooped that he was bent almost double. His boots, his threadbare black suit, his white shirt, and his black felt hat were all very neat; like his house and his garden. Indeed, he was immaculately clean from head to foot, except for his wrinkled little face. It was in great part covered with stubbly gray hair, that looked more like an animal's fur than a proper human beard.

"It was old Paddy Moynihan himself," said the sergeant in a solemn tone, "that they brought home on the cart."

The Pedlar laughed drily in his throat, making a sound that was somewhat like the bleating of a goat, plaintive and without any merriment.

"Ho! Ho! Did the shameless scoundrel get drunk again?" he said in a thin high-pitched voice. "Two months ago, he got speechless in Richie Tallons's pub with two sheep jobbers from Castlegorm. He had to be taken home on Phil Manion's ass cart. There wasn't room for the whole of him on the cart. Two lads had to follow along behind, holding up the lower parts of his legs."

"Old Paddy is dead," the sergeant said in a stern tone.

The Pedlar became motionless for a few moments on hearing this news, with his shrewd blue eyes looking upwards at the sergeant's face from beneath his bushy grey eyebrows. Then his heels began once more to beat their minute tattoo and his fingers moved tremulously along the surface of the blackthorn stick, up and down, as if it were a pipe from which they were drawing music.

"I'll ask God to have mercy on his soul," he said coldly, "but I won't say that I'm sorry to hear he's dead. Why should I? To tell you the honest truth, the news that you bring lifts a great weight off my mind. How did he die?"

He again laughed drily in his throat, after the sergeant had told him the manner of old Moynihan's death. His laughter now sounded gay.

"It must have been his weight that killed him," he said, "for John Delaney, a carpenter that used to live in Srulane long ago, fell down at that very same place without hurting himself in the least. It was a terrible night, about forty years ago. Delaney was coming home alone from a funeral at Tirnee, where he had gone to make the coffin. As usual, he was dead drunk, and never let a word out of him as he fell. He stayed down there in the hole for the rest of that night and all next day. He crawled out of it at nightfall, as right as rain. That same Delaney was the king of all drunkards. I remember one time he fell into a coffin he was making for an old woman at ..."

"I must warn you," Sergeant Toomey interrupted, "that Paddy Moynihan made certain allegations against you, in the presence of Joe Finnerty here, shortly before he died. They were to the effect that you had ..."

"Ho! Ho! Bad cess to the scoundrel!" The Pedlar interrupted in turn. "He's been making allegations against me all his life. He's been tormenting me, too. God forgive me! I've hated that man since I was a child."

"You've hated him all that time?" said the sergeant.

"We were the same age," said The Pedlar. "I'll be seventy-nine next month. I'm only a few weeks older than Paddy. We started going to school on the very same day. He took a violent dislike to me from the first moment he laid eyes on me. I was born stooped, just the same as I am now. I was delicate into the bargain and they didn't think I'd live. When I was seven or eight years old, I was no bigger than a dwarf. On the other hand, Paddy Moynihan was already a big hefty block of a lad. He was twice the size of other boys his own age. He tortured me in every way that he could. His favorite trick was to sneak up behind me and yell into my ear. You know what a powerful voice he had as a grown man. Well! It was very nearly as powerful when he was a lad. His yell was deep and rumbling, like the roar of an angry bull. I always fell down in a fit whenever he sneaked up behind me and yelled into my ear."

"That was no way to treat a delicate lad," said the sergeant in a sympathetic tone. "It was no wonder that you got to hate him."

"Don't believe a word of what he's telling you," said Finnerty to the sergeant. "Paddy Moynihan never did anything of the sort."

The Pedlar again became motionless for a few seconds, as he looked at Finnerty's legs. Then he resumed his dance and turned his glance back to the sergeant's face.

"He did worse things to me," he said. "He made the other scholars stand around me in a ring and beat my bare feet with little pebbles. He used to laugh at the top of his voice while he watched them do it. If I tried to break out of the ring, or sat down on the ground and put my feet under me, he'd threaten me with worse torture. 'Stand there,' he'd say, 'or I'll keep shouting into your ear until you die.' Of course, I'd rather let them go on beating me than have him do the other thing. Oh! God! The shouting in my ear was a terrible torture. I used to froth at the mouth so much, when I fell down, that they thought for a long time I had epilepsy."

"You old devil!" cried Finnerty angrily. "You should be ashamed of yourself for telling lies about the dead."

"Let him have his say," the sergeant said to Finnerty. "Every man has a right to say what he pleases on his own threshold."

"He had no right to speak ill of the dead, all the same," said

Finnerty, "especially when there isn't a word of truth in what he says. Sure, it's well known that poor old Paddy Moynihan, Lord have mercy on him, wouldn't hurt a fly. There was no more harm in him than in a babe unborn."

"Take it easy, Joe," said the sergeant. "There are two sides to every story."

Then he turned to The Pedlar and added:

" 'Faith, you had cause to hate Moynihan, all right. No wonder you planned to get revenge on him."

"I was too much afraid of him at that time," said The Pedlar, "to think of revenge. Oh! God! He had the life nearly frightened out of me. He and his gang used to hunt me all the way home from school, throwing little stones at me and clods of dirt. 'Pedlar, Pedlar, Pedlar,' they'd shout and they coming after me."

"Musha, bad luck to you," said Finnerty, "for a cunning old rascal, trying to make us believe it was Paddy Moynihan put the scholars up to shouting 'Pedlar' after you. Sure, everybody in the parish has shouted 'Pedlar' after a Counihan at one time or other and thought nothing of it. Neither did the Counihans. Why should they? They've all been known as 'The Pedlars' from one generation to another, every mother's son of them."

The sergeant walked over to the open doorway and thrust his head into the kitchen.

"Leave the man alone," he said to Finnerty.

The fireplace, the dressers that were laden with beautiful old brown delftware and the flagged floor were all spotlessly clean and brightly polished.

"Ah! Woe!" The Pedlar cried out in a loud voice, as he began to rock himself like a lamenting woman. "The Counihans are all gone except myself and I'll soon be gone, too, leaving no kith or kin behind me. The day of the wandering merchant is now done. He and his ass will climb no more up from the sea along the stony mountain roads, bringing lovely bright things from faraway cities to the wild people of the glens. Ah! Woe! Woe!"

"If you were that much afraid of Moynihan," said the sergeant, as he walked back from the doorway to The Pedlar's stool, "it must have been the devil's own job for you to get revenge on him."

The Pedlar stopped rocking himself and looked up sideways at the sergeant, with a very cunning smile on his little bearded face.

"It was easy," he whispered in a tone of intense pleasure, "once I had learned his secret."

"What secret did he have?" said the sergeant.

"He was a coward," said The Pedlar.

"A coward!" cried Finnerty. "Paddy Moynihan a coward!"

"Keep quiet, Joe," said the sergeant.

"I was nineteen years of age at the time," said The Pedlar, "and in such a poor state of health that I was barely able to walk. Yet I had to keep going. My mother, Lord have mercy on her, had just died after a long sickness, leaving me alone in the world with hardly a penny to my name. I was coming home one evening from Ballymullen, with a load of goods in my ass's creels, when Moynihan came along and began to torment me. 'Your load isn't properly balanced,' he said. 'It's going to overturn.' Then he began to pick up loose stones from the road and put them into the creels, first into one and then into the other, pretending that he was trying to balance the load. I knew very well what he had in mind, but I said nothing. I was speechless with fright. Then he suddenly began to laugh and he took bigger stones from the wall and threw them into the creels, one after the other. Laughing at the top of his voice, he kept throwing in more and more stones, until the poor ass fell down under the terrible weight. That was more than I could bear. In spite of my terror, I picked up a stone and threw it at him. It wasn't much of a stone and I didn't throw it hard, but it struck him in the cheek and managed to draw blood. He put up his hand and felt the cut. Then he looked at his fingers. 'Lord God!' he said in a weak little voice. 'Blood is coming from my cheek. I'm cut.' Upon my soul, he let a terrible yell out of him and set off down the road towards the village as fast as he could, with his hand to his cheek and he screaming like a frightened girl. As for me, 'faith, I raised up my ass and went home happy that evening. There was a little bird singing in my heart, for I knew that Moynihan would never again be able to torture me."

"Right enough," said the sergeant, "you had him in your power after that. You had only to decide . . ."

"Best of all, though," The Pedlar interrupted excitedly, "was when I found out that he was mortally afraid of bees. Before that, he was able to steal all my fruit and vegetables while I was out on the roads. It was no use keeping a dog. The sight of him struck terror into the fiercest dog there ever was."

"You wicked old black spider!" said Finnerty. "Why do you go on telling lies about the dead?"

"Keep quiet, Joe," said the sergeant. "Let him finish his story!"

"All animals loved Moynihan," said Finnerty, "because he was gentle with them. They knew there was no harm in him. Children loved him, too. Indeed, every living creature was fond of the poor old fellow except this vindictive little cripple, who envied his strength and his good nature and his laughter. It was his rollicking laughter, above all else, that aroused the hatred of this cursed little man."

"So you got bees," the sergeant said to The Pedlar.

"I bought three hives," The Pedlar said, "and put them here in the garden. That did the trick. Ho! Ho! The ruffian has suffered agonies on account of those bees, especially since the war made food scarce in the shops. Many is the good day's sport I've had, sitting here on my stool, watching him go back and forth like a hungry wolf, with his eyes fixed on the lovely fruit and vegetables that he daren't touch. Even so, I'm glad to hear he's dead."

"You are?" said Sergeant Toomey.

"It takes a load off my mind," The Pedlar said.

"It does?" said the sergeant.

"Lately," said The Pedlar, "I was beginning to get afraid of him again. He was going mad with hunger. You can't trust a madman. In spite of his cowardice, he might attack me in order to rob my house and garden."

"Was that why you decided to poison him?" said the sergeant.

The Pedlar started violently and became motionless, with his upward-glancing eyes fixed on the sergeant's chest. He looked worried for a moment. Then his bearded face became suffused with a cunning smile and his palsied limbs resumed their uncouth dance. The metaled heels of his boots now made quite a loud and triumphant sound as they beat upon the flagstone.

"You are a clever man, Sergeant Toomey," he whispered in a sneering tone, "but you'll never be able to prove that I'm guilty of having caused Paddy Moynihan's death."

"He was in your house today," said the sergeant.

"He was," said The Pedlar.

"Did you give him anything?" said the sergeant.

"I gave him nothing," said The Pedlar.

"You might as well tell the truth," said the sergeant. "When the doctor comes back this evening, we'll know exactly what old Moynihan had for his last meal."

"I can tell you that myself," said The Pedlar.

"You can?" said the sergeant.

"He burst into my kitchen," said The Pedlar, "while I was frying a few potatoes with some of the bacon fat that I collect in a bowl. 'Where did you get the bacon?' he said. He loved bacon and he was furious because there was none to be had in the shops. 'I have no bacon,' I said. 'You're a liar,' said he. 'I can smell it.' I was afraid to tell him the truth, for fear he might ransack the house and find my bowl of bacon fat. Then he'd kill me if I tried to prevent him from marching off with it. So I told him it was candles I was frying with the potatoes. God forgive me, I was terribly frightened by the wild look in his eyes. So I told him the first thing that came into my head, in order to get him out of the house. 'Candles!' he said. 'In that case, I'll soon be eating fried potatoes myself.' Then he ran out of the house. I locked the door as soon as he had gone. Not long afterwards, he came back and tried to get in, but I pretended not to hear him knocking. 'You old miser!' he shouted, as he gave the door a terrible kick that nearly took it off its hinges. 'I have candles myself now. I'll soon be as well fed as you are.' He kept laughing to himself as he went away. That was the last I saw or heard of him."

"You think he ate the candles?" said the sergeant.

"I'm certain of it," said The Pedlar. "He'd eat anything."

The sergeant folded his arms across his chest and stared at The Pedlar in silence for a little while. Then he shook his head.

"May God forgive you!" he said.

"Why do you say that?" The Pedlar whispered softly.

"You are a very clever man," said the sergeant. "There is nothing that the law can do to a man as clever as you, but you'll have to answer for your crime to Almighty God on the Day of Judgment all the same."

Then he turned to Finnerty and said sharply:

"Come on, Joe. Let's get out of here."

Finnerty spat on the ground at The Pedlar's feet.

"You terrible man!" he said. "You wicked dwarf! You'll roast in hell for all eternity in payment for your crime."

Then he followed the sergeant down along the narrow flagged path that divided the garden.

"Ho! Ho!" The Pedlar cried in triumph as he stared after them. "Ho! Ho! My lovelies! Isn't it great to hear the mighty of this earth asking for God's help to punish the poor? Isn't it great to see the law of the land crying out to God for help against the weak and the persecuted."

He broke into a peal of mocking laughter, which he suddenly cut short.

"Do ye hear me laugh out loud?" he shouted after them. "No man heard me laugh like this in all my life before. I'm laughing out loud, because I fear neither God nor man. This is the hour of my delight. It is, 'faith. It's the hour of my satisfaction."

He continued to laugh at intervals, on a shrill high note, while the two men went down the flagged path to the gate and then turned right along the road that led back to Moynihan's sordid cottage.

"Ho! Ho!" he crowed between the peals of laughter. "I have a lovely satisfaction now for all my terrible shame and pain and sorrow. I can die in peace."

The metaled heels of his boots now beat a frantic tattoo upon the flagstones and his palsied hands continued to move back and forth over the surface of his blackthorn stick, as if it were a pipe from which they were drawing music.

Elizabeth Bowen (1899–1973)

Elizabeth Bowen was born in Dublin in 1899. Both her mother and father came from old Anglo-Irish families. Her father's ancestral home, Bowen's Court, near Cork, was inherited by Elizabeth in 1930. Her father, a barrister and legal historian, was an unstable man given to nervous breakdowns, and Elizabeth spent an insecure childhood in Ireland and England. After her marriage in 1923 she lived mainly in London, though she returned frequently to Cork. In 1952 she settled at Bowen's Court for eight years. By that time she had already written most of her best work, the novels The Last September *(1929),* The House in Paris *(1935),* The Death of the Heart *(1938), and* The Heat of the Day *(1949), and the short story collections* The Cat Jumps *(1934),* Look at All Those Roses *(1941), and* The Demon Lover *(1945). She published her tenth and final novel,* Eva Trout *(1969), four years before her death in London. "Summer Night" is taken from* Look at All Those Roses *and is included in the recent collection made by her biographer, Victoria Glendinning,* The Irish Stories of Elizabeth Bowen *(1978).*

Summer Night

As the sun set its light slowly melted the landscape, till everything was made of fire and glass. Released from the glare of noon, the haycocks now seemed to float on the aftergrass: their freshness penetrated the air. In the not far distance hills with woods up their flanks lay in light like hills in another world—it would be a pleasure of heaven to stand up there, where no foot ever seemed to have trodden, on the spaces between the woods soft as powder dusted over with gold. Against those hills, the burning red rambler roses in cottage gardens along the roadside looked earthy—they were too near the eye.

The road was in Ireland. The light, the air from the distance, the air of evening rushed transversely through the open sides of the car. The rims of the hood flapped, the hood's metal frame rattled as the tourer, in great bounds of speed, held the road's darkening magnetic center streak. The big shabby family car was empty but for its small driver—its emptiness seemed to levitate it—on its back seat a coat slithered about, and a dressing case bumped against the seat. The driver did not relax her excited touch on the wheel: now and then while she drove she turned one wrist over, to bring the watch worn on it into view, and she gave the mileage marked on the yellow signposts a flying, jealous, half-inadvertent look. She was driving parallel with the sunset: the sun slowly went down on her right hand.

The hills flowed round till they lay ahead. Where the road bent for its upward course through the pass she pulled up and lighted a cigarette. With a snatch she untwisted her turban; she shook her hair free and threw the scarf behind her into the back seat. The draft of the pass combed her hair into coarse strands as the car hummed up in second gear. Behind one brilliantly outlined crest the sun had now quite gone; on the steeps of bracken, in the electric shadow, each frond stood out and climbing goats turned their heads. The car came up on a lorry, to hang on its tail, impatient, checked by turns of the road. At the first stretch the driver smote her palm on the horn and shot past and shot on ahead again.

The small woman drove with her chin up. Her existence was in her hands on the wheel and in the sole of the foot in which she felt, through the sandal, the throbbing pressure of the accelerator. Her face, enlarged by blown-back hair, was as overbearingly blank as the face of a figurehead; her black eyebrows were ruled level, and her eyes, pupils dilated, did little more than reflect the low burn of daylight along horizons, the luminous shades of the half-dark.

Clear of the pass, approaching the county town, the road widened and straightened between stone walls and burnished, showering beech. The walls broke up into gateways and hoardings and the suburbs began. People in modern building estate gardens let the car in a hurry through their unseeing look. The raised footpaths had margins of grass. White and gray rows of cottages under the pavement level let woodsmoke over their half-doors: women and old men sat outside the doors on boxes, looking down at their knees; here and there a bird sprang in a cage tacked to a wall. Children chasing balls over the roadway shot whooping right and left of the car. The refreshed town, unfolding streets to its center, at this hour slowly heightened, cooled; streets and stones threw off a gray-pink glare, sultry lasting ghost of the high noon. In this dayless glare the girls in bright dresses, strolling, looked like color photography.

Dark behind all the windows: not a light yet. The ingoing perspective looked meaning, noble and wide. But everybody was elsewhere—the polished street was empty but cars packed both the curbs under the trees. What was going on? The big tourer dribbled, slipped with animal nervousness between the static, locked cars each side of its way. The driver peered left and right with her face narrow, glanced from her wristwatch to the clock in the tower, sucked her lip, maneuvered for somewhere to pull in. The A.A. sign of the hotel hung out from under a balcony, over the steps. She edged in to where it said DO NOT PARK.

At the end of the hotel hall one electric light from the bar shone through a high-up panel: its yellow sifted onto the dusty dusk and a moth could be seen on the glass pane. At the door end came in street daylight, to fall weakly on prints on the oiled walls, on the magenta announcement strip of a cinema, on the mahogany bench near the receptionist's office, on the hatstand with two forgotten hats. The woman who had come breathlessly up the steps felt in her face a wall of indifference. The impetuous click of her heeled sandals on the linoleum brought no one to the receptionist's desk, and the drone of two talkers in the bar behind the glass panel seemed, like the light, to be blotted up, word by word. The little woman attacked the desk with her knuckles. "Is there nobody there—I say? Is there nobody *there?*"

"I am, I am. Wait now," said the hotel woman, who came impassively through the door from the bar. She reached up a hand and fumbled the desk light on, and by this with unwondering negligence studied the customer—the childish, blown little woman with wing-like eyebrows and eyes still unfocused after the long road. The hotel woman, bust on the desk, looked down slowly at the bare legs, the crumple-hemmed linen coat. "Can I do anything for you?" she said, when she had done.

"I want the telephone—want to put through a call!"

"You can of course," said the unmoved hotel woman. "Why not?" she added after consideration, handing across the keys of the telephone cabinet. The little woman made a slide for the cabinet: with her mouth to the mouthpiece, like a conspirator, she was urgently putting her number through. She came out then and ordered herself a drink.

"Is it long distance?"

"Mm-mm . . . What's on here? What are all those cars?"

"Oh, this evening's the dog racing."

"Is it?"

"Yes, it's the dog racing. We'd a crowd in here, but they're all gone on now."

"I wondered who they were," said the little woman, her eyes on the cabinet, sipping at her drink.

"Yes, they're at the dog racing. There's a wonderful crowd.

But I wouldn't care for it," said the hotel woman, fastidiously puckering up her forehead. "I went the one time, but it didn't fascinate me."

The other forgot to answer. She turned away with her drink, sat down, put the glass beside her on the mahogany bench and began to chafe the calves of her bare legs as though they were stiff or cold. A man clasping sheets of unfurled newspaper pushed his way with his elbow through the door from the bar. "What it says here," he said, shaking the paper with both hands, "is identically what I've been telling you."

"That proves nothing," said the hotel woman. "However, let it out of your hand." She drew the sheets of the paper from him and began to fold them into a wad. Her eyes moved like beetles over a top line. "That's an awful battle . . ."

"What battle?" exclaimed the little woman, stopping rubbing her legs but not looking up.

"An awful air battle. Destroying each other," the woman added, with a stern and yet voluptuous sigh. "Listen, would you like to wait in the lounge?"

"She'd be better there," put in the man who had brought the paper. "Better accommodation." His eyes watered slightly in the electric light. The little woman, sitting upright abruptly, looked defiantly, as though for the first time, at the two watching her from the desk. "Mr. Donovan has great opinions," said the hotel woman. "Will you move yourself out of here?" she asked Mr. Donovan. "This is very confined— *There's* your call, now!"

But the stranger had packed herself into the telephone box like a conjuror's lady preparing to disappear. *"Hullo?"* she was saying. "Hullo! I want to speak to—"

"—You are," the other voice cut in. "All right? Anything wrong?"

Her face flushed all over. "You sound nearer already! I've got to C——."

The easy, calm voice said: "Then you're coming along well."

"Glad, are you?" she said, in a quiver.

"Don't take it too fast," he said. "It's a treacherous light. Be easy, there's a good girl."

"You're a fine impatient man." His end of the line was silent. She went on: "I might stay here and go to the dog racing."

"Oh, is that tonight?" He went on to say equably (having stopped, as she saw it, and shaken the ash off the tip of his cigarette), "No, I shouldn't do that."

"Darling . . ."

"Emma . . . How is the Major?"

"He's all right," she said, rather defensively.

"I see," he said. "Everything quite O.K.?"

"In an hour, I'll be . . . where do you live."

"First gate on the left. Don't kill yourself, there's a good girl. Nothing's worth that. Remember we've got the night. By the way, where are you talking?"

"From the hotel." She nursed the receiver up close to her face and made a sound into it. Cutting that off she said: "Well, I'll hang up. I just . . ."

"Right," he said—and hung up.

Robinson, having hung up the receiver, walked back from the hall to the living room where his two guests were. He still wore a smile. The deaf woman at the table by the window was pouring herself out another cup of tea. "That will be very cold!" Robinson shouted—but she only replaced the cosy with a mysterious smile. "Let her be," said her brother. "Let her alone!"

The room in this uphill house was still light: through the open window came in a smell of stocks from the flower beds in the lawn. The only darkness lay in a belt of beech trees at the other side of the main road. From the grate, from the coal of an unlit fire came the fume of a cigarette burning itself out. Robinson still could not help smiling: he reclaimed his glass from

the mantelpiece and slumped back with it into his leather armchair in one of his loose, heavy, good-natured attitudes. But
Justin Cavey, in the armchair opposite, still looked crucified at
having the talk torn. "Beastly," he said, "you've a beastly telephone." Though he was in Robinson's house for the first time,
his sense of attraction to people was marked, early, by just this
intransigence and this fretfulness.

"It is and it's not," said Robinson. That was that. "Where
had we got to?" he amiably asked.

The deaf woman, turning round from the window, gave the
two men, or gave the air between them, a penetrating smile.
Her brother, with a sort of lurch at his pocket, pulled out a
new packet of cigarettes: ignoring Robinson's held-out cigarette case he frowned and split the cellophane with his thumbnail. But, as though his sister had put a hand on his shoulder,
his tension could be almost seen to relax. The impersonal, patient look of the thinker appeared in his eyes, behind the spectacles. Justin was a city man, a blackcoat, down here (where his
sister lived) on holiday. Other summer holidays before this he
had traveled in France, Germany, Italy: he disliked the chaotic
"scenery" of his own land. He was down here with Queenie
this summer only because of the war, which had locked him in:
duty seemed to him better than failed pleasure. His father had
been a doctor in this place; now his sister lived on in two
rooms in the square—for fear Justin should not be comfortable
she had taken a room for him at the hotel. His holiday with his
sister, his holiday in this underwater, weedy region of memory,
his holiday on which, almost every day, he had to pass the
doors of their old home, threatened Justin with a pressure he
could not bear. He had to share with Queenie, as he shared the
dolls' house meals cooked on the oil stove behind her sitting-
room screen, the solitary and almost fairylike world created by
her deafness. Her deafness broke down his only defense, talk.
He was exposed to the odd, immune, plumbing looks she was
for ever passing over his face. He could not deflect the tilted

blue of her eyes. The things she said out of nowhere, things with no surface context, were never quite off the mark. She was not all solicitude; she loved to be teasing him.

In her middle age Queenie was very pretty: her pointed face had the coloring of an imperceptibly fading pink-and-white sweet pea. This hot summer her artless dresses, with their little lace collars, were mottled over with flowers, mauve and blue. Up the glaring main street she carried a *poult-de-soie* parasol. Her rather dark first-floor rooms faced north, over the square with its grass and lime trees: the crests of great mountains showed above the opposite façades. She would slip in and out on her own errands, as calm as a cat, and Justin, waiting for her at one of her windows, would see her cross the square in the noon sunshine with hands laced over her forehead into a sort of porch. The little town, though strung on a through road, was an outpost under the mountains: in its quick-talking, bitter society she enjoyed, to a degree that surprised Justin, her privileged place. She was woman enough to like to take the man Justin round with her and display him; they went out to afternoon or to evening tea, and in those drawing rooms of tinted lace and intently staring family photographs, among octagonal tables and painted cushions, Queenie, with her cotton gloves in her lap, well knew how to contribute, while Justin talked, her airy, brilliant, secretive smiling and looking on. For his part, he was man enough to respond to being shown off— besides, he was eased by these breaks in their tête-à-tête. Above all, he was glad, for these hours or two of chatter, not to have to face the screen of his own mind, on which the distortion of every one of his images, the war-broken towers of Europe, constantly stood. The immolation of what had been his own intensely had been made, he could only feel, without any choice of his. In the heart of the neutral Irishman indirect suffering pulled like a crooked knife. So he acquiesced to, and devoured, society: among the doctors, the solicitors, the auctioneers, the bank people of this little town he renewed old acquaintanceships and developed new. He was content to bloom, for this settled number of weeks—so unlike was this to his monkish life in the city—in a sort of tenebrous popularity. He attempted to check his solitary arrogance. His celibacy and his studentish manner could still, although he was past forty, make him acceptable as a young man. In the mornings he read late in his hotel bed; he got up to take his solitary walks; he returned to flick at his black shoes with Queenie's duster and set off with Queenie on their tea-table rounds. They had been introduced to Robinson, factory manager, in the hall of the house of the secretary of the tennis club.

Robinson did not frequent drawing rooms. He had come here only three years ago, and had at first been taken to be a bachelor—he was a married man living apart from his wife. The resentment occasioned by this discovery had been aggravated by Robinson's not noticing it: he worked at very high pressure in his factory office, and in his off times his high-powered car was to be seen streaking too gaily out of the town. When he was met, his imperturbable male personality stood out to the women unpleasingly, and stood out most of all in that married society in which women aspire to break the male in a man. Husbands slipped him in for a drink when they were alone or shut themselves up with him in the dining room. Justin had already sighted him in the hotel bar. When Robinson showed up, late, at the tennis club, his manner with women was easy and teasing, but abstract and perfectly automatic. From this had probably come the legend that he liked women "only in one way." From the first time Justin encountered Robinson, he had felt a sort of anxious, disturbed attraction to the big, fair, smiling, offhand, cold-minded man. He felt impelled by Robinson's unmoved physical presence into all sorts of aberrations of talk and mind; he committed, like someone waving an anxious flag, all sorts of absurdities, as though this type of creature had been a woman; his talk became exaggeratedly cerebral, and he became prone, like a perverse person in love, to expose all his own piques, crotchets, and weaknesses. One night in the hotel bar with Robinson he had talked until he burst into tears. Robinson had on him the touch of some foreign sun. The acquaintanceship—it could not be called more—was no more than an accident of this narrowed summer. For Justin it had taken the place of travel. The two men were so far off each other's beat that in a city they would certainly not have met.

Asked to drop in some evening or any evening, the Caveys had tonight taken Robinson at his word. Tonight, the night of the first visit, Justin's high, rather bleak forehead had flushed from the moment he rang the bell. With Queenie behind his shoulder, in muslin, he had flinched confronting the housekeeper. Queenie, like the rest of the town ladies, had done no more till now than go by Robinson's gate.

For her part, Queenie showed herself happy to penetrate into what she had called "the china house." On its knoll over the main road, just outside the town, Bellevue did look like china up on a mantelpiece—it was a compact, stucco house with moldings, recently painted a light blue. From the lawn set with pampas and crescent-shaped flower beds the hum of Robinson's motor mower passed in summer over the sleepy town. And when winter denuded the trees round them the polished windows, glass porch, and empty conservatory sent out, on mornings of frosty sunshine, a rather mischievous and uncaring flash. The almost sensuous cleanness of his dwelling was reproduced in the person of Robinson—about his ears, jaw, collar, and close-clipped nails. The approach the Caveys had walked up showed the broad, decided tire prints of his car.

"Where had we got to?" Robinson said again.

"I was saying we should have to find a new form."

"Of course you were," agreed Robinson. "That was it." He nodded over the top of Justin's head.

"A new form for thinking and feeling . . ."

"But one thinks what one happens to think, or feels what

one happens to feel. That is as just so happens—I should have thought. One either does or one doesn't?"

"One doesn't!" cried Justin. "That's what I've been getting at. For some time we have neither thought nor felt. Our faculties have slowed down without our knowing—they had stopped without our knowing! We know now. Now that there's enough death to challenge being alive we're facing it that, anyhow, we don't live. We're confronted by the impossibility *of* living—unless we can break through to something else. There's been a stop in our senses and in our faculties that's made everything round us so much dead matter—and dead matter we couldn't even displace. We can no longer express ourselves: what we say doesn't even approximate to reality; it only approximates to what's been said. I say, this war's an awful illumination; it's destroyed our dark; we have to see where we are. Immobilized, God help us, and each so far apart that we can't even try to signal each other. And our currency's worthless—our 'ideas,' so on, so on. We've got to mint a new one. We've got to break through to the new form—it needs genius. We're precipitated, this moment, between genius and death. I tell you, we must have genius to live at all."

"I am certainly dished, then," said Robinson. He got up and looked for Justin's empty glass and took it to the sideboard where the decanters were.

"We have it!" cried Justin, smiting the arm of his chair. "I salute your genius, Robinson, but I mistrust my own."

"That's very nice of you," said Robinson. "I agree with you that this war makes one think. I was in the last, but I don't remember thinking: I suppose possibly one had no time. Of course, these days in business one comes up against this war the whole way through. And to tell you the truth," said Robinson, turning round, "I do like my off times to *be* my off times, because with this and then that they are precious few. So I don't really think as much as I might—though I see how one might always begin. You don't think thinking gets one a bit rattled?"

"I don't think!" said Justin violently.

"Well, you should know," said Robinson, looking at his thumbnail. "I should have thought you did. From the way you talk."

"I couldn't think if I wanted: I've lost my motivation. I taste the dust in the street and I smell the limes in the square and I beat round inside this beastly shell of the past among images that all the more torment me as they lose any sense that they had. As for feeling—"

"You don't think you find it a bit slow here? Mind you, I haven't a word against this place but it's not a place I'd choose for an off time—"

"—My dear Robinson," Justin said, in a mincing, school-masterish tone, "You seem blind to our exquisite sociabilities."

"Pack of old cats," said Robinson amiably.

"You suggest I should get away for a bit of fun?"

"Well, I did mean that."

"I find my own fun," said Justin, "I'm torn, here, by every single pang of annihilation. But that's what I look for; that's what I want completed; that's the whole of what I want to embrace. On the far side of the nothing—my new form. Scrap 'me'; scrap my wretched identity and you'll bring to the open some bud of life. I *not* 'I'—I'd be the world . . . You're right: what you would call thinking does get me rattled. I only what you call think to excite myself. Take myself away, and I'd *think*. I might see; I might feel purely; I might even love—"

"Fine," agreed Robinson, not quite easy. He paused and seemed to regard what Justin had just said—at the same time, he threw a glance of perceptible calculation at the electric clock on the mantelpiece. Justin halted and said: "You give me too much to drink."

"You feel this war may improve us?" said Robinson.

"What's love like?" Justin said suddenly.

Robinson paused for just less than a second in the act of lighting a cigarette. He uttered a shortish, temporizing, and, for him, unnaturally loud laugh.

Queenie felt the vibration and turned round, withdrawing her arm from the windowsill. She had been looking intently, between the clumps of pampas, down the lawn to the road: cyclists and walkers on their way into town kept passing Robinson's open gate. Across the road, above the demesne wall, the dark beeches let through glitters of sky, and the color and scent of the mown lawn and the flowers seemed, by some increase of evening, lifted up to the senses as though a new current flowed underneath. Queenie saw with joy in her own mind what she could not from her place in the window see—the blue china house, with all its reflecting windows, perched on its knoll in the brilliant, fading air. They are too rare—visions of where we are.

When the shock of the laugh made her turn round, she still saw day in Robinson's picture frames and on the chromium fingers of the clock. She looked at Robinson's head, dropped back after the laugh on the leather scroll of his chair: her eyes went from him to Justin. "Did you two not hit it off?"

Robinson laughed again, this time much more naturally: he emitted a sound like that from inside a furnace in which something is being consumed. Letting his head fall sideways towards Queenie, he seemed to invite her into his mood. "The way things come out is sometimes funny," he said to Justin, "if you know what I mean."

"No, I don't," Justin said stonily.

"I bet your sister does."

"You didn't know what I meant. Anything I may have said about your genius I do absolutely retract."

"Look here, I'm sorry," Robinson said, "I probably took you up all wrong."

"On the contrary: the mistake was mine."

"You know, it's funny about your sister: I never can realize she can't hear. She seems so much one of the party. Would she be fond of children?"

"You mean, why did she not marry?"

"Good God, no—I only had an idea . . ."

Justin went on: "There was some fellow once, but I never heard more of him. You'd have to be very oncoming, I daresay, to make any way with a deaf girl."

"No, I meant my children," said Robinson. He had got up, and he took from his mantelpiece two of the photographs in silver frames. With these he walked down the room to Queenie, who received them with her usual eagerness and immediately turned with them to the light. Justin saw his sister's profile bent forward in study and saw Robinson standing above her leaning against the window frame. When Robinson met an upward look from Queenie he nodded and touched himself on the chest. "I can see that—aren't they very like you?" she said. He pointed to one picture then held up ten fingers, then to the other and held up eight. "The fair little fellow's more like you, the bold one. The dark one has more the look of a girl—but he will grow up manly, I daresay . . ." With this she went back to the photographs: she did not seem anxious to give them up, and Robinson made no movement to take them from her— with Queenie the act of looking was always reflective and slow. To Justin the two silhouettes against the window looked wedded and welded by the dark. "They are both against me," Justin thought. "She does not hear with her ears, he does not hear with his mind. No wonder they can communicate."

"It's a wonder," she said, "that you have no little girl."

Robinson went back for another photograph—but, standing still with a doubtful look at Queenie, he passed his hand, as though sadly expunging something, backwards and forwards across the glass. "She's quite right; we did have a girl," he said. "But I don't know how to tell her the kid's dead."

* * *

Sixty miles away, the Major was making his last round through the orchards before shutting up the house. By this time the bronze-green orchard dusk was intense; the clumped curves of the fruit were hardly to be distinguished among the leaves. The brilliance of evening, in which he had watched Emma driving away, was now gone from the sky. Now and then in the grass his foot knocked a dropped apple—he would sigh, stoop rather stiffly, pick up the apple, examine it with the pad of his thumb for bruises, and slip it, tenderly as though it had been an egg, into a baggy pocket of his tweed coat. This was not a good apple year. There was something standardized, uncomplaining about the Major's movements—you saw a tall, unmilitary-looking man with a stoop and a thinnish, drooping mustache. He often wore a slight frown, of doubt or preoccupation. This frown had intensified in the last months.

As he approached the house he heard the wireless talking, and saw one lamp at the distant end of the drawing room where his aunt sat. At once, the picture broke up—she started, switched off the wireless, and ran down the room to the window. You might have thought the room had burst into flames. "Quick!" she cried. "Oh, gracious, quick!—I believe it's the telephone."

The telephone was at the other side of the house—before he got there he heard the bell ringing. He put his hands in his pockets to keep the apples from bumping as he legged it rapidly down the corridor. When he unhooked on his wife's voice he could not help saying haggardly: "You all right?"

"Of course. I just thought I'd say good night."

"That was nice of you," he said, puzzled. "How is the car running?"

"Like a bird," she said in a singing voice. "How are you all?"

"Well, I was just coming in; Aunt Fran's in the drawing room listening to something on the wireless, and I made the children turn in half an hour ago."

"You'll go up to them?"

"Yes, I was just going." For a moment they both paused on the line, then he said: "Where have you got to now?"

"I'm at T—— now, at the hotel in the square."

"At T——? Aren't you taking it rather fast?"

"It's a lovely night; it's an empty road."

"Don't be too hard on the car, she—"

"Oh, I know," she said, in the singing voice again. "At C—— I did try to stop, but there was a terrible crowd there: dog racing. So I came on. Darling . . . ?"

"Yes?"

"It's a lovely night, isn't it?"

"Yes, I was really quite sorry to come in. I shall shut up the house now, then go up to the children; then I expect I'll have a word or two with Aunt Fran."

"I see. Well, I'd better be pushing on."

"They'll be sitting up for you, won't they?"

"Surely," said Emma quickly.

"Thank you for ringing up, dear: it was thoughtful of you."

"I was thinking about you."

He did not seem to hear this. "Well, take care of yourself. Have a nice time."

"Good night," she said. But the Major had hung up.

In the drawing room Aunt Fran had not gone back to the wireless. Beside the evening fire lit for her age, she sat rigid, face turned to the door, plucking round and round the rings on her left hand. She wore a foulard dress, net jabot, and boned-up collar, of the type ladies wear to dine in private hotels. In the lamplight her waxy features appeared blurred, even effaced. The drawing room held a crowd of chintz-covered chairs, inlaid tables, and wool-worked stools; very little in it was antique, but nothing was strikingly up-to-date. There were cabinets of not rare china, and more blue-and-white plates, in metal clamps, hung in lines up the walls between watercolors. A vase of pink roses arranged by the governess already dropped petals on the piano. In one corner stood a harp with two broken strings—when a door slammed or one made a sudden movement this harp gave out a faint vibration or twang. The silence for miles around this obscure country house seemed to gather inside the folds of the curtains and to dilute the indoor air like a mist. This room Emma liked too little to touch already felt the touch of decay; it threw lifeless reflections into the two mirrors—the walls were green. Aunt Fran's body was stranded here like some object on the bed of a pool that has run dry. The magazine that she had been looking at had slipped from her lap to the black fur rug.

As her nephew appeared in the drawing-room door Aunt Fran fixed him urgently with her eyes. *"Nothing wrong?"*

"No, no—that was Emma."

"What's happened?"

"Nothing. She rang up to say good night."

"But she had said good night," said Aunt Fran in her troubled way. "She said good night to us when she was in the car. You remember, it was nearly night when she left. It seemed late to be starting to go so far. She had the whole afternoon, but she kept putting off, putting off. She seemed to me undecided up to the very last."

The Major turned his back on his aunt and began to unload his pockets, carefully placing the apples, two by two, in a row along the chiffonier. "Still, it's nice for her having this trip," he said.

"There was a time in the afternoon," said Aunt Fran, "when I thought she was going to change her mind. However, she's there now—did you say?"

"Almost," he said, "not quite. Will you be all right if I go and shut up the house? And I said I would look in on the girls."

"Suppose the telephone rings?"

"I don't think it will, again. The exchange will be closing, for one thing."

"This afternoon," said Aunt Fran, "it rang four times."

She heard him going from room to room, unfolding and barring the heavy shutters and barring and chaining the front door. She could begin to feel calmer now that the house was a fortress against the wakeful night. "Hi!" she called, "don't forget the window in here"—looking back over her shoulder into the muslin curtains that seemed to crepitate with dark air. So he came back, with his flat, unexpectant step. "I'm not cold," she said, "but I don't like dark coming in."

He shuttered the window. "I'll be down in a minute."

"Then we might sit together?"

"Yes, Aunt Fran: certainly."

The children, who had been talking, dropped their voices when they heard their father's step on the stairs. Their two beds creaked as they straightened themselves and lay silent, in social, expectant attitudes. Their room smelled of toothpaste; the white presses blotted slowly into the white walls. The window was open, the blind up, so in here darkness was incomplete—obscured, the sepia picture of the Good Shepherd hung over the mantelpiece. "It's all right" they said, "we are quite awake." So the Major came round and halted between the two beds. "Sit on mine," said Di nonchalantly. "It's my turn to have a person tonight."

"Why did Mother ring up?" said Vivie, scrambling up on her pillow.

"Now how on earth did *you* know?"

"We knew by your voice—we couldn't hear what you said. We were only at the top of the stairs. Why did she?"

"To tell me to tell you to be good."

"She's said that," said Vivie, impatient. "What did she say truly?"

"Just good night."

"Oh. Is she there?"

"Where?"

"Where she said she was going to."

"Not quite—nearly."

"Goodness!" Di said; "it seems years since she went." The two children lay cryptic and still. Then Di went on: "Do you know what Aunt Fran said because Mother went away without any stockings?"

"No," said the Major, "and never mind."

"Oh, *I* don't mind," Di said, "I just heard." "And I heard," said Vivie: she could be felt opening her eyes wide, and the Major could just see, on the pillow, an implacable miniature of his wife's face. Di went on: "She's so frightened something will happen."

"Aunt Fran is?"

"She's always frightened of that."

"She is very fond of us all."

"Oh," burst out Vivie, "but Mother likes things to happen. She was whistling all the time she was packing up. Can't *we* have a treat tomorrow?"

"Mother'll be back tomorrow."

"But *can't* we have a treat?"

"We'll see; we'll ask Mother," the Major said.

"Oh, yes, but suppose she didn't come back?"

"Look, it's high time you two went to sleep."

"We can't: we've got all sorts of ideas ... *You* say something, Daddy. Tell us something. Invent."

"Say what?" said the Major.

"Oh goodness," Vivie said; *"something.* What do you say to Mother?"

He went downstairs to Aunt Fran with their dissatisfied kisses stamped on his cheek. When he had gone Di fanned herself with the top of her sheet. "What makes him so disappointed, do you know?"

"I know, he thinks about the war."

But it was Di who, after the one question, unlocked all over and dropped plumb asleep. It was Vivie who, turning over and

over, watched in the sky behind the cross of the window the
tingling particles of the white dark, who heard the moth between the two window sashes, who fancied she heard apples
drop in the grass. One arbitrary line only divided this child
from the animal: all her senses stood up, wanting to run the
night. She swung her legs out of bed and pressed the soles of
her feet on the cool floor. She got right up and stepped out of
her nightdress and set out to walk the house in her skin. From
each room she went into the human order seemed to have
lapsed—discovered by sudden light, the chairs and tables
seemed set round for a mouse's party on a gigantic scale. She
stood for some time outside the drawing-room door and heard
the unliving voices of the Major and Aunt. She looked
through the ajar door to the kitchen and saw a picked bone
and a teapot upon the table and a maid lumped mute in a
man's arms. She attempted the front door, but did not dare to
touch the chain: she could not get out of the house. She returned to the schoolroom, drawing her brows together, and
straddled the rocking horse they had not ridden for years. The
furious bumping of the rockers woke the canaries under their
cover: they set up a wiry springing in their cage. She dis-
mounted, got out the box of chalks, and began to tattoo her
chest, belly, and thighs with stars and snakes, red, yellow, and
blue. Then, taking the box of chalks with her, she went to her
mother's room for a look in the long glass—in front of this she
attempted to tattoo her behind. After this she bent right down
and squinted, upside down between her legs, at the bedroom—the electric light over the dressing table poured into
the vacantly upturned mirror and on to Emma's left-behind silver things. The anarchy she felt all through the house tonight
made her, when she had danced in front of the long glass,
climb up to dance on the big bed. The springs bounced her
higher and higher; chalk dust flew from her body onto the
fleece of the blankets, onto the two cold pillows that she was

trampling out of their place. The bed castors lunged, under her springing, over the threadbare pink bridal carpet of Emma's room.

Attacked by the castors, the chandelier in the drawing room tinkled sharply over Aunt Fran's head.

She at once raised her eyes to the ceiling. "Something has got in," she said calmly—and, rising, made for the drawing-room door. By reflex, the Major rose to stop her: he sighed and put his weak whiskey down. "Never mind," he said, "Aunt Fran. It's probably nothing. I'll go."

Whereupon, his Aunt Fran wheeled round on him with her elbows up like a bird's wings. Her wax features sprang into stony prominence. "It's never me, never me, never me! Whatever *I* see, whatever *I* hear it's 'nothing,' though the house might fall down. You keep everything back from me. No one speaks the truth to me but the man on the wireless. Always things being said on the telephone, always things being moved about, always Emma off at the end of the house singing, always the children hiding away. I am never told, never told, never told. I get the one answer, 'Nothing.' I am expected to wait here. No one comes near the drawing room. I am never allowed to go and see!"

"If that's how you feel," he said, "do certainly go." He thought: it's all right, I locked the house.

So it was Aunt Fran's face, with the forehead lowered, that came by inches round Emma's door. She appeared to present her forehead as a sort of a buffer, obliquely looked from below it, did not speak. Her glance, arriving gradually at its object, took in the child and the whole room. Vivie paused on the bed, transfixed, breathless, her legs apart. Her heart thumped; her ears drummed; her cheeks burned. To break up the canny and comprehensive silence she said loudly: "I am all over snakes."

"So this is what . . ." Aunt Fran said. "So this is what . . ."

"I'll get off this bed, if you don't like."

"The bed you were born in," said Aunt Fran.

Vivie did not know what to do; she jumped off the bed saying. "No one told me not to."

"Do you not know what is wicked?" said Aunt Fran—but with no more than estranged curiosity. She approached and began to try to straighten the bed, her unused hands making useless passes over the surface, brushing chalk dust deeper into the fleece. All of a sudden, Vivie appeared to feel some majestic effluence from her aunt's person: she lagged round the bed to look at the stooping, set face, at the mouth held in a curve like a dead smile, at the veins in the downcast eyelids and the backs of the hands. Aunt Fran did not hurry her ceremonial fumbling; she seemed to exalt the moment that was so fully hers. She picked a pillow up by its frill and placed it high on the bolster.

"That's Mother's pillow," said Vivie.

"Did you say your prayers tonight?"

"Oh, *yes.*"

"They didn't defend you. Better say them again. Kneel down and say to Our Lord—"

"In my skin?"

Aunt Fran looked directly at, then away from, Vivie's body, as though for the first time. She drew the eiderdown from the foot of the bed and made a half-blind sweep at Vivie with it, saying: "Wrap up, wrap up." "Oh, they'll come off—my snakes!" said Vivie, backing away. But Aunt Fran, as though the child were on fire, put into motion an extraordinary strength—she rolled, pressed, and pounded Vivie up in the eiderdown until only the prisoner's dark eyes, so like her mother's, were left free to move wildly outside the great sausage, of padded taffeta, pink.

Aunt Fran, embracing the sausage firmly, repeated: "Now say to Our Lord—"

* * *

Shutting the door of her own bedroom, Aunt Fran felt her heart beat. The violence of the stranger within her ribs made her sit down on the ottoman—meanwhile, her little clock on the mantelpiece loudly and, it seemed to her, slowly ticked. Her window was shut, but the pressure of night silence made itself felt behind the blind, on the glass.

Round the room, on ledges and brackets, stood the fetishes she traveled through life with. They were mementoes—photos in little warped frames, musty, round straw boxes, china kittens, palm crosses, the three Japanese monkeys, *bambini,* a Lincoln Imp, a merry-thought pen wiper, an ivory spinning wheel from Cologne. From these objects the original virtue had by now almost evaporated. These gifts' givers, known on her lonely journey, were by now faint as their photographs: she no longer knew, now, where anyone was. All the more, her nature clung to these objects that moved with her slowly towards the dark.

Her room, the room of a person tolerated, by now gave off the familiar smell of herself—the smell of the old. A little book wedged the mirror at the angle she liked. When she was into her ripplecloth dressing gown she brushed and plaited her hair and took out her teeth. She wound her clock and, with hand still trembling a little, lighted her own candle on the commode, then switched off her nephew's electric light. The room contracted round the crocus of flame as she knelt down slowly beside her bed—but while she said the Lord's Prayer she could not help listening, wondering what kept the Major so long downstairs. She never felt free to pray till she had heard the last door shut, till she could relax her watch on the house. She never could pray until they were *all* prostrate—loaned for at least some hours to innocence, sealed by the darkness over their lids.

Tonight she could not attempt to lift up her heart. She could, however, abase herself, and she abased herself for them all. The evil of the moment down in the drawing room, the moment when she had cried, "It is never me!" clung like a smell to her, so closely that she had been eager to get her clothes off, and did not like, even now, to put her hands to her face.

Who shall be their judge? Not I.

The blood of the world is poisoned, feels Aunt Fran, with her forehead over the eiderdown. Not a pure drop comes out at any prick—yes, even the heroes shed black blood. The solitary watcher retreats step by step from his post—who shall stem the black tide coming in? There are no more children: the children are born knowing. The shadow rises up the cathedral tower, up the side of the pure hill. There is not even the past: our memories share with us the infected zone; not a memory does not lead up to this. Each moment is everywhere, it holds the war in its crystal; there is no elsewhere, no other place. Not a benediction falls on this apart house of the Major; the enemy is within it, creeping about. Each heart here falls to the enemy.

So this is what goes on ...

Emma flying away—and not saying why, or where. And to wrap the burning child up did not put out the fire. You cannot look at the sky without seeing the shadow, the men destroying each other. What is the matter tonight—is there a battle? This is a threatened night.

Aunt Fran sags on her elbows; her knees push desperately in the woolly rug. She cannot even repent; she is capable of no act; she is undone. She gets up and eats a biscuit, and looks at the little painting of Mont Blanc on the little easel beside her clock. She still does not hear the Major come up to bed.

Queenie understood that the third child, the girl, was dead: she gave back the photograph rather quickly, as though unbearable sadness emanated from it. Justin, however, came down the room and looked at the photograph over Robinson's shoulder—at the rather vulgar, frank, blonde little face. He found it hard to believe that a child of Robinson's should have chosen the part of death. He then went back to the table and picked up, with a jerky effrontery, the photographs of the two little boys. "Do they never come here?" he said. "You have plenty of room for them."

"I daresay they will; I mean to fix up something. Just now they're at Greystones," Robinson said—he then looked quite openly at the clock.

"With their mother?" Justin said, in a harsh impertinent voice.

"Yes, with my wife."

"So you keep up the two establishments?"

Even Robinson glanced at Justin with some surprise. "If you call it that," he said indifferently. "I rather landed myself with this place, really—as a matter of fact, when I moved in it looked as though things might work out differently. First I stopped where you are, at the hotel, but I do like to have a place of my own. One feels freer, for one thing."

"There's a lot in that," said Justin, with an oblique smile. "Our local ladies think you keep a Bluebeard's castle up here."

"What, corpses?" Robinson said, surprised.

"Oh yes, they think you're the devil."

"Who, me?" replied Robinson, busy replacing photographs on the mantelpiece. "That's really very funny: I'd no idea. I suppose they may think I've been pretty slack—but I'm no good at teafights, as a matter of fact. But I can't see what else can be eating them. What ought I to do then? Throw a party here? I will if your sister'll come and pour out tea—but I don't think I've really got enough chairs . . . I hope," he added, looking at Queenie, *"she* doesn't think it's not all aboveboard here?"

"You're forgetting again: she misses the talk, poor girl."

"She doesn't look very worried."

"I daresay she's seldom been happier. She's built up quite a romance about this house. She has a world to herself—I could envy her."

Robinson contrived to give the impression that he did not wish to have Queenie discussed—partly because he owned her, he understood her, partly because he wished to discuss nothing: it really was time for his guests to go. Though he was back again in his armchair, regard for time appeared in his attitude. Justin could not fail to connect this with the telephone and the smile that had not completely died. It became clear, staringly clear, that throughout the evening his host had been no more than marking time. This made Justin say, "Yes" (in a loud, pertinacious voice), "this evening's been quite an event for us. Your house has more than its legend, Robinson; it has really remarkable character. However, all good things—" Stiff with anger, he stood up.

"Must you?" said Robinson, rising, "I'm so sorry."

Lighting-up time, fixed by Nature, had passed. The deaf woman, from her place in the window, had been watching lights of cars bend over the hill. Turning with the main road, that had passed the foot of the mountains, each car now drove a shaft of extreme brilliance through the dark below Robinson's pampas grass. Slipping, dropping with a rush past the gate, illuminating the dust on the opposite wall, car after car vanished after its light—there was suddenly quite a gust of them, as though the mountain country, before sleeping, had stood up and shaken them from its folds. The release of movement excited Queenie—that and the beat of light's wings on her face. She turned round very reluctantly as Justin approached and began to make signs to her.

"Why, does Mr. Robinson want us to go?" she said.

"That's the last thing I want!" shouted Robinson.

("She can't hear you.")

"Christ . . ." said Robinson, rattled. He turned the lights on—the three, each with a different face of despair, looked at each other across the exposed room, across the tea tray on the circular table and the superb leather backs of the chairs. "My brother thinks we've kept you too long," she said—and as a lady she looked a little shaken, for the first time unsure of her-self. Robinson would not for worlds have had this happen; he strode over and took and nursed her elbow, which tensed then relaxed gently inside the muslin sleeve. He saw, outdoors, his window cast on the pampas, saw the whole appearance of shat-tered night. She looked for reassurance into his face, and he saw the delicate lines in hers.

"And look how late it's got, Mr. Robinson!"

"It's not that," he said in his naturally low voice, "But—"

A car pulled up at the gate. Alarmed by the lit window it cut its lights off and could be felt to crouch there, attentive, docile, cautious, waiting to turn in. "Your friend is arriving," Justin said.

On that last lap of her drive, the eighteen miles of flat road along the base of the mountains, the last tingling phase of darkness had settled down. Grassy sharpness passed from the mountains' outline, the patches of firs, the gleam of watery ditch. The west sky had gradually drunk its yellow and the ridged heights that towered over her right hand became im-mobile cataracts, sensed not seen. Animals rising out of the ditches turned to Emma's headlamps green lamp-eyes. She felt the shudder of night, the contracting bodies of things. The quick air sang in her ears; she drove very fast. At the crossroads above Robinson's town she pulled round in a wide swerve: she saw the lemon lights of the town strung along under the black trees, the pavements, and the pale, humble houses below her in a faint, mysterious glare as she slipped down the funnel of hill to Robinson's gate. (The first white gate on the left, you can-not miss it, he'd said.) From the road she peered up the lawn and saw, between pampas tufts, three people upright in his lit room. So she pulled up and switched her lights and her engine off and sat crouching in her crouching car in the dark—night began to creep up her bare legs. Now the glass porch sprang into prominence like a lantern—she saw people stiffly saying good-bye. Down the drive came a man and woman almost in flight; not addressing each other, not looking back—putting the back of a fist to her mouth quickly Emma checked the uprush of an uncertain laugh. She marked a lag in the steps— turning their heads quickly the man and woman looked with involuntary straightness into the car, while her eyes were glued to their silhouettes. The two turned down to the town and she turned in at the gate.

Farouche, with her tentative little swagger and childish, pleading air of delinquency, Emma came to a halt in Robinson's living room. He had pulled down the blind. She kept recoiling and blinking and drawing her fingers over her eyes, till Robinson turned off the top light. "Is that that?" There was only the reading lamp.

She rested her shoulder below his and grappled their enlaced fingers closer together as though trying to draw calmness from him. Standing against him, close up under his height, she held her head up and began to look round the room. "You're whistling something," she said, after a moment or two.

"I only mean, take your time."

"Why, am I nervous?" she said.

"Darling, you're like a bat in out of the night. I told you not to come along too fast."

"I see now, I came too early," she said. "Why didn't you tell me you had a party? Who were they? What were they doing here?"

"Oh, they're just people in this place. He's a bit screwy and she's deaf, but I like them, as a matter of fact."

"They're mackintoshy sort of people," she said. "But I always thought you lived all alone . . . Is there anyone else in the house now?"

"Not a mouse," said Robinson, without change of expression. "My housekeeper's gone off for the night."

"I see," said Emma. "Will you give me a drink?"

She sat down where Justin had just been sitting, and, bending forward with a tremulous frown, began to brush ash from the arm of the chair. You could feel the whole of her hesitate. Robinson, without hesitation, came and sat easily on the arm of the chair from which she had brushed the ash. "It's sometimes funny," he said, "when people drop in like that. 'My God,' I thought when I saw them, 'what an evening to choose.' " He slipped his hand down between the brown velvet cushion and Emma's spine, then spread the broad of his hand against the small of her back. Looking kindly down at her closed eyelids he went on: "However, it all went off all right. Oh, and there's one thing I'd like to tell you—that chap called me a genius."

"How would he know?" said Emma, opening her eyes.

"We never got that clear. I was rather out of my depth. His sister was deaf ..." here Robinson paused, bent down and passed his lips absently over Emma's forehead. "Or did I tell you that?"

"Yes, you told me that ... Is it true that this house is blue?"

"You'll see tomorrow."

"There'll hardly be time, darling; I shall hardly see this house in the daylight. I must go on to—where I'm supposed to be."

"At any rate, I'm glad that was all O.K. They're not on the telephone, where you're going?"

"No, it's all right; they're not on the telephone ... *You'll* have to think of something that went wrong with my car."

"That will all keep," said Robinson. "Here you are."

"Yes, here I am." She added: "The night was lovely," speaking more sadly than she knew. Yes, here she was, being settled down to as calmly as he might have settled down to a meal. Her naivety as a lover ... She could not have said, for instance, how much the authoritative male room—the electric clock, the sideboard, the unlit grate, the cold of the leather chairs—put, at every moment when he did not touch her, a gulf between her and him. She turned her head to the window. "I smell flowers."

"Yes, I've got three flower beds."

"Darling, for a minute could we go out?"

She moved from his touch and picked up Queenie's tea tray and asked if she could put it somewhere else. Holding the tray (and given countenance by it) she halted in front of the photographs. "Oh . . ." she said. "Yes. Why?" "I wish in a way you hadn't got any children." "I don't see why I shouldn't have: you have."

"Yes, I . . . But Vivie and Di are not so much *like* children—"

"If they're like you," he said, "those two will be having a high old time, with the cat away—"

"Oh darling, I'm not the cat."

In the kitchen (to put the tray down) she looked round: it shone with tiling and chromium and there seemed to be switches in every place. "What a whole lot of gadgets you have," she said. "Look at all those electric . . ." "Yes I like them." "They must cost a lot of money. My kitchen's all over black lead and smoke and hooks. My cook would hate a kitchen like this."

"I always forget that you have a cook." He picked up an electric torch and they went out. Going along the side of the house, Robinson played a mouse of light on the wall. "Look, really blue." But she only looked absently. "Yes—But have I been wrong to come?" He led her off the gravel onto the lawn, till they reached the edge of a bed of stocks. Then he firmly said: "That's for you to say, my dear girl."

"I know it's hardly a question—I hardly know you, do I?"

"We'll be getting to know each other," said Robinson.

After a minute she let go of his hand and knelt down abruptly beside the flowers: she made movements like scooping the scent up and laving her face in it—he, meanwhile, lighted a cigarette and stood looking down. "I'm glad you like my garden," he said. "You feel like getting fond of the place?"

"You say you forget that I have a cook."

"Look, sweet, if you can't get that off your mind you'd better get in your car and go straight home ... But you will."

"Aunt Fran's so old, too old; it's not nice. And the Major keeps thinking about the war. And the children don't think I am good; I regret that."

"You have got a nerve," he said, "but I love that. You're with me. Aren't you with me?—Come out of that flower bed."

They walked to the brow of the lawn; the soft feather-plumes of the pampas rose up a little over her head as she stood by him overlooking the road. She shivered. "What are those trees?" "The demesne—I know they burnt down the castle years ago. The demesne's great for couples." "What's in there?" "Nothing, I don't think; just the ruin, a lake ..."

"I wish—"

"Now, what?"

"I wish we had more time."

"Yes: we don't want to stay out all night."

So taught, she smothered the last of her little wishes for consolation. Her shyness of further words between them became extreme; she was becoming frightened of Robinson's stern, experienced delicacy on the subject of love. Her adventure became the quiet practice with him. The adventure (even, the pilgrimage) died at its root, in the childish part of her mind. When he had headed her off the cytherean terrain—the leaf-drowned castle ruin, the lake—she thought for a minute he had broken her heart, and she knew now he had broken her fairytale. He seemed content—having lit a new cigarette—to wait about in his garden for a few minutes longer: not poetry but a sort of tactile wisdom came from the firmness, lawn, under their feet. The white gateposts, the boles of beeches above the dust-whitened wall were just seen in reflected light from the town. There was no moon, but dry, tense, translucent darkness: no dew fell.

* * *

Justin went with his sister to her door in the square. Quickly, and in their necessary silence, they crossed the grass under the limes. Here a dark window reflected one of the few lamps, there a shadow crossed a lit blind, and voices of people moving under the trees made a reverberation in the box of the square. Queenie let herself in; Justin heard the heavy front door drag shut slowly across the mat. She had not expected him to come in, and he did not know if she shared his feeling of dissonance, or if she recoiled from shock, or if she were shocked at all. Quitting the square at once, he took the direct way to his hotel in the main street. He went in at the side door, past the bar in which he so often encountered Robinson.

In his small, harsh room he looked first at his bed. He looked, as though out of a pit of sickness, at his stack of books on the mantelpiece. He writhed his head round sharply, threw off his coat and began to unknot his tie. Meanwhile he beat round, in the hot light, for some crack of outlet from his constriction. It was at his dressing table, for he had no other, that he began and ended his letter to Robinson: the mirror screwed to the dressing table constituted a witness to this task—whenever his look charged up it met his own reared head, the flush heightening on the bridge of the nose and forehead, the neck from which, as though for an execution, the collar had been taken away.

My dear Robinson: Our departure from your house (Belle-vue, I think?) tonight was so awkwardly late, and at the last so hurried, that I had inadequate time in which to thank you for your hospitality to my sister and to myself. That we exacted this hospitality does not make its merit, on your part, less. Given the inconvenience we so clearly caused you, your forbearance with us was past praise. So much so that (as you may be glad to hear) my sister does not appear to realize how very greatly we were *de trop*. In my own case—which is just—the same cannot be said. I am conscious that, in spite of her disability, she did at least prove a less wearisome guest than I.

My speculations and queries must, to your mind, equally seem absurd. This evening's fiasco has been definitive: I think it better our acquaintance should close. You will find it in line with my usual awkwardness that I should choose to state this decision of mine at all. Your indifference to the matter I cannot doubt. My own lack of indifference must make its last weak exhibition in this letter—in which, if you have fine enough nostrils (which I doubt), every sentence will almost certainly stink. In attempting to know you I have attempted to enter, and to comport myself in, what might be called an area under your jurisdiction. If my inefficacies appeared to you ludicrous, my curiosities (as in one special instance tonight) appeared more revolting. I could gauge (even before the postscript outside your gate) how profoundly I had offended you. Had we either of us been gentlemen, the incident might have passed off with less harm.

My attempts to know you I have disposed of already. My wish that you should know me has been, from the first, ill found. You showed yourself party to it in no sense, and the trick I played on myself I need not discuss. I acted and spoke (with regard to you) upon assumptions you were not prepared to warrant. You cannot fail to misunderstand what I mean when I say that a year ago this might not have happened to me. But—the assumptions on which I acted, Robinson, are becoming more general in a driven world than you yet (or may ever) know. The extremity to which we are each driven must be the warrant for what we do and say.

My extraordinary divagation towards you might be said to be, I suppose, an accident of this summer. But there are no accidents. I have the fine (yes) fine mind's love of the fine plume, and I meet no fine plumes down my own narrow street. Also, in this place (birthplace) you interposed your solidity between me and what might have been the full effects of an exacerbating return. In fact, you had come to constitute for me a very genuine holiday. As things are, my five remaining days here will have to be seen out. I shall hope not to meet you, but must fear much of the traplike size of this town. (You need not, as I mean to, avoid the hotel bar.) Should I, however, fail to avoid you, I shall again, I suppose, have to owe much, owe any face I keep, to your never-failing imperviousness. Understand that it will be against my wish that I reopen this one-sided account.

I wish you good night. Delicacy does not deter me from adding that I feel my good wish to be superfluous. I imagine that, incapable of being haunted, you are incapable of being added to. Tomorrow (I understand) you will feel fine, but you will not know any more about love. If the being outside your gate came with a question, it is possible that she should have come to me. If I had even seen her she might not go on rending my heart. As it is, as you are, I perhaps denounce you as much on her behalf as my own. Not trying to understand, you at least cannot misunderstand the mood and hour in which I write. As regards my sister, please do not discontinue what has been your even kindness to her: she might be perplexed. She has nothing to fear, I think.

Accept, my dear Robinson (without irony) my kind regards,

J.C.

Justin, trembling, smote a stamp on this letter. Going down as he was, in the hall he unhooked his mackintosh and put it over his shirt. It was well past midnight; the street, empty, lay in dusty reaches under the few lamps. Between the shutters his step raised an echo; the cold of the mountains had come down;

two cats in his path unclinched and shot off into the dark. On his way to the letterbox he was walking towards Bellevue; on his way back he still heard the drunken woman sobbing against the telegraph pole. The box would not be cleared till tomorrow noon.

Queenie forgot Justin till next day. The house in which her rooms were was so familiar that she went upstairs without a pause in the dark. Crossing her sitting room she smelled oil from the cooker behind the screen: she went through an arch to the cubicle where she slept. She was happy. Inside her sphere of silence that not a word clouded, the spectacle of the evening at Bellevue reigned. Contemplative, wishless, almost without an "I," she unhooked her muslin dress at the wrists and waist, stepped from the dress, and began to take down her hair. Still in the dark, with a dreaming sureness of habit, she dropped hairpins into the heart-shaped tray.

This was the night she knew she would find again. It had stayed living under a film of time. On just such a summer night, once only, she had walked with a lover in the demesne. His hand, like Robinson's, had been on her elbow, but she had guided him, not he her, because she had better eyes in the dark. They had gone down walks already deadened with moss, under the weight of July trees; they had felt the then fresh aghast ruin totter above them; there was a moonless sky. Beside the lake they sat down, and while her hand brushed the ferns in the cracks of the stone seat emanations of kindness passed from him to her. The subtle deaf girl had made the transposition of this nothing or everything into an everything—the delicate deaf girl that the man could not speak to and was afraid to touch. She who, then so deeply contented, kept in her senses each frond and breath of that night, never saw him again and had soon forgotten his face. That had been twenty years ago, till tonight when it was now. Tonight it was Robinson who, guided by Queenie down leaf tunnels, took the place on the stone seat by the lake.

The rusted gates of the castle were at the end of the square. Queenie, in her bed facing the window, lay with her face turned sideways, smiling, one hand lightly against her cheek.

Sean O'Faolain (1900–1991)

Sean O'Faolain was born John Whelan in 1900, *in Dublin, but he grew up in Cork. His father was a constable in the Royal Irish Constabulary and his mother took in lodgers. O'Faolain in his autobiography* Vive Moi! (1964) *described his family as "shabby genteels at the lowest possible social level." O'Faolain was educated at Cork schools, and came under the influence of Daniel Corkery, joining the Cork Dramatic Society, and increasing his Gaelic, which he had begun in school. Shortly after entering University College, Cork, he joined the Irish Volunteers, and served during the Civil War as censor for the Cork* Examiner *and as publicity director for the I.R.A. After the Republican loss, he eventually finished a B.A. and an M.A. at University College, Cork, and went on to earn an M.A. at Harvard University. After a short teaching career, he became a full-time writer, publishing in* 1932 *his first book,* Midsummer Night Madness, *a collection of stories partly based on his Civil War experiences. Now considered one of Ireland's leading men of letters, he has published novels; short stories; biographies; literary criticism, including one of the rare full-length studies of the short story* (The Short Story, 1948); *an excellent cultural history* (The Irish, 1947); *travel books; and translations. For six years in the 1940s he was editor of one of Ireland's major literary magazines,* The Bell. *Among O'Faolain's collections of short stories are* A Purse of Coppers (1937), I Remember! I Remember! (1961), The Heat of the Sun (1966), The Talking Trees (1971), *and* Foreign Affairs (1976). The Collected Stories *appeared in* 1983. *In* 1979 *he published his fourth novel,* And Again? *His other novels are* A Nest of Simple Folk (1934), Bird Alone (1936), *and* Come Back to Erin (1940). *"Falling Rocks, Narrowing*

Road, Cul-de-Sac, Stop" is taken from Foreign Affairs *and marks a new direction in a particularly Irish genre, the literary yarn.*

Falling Rocks, Narrowing Road, Cul-de-sac, Stop

The day Morgan Myles arrived in L—— as the new county librarian he got a painful boil under his tongue. All that week he was too busy settling into his new quarters to do anything about it beyond dribbling over his mother's hand mirror into a mouth as pink and black as a hotel bathroom. Otherwise he kept working off the pain and discomfort of it in outbursts of temper with his assistant, Marianne Simcox, a frail, long-legged, neurotically efficient, gushingly idealistic, ladylike (that is to say, Protestant) young woman whom he hated and bullied from the first moment he met her. This, however, could have been because of his cautious fear of her virginal attractiveness.

On his fourth day in the job he was so rude to her that she turned on him, called him a Catholic cad, and fled sobbing behind the stacks. For fifteen minutes he went about his work humming with satisfaction at having broken her ladylike ways; but when she failed to come trotting to his next roar of command, he went tearing around the stacks in a fury looking for her. He was horrified to find her sitting on the floor of the Arts Section still crying into her mouse-sized handkerchief. With a groan of self-disgust he sat on the floor beside her, put his arm around her shoulder, rocked her as gently as if she was a kid of twelve, told her he was a bastard out of hell, that she was the most efficient assistant he had ever had in his life, and that from this time on they would be doing marvelous things together with "our library." When she had calmed, she apologized for being so rude, and thanked him so formally, and so courteously, and in such a ladylike accent that he decided that she was a born bitch and went off home in a towering temper to his mother who, seeing the state her dear boy was in, said, "Wisha, Morgan love, why don't you take that gumboil of yours to a doctor and show it to him. You're not your natural nice self at all. You're as cranky as a bag of cats with it."

At the word *doctor* Morgan went pale with fear, bared his teeth like a five-barred gate, and snarled that he had no intention of going next nor nigh any doctor in this one-horse town. "Anyway," he roared, "I hate all doctors. Without exception of age or sex. Cods and bluffers they are, the whole lot of them. And you know well that all any doctor ever wants to do with any patient is to take X rays of his insides, order him into hospital, take the clothes down off of him, stick a syringe into his backside and before the poor fathead knows where he is there'll be half a dozen fellows in white nightshirts sawing away at him like a dead pig. It's just a gumboil. It doesn't bother me one bit. I've had dozens of them in my time. It's merely an Act of God. Like an earthquake, or a crick in the neck. It will pass."

But it did not pass. It went on burning and smarting until one windy sunstruck afternoon in his second week when he was streeling miserably along the Dublin Road, about a mile beyond the town's last untidy lot, beside its last unfinished suburban terrace. About every ten minutes or so, the clouds opened and the sun flicked and vanished. He held the collar of his baggy, tweed overcoat humped about his neck. His tongue was trying to double back acrobatically to his uvula. Feeling as lost and forlorn as the grey heron he saw across the road standing by the edge of a wrinkled loch, he halted to compose. *"O long-legged bird by your ruffled lake / Alone as I, as bleak of eye, opaque . . ."* As what? He unguardedly rubbed his under-tongue on a sharp tooth, cursed, the sun winked, and he was con-

fronted by one of destiny's infinite options. It was his moment
of strength, of romance, of glamour, of youth, of sunshine on a
strange shore. A blink of sunlight fell on a brass plate fastened
to the red-brick gate pillar beside him, DR. FRANCIS BREEN.

The gate was lined with sheet metal. Right and left of it
there was a high cut-stone wall backing on a coppice of rain-
black macrocarpa that extended over the grass-grown border of
the road. The house was not visible. He squeaked the gate
open, peered timidly up a short curved avenue at it, all in red
brick, tall, turreted, and bay-windowed. An empty-looking conservatory hooped against one side of it (intended, presumably,
for the cultivation of rare orchids). Along the other side, a
long veranda (intended, doubtless, to shelter Doctor Francis
Breen from Ireland's burning tropical sun). He opened his
mouth wide as he gazed, probed with his finger for the sore
spot, and found it.

It did not look like a house where anybody would start cutting anybody up. It did not look like a doctor's house at all. It
looked more like a gentleman's residence. Although he did remember the American visitor to Dublin who said to him that
every Irish surgery looked as if it had been furnished by Dr.
Watson for Sherlock Holmes. As he cautiously entered the avenue he observed that the gate bore a perpendicular column of
five warning signs in blue lettering on white enamel. NO DOGS.
NO CANVASSERS. NO HAWKERS. NO CIRCULARS. SHUT THE
GATE. He advanced on the house, his fists clenched inside his
overcoat pockets, his eyebrows lifted to indicate his contempt
for all doctors. Twice on the way to the front door he paused,
as if to admire the grounds, really to assure himself that no dog
had failed to read the NO DOGS sign: a born city man, he feared
all living animals. He was very fond of them in poetry. He took
the final step upwards to the stained-glass door, stretched out
his index finger, to tip, to tempt, to test, to press the brass bell
knob. (An enamel sign beneath it said, TRADESMEN TO THE
REAR.) His mother had spoken of a deficiency. She had also

mentioned pills. He would ask this sawbones for a pill, or for a soothing bottle. He would not remove his shirt for him. And he would positively refuse to let down his pants. "Where," he foresaw himself roaring, "do you think I have this boil?"

A shadow appeared behind the door. He looked speculatively over his glasses at the servant who partly opened it. She was gray and settled, but not old, dressed in black bombazine, wearing a white starched apron with shoulder frills. When he asked for the doctor she immediately flung the door wide open as if she had been eagerly expecting him for years and years; then, limping eagerly ahead of him, dot and carry one down a softly upholstered corridor, she showed him into what she called "the dachtar's sargery," quacking all about "what an ahful co-eld dayeh it iss Gad bliss itt" in what he had already scornfully come to recognize as the ducks' dialect of this sodden, mist-shotten dung heap of the Shannon's delta.

Left to himself he had time only to be disturbed by the sight of one, two, three barometers side by side on the wall, and one, two, three, four clocks side by side on the mantelpiece; relieved by an opposite wall lined with books; and enchanted by a dozen daintily tinted lithographs of flying moths and half a dozen hanging glass cases displaying wide-winged butterflies pinned against blue skies, when the door was slammed open by a tall, straight, white-haired, handsome, military-looking man, his temper at boiling point, his voice of the barrack square, the knuckles of his fist white on the doorknob as if he were as eager to throw out his visitor as his Bombazine had been to welcome him in. Morgan noted that his eyes were quiet as a novice of nuns, and that his words were as polite, and remembered hearing somewhere that when the Duke of Wellington gave his order for the final charge at Waterloo his words to his equerry had been, "The Duke of Wellington presents his compliments to Field Marshal von Blücher and begs him to be so kind as to charge like blazes."

"Well, sir?" the doctor was saying. "Would you be so kind

as to tell me what you mean by entering my house in this cavalier fashion? Are you an insurance salesman? Are you distrib-
uting circulars? Are you promoting the *Encyclopaedia Britan-
nica?* Are you a hawker? A huckster? A Jehovah's Witness?"

At these words Morgan's eyes spread to the rims of his lake-
size glasses. He felt a heavenly sunlight flooding the entire
room. He raised two palms of exultant joy. More than any
other gift of life, more than drink, food, girls, books, nicotine,
coffee, music, more even than poetry and his old mother
(whom he thought of, and saw through, as if she were a
stained glass image of the Mother of God), he adored all
cranks, fanatics, eccentrics and near-lunatics, always provided
that they did not impinge on his personal comfort, in which
case he would draw a line across them as fast as a butcher cuts
off a chicken's head. More than any other human type he de-
spised all men of good character, all solid citizens, all well-
behaved social men, all mixers, joiners, hearty fellows, and jolly
good chaps, always provided that he did not require their assistance in his profession as librarian, in which case he would
cajole them and lard them and lick them like a pander, while
utterly despising himself, and his job, for having to tolerate
such bores for one moment. But here before his eyes was a figure of purest gold. If there were any other such splendid crack-
pots in L—— then this was heaven, nor was he ever to be out
of it.

"But," he protested gaily, "you are a doctor! I have a gumboil! We are the perfect match."

The old man moaned as if he had been shot through by an
arrow of pain.

"It is true that I am, by letters patent, a man licensed to
practice the crude invention called medicine. But I have never
practiced, I have never desired to practice, and I never do intend to practice medicine. I know very well, sir, what you want
me to do. You want me to look down your throat with an
electric torch and make some such solemn, stupid, and mean-

ingless remark as 'You have a streptococcal infection.' Well,"
he protested, "I will do nothing of the kind for you. Why
should I? It might be only a symptom. Next week you might
turn up with rheumatic heart disease, or a latent kidney disease,
as people with strep throats have been known to do. You talk
airily of a gumboil. You may well be living in a fool's paradise,
sir. Even supposing I were to swab strep out of your throat and
grow it on a culture medium, what would that tell me about
the terrible manifold, creeping, subtle, lethal disease processes
that may be going on at this moment in the recesses of your
body as part of that strep infection, or set off by it? The only
thing I, or any other doctor—bluffers and liars that we all
are—could honestly say to you would be the usual evasion.
'Gargle with this bottle three times a day and come back in a
week.' By which time Nature or God would have in any case
cured you without our alleged assistance. I know the whole
bag of tricks from the Hippocratic collection, the treatises of
Galen and the Canon of Avicenna down. I suppose you imagine that I spent all my years in Dublin and Vienna studying
medicine. I spent them studying medicos. I am a neurologist.
Or I was a neurologist until I found that what true medicine
means is true magic. Do you know how to remove a wart?
You must wait on the roadway to the cemetery until a funeral
passes, and say, 'Corpse, corpse, take away my wart.' And your
wart will go, sir! That is true medicine. I believe in miracles
because I have seen them happen. I believe in God, prayer, the
imagination, the destiny of the Irish, our bottomless racial
memory—and in nothing else."

Morgan's left hand was circling his belly in search of manifold, creeping, secret diseases.

"But, surely to God, doctor," he whined, "medical science
can do *something* for a gumboil?"

"Aha! I know what you're up to now. X rays! That's the
mumbo-jumbo every patient wants. And neither will I suggest,
as you would probably like me to suggest, that you should go

to hospital. All you would do there would be either to pass your infection to some other patient or pick up his infection from him. I will have nothing to do with you, sir. And please keep your distance. I don't want your beastly infection. If you want to mess about with your gumboil you will have to go to a doctor. If you wish me to pray for your gumboil I will pray for it. But I refuse to let you or anybody else turn me into the sort of mountebank who pretends he can cure any tradesman's sore toe or any clerk's carbuncle in one second with a stroke of his pen and a nostrum from the chemist's shop. Good afternoon to you, sir. You are now in the hands of God!"

Morgan, stung by arrogance and enraged by fear, roared back a line fit for his memoirs.

"And good afternoon to you, sir! From one who is neither clerk nor tradesman, higgler nor hawker, huckster nor hound-dog, but, by God's grace, a poet whose poems will live long after," hand waving, "your butterflies have been devoured by the jaws of your moths."

The old man's rage vanished like a ghost at cockcrow. He closed the door gently behind him.

"A poet?" he asked quietly. "Now, this is most interesting." Courteously he indicated a chair. "Won't you sit down? Your name is?"

"Morgan Myles," Morgan Myles boomed as if he were a majordomo announcing Lord Byron.

"Mine is Francis Breen. Yours is more euphonious. I can see it already on your first book of verses. But a poet should have three names. Like American politicians. Percy Bysshe Shelley. George Gordon Byron. Thomas Stearns Eliot. William Butler Yeats. Ella Wheeler Wilcox. Richard Milhous Nixon. You have a second name? Taken at your Confirmation? Arthur? There we have it! *First Poems*. By Morgan Arthur Myles!"

Morgan, like most men who are adept at flattering others, could never resist flattery himself. He waggled his bottom like a dog. His grin was coy but cocksure. Three minutes later the doctor was tenderly parting his lips and illuminating the inside of his mouth. He extinguished the torch. He lifted his eyes and smiled into Morgan's.

"Well, Doc?" Morgan asked fearfully. "What did you see there?"

"You are not even," his new-found friend smiled, "about to give birth to a couplet. Just a blister." He sat to his desk. "I will give you a prescription for a gargle. Rinse you mouth with this three times a day. And come back to me in a week. But if you wish to get better sooner come sooner, any evening for a drink and a chat. I have no friends in L——."

"Nor have I!"

Within a week they were bosom cronies.

From start to finish it was a ridiculous friendship. Indeed, from that day onwards, to the many of us who saw them every day after lunch walking along O'Connell Street arm in arm like father and son, or nose to nose like an aging ward boss with a young disciple, it seemed an unnatural business. Can the east wind, we asked one another in wonder, lie down with the west wind? A cormorant mate with a herring? A heron with a hare? An end with a beginning? We gave their beautiful friendship three months. As a matter of fact we were only two years and eleven months out.

Even to look at they were a mismatch: the doctor straight and spare as a spear, radiating propriety from every spiky bone of his body, as short of step as a woman, and as carefully dressed from his wide-brimmed bowler hat to the rubber tip of his mottled, gold-headed malacca cane; the poet striding beside him, halting only to swirl his flabby tweeds; his splendid hydrocephalic head stretched behind his neck like a balloon; his myopic eyes glaring at the clouds over the roofs through the thick lenses of his glasses; a waterfall of black hair permanently frozen over his left eye, his big teeth laughing, his big voice booming, he looked for all the world like a peasant Yeats in a

poor state of health. The only one of us who managed to produce any sort of explanation was our amateur psychiatrist, Father Tim Buckley, and we never took him seriously anyway.
He said, with an episcopal *sprinkle me O Lord with hyssop* wave of
his hand, "They have invented one another."

Now, we knew from experience that there was only one way
to handle Tim Buckley. If he said some fellow was a homosexual because he had fallen in love with his hobbyhorse when he
was five you had to say at once, "But, Tim, why did he fall in
love with his hobbyhorse when he was five?" If he said that it
was because the poor chap hated his mother and loved his father you had to say, at once, "But, Tim, why did he hate his
ma and love his da?" If he then said that it was natural for
every child to prefer one parent to another, you had to say at
once, "But, Tim, why . . ." And so on until he lost his temper
and shut up. This time, however, he was ready for our coun-
terattack.

"They have invented one another," he said, "for mutual support because they are both silently screaming for freedom.
Now what is the form of slavery from which all human beings
most want to be free?"

"Sex," we conceded, to save time, knowing our man.

"Passion!" he amended. "For this agony there are only three
solutions. The first is sin, which," he grinned, "I am informed
on the best authority is highly agreeable but involves an awful
waste of time. I mean if you could hang a girl up in the closet
every time you were finished with her that would be very con-
venient, but. Then there is marriage, which as Shaw said is the
perfect combination of maximum temptation and maximum
opportunity. And there is celibacy of which, I can say with authority, as the only member of the present company who
knows anything at all about it, that it bestows on man the
qualified freedom of a besieged city where one sometimes has
to eat rats. Of our two friendly friends the older man needs
approval for his lifelong celibacy. The younger man needs en-

288 MODERN IRISH SHORT STORIES

couragement to sustain his own. Or so they have chosen to imagine. In fact neither of them really believes in celibacy at all. Each has not only invented the other. He has invented himself."

Our silence was prolonged.

"Very well," he surrendered. "In that case thicken your own plot!"

Of course, we who had known Frank Breen closely ever since we were kids together in L—— knew that there was nothing mysterious about him: he had simply always been a bit balmy, even as a four-eyed kid. When his parents sent him to school in England we saw much less of him; still less when he went to Dublin for his M.B., and from there on to Austria for his M.D. After he came back to L—— to settle down for life in the old Breen house on the Dublin Road on the death of his father, old Doctor Frank, and of his mother, we hardly saw him at all. We knew about him only by hearsay, chiefly through the gossip of his housekeeper, Dolly Lynch, passed on to Claire Coogan, Father Tim Buckley's housekeeper, and glee-fully passed on by him to the whole town.

That was how the town first heard that the brass plate on his gate pillar—his father's, well polished by chamois and dulled by weather—would never again mean that there was a doctor behind it; about his four clocks and his three barometers; about his collection of moths and butterflies; about the rope ladder he had coiled in a red metal box under every bedroom window; about his bed always set two feet from the wall lest a bit of cornice should fall on his head during the night; about the way he looked under the stairs for hidden thieves every night before going to bed; that his gold-knobbed malacca cane contained a sword; that he never arrived at the railway station less than half an hour before his train left; that he hung his pajamas on a clothes hanger; had handmade wooden trees for every pair of his handmade boots; that he liked to have his bootlaces washed and ironed; that his vest-pocket watch told the time, the date, the day, the year, the points of the compass, and contained an alarm buzzer that he was always setting to remind him of something important he wanted to do later on, but whose nature he could never remember when the buzzer hummed over his left gut—very much the way a wife will leave her wedding ring at night on her dressing table to remind her in the morning of something that by then she has incontinently forgotten.

So! A bit odd. Every club in the world must have elderly members like him—intelligent and successful men of whose oddities the secretary will know one, the headwaiter another, the bartender a third, their fellow members smile at a fourth. It is only their families, or if they live for a long time in a small town their townsfolk, who will, between them, know the lot. Frank Breen might have gone on in his harmless, bumbling way to the end of his life if that brass plate of his had not winked at Morgan Myles, and if Father Tim Buckley—was he jealous?—had not decided to play God.

Not that we ever called him "Father Tim Buckley." He was too close to us, too like one of ourselves for that. We called him Tim Buckley, or Tim, or even, if the whiskey was fluming, Bucky. He was not at all like the usual Irish priest who is as warm as toast and as friendly and understanding as a brother until you come to the sixth commandment, and there is an end to him. Tim was like a man who had dropped off an international plane at Shannon; not a Spencer Tracy priest from downtown Manhattan, all cigar and white cuffs, parish computer and portable typewriter, fists and feet, and there is the end to him; perhaps more like an unfrocked priest from Bolivia or Brazil, so ungentlemanly in his manners as to have given acute pain to an Evelyn Waugh and so cheerful in spite of his scars as to have shocked a Graham Greene; or still more like, among all other alternatives, a French workers' priest from

Liège; or in other words, as far as we were concerned, the right
man in the right place and as far as the bishop was concerned, a
total disaster. He was handsome, ruddy, and full-blooded in a
sensual way, already so heavy in his middle thirties that he had
the belly, the chins, and (when he lost his temper) something
of the voracity of Rodin's ferocious statue of Balzac in his
dressing gown; but he was most himself when his leaden-lidded
eyes glistened with laughter, and his tiny mouth, crushed between the peonies of his cheeks, reminded you of a small boy
whistling after his dog, or of some young fellow saucily making a kiss-mouth across the street to his girl. His hobby was
psychoanalysis.

His analysis of the doctor was characteristic. He first pointed
out to us, over a glass of malt, the sexual significance of pocket
watches, so often fondled and rubbed between the fingers. He
merely shrugged at the idea of ladders unfolding from red con-
tainers, and said that swords being in sword sticks needed no
comment. Clocks and barometers were merely extensions of
pocket watches. (The wristwatch, he assured us, was one of the
great sexual revolutions of our age—it brought everything out
in the open.) But, above all, he begged us to give due attention
to Frank Breen's mother complex—evident in his love of se-
clusion behind womblike walls, dark trees, a masked gate; and
any man must have a terrible hate for his father who mock-
ingly leaves his father's brass plate on a pillar outside his home
while publicly refusing to follow his father's profession inside
it. ("By the way, can we ignore that NO DOGS sign?") The
looking for thieves under the stairs at night, he confessed,
puzzled him for the moment. Early arrival for trains was an obvious sign of mental insecurity. "Though, God knows," laughing in his fat, "any man who doesn't feel mentally insecure in
the modern world must be out of his mind." As for this beautiful friendship, that was a classical case of narcissism: the older
man in love with an image of his own lost and lonely youth.

"Any questions?"

No wonder he was the favorite confessor of all the nubile girls in town, not (or not only) because they thought him handsome but because he was always happy to give them the most disturbing explanations for their simplest misdemeanors. "I kissed a boy at a dance, Father," they would say to some other priest and, as he boredly bade them say three Hail Marys for their penance, they would hear the dark slide of the confessional move dismissively across their faces. Not so with Father Tim! He would lean his cheek against the grille and whisper, "Now, my dear child, in itself a kiss is an innocent and beautiful act. Therefore the only reason prompting you to confess it as a sin must refer to the manner in which the kiss was given and the spirit in which it was received, and in this you may be very wise. Because, of course, when we say *kiss*, or *lips*, we may—one never knows for certain—be thinking of something quite different . . ." His penitents would leave his box with their faces glowing, and their eyes dazed. One said that he made her feel like a Magdalen with long floating hair. Another said he made her want to go round L—— wearing a dark veil. A third (who was certain to come to a bad end) said he had revealed to her the *splendeurs et misères de l'amour*. And a fourth, clasping her palms with delight, giggled that he was her Saint Rasputin.

We who met him in our homes, with a glass in his fist and his Roman collar thrown aside, did not worry about what he told our daughters. We had long since accepted him as an honest, innocent, unworldly man who seemed to know a lot about sex-in-the-head—and was always very entertaining about it—but who knew sweet damn all about love-in-the-bed, not to mention love at about eleven o'clock at night when your five kids are asleep and the two of you are so edgy from adding up the household accounts that by the time you have decided once again that the case is hopeless all "to go to bed" means is to go sound asleep. But we did worry about him. He was so outspoken, so trustful of every stranger, had as little guard over his

tongue as a sailor ashore, that we could foresee the day when
his bishop would become so sick of getting anonymous letters
about him that he would shanghai him to some remote punishment curacy on the backside of Slievenamuck.

We would try to frighten him into caution by telling him
that he would end up there, exiled to some spot so insignifi-
cant that it would not be marked even on one of those nostal-
gic one-inch-to-the-mile British Ordnance maps of 1899 that
still—indifferent to the effects of time and history, of gunshot
and revolution—record every burned-out constabulary barracks, destroyed mansion, abandoned branch railway, eigh-
teenth century "inn," disused blacksmith's hovel, silenced
windmill, rook-echoing granary, or "R. C. Chapel," where, we
would tell him, is where our brave Bucky would then be, in a
bald-face presbytery, altitude 1,750 feet, serving a cement-faced
chapel, beside an anonymous crossroads, without a tree in sight
for ten miles, stuck for life as curator, nurse, and slave of some
senile parish priest. He would just raise his voice to spit scorn
at us; like the night he gobbled us up in a rage:

"And," he roared, "if I can't say what I think how the hell
am I going to live? Am I free or am I not free? Am I to lie
down in the dust and be gagged and handcuffed like a slave?
Do ye want me to spend my whole life watching out for traffic
signs? Falling rocks! Narrowing Road! Cul-de-sac! Stop! My
God, are ye men or are ye mice?"

"Mice!" we roared back with one jovial voice and dispelled
the tension in laughter so loud that my wife looked up in
fright at the ceiling and said, "Sssh! Ye bastards! If ye wake the
kids I'll make every one of ye walk the floor with them in yeer
arms till three in the morning. Or do ye think ye're starting
another revolution in yeer old age?"

"We could do worse," Tim smiled into his double chin.

Whenever he smiled like that you could see the traffic signs
lying right and left of him like idols overthrown.

*   *   *

It was a Sunday afternoon in May. The little island was deserted. He was lying on the sun-warmed grass between the other two, all three on their backs, in a row, their hats on their faces. They were neither asleep nor awake. They were breathing as softly as the lake at their feet. They had driven at their ease that morning to the east side of the lake past the small village of Mountshannon, now looking even smaller across the level water, rowed to the island (Tim Buckley at the oars), delighted to find every hillocky green horizon slowly bubbling with cumulus clouds. They had inspected the island's three ruined churches, knee-deep in nettles and fern, and its tenth-century Round Tower that had stood against the morning sun as dark as a factory chimney. They had photographed the ruins, and one another, and then sat near the lake and the boat to discuss the excellent lunch that Dolly Lynch always prepared for "the young maaaster" on these Sunday outings: her cold chicken and salad, her handmade mayonnaise, her own brown bread and butter, the bottle of Liebfraumilch that Frank had hung by a string in the lake to cool while they explored the island, her double roasted French coffee, flavored, the way the maaaster always liked it, with chicory and a suspicion of cognac. It was half an hour since they had lain back to sleep. So far everything about the outing had been perfect. No wonder Morgan had jackknifed out of bed that morning at eight o'clock, and Frank Breen wakened with a smile of special satisfaction.

Before Morgan came, exactly two years and eleven months ago, it had been the doctor's custom, at the first call of the cuckoo, to take off now and again (though never too often to establish a precedent), on especially fine Sundays like this, with Father Timothy Buckley in Father Timothy's roomy second-hand Peugeot—Frank did not drive—in search of moths and butterflies, or to inspect the last four walls, perhaps the last three walls, of some eighth-century Hiberno-Romanesque churchlet, or the rotting molar of some Norman castle smelling of cow dung, purple mallow, meadowsweet, and the woodsmoke of the last tinkers who had camped there. After Morgan came he had begun to drive off every fine Sunday with Morgan in Morgan's little Ford Prefect. Still, *noblesse oblige,* and also if the journey promised to be a rather long one, he had about twice a year suggested to Morgan that they might invite Father Timothy to join them; and Tim had always come, observing with amusement that they indulgently allowed him to bring his own car, and that they would, after loud protestations, allow him to do all the driving, and that he also had to persuade them forcibly to allow him to pack the luggage on the seat beside him, so as to leave plenty of room—at this point they would all three laugh with the frankest irony—for their lordships' bottoms in the soft and roomy rear of the Peugeot. This luggage consisted of Frank's two butterfly nets, in case one broke, three binoculars and three cameras, one for each, two umbrellas for himself and Morgan, the bulging lunch basket for them all, two foam-rubber cushions, one for his poor old back, one for Morgan's poor young back, and a leather-backed carriage rug so that the dear boy should not feel the cold of the grass going up through him while he was eating his lunch and enjoying—as he was now enjoying—his afternoon siesta.

Retired, each one, into his own secret shell of sleep, they all three looked as dead as they would look in fifteen years' time in one of the photographs they had just taken of themselves. The day had stopped. The film of the climbing towers of clouds had stopped. The lake was silent. The few birds and the three cows they had seen on the island were dozing. Thinking had stopped. Their three egos had stopped. Folktales say that when a man is asleep on the grass like that, a tiny lizard may creep into his mouth, devour his tongue, and usurp its power. After about an hour of silence and dozing some such lizard spoke from the priest's mouth. Afterwards he said that he had been dreaming of the island's hermits, and of what he called the shortitude and latitude of life, and of how soon it stops, and that those two selfish bastards beside him were egotistical sinners, too concerned with their comfort as adolescents to assert their dignity as men. "And I?" he thought with a start, and woke.

"In Dublin last month," his lizard said hollowly into his hat, "I saw a girl on a horse on a concrete street."

"What?" Morgan asked drowsily, without stirring.

"A girl on a horse," Tim said, removing his hat, and beholding the glorious blue sky. "It was the most pathetic sight I ever saw."

"Why pathetic?" Morgan asked, removing his hat and seeing the blue Pacific sweep into his ken.

"She was riding on a concrete street, dressed as if she was riding to hounds. The fantasy of it was pathetic. Miles away from green fields. But all the girls are gone mad on horses nowadays. I wish somebody would tell them that all they're doing is giving the world a beautiful example of sexual transference. They have simply transferred their natural desire for a man to a four-legged brute."

"Balderdash," said Morgan, and put back his hat as Frank patiently lifted his to ask the blueness what all the poor girls who haven't got horses do to inform the public of their adolescent desires.

"They have cars," Tim said, and sat up slowly, the better to do battle. Morgan sat up abruptly.

"So," he demanded, "every time I drive a car I become a homosexual?"

Tim considered the matter judicially.

"Possibly," he agreed. "But not necessarily. There are male cars for women, and female cars for men. For women? Clubman, Escort, Rover, Consort, Jaguar, Triumph. Fill 'em up and drive them at seventy miles an hour! What fun! For men? Giulietta. Whose Romeo? Morris Minor. The word means moor—symbolical desire for a small negress. Mercedes? Actually that is

Mrs. Benz's name. Also means Our Lady of Mercy. Symbolical desire for a large virgin. Ford Consul? Consuela, Our Lady of Consolations. Volvo? Vulva. Volkswagen. Double V. Symbolical . . ."

"Well of all the filthy minds!" Morgan roared.

The doctor sat up with a sigh. His siesta was ruined. His anger was hot upon his humor and his honor.

"I do think, Father Timothy, that you, as a priest of God . . ."

Tim scrambled to his feet, high above him, black as a wine tun against the pale sheen of the lake.

"A priest, a presbyter, an elder, a sheikh, an old man, a minister, a pastor of sheep? What does that mean? Something superior, elegant, stainless, and remote from life like yourself and Master Poet here? An angel, a seraph, a saint, a mystic, a eunuch, a cherubim, a morning star? Do I look like it? Or like a man fat from eating too much, wheezy from smoking too much, sick and tired from trying to do the job he was called on to do? A priest of God is a man with a bum and a belly, and everything that hangs out of a belly or cleaves it, with the same appetites and desires, thirsts and hungers as the men and women, the boys and the girls he lives and works with. It may be very nice for you to look at us before the altar in Saint Jude's all dressed up in our golden robes, swinging a censer, and to think, 'There is heavenly power, there is magic.' But I have no power. I'm nothing alone. I merely pretend to a power that is an eternity beyond me. When I was in Rome, as a student, a priest in Southern Italy went mad, ran down to the bakery to turn the whole night's baking into the body of God, and from there to the wine factory to turn every flask and vat of flowing wine into the blood of the Lord. But did he? Of course not. Alone he hadn't the power to make a leaf of basil grow. But I will pretend to any boy or girl who is troubled or in misery that I have all the power in heaven to cure them, do mumbo-jumbo, wave hands, say hocus pocus, anything if it will only give them peace. And if that doesn't work I tell them the truth."

"You are shouting, Father," Doctor Frank said coldly.

Tim controlled himself. He sat down again. He laughed.

"Ye don't want to hear the truth. Too busy romanticizing, repressing, rationalizing, running away, when everybody knows the pair of ye think of nothing but women from morning to night! Your moths, Frank, that come out in the twilight, your easy girls, your lights o' love, fluttering against your windowpanes? Do you want me to believe that you never wish you could open the window to let one in? I saw you, Morgan, the other day in the library fawning over that unfortunate virgin Simcox, and a child could see what was in the minds of the pair of ye. And what do you think she thinks she's doing every time she goes out to the yard to wash the backside of your car with suds and water? Why don't you be a man, Morgan, and face up to it—one day you'll have to be spliced. It's the common fate of all mankind."

"It hasn't been yours, Father," Frank snapped.

"Because I took a vow and kept to it, logically."

"Pfoo!" Morgan snarled at him. "You know damned well that logic has as much to do with marriage as it has with music."

Tim looked at him with the air of a small boy who is thinking what fun it would be to shove his Auntie Kitty down the farmyard well.

"You know," he said slyly, "you should ask Fräulein Keel about that the next time she is playing the *Appassionata* for you," and was delighted to observe the slow blush that climbed up Morgan's face and the black frown that drew down the doctor's eyebrows. The silence of his companions hummed. He leaned back.

It was about two months ago since Frau Keel had come to L—— with her daughter Imogen and her husband Georg, an electrical engineer in charge of a new German factory at the

Shannon Free Airport complex. He was about fifty and a Roman Catholic, which was presumably why he had been chosen for this Irish job. His wife was much younger; blonde, handsome, curly-headed, well-corseted, with long-lashed eyes like a cow. Hera-eyed, Morgan said; dopey, Frank said; false lashes, Tim Buckley said. She was broad of bosom and bottom, strong-legged as a peasant and as heavy-shouldered, one of those abundant, self-indulgent, flesh-folding bodies that Rubens so loved to paint in their pink skin. Imogen was quite different; small, black-avised, black-haired, her skin like a bit of burned cork. She was a *belle laide* of such intensity, so packed and powerful with femininity that you felt that if you were to touch her with one finger she would hoop her back and spring her arms around you like a trap. Morgan had met her in the library, let her talk about music, found himself invited by her mother to hear her play, and unwisely boasted about it to Tim Buckley.

In the sullen silence he heard the lake sucking the stones of the beach. The clouds were less bright. The doctor said primly that he wanted to try his hand with his butterfly net. Morgan said gruffly that he wanted to take some more pictures before the sun went down. Together they walked away across the island. Tim reached for his breviary and began to read the office of the day. "Let us then be like newborn children hungry for the fresh milk . . ."

The delicate India paper of his breviary whispered each time he turned a page. Presently a drop of rain splashed on his knuckles. He looked about him. The sun still touched the island but nowhere else. The lake hissed at the shore. He stood on a rock but could see no sign of his companions. Were they colloguing with the seventh century? He packed the lunch basket, rolled up the rugs, loaded the cargo, sat in the stern of the boat, opened an umbrella, lit his pipe, and waited. He was sick of them. No doubt when slaves fall in love they feel more free . . .

They returned slowly and silently. Little was said as he rowed them to the mainland, and less on the way back to L—— because the rain became a cloudburst, and he was alone peering into it. On previous excursions he had always been invited to dine with them. He knew he would not be this evening: a snub that Morgan aggravated by assuring him that they must all meet soon again "on a more propitious occasion." He gave them a cheerful good-bye and drove off along the rain-dancing asphalt. To the devil with their four-course dinner. His freedom was more important to him. Anyway there were a dozen houses in town where the wife would be delighted to give him a plate of bacon and eggs.

Frank said nothing until he had poured their usual aperitif—a stout dollop of malt.

"That," he said as he handed the glass of whiskey to Morgan deep in the best armchair on the side of the turf fire, "is probably the last·time we shall meet his reverence socially."

Morgan looked portentously over his glasses at the fire.

"A terrible feeling sometimes assails me," he said, smacking each sibilant, "that Timothy John Buckley has a coarse streak in him."

Frank took the opposite armchair.

"I would call it a grave lack of tact. Even presuming that La Keel has not already told him that she is a patient of mine."

"Imogen?" said Morgan, sitting straight up. "Good God! Is there something wrong with her?"

"Imogen? Oh, you mean the child? I was referring to the mother."

Morgan sat back.

"Oh, and what's wrong with that old battle-ax? Are you beginning to take patients?"

Frank frowned.

"I have done my best to avoid it. The lady, and her husband, ever since they heard that I studied neurology in Vienna, have been very persistent. As for what is wrong, I should not, ethically speaking as a doctor, discuss the affairs of any patient, but, in this case, I think I may safely speak to you about the matter. Aye. Because I can trust you. And Bee. Because there is nothing whatsoever wrong with the lady."

"Then why did she come to consult you?"

Frank answered this one even more stiffly.

"She speaks of her cycles."

Morgan, like an old lady crossing a muddy road, ventured between the pools of his inborn prudishness, his poetic fastidiousness, and his natural curiosity:

"Do you by any chance mean she has some sort of what they call woman trouble?"

"If you mean the menopause, Madame Keel is much too young for that. She means emotional cycles. Elation-depression. Vitality-debility. Exultation-despair. The usual manic-depressive syndrome. She says that ever since she came to Ireland she has been melancholy."

"Jaysus! Sure, aren't we all melancholy in Ireland? What I'd say that one needs is a few good balls of malt every day or a dose or two of cod liver oil. If I were you, Frank, I'd pack her off about her business."

The doctor's body stirred restively.

"I have made several efforts to detach myself. She insists that I give her comfort."

Morgan looked over his glasses at his friend.

"And what kind of comfort would that be?" he asked cautiously.

"That," his friend said, a trifle smugly, "is scarcely for me to say."

Morgan glared into his glass. For a moment he wished Bucky was there to crash through the ROAD NARROWS sign, the CUL-DE-SAC, the FALLING ROCKS.

"It is a compliment to you," he said soapily.

"I take small pride in it, Morgan. Especially since she tells me that she also gets great comfort from her pastor."

Morgan rose to his feet, dark as a thundercloud, or as a Jove who had not shaved for a week.

"What pastor?" he demanded in his deepest basso.

"You have guessed it. Our companion of today. The Reverend Timothy Buckley. He also gives great comfort to Herr Keel. And to the girl. He holds sessions."

Jehovah's thunder-rumble rolled.

"Sessions?"

"It is apparently the latest American-Dutch ecumenical idea. Group confessions."

"The man," Morgan boomed, "must be mad! He is worse than mad. Who was it called him Rasputin? He was born to be hanged! Or shot! Or poisoned! That man is e-e-e-evil. Frank! You must stop this monstrous folly at once. Think of the effect on that innocent poor child."

"I have no intention whatsoever of interfering," Frank fluttered. "It's a family affair. I have no least right to interfere. And I suspect she is not in the least innocent. And she is not a child. She is eighteen."

"Frank!" Morgan roared. "Have you *no* principles?"

A mistake. It is not a nice question to be asked by anybody. Suppose Morgan had been asked by somebody if he had any principles himself! How does any of us know what his principles are? Nobody wants to have to start outlining his principles at a word of command.

"I begin to fear," Frank said huffily, "that in all this you are not thinking of me, nor of Frau Keel, nor of Herr Keel, nor of my principles, nor of any principles whatever, but solely of the sexual attractions of Fräulein Keel. She has hairy legs. A well-known sign of potency."

At which moment of dead silence Dolly Lynch opened the door, put in her flushed face and in her slow, flat, obsequious

Shannon voice, said, "Dinner is i-now-eh sarvedeh, Dachtar." Her employer glared at her. Why was she looking so flushed? The foul creature had probably been outside the door for the last three minutes listening to the rising voices. By tomorrow the thing would be all over the town.

They entered the dining room in silence. She served them in silence. When she went out they maintained silence, or said small polite things like, "This spring lamb is very tender," or "Forced rhubarb?" The silences were so heavy that Morgan felt obliged to retail the entire life of Monteverdi. Immediately after the coffee, in the drawing room, he said he had better go home to his mother, and, with fulsome thanks for a splendid lunch and a marvelous dinner, he left his friend to his pipe and, if he had any, his principles.

Morgan did not drive directly to his cottage on the Ennis Road. He drove to the library, extracted from the music section a biography of Monteverdi, and drove to the Keels' flat in O'Connell Square. It was Frau Keel, majestic as Brünnhilde, who opened the door, received the book as if it were a ticket of admission, and invited him to come in. To his annoyance he found Buckley half-filling a settee, winking cheerfully at him, smoking a cigar, a coffee in his paw, a large brandy on a small table beside him. Herr Keel sat beside him, enjoying the same pleasures. Through the dining-room door he caught a glimpse of Imogen with her back to him, clearing the dinner table, her oily black hair coiled as usual on either side of her cheeks. As she leaned over the table he saw the dimpled backs of her knees. She was not wearing stockings. The dark down on her legs suggested the untamed forests of the north.

"Aha!" Herr Keel cried, in (for so ponderous a man) his always surprising countertenor. "It is Mister Myles. You are most welcome. May I offer you a coffee and a good German cigar? We had just begun a most interesting session."

Morgan beamed and bowed ingratiatingly. He almost

clicked his heels in his desire to show his pleasure and to conceal the frightening thought: "Is this one of Bucky's sessions?" He beamed as he received the cigar and a brandy from Herr Keel, who bowed in return. He bowed as he accepted a coffee from Frau Keel, who beamed in return before she went back to her own place on a small sofa of the sort that the French—so he found out next day from a History of Furniture—call a *canapé*, where she was presently joined by Imogen. Thereafter he found that whenever he glanced (shyly) at Frau Keel she was staring anxiously and intently at Buckley, and whenever he glanced (shyly) at Imogen she was looking at himself with a tiny smile of what, crestfallen, he took to be amusement until she raised her hairy eyebrows and slowly shook her midnight head, and he heard a beautiful noise like a bomb exploding inside his chest at the thought that this black sprite was either giving him sympathy or asking sympathy from him. Either would be delightful. But, then, her eyebrows suddenly plunged, she shook her head threateningly, her smile curled, anger and disapproval sullied her already dark eyes.

"As I was saying," Father Tim was saying, magisterially waving his cigar, "if adultery is both a positive fact and a relative term, so is marriage. After all, marriage is much more than what The Master of the Sentences called a *conjunctio viri et mulieris*. It is also a union of sympathy and interest, heart and soul. Without these marriage becomes licensed adultery."

"I agree," Frau Keel sighed. "But no woman ever got a divorce for that reason."

Buckley pursed his little mouth into a provocative smile. "In fact people do divorce for that very reason. Only they call it mental cruelty."

"Alas," said Brünnhilde, "according to our Church, there is no such sin as mental cruelty and therefore there is no divorce."

"There are papal annulments," Herr Keel said to her coldly, "if you are interested in such things."

"I am very interested," she said to him as frigidly, which was not the kind of warm domestic conversation that Morgan had read about in books.

"You were about to tell us, Father Tim," Imogen said, "what you consider unarguable grounds for the annulment of a marriage."

Sickeningly Buckley beamed at the girl; fawningly she beamed back. *She!* The Hyrcanian tigress! Had this obese sensualist mesmerized the whole lot of them? But he could not, as Buckley calmly began to enumerate the impediments to true wedlock, center his mind on what was being said, so dumbfounded was he to find that nobody but himself seemed to be forming images of the hideous realities of what he now heard. All he could do was to gulp his brandy, as any man of the world might in such circumstances, and struggle to keep his eyes from Imogen's hirsute legs. (Where had he read that Charles XII had a woman in his army whose beard was two feet long?)

"It is not," Buckley said, "a true marriage if it has been preceded by rape. It is not a true marriage if either or both parties are certifiable lunatics. It is not," here he glanced at Keel, "a genuine marriage if the father marries the daughter," smiling at Imogen, "or if the sister marries the brother. It is not marriage if by error either party marries the wrong person, which can happen when a number of people are being married simultaneously. If either party has previously murdered the wife or husband of the other party it is not really a very good marriage. Nor if either party persuades the other party into adultery beforehand by a promise of marriage afterwards. It is not marriage if the male party is impotent both antecedently and perpetually. Nor if a Christian marries a Jew or other heathen . . ."

At which point they all started talking together, Imogen declaring passionately, "I would marry a Jew if I damn well wanted to," and Georg Keel demanding, "How can you prove impotency?" and Frau Keel protesting with ringed fingers,

"Kein Juden! Kein Juden!" Buckley laughingly crying out, "I agree, I agree," and Morgan wailing that it was all bureaucratic balderdash, all quashed suddenly into silence by the prolonged ringing of the doorbell. Keel glanced at his watch and said testily, "Who on earth . . . ?" Imogen, unwilling to lose a fraction of the fight, rushed to the door and led in the latecomer. It was the doctor.

Morgan had to admire his comportment. Though he must have been much taken aback to see all his problems personified before him, the old boy did not falter for a moment in his poise and manners. He formally apologized for his late call to Frau Keel, who revealed her delight in his visit by swiftly patting her hair as she passed a mirror, making him sit beside her, fluttering to Imogen to sit beside Morgan, and yielding him a brandy glass between her palms as if it were a chalice. He accepted it graciously, he did not allow it to pass over him, he bowed like a cardinal, he relaxed into the company, legs crossed, as easily as if he were the host and they his guests. Morgan observed that the cuffs of his trousers were wet. He had walked here in the rain. He must be feeling greatly upset.

"Are you a friend of this dirty old doctor?" Imogen whispered rapidly to Morgan.

"I know him slightly. I like you very much, Imogen."

"He is a vurm!" she whispered balefully. "You are another vurm. You both turned Father Tim from the door without a meal."

"Neither," said Tim, resuming control, "is it a marriage if it is clandestine, that is, performed secretly."

"I would marry in secret if I wanted to," like a shot from Imogen.

"It wasn't my house," Morgan whispered. "I wanted him to stay."

"What does 'secret' mean?" Keel asked petulantly.

"I know you lie," she whispered.

"It means failing to inform your parish priest."

"That's more bureaucratic fiddlesticks!" Morgan said, and an electric shock ran up his thigh when Imogen patted it approvingly.

"So," Tim said dryly to him, "the Empress Josephine thought, but her failure to obey the regulation meant that the Pope was able to allow the Emperor to eject her from his bed and marry again."

"Then," Keel agreed, "it is a wise precaution."

"It's bosh!" Morgan declared. "And cruel bosh."

"Good man!" said Imogen, and gave him another shock, while Frau Keel turned inquiringly to her pastor who said that the rule might be useful to prevent bigamy but was really no reason for dissolving a marriage, whereat she said, "Then it is bosh!" and her husband, outraged, proclaimed, "In my house I will allow nobody to say I am defending bosh!"

She waved him aside, clasped her paws, beamed at Father Timothy, and cried, "And now, for adultery!"

"Alas, Madame, adultery by either party is not sufficient cause to annul a marriage."

"So we women are trapped!"

"While you men," charged Imogen, glaring around her, "can freely go your adulterous ways."

The doctor intervened mildly.

"Happily none of this concerns anybody in this room."

"How do you know what concerns me?" she challenged, jumping to her feet, her gripped fists by her lean flanks, her prowlike nose pointing about her like a setter. "I, Imogen Keel, now, at this moment, vant to commit adultery with somebody in this room."

Morgan covered his face in his hands. O God! The confessions! She means me. What shall I say? That I want to kiss her knees?

"Imogen!" Keel blazed at her. "I will not permit this. In delicacy! Not to say, in politeness!"

"Please, Georg!" his wife screamed. "Not again!" She turned to the company. "Always I hear this appeal to politeness and delicacy. It is an excuse. It is an evasion. It is an alibi."

"Aha!" Imogen proclaimed, one hand throwing towards her father's throat an imaginary flag or dagger. "But he has always been excellent at alibis."

Keel slammed his empty brandy glass on the coffee table so hard that its stem snapped. "How fiery she is!" Morgan thought. What a heroic way she has of rearing her head back to the left and lifting her opposite eyebrow to the right. A girl like that would fight for her man to her death—or, if he betrayed her, to his. Has she, he wondered, hair on her back. Father Tim, amused by the whole scene, was saying tactfully but teasingly, "Imogen there is one other injustice to women that you must hear about. It is that you will in most countries not be permitted to marry, no matter how much you protest, until you have arrived at the age of twelve and your beloved at the age of fourteen."

She burst into laughter. They all laughed with relief.

"Finally," he said tristfully, "priests may not marry at all."

"They are nevertheless doing so," the girl commented pertly.

He looked at her, seemed to consider saying something, drank the last drop of his coffee, and did not say it. Frau Keel said it for him, compassionately.

"Only by giving up their priesthood."

"Or more," he agreed in a subdued voice.

"The whole caboodle," Imogen mocked.

They talked a little about current examples of priests who had given up everything. The subject trailed away. Keel looked at the window. "Rain," he sighed, in so weary a voice that the doctor at once rose, and all the others with him. As the group dissolved towards the entrance hall of the apartment Morgan found himself trailing behind with Imogen.

"What have you against the doctor?" he asked her.

"He is just like my father. And I hate my father. The only good thing I say about your doctor is that he helps my mother to put up with my father."

He must drive old Frank home—he must go on helping Frau Keel; they must talk about the best way to handle Buckley in future; they must have Georg Keel on one of their excursions; if the girl was lonely perhaps Keel would like to bring her with them. She was a superb, a wonderful, a marvelous girl, so heroic, so wild, so passionate. The very first thing they must do was to have Buckley to dinner, and maybe Buckley would bring the girl with him . . . Just then he heard Frank ask Keel if it was too late for them to have a brief word together before he left. If this meant the old fool was falling back on some ridiculous, bloody point of principle about treating Frau Keel . . . As he was making his way towards his friend to offer him a lift home Frau Keel absently shook his hand, handed him his hat, opened the door, bade him good night, and the door closed on her voice suggesting to Imogen to drive the good Father to his presbytery in her little car. A minute later he was in the street cursing.

There was not a soul in sight. The rain hung like vests around the lamplights of O'Connell Street. When his car refused to start his rage boiled against that stupid cow Marianne Simcox who must have let water (or something) get into the petrol. After many fruitless zizzings from the starter he saw Imogen's little blue car with the priest aboard shoot past in a wake of spray. More zizzings, more pulling at the choke, a long rest to deflood the carburetor, and the engine roared into life, just as Keel's Mercedes, with the doc aboard, vanished through the rain towards the bridge and the Dublin Road. He circled wildly, followed their taillights, halted twenty yards behind them outside Frank's house, doused his lights, saw him get out and Keel drive away. He ran forward to where Frank was unlocking his iron gate, and clutched his arm beseechingly.

"Frank! I simply must talk to you about Buckley. What is he

doing to all those people? What is he doing to that Imogen girl? For God's sake what's going on in that Keel family? I won't sleep a wink unless you tell me all you know about them."

The doctor marveled at him for a moment and then returned to his unlocking.

"I do not feel disposed," he said in his haughtiest voice, holding the gate six inches ajar for the length of his reply, "to discuss such matters at twelve o'clock at night, on an open road, under a downpour of rain, and all the less so since, so far as I can see, nothing is, as you so peculiarly put it, 'going on' that is of any interest to me. Everything seems perfectly normal and in order in the Keel family, except that Herr Keel is a total idiot who seems unable to control his wife, that she seems to me to have developed a most unseemly sexual interest in Father Timothy Buckley, that she is intent on divorcing her husband, that their daughter, who is both impertinent and feckless, is a nymphomaniac, who has quite obviously decided to seduce you, and that I am very glad to say that I need never again lay eyes on them for the rest of my natural life. And, now, sir, good night to you."

With which he entered his drive, banged the metaled gate behind him, and his wet footsteps died into a voice from his front door wailing, "Oh, dachtar, dachtar! Wait for me! I have the umbrella here for you. You'll be dhrowneded all together with that aaahful rain . . ."

Morgan spat on the gate, turned, and raced for his car, which resolutely refused to start. He implored it until its exhausted starter died into the silence of a final click. He got out, kicked its door soundly, and then overwhelmed by all the revelations he had just heard, especially the one about Imogen and himself, he walked home through the empty streets of L——, singing love songs from the *Barber* and *Don Giovanni* at the top of his voice to the summer rain.

*   *   *

One of the more pleasantly disconcerting things about will-ful man is that his most table-thumping decisions rarely con-clude the matter in hand. There is always time for a further option. Every score is no better than halftime. *Viz:*

1. That July our poor, dear friend Tim Buckley left us for a chin pimple of a village called Four Noughts (the vulgariza-tion of a Gaelic word meaning Stark Naked) on the backside of Slievenamuck. We loyally cursed His Lordship the bishop, while feeling that he had had no option. For weeks the dogs in the streets had been barking, "Im-o-gen Keel." At the farewell party Tim assured us that the bish had neither hand, act, nor part in it. He had himself asked His Lordship for a transfer. He asked us to pray for him. He said sadly that he believed he was gone beyond it. The die was cast, the Rubicon crossed, it was the Ides of March, and so forth and so on.

One effect of this event (Dolly Lynch reporting, after her usual survey of her master's wastepaper basket) was that Mister Myles had been invited to dinner with the dachtar at his ear-liest convenience.

2. That August we heard that Frau Keel was claiming a sepa-ration from her husband *a mensa et a thoro;* that she was also applying for a papal annulment of her marriage on the ground of his impotence, which meant that she was ready to swear that Imogen was not his child. Herr Keel, we gathered, had knocked her down, broken one of her ribs with a kick, and left for Stuttgart swearing that he would foil her if it cost him his last deutschmark.

Mister Myles was by now dining every week with the doctor, who was also (Dolly Lynch's knuckle suspended outside the dining-room door) seeing Frau Keel regularly, who (Dolly Lynch's hand on the doorknob) was also in constant consulta-tion, through Imogen, with Father Tim Buckley in his exile on Slievenamuck.

3. That September Tim Buckley disappeared from Four

Noughts, Imogen Keel disappeared from the Keel flat, and both were reported to have been seen at Shannon Airport boarding a plane for Stockholm. This blow brought us down. Tim's way of living life had been to tell us how to live it. Now that he was starting to live it himself he was no better than any of us. He was the only one of us who had both faced and been free of the world of men, of women, of children, of the flesh. Now we knew that it cannot be done. You must not put your toe into the sea if you do not want to swim in it.

Myles was by now dining with Frank Breen three times a week, friendship glued by gossip.

4. October. Dreadful news from Stuttgart. Herr Keel had accidentally killed himself while cleaning a shotgun. When the news came Morgan was having tea with Frau Keel. She collapsed, calling for the doctor. Morgan drove at once to Frank's house and brought him back to her. For the rest of that month Myles was dining every night with the doctor.

5. By November Dolly Lynch reported that Mister Myles had stopped dining with the doctor, but Mrs. Keel, she spat, was coming as often as "tree taimes every bluddy wee-uk." When we heard this we looked at one another. Our eyes said, "Could it be possible?" We asked Morgan. He was in no doubt about it.

"Buckley was right!" he stormed. "The man is a sexual maniac! A libertine! A corrupter of women! A traitor and a liar. As that foolish woman will discover before the year is out."

It was a spring wedding, and the reception was one of the gayest, most crowded, most lavish the town had ever seen. The metal sheeting was gone from the gate, the cypresses cut down, the warning signs inside the gate removed, the brass plate removed, the conservatory packed with flowers, the only drink served was champagne. The doctor became Frank to every Tom and Harry. For the first time we found out that his wife's name was Victorine. With his hair tinted he looked ten years younger. Long before the reception ended he was going around whispering to everybody, as a dead secret, that Victorine was expecting.

6. Morgan, naturally, did not attend the wedding. He took off for the day with Marianne Simcox, and they have since been taking off every fine Sunday in her red Mustang, together with Morgan's mother, in search of faceless churchlets in fallow fields where the only sound is the munching of cattle. His mother prepares the lunch. Marianne reads out his own poems to him. They both feed him like a child with tidbits from their fingers. But who knows the outcome of any mortal thing? Buckley—there is no denying it—had a point when he insisted that man's most ingenious invention is man, that to create others we must first imagine ourselves, and that to keep us from wandering, or wondering, in some other direction where a greater truth may lie, we set up all sorts of roadblocks and traffic signals. Morgan has told his Marianne that he has always admired the virginal type. It is enough to put any girl off her stroke. A wink of a brass plate in a country road set him off on one tack. A wink from her might set him off on another. What should she do? Obey his traffic signs, or acknowledge the truth—that he is a born liar—and start showing him a glimpse of thigh?

Heaven help the women of the world, always wondering what the blazes their men's next graven image will be.

Frank O'Connor (1903–1966)

Frank O'Connor was born Michael O'Donovan in Cork in 1903. His early life was marked by rock-bottom poverty and by his father's struggles with drink and work. But there were compensations, both in his family and in Cork City, as O'Connor movingly describes in the first volume of his autobiography, An Only Child *(1961). He had to quit the Christian Brothers' school before he was fourteen, but his early education was supplemented, and strongly influenced, by Daniel Corkery. After a series of odd jobs he joined the Republican forces during the Civil War and was captured. In the Free State jail he improved his Gaelic, and mastered it to such a degree that he won a national prize with an essay in Gaelic on Turgenev. He later became a professional librarian, went to Dublin, and began publishing poems and translations in George Russell's* The Irish Statesman *and in Seumas O'Sullivan's* Dublin Magazine. *He met Yeats, who encouraged him to continue his translations from Gaelic and had him appointed director of the Abbey Theatre, a position he resigned in 1939. Though O'Connor has written two novels,* The Saint and Mary Kate *(1932) and* Dutch Interior *(1940), he has concentrated on the writing—and rewriting—of short stories, and he is now recognized as one of the modern masters of the form. Sean O'Faolain has written that O'Connor was "the finest craftsman in the art of the short story Ireland has produced." Among his collections of stories are* Guests of the Nation *(1931),* Bones of Contention *(1936),* Crab Apple Jelly *(1944),* The Common Chord *(1947),* Traveller's Samples *(1951), and* Domestic Relations *(1957). His* Collected Stories *appeared in 1981. O'Connor has also published studies of the novel and of the short story, a survey of Irish literature, and several travel books. His translations from Gaelic are collected in* Kings, Lords and Commons *(1959). "In the Train," Patrick Kavanagh's favorite O'Connor story, is taken from* Bones of Contention.

In the Train

I

"There!" said the sergeant's wife. "You would hurry me."

"I always like being in time for a train," replied the sergeant, with the equability of one who has many times before explained the guiding principle of his existence.

"I'd have had heaps of time to buy the hat," added his wife.

The sergeant sighed and opened his evening paper. His wife looked out on the dark platform, pitted with pale lights under which faces and faces passed, lit up and dimmed again. A uniformed lad strode up and down with a tray of periodicals and chocolates. Farther up the platform a drunken man was being seen off by his friends.

"I'm very fond of Michael O'Leary," he shouted. "He is the most sincere man I know."

"I have no life," sighed the sergeant's wife. "No life at all. There isn't a soul to speak to; nothing to look at all day but bogs and mountains and rain—always rain! And the people! Well, we've had a fine sample of them, haven't we?"

The sergeant continued to read.

"Just for the few days it's been like heaven. Such interesting people! Oh, I thought Mr. Boyle had a glorious face! And his voice—it went through me."

The sergeant lowered his paper, took off his peaked cap, laid it on the seat beside him, and lit his pipe. He lit it in the old-fashioned way, ceremoniously, his eyes blinking pleasurably like a sleepy cat's in the match flare. His wife scrutinized each face that passed and it was plain that for her life meant faces and people and things and nothing more.

"Oh, dear!" she said again. "I simply have no existence. I was educated in a convent and play the piano; my father was a literary man, and yet I am compelled to associate with the lowest types of humanity. If it was even a decent town, but a village!"

"Ah," said the sergeant, gapping his reply with anxious puffs, "maybe with God's help we'll get a shift one of these days." But he said it without conviction, and it was also plain that he was well pleased with himself, with the prospect of returning home with his pipe and his paper.

"Here are Magner and the others," said his wife as four other policemen passed the barrier. "I hope they'll have sense enough to let us alone. . . . How do you do? How do you do? Had a nice time, boys?" she called with sudden animation, and her pale, sullen face became warm and vivacious. The policemen smiled and touched their caps but did not halt.

"They might have stopped to say good evening," she added sharply, and her face sank into its old expression of boredom and dissatisfaction. "I don't think I'll ask Delancey to tea again. The others make an attempt but, really, Delancey is hopeless. When I smile and say, 'Guard Delancey, wouldn't you like to use the butter knife?' he just scowls at me from under his shaggy brows and says without a moment's hesitation, 'I would not.'"

"Ah, Delancey is a poor slob," the sergeant said affectionately.

"Oh, yes, but that's not enough, Jonathan. Slob or no slob, he should make an attempt. He's a young man; he should have a dinner jacket at least. What sort of wife will he get if he won't even wear a dinner jacket?"

"He's easy, I'd say. He's after a farm in Waterford."

"Oh, a farm! A farm! The wife is only an incidental, I suppose?"

"Well, now, from all I hear she's a damn nice little incidental."

"Yes, I suppose many a nice little incidental came from a farm," answered his wife, raising her pale brows. But the irony was lost on him.

"Indeed yes, indeed yes," he said fervently.

"And here," she added in biting tones, "come our charming neighbors."

Into the pale lamplight stepped a group of peasants. Not such as one sees near a capital but in the mountains and along the coasts. Gnarled, wild, with turbulent faces, their ill-cut clothes full of character, the women in pale brown shawls, the men wearing black sombreros and carrying big sticks, they swept in, ill at ease, laughing and shouting defiantly. And so much part of their natural environment were they that for a moment they seemed to create about themselves rocks and bushes, tarns, turf-ricks, and sea.

With a prim smile the sergeant's wife bowed to them through the open window.

"How do you do? How do you do?" she called. "Had a nice time?"

At the same moment the train gave a jolt and there was a rush in which the excited peasants were carried away. Some minutes passed; the influx of passengers almost ceased, and a porter began to slam the doors. The drunken man's voice rose in a cry of exultation.

"You can't possibly beat O'Leary," he declared. "I'd lay down my life for Michael O'Leary."

Then, just as the train was about to start, a young woman in a brown shawl rushed through the barrier. The shawl, which came low enough to hide her eyes, she held firmly across her mouth, leaving visible only a long thin nose with a hint of pale flesh at either side. Beneath the shawl she was carrying a large parcel.

She looked hastily around; a porter shouted to her and

pushed her towards the nearest compartment, which happened to be that occupied by the sergeant and his wife. He had actually seized the handle of the door when the sergeant's wife sat up and screamed.

"Quick! Quick!" she cried. "Look who it is! She's coming in. Jonathan! Jonathan!"

The sergeant rose with a look of alarm on his broad red face. The porter threw open the door, with his free hand grasping the woman's elbow. But when she laid eyes on the sergeant's startled face she stepped back, tore herself free, and ran crazily up the platform. The engine shrieked; the porter slammed the door with a curse; somewhere another door opened and shut, and the row of watchers, frozen into effigies of farewell, now dark now bright, began to glide gently past the window, and the stale, smoky air was charged with the breath of open fields.

II

The four policemen spread themselves out in a separate compartment and lit cigarettes.

"Poor old Delancey!" Magner said with his reckless laugh. "He's cracked on her all right."

"Cracked on her," agreed Fox. "Did ye see the eye he gave her?"

Delancey smiled sheepishly. He was a tall, handsome, black-haired young man with the thick eyebrows described by the sergeant's wife. He was new to the force and suffered from a mixture of natural gentleness and country awkwardness.

"I am," he said in his husky voice. "The devil admire me, I never hated anyone yet, but I think I hate the living sight of her."

"Oh now, oh now!" protested Magner.

"I do. I think the Almighty God must have put that one into the world with the one main object of persecuting me."

"Well indeed," said Foley, "'tis a mystery to me how the sergeant puts up with her. If any woman up and called me by an outlandish name like Jonathan when everyone knew my name was plain John I'd do fourteen days for her—by God, I would, and a calendar month."

The four men were now launched on a favorite topic that held them for more than a hour. None of them liked the sergeant's wife and all had stories to tell against her. From these there emerged the fact that she was an incurable scandalmonger and mischief-maker who couldn't keep quiet about her own business, much less about that of her neighbors. And while they talked the train dragged across a dark plain, the heart of Ireland, and in the moonless night tiny cottage windows blew past like sparks from a fire, and a pale simulacrum of the lighted carriages leaped and frolicked over hedges and fields. Magner shut the window and the compartment began to fill with smoke.

"She'll never rest till she's out of Farranchreesht," he said.

"That she mightn't!" groaned Delancey.

"How would you like the city yourself, Dan?" asked Magner.

"Man dear," exclaimed Delancey with sudden brightness, "I'd like it fine. There's great life in a city."

"You're welcome to it," said Foley, folding his hands across his paunch.

"Why so? What's wrong with it?"

"I'm better off where I am."

"But the life!"

"Life be damned! What sort of life is it when you're always under someone's eye? Look at the poor devils in court."

"True enough, true enough," agreed Fox.

"Ah, yes, yes," said Delancey, "but the adventures they have!"

"What adventures?"

"There was a sergeant in court only yesterday telling me one thing that happened himself. 'Twas an old maid without a soul in the world that died in an old loft on the quays. The sergeant put a new man on duty outside the door while he went back to report, and all he had to do was kick the door and frighten off the rats."

"That's enough, that's enough!" cried Foley.

"Yes, yes, but listen now, listen can't you?" cried Delancey. "He was there ten minutes with a bit of candle when the door at the foot of the stairs began to open. 'Who's there?' says he, getting a bit nervous. 'Who's there I say?' No answer, and still the door kept opening. Then he gave a laugh. What was it only an old cat? 'Puss, puss,' says he, 'come on up, puss.' Then he gave another look and the hair stood up on his head. There was another bloody cat coming in. 'Get out!' says he to scare them, and then another cat came in and then another, and in his fright he dropped the candle. The cats began to hiss and bawl and that robbed him of the last stitch of sense. He made down the stairs, and if he did he trod on a cat, and went down head over heels, and when he tried to grip something 'twas a cat he gripped, and he felt the claws tearing his face. He was out for three weeks after."

"That's a bloody fine adventure," said Foley with bitter restraint.

"Isn't it though?" Delancey said eagerly. "You'd be a long time in Farranchreesht before anything like that would happen you."

"That's the thing about Farranchreesht, lad," said Magner. " 'Tis a great ease to be able to put on your cap and go for a drink any hour of the day or night."

"Yes," added Foley, "and to know the worst case you're likely to have in ten years is a bit of a scrap about politics."

"I don't know," Delancey sighed dreamily. "Chrisht, there's great charm about the Criminal Courts."

"Damn the much they had for you when you were in the box," growled Foley.

"I know, sure, I know," admitted Delancey crestfallen. "I was sweating."

"Shutting your eyes you were," said Magner, "like a kid afraid he was going to get a box on the ear."

"Still," said Delancey, "this sergeant I'm talking about, he said after a while you wouldn't mind that no more than if 'twas a card party. He said you'd talk back to the judge as man to man."

"I daresay that's true," agreed Magner.

There was silence in the smoky compartment that jolted and rocked on its way across Ireland, and the four occupants, each touched with that morning wit which afflicts no one so much as state witnesses, thought of how they'd speak to the judge now if only they had him before them as man to man. They looked up to see a fat red face behind the door, and a moment later it was dragged back.

"Is this my carriage, gentlemen?" asked a meek and boozy voice.

"No, 'tisn't. Go on with you!" snapped Magner.

"I had as nice a carriage as ever was put on a railway train," said the drunk, leaning in, "a handsome carriage, and 'tis lost."

"Try farther on," suggested Delancey.

"Ye'll excuse me interrupting yeer conversation, gentlemen."

"That's all right, that's all right."

"I'm very melancholic. My best friend, I parted him this very night, and 'tis unknown to anyone, only the Almighty and Merciful God (here the drunk reverently raised his bowler hat and let it slide down the back of his neck to the floor) if I'll ever lay eyes on him again in this world. Good night, gentlemen, and thanks, thanks for all yeer kindness."

As the drunk slithered away up the corridor Delancey laughed. Fox, who had remained thoughtful, resumed the conversation where it had left off.

"Delancey wasn't the only one that was sweating," he said.

"He was not," agreed Foley. "Even the sergeant was a bit shook."

"He was very shook. When he caught up the poison mug to identify it he was shaking, and before he could put it down it danced a jig on the table."

"Ah, dear God, dear God," sighed Delancey, "what killed me most entirely was the bloody old model of the house. I didn't mind anything else only the house. There it was, a living likeness, with the bit of grass in front and the shutter hanging loose, and every time I looked at it I was in the back lane in Farranchreesht, and then I'd look up and see the lean fellow in the wig pointing his finger at me."

"Well, thank God," said Foley with simple devotion, "this time tomorrow I'll be in Ned Ivers's back with a pint in my fist."

Delancey shook his head, a dreamy smile playing upon his dark face.

"I don't know," he said. " 'Tis a small place, Farranchreesht; a small, mangy old place with no interest or advancement in it." His face lit up as the sergeant appeared in the corridor. "Here's the sergeant now," he said.

"He wasn't long getting tired of Julietta," whispered Magner maliciously.

The door was pushed back and the sergeant entered, loosening the collar of his tunic. He fell into a corner seat, crossed his legs, and accepted the cigarette which Delancey proffered.

"Well, lads," he exclaimed. "What about a jorum?"

"Isn't it remarkable?" said Foley. "I was only just talking about it."

"I have noted before now, Peter," said the sergeant, "that you and me have what might be called a simultaneous thirst."

III

The country folk were silent and exhausted. Kendillon drowsed now and then, but he suffered from blood pressure, and after a while his breathing grew thicker and stronger till at last it exploded in a snort and he started up, broad awake and angry. In the silence rain spluttered and tapped along the roof and the dark windowpanes streamed with shining runnels of water that trickled to the floor. Moll Mhor scowled, her lower lip thrust out. She was a great flop of a woman with a big, coarse, powerful face. The other two women whose eyes were closed had their brown shawls drawn tight about their heads, but Moll's was round her shoulders and the gap above her breasts was filled with a blaze of scarlet.

"Aren't we home yet?" Kendillon asked crossly, starting awake after one of his drowsing fits.

Moll glowered at him.

"No, nor won't be. What scour is on you?"

"My little house," moaned Kendillon.

"My little house," mimicked Moll. " 'Twasn't enough for you to board the windows and put barbed wire on the gate."

" 'Tis all very well for you that have someone to mind yours for you," he snarled.

One of the women laughed softly and turned a haggard virginal face within the cowl of her shawl.

" 'Tis that have me laughing," she explained apologetically. "Tim Dwyer this week past at the stirabout pot."

"And making the beds," chimed in the third woman.

"And washing the children's faces! Glory be to God, he'll be mad."

"Ay," said Moll, "and his chickens running off with Thade Kendillon's roof."

"My roof is it?" he asked.

"Yes."

" 'Tis a good roof," he said roughly. " 'Tis a better roof than ever was seen over your head since the day you married."

"Oh, Mary my mother!" sighed Moll, " 'tis a great pity of me this three hours and I looking at the likes of you instead of my own fine bouncing man."

" 'Tis a new thing to hear you praising Sean then," said a woman.

"I wronged him," Moll said contritely. "I did so. I wronged him before God and the world."

At this moment the drunken man pulled back the door of the compartment and looked from face to face with an expression of deepening melancholy.

"She's not here," he said in disappointment.

"Who's not here, mister?" asked Moll with a wink at the others.

"I'm looking for my own carriage, ma'am," said the drunk with melancholy dignity, "and whatever the bloody hell they done with it, 'tis lost. The railways in this country are gone to hell."

"Wisha, if that's all that's worrying you, wouldn't you sit here with me?" asked Moll. "I'm here so long I'm forgetting what a real man looks like."

"I would with great pleasure," replied the drunk politely, "but 'tisn't only the carriage. 'Tis my traveling companion. I'm a lonely man; I parted my best friend this very night; I found one to console me, and then when I turned my back—God took her!"

And with a dramatic gesture he closed the door and continued on his way. The country folk sat up, blinking. The smoke of the men's pipes filled the compartment and the heavy air was laden with the smell of homespun and turf smoke, the sweet pungent odor of which had penetrated every fiber of their clothes.

"Listen to the rain!" said one of the women. "We'll have a wet walk home."

" 'Twill be midnight before we're in," said another.

"Ah, what matter sure when the whole country will be up? There'll be a lot of talking done in Farranchreesht tonight."

"A lot of talking and no sleep."

"Oh, Farranchreesht! Farranchreesht!" cried the young woman with the haggard face, the ravaged lineaments of which were suddenly transfigured. "Farranchreesht and the sky over you, I wouldn't change places with the Queen of England to-night!"

And suddenly Farranchreesht, the bare bogland with the humpbacked mountain behind, the little white houses and the dark fortifications of turf that made it seem like the flame-blackened ruin of some mighty city, all was lit up in their minds. An old man sitting in a corner, smoking a broken clay pipe, thumped his stick on the floor.

"Well now," said Kendillon darkly, "wasn't it great impudence in her to come back?"

"Wasn't it indeed?" echoed one of the women.

"I'd say she won't be there long," he went on knowingly.

"You'll give her the hunt, I suppose?" asked Moll politely, too politely.

"If no one else do, I'll give her the hunt myself. What right have she in a decent place?"

"Oh, the hunt, the hunt," agreed a woman. "Sure, no one could ever darken her door again."

"And what the hell did we tell all the lies for?" asked Moll with her teeth on edge to be at Kendillon. "Thade Kendillon there swore black was white."

"What else would I do, woman? There was never an informer in my family."

"I'm surprised to hear it," said Moll vindictively, but the old man thumped his stick three or four times for silence.

"We all told our story," he said, "and we told it well. And no one told it better than Moll. You'd think to hear her she believed it herself."

"I declare to God I very nearly did," she said with a wild laugh.

"I seen great changes in my time, great changes," the old man said, shaking his head, "and now I see a greater change still."

A silence followed his words. There was profound respect in all their eyes. The old man coughed and spat.

"What change is that, Colm?" asked Moll.

"Did any of ye ever think the day would come when a woman in our parish would do the like of that?"

"Never, never."

"But she might do it for land?"

"She might."

"Or for money?"

"She might so."

"She might indeed. When the hunger is money people kill for the money; when the hunger is land people kill for the land. But what are they killing for now? I tell ye, there's a great change coming. In the ease of the world people are asking more. When I was a boy in the barony if you killed a beast you made six pieces of it, one for yourself and the rest for the neighbors. The same if you made a catch of fish. And that's how it was with us from the beginning of time. But now look at the change! The people aren't as poor or as good or as generous or as strong."

"Or as wild," added Moll with a vicious glance at Kendillon. "'Tis in the men you'd mostly notice the change."

The door opened and Magner, Delancey, and the sergeant entered. Magner was already drunk.

"I was lonely without you, Moll," he said. "You're the biggest and brazenest and cleverest liar of the lot and you lost me my sergeant's stripes, but I'll forgive you everything if you'll give us one bar of the 'Colleen Dhas Roo.'"

IV

"I'm a lonely man," said the drunk. "And I'm going back to a lonely habitation."

"My best friend," he continued, "I left behind me—Michael O'Leary, the most sincere man I know. 'Tis a great pity you don't know Michael and a great pity Michael don't know you. But look at the misfortunate way things happen! I was looking for someone to console me, and the moment I turned my back you were gone."

He placed his hand solemnly under the woman's chin and raised her face to the light. With the other hand he stroked her cheeks.

"You have a beautiful face," he said reverently, "a beautiful face. But what's more important, you have a beautiful soul. I look into your eyes and I see the beauty of your nature. Allow me one favor. Only one favor before we part."

He bent and kissed her. Then he picked up his bowler which had fallen once more, put it on back to front, took his dispatch case, and got out.

The woman sat on alone. Her shawl was thrown open and beneath it she wore a bright blue blouse. The carriage was cold, the night outside black and cheerless, and within her something had begun to contract that threatened to crush the very spark of life in her. She could no longer fight it off even when for the hundredth time she went over the scenes of the previous day; the endless hours in the dock, the wearisome questions and speeches she could not understand, and the long wait in the cells till the jury returned. She felt again the shiver of mortal anguish that went through her when the chief warder beckoned angrily from the stairs and the wardress, glancing hastily in a hand mirror, pushed her forward. She saw the jury with their expressionless faces. She was standing there alone, in nervous twitches jerking back the shawl from her face to give herself air. She was trying to say a prayer but the words were being drowned in her mind by the thunder of nerves, crashing and bursting. She could feel one which had escaped dancing madly at the side of her mouth, but was powerless to recapture it.

"The verdict of the jury is that Helena Maguire is not guilty." Which was it? Death or life? She could not say. "Silence! Silence!" shouted the usher though no one had tried to say anything. "Any other charge?" asked a weary voice. "Release the prisoner." "Silence!" shouted the usher again. The chief warder opened the door of the dock and she began to run. When she reached the steps she stopped and looked back to see if she was being followed. A policeman held open a door and she found herself in an ill-lit, drafty stone corridor. She stood there, the old shawl about her face. The crowd began to emerge. The first was a tall girl with a rapt expression as though she were walking on air. When she saw the woman she halted, her hands went up in an instinctive gesture, as though to feel her, to caress her. It was that look of hers, that gait as of a sleepwalker that brought the woman to her senses. . . .

But now the memory had no warmth in her mind, and the something within her continued to contract, smothering her with loneliness, shame, and fear. She began to mutter crazily to herself. The train, now almost empty, was stopping at every little wayside station. Now and again a blast from the Atlantic pushed at it as though trying to capsize it.

She looked up as the door slammed open and Moll came in, swinging her shawl behind her.

"They're all up the train. Wouldn't you come?"

"No, no, I couldn't."

"Why couldn't you? Who are you minding? Is it Thade Kendillon?"

"No, no, I'll stop as I am."

"Here, take a sup of this." Moll fumbled in her shawl and produced a bottle of liquor as pale as water. "Wait till I tell you what Magner said! That fellow is a limb of the devil. 'Have you e'er a drop, Moll?' says he. 'Maybe I have,' says I. 'What is it?' says he. 'For God's sake, baptize it quick and call it whiskey.' "

The woman took the bottle and put it to her lips. She shivered as she drank.

" 'Tis a good drop," said Moll approvingly.

Next moment there were loud voices in the corridor. Moll grabbed the bottle and hid it under her shawl. But it was only

Magner, the sergeant, and Delancey. After them came the two countrywomen, giggling. Magner held out his hand.

"Helena," he said, "accept my congratulations."

She took his hand, smiling awkwardly.

"We'll get you the next time though," he added.

"Musha, what are you saying, mister?"

"Not a word. You're a clever woman, a remarkable woman, and I give you full credit for it. You threw dust in all our eyes."

"Poison is supposed to be an easy thing to trace but it beat me to trace it," said the sergeant, barely concealing his curiosity.

"Well, well, there's things they're saying about me!" she said with a nervous laugh.

"Tell him," advised Magner. "There's nothing he can do to you now. You're as safe as the judge himself. Last night when the jury came in with the verdict you could have stood there in the dock and said: 'Ye're wrong. I did it. I got the stuff in such and such a place. I gave it to him because he was old and dirty and cantankerous and a miser. I did it and I'm proud of it.' You could have said every word of that and they couldn't have laid a finger on you."

"Indeed, what a thing I'd say!"

"Well, you could."

"The law is truly a remarkable phenomenon," said the sergeant, who was also rather squiffy. "Here you are, sitting at your ease at the expense of the state, and for one simple word of a couple of letters you could be up in Mountjoy, waiting for the rope and the morning jaunt."

The woman shuddered. The young woman with the ravaged face looked up.

" 'Twas the holy will of God," she said.

" 'Twas all the bloody lies Moll Mhor told," replied Magner.

" 'Twas the will of God."

"There was many hanged in the wrong," said the sergeant.

"Even so, even so, 'twas God's will."

"You have a new blouse, Helena," said the other woman in an envious tone.

"I seen it last night in a shop on the quays."

"How much was it?"

"Honor of God!" exclaimed Magner, looking at the woman in stupefaction. "Is that all you had to think of? You should have been on your bended knees before the altar."

"And sure I was," she answered indignantly.

"Women!" exclaimed Magner with a gesture of despair. He winked at Moll and they retired to the next compartment. But the interior was reflected clearly in the corridor window, and the others could see the pale quivering image of the policeman lift the bottle to his lips and blow a long silent blast on it. The young woman who had spoken of the blouse laughed.

"There'll be one good day's work done on the head of the trial," she said.

"How so?" asked the sergeant.

"Dan Canty will make a great brew of poteen while he have all yeer backs turned."

"I'll get Dan Canty yet," replied the sergeant stiffly.

"You will, the way you got Helena."

"I'll get him yet," he said as he consulted his watch. "We'll be in in another quarter of an hour. 'Tis time we were all getting back to our respective compartments."

Magner entered and the other policemen rose. The sergeant fastened his collar and buckled his belt. Magner swayed, holding the doorframe, a mawkish smile on his thin, handsome, dissipated face.

"Well, good night to you now, ma'am," said the sergeant primly. "I'm as glad for all our sakes things ended as they did."

"Good night, Helena," said Magner, bowing low and promptly tottering. "There'll be one happy man in Farranchreesht tonight."

"Come on, Joe," protested the sergeant.

"One happy man," Magner repeated obstinately. " 'Tis his turn now."

"You're drunk, man," said Delancey.

"You wanted him," Magner said heavily. "Your people wouldn't let you have him but you have him now in spite of them all."

"Do you mean Cady Driscoll?" hissed the woman with sudden anger, leaning towards Magner, the shawl tight about her head.

"Never mind who I mean. You have him."

"He's no more to me now than the salt sea."

The policemen went out first, the women followed, Moll Mhor laughing boisterously. The woman was left alone. Through the window she could see little cottages stepping down over wet and naked rocks to the water's edge. The flame of life had narrowed in her to a pinpoint, and she could only wonder at the force that had caught her up, mastered her, and then thrown her aside.

"No more to me," she repeated dully to her own image in the glass, "no more to me than the salt sea."

Patrick Kavanagh (1904–1967)

Patrick Kavanagh was born in Inniskeen, County Monaghan, in 1904. He was the son of a farmer and cobbler who is one of the figures in The Green Fool (1938). *Kavanagh went to Dublin in the early 1930s, and, aided and encouraged by George Russell, he published his first book of poetry,* Ploughman and Other Poems (1936). *During World War II he wrote one of his best works, the long poem "The Great Hunger" (1942). Now recognized as one of Ireland's major poets after Yeats, he also wrote a fine novel,* Tarry Flynn (1948), *and various essays and pamphlets. His poems are gathered in* Collected Poems (1964), *and his prose in* Collected Pruse (1967). *"George" is taken from the autobiographical sequence of story sketches that form* The Green Fool.

George

I was fond of visiting the neighbors' houses. Nobody was ever so busy that he couldn't give you a "while of his crack."

Once a week at least I visited old George. George was a cripple, a once savage man who had mellowed into a teller of fairy tales. He believed in the fairies. He was poor. Once I was sitting in his kitchen listening to his wonder tales. I put leading questions sometimes when George was in bad humor.

"What do you think of Dromore?"

"Aw, Dromore is a gentle place," he said. "The Banshee . . .

Josie, Josie," George called his daughter, "put out that cat and don't have him atin' the blessed stirabout." The big black-and-white cat was trying to lift the lid off the stirabout pot.

"It'll not do Jamsie a bit a harm," his daughter said.

George looked from his daughter to me with a mournful look. "In my youthful days," he said, "the children would do as they were bid. Now the youths that's going have no care, no consarn for the oul' folk."

The cat, Jamsie, was at the pot again. "Oh, ye tarlin villain," George cried, and he flung a piece of coal at the cat.

George lived on a five-acre farm. He talked big.

"Five and thirty years ago I was in the Fair of Mullingar in the County Wicklow," he would begin. He was weak on geography. "I had a three-year-oul' horse there."

"Don't be makin' a cod of yerself," his daughter said.

"Aw, ye tarlin faggot," he screamed. He had a hot temper.

"Paddy," he addressed me, "no one in God's world knows what I have to put up with." His daughter had gone out, and when she returned George asked: "Did she lay yet?"

"No, she's houldin' to it still."

"Did ye look under the marley hen?"

The daughter put on an edge. "Don't ye know as well as I do," she cried, "that the marley hen is lookin' hatch."

"Ye don't smoke the tobacco, nor yer da anayther," George said to me.

"An odd pipeful," I said.

"Yer lucky can do without it," he said. "I didn't get a pull of a pipe since yesterday afore dinner. If that hen would lay we'd have the makings of a dozen eggs for the shop and Katie could get me an ounce. Tenpence an ounce—and it's daylight robbery. Go out again," he spoke to his daughter, "and have another look."

"No, I'll do no such thing," she said. "Liftin' the hen be the tail will put her from layin' altogether."

"Very well then," George sighed resignedly.

Then from the hen house there came the heart-gladdening cackle of a hen. George brightened up. He looked as happy as turnips in July after rain.

"Thanks be to the Almighty," he said. He took his blackened clay pipe from the hole in the hob and looked into the bowl.

"There's just one wee smoke in it," he said, "just one wee smoke, and if I had to smoke that and had no more I'd be in a bad way: it stood between me and the divil."

He lit up, and his memories danced in the rings of tobacco smoke.

"Aw, Paddy," he began, "in my youthful days times weren't like they are now. I worked for Charlie Kenny at sevenpence a day. From six o'clock in the mornin' till seven in the evenin': the youths that's going now couldn't stand that."

"You were a tight hardy fella, I heard people to say," I said.

"Who was sayin' that?" he asked.

Nobody ever said it, but I wanted to give my praise a background.

"Yer own da was a tight wee fella," he said. "He reared and schooled a big family of yez be his trade. A great wee man was the Kavanagh."

His daughter was on her way to the huckster's shop.

As he puffed at his pipe I could see the fairies peering out like angels in a tomboy mood.

"Aw, Paddy," he said, "this part of Ireland is a gentle spot. It isn't right to be trampin' the fields at nightfall except on good business. The Wee Fellas be about."

The cat was staring up at old George. "Get outa me sight," he told the cat. He didn't like to see a cat staring him.

"The cat's a quare article," he said. "I'd be afraid he'd start to talk to me."

"Your grandmother walked to Dublin in a day," I said. The story of her walking powers was still current coin of conversation among the old folk.

"She did that," he said, "and back the same day. She had a letter for Charlie Kenny. But that was nothin' to her walkin' to the town of Monaghan every day when me grand-uncle was in jail for a little trifle."

I had heard the story before, but I expressed suitable wonder. George told me.

"Me grand-uncle was in Monaghan jail for a debt of eleven shillings. Me granny brought him his dinner of champ every day. Twenty-one and a half Irish miles to Monaghan, she'd have the champ warm enough to melt the butter. Sure, the youths that's goin' now are . . ."

Just then his daughter arrived with the tobacco. He surveyed the plug with a knowing eye.

"A bad ounce," he said. "I don't like to see the rider on an ounce."

The plug of tobacco had been cut lightweight off the coil and a slip of tobacco was stuck on with a rivet. This was the rider. He stuck the tobacco in his greasy waistcoat pocket. "Aw well, we'll have to be doin' with it," he said.

We could see from George's window all the people passing on the County Road. George had wonderful sight for a man of seventy. A woman passed.

"Oul' Betty goin' for her pension," George said. A man passed. "Pat the Wrastler," George stated. "Did I ever tell ye how he came to wear that name?" he asked.

"About a thousand times," the daughter butted in.

"You shut yer big mouth," her father said.

"I never heard a word about that," I said.

"Aw sure, nobody gives in to anythin' now," he began. "The youths that's goin' now know more than the oul' people. Pat was goin' home late one evenin' in the month of June. When he came to the dark part of the road at Rocksavage Avenue he chanced to look through the trees. The Moon was shinin' on the grass. The Wee Fellas were kickin' a football. 'Come out here,' says the captain to Pat. Pat went out. Every time he tried

to folly the ball he got a riser that sent him on his mouth and
nose a perch away. And mind ye, Pat was no aisy man to
throw. So when Pat was lavin' the captain of the Wee Fellas
called him to one side and says he to Pat: 'Pat, the longest day
ye live no man will be able to down ye.' And not a man or men
could ever down Pat from that day to this."

"Such rubbish," the daughter said.

Old George gave her a wild stare. "Aw, the youths that's
goin' now are a quare pack."

He became silent for a while. Then he asked: "Are ye on the
sate these days?" He meant was I at the cobbling trade.

"An odd day," I said.

"Stick to the sate," he advised me, "yer da made a good livin'
from his trade. Can ye cut out yet?"

"Don't ye know right well he can cut out a pair of boots,"
the daughter said. "What d'ye think he is?"

"Who's talkin' to you?" the father said. "Have ye yer pigs
near ready for the hammer?"

"We're killing next week."

"Yer mother is a great feeder of the pig," he said. "A notorious great woman is Biddy."

A whirl-blast danced outside, lifting stray straws from the
street. George took off his greasy soot-black cap. "The day is
Wednesday, God speed them," he said. The whirlwind was to
old George the fairies traveling across country.

George believed in all the old things—ghosts, fairies, horses,
scythes, sickles, and flails, and he hated the modern equivalents
of these things. "They have the country destroyed," he said,
"things are goin' too fast." And then he said, with a touch of
suspicion: "Did ye see Johnnie lately?"

Johnnie was a near neighbor of ours.

"I saw him this very day," I said.

George bowed his head till his shaggy beard was all crumpled against his waistcoat.

"Johnnie is a boyo," he said when he looked up. George

didn't like our neighbor Johnnie of the Parables. Johnnie had a dry, logical humor, which squeezed to suffocation George's fairies and ghosts. Johnnie often told me stories that reflected on the comical side of George's face.

"Aw, Paddy, Johnnie is a boyo."

In the middle of two of George's three fields there grew lone bushes, huge thorn trees, thirty feet high. Although he was poor as a hawk and was often scarce of fire, George never even dreamt of cutting these bushes. One dark night a fellow climbed up one of the trees and flashed an electric torch about. George, from his window, saw and was confirmed in his faith.

The year his wife died a limb had broken from one of the lone bushes. George shook his head and prepared for the worst.

"I hear there's a ridge of oats missed in Meigan's field," I said to George.

"Is that the truth?" he questioned solemnly.

"It's missed, all right," the daughter corroborated truthfully. A missed ridge of corn or drill of potatoes was an ill omen.

"I wonder which of them is goin' to die?" he said. "Dacent unmeddlin' people—I'd be long sarry and a week sick to see them in trouble."

"The ridge is missed, at any rate," I said.

"Well, that's enough," George said. "It's the surest sign of a death in a family."

We were still discussing the missed ridge when Caraher arrived. Caraher was the only beggar-man we had. He wasn't a common beggar, but a sort of gentleman collector of potatoes. He remembered his once-upon-a-time respectability and it seemed a heavier load than his bag. He was dull as respectable people usually are. When he was drunk he sang:

"Show me the Scotsman that won't love the thistle,
    Show me the Englishman that won't love the rose,
    But show me the true-born son of oul' Ireland
    That won't love the place where the shamrock grows."

He was sober on this occasion, so he uttered his sober statement: "Howld yer horses still, for God loves the childre."

I left for home. When I got there mother and a neighborman were leaning over the piggery wall examining the pigs.

"Where were ye?" she said.

"Over in old George's," I answered.

Patrick Boyle (1905–1982)

Patrick Boyle was born in County Antrim in 1905. A bank official for most of his life, Boyle published his first book only after he had retired from his position as bank manager in County Wexford. This was a collection of short stories entitled At Night All Cats Are Grey *(1966). Later he published a novel,* Like Any Other Man *(1966), and two more collections of short stories,* All Looks Yellow to the Jaundiced Eye *(1969) and* A View From Calvary *(1976).*

Pastorale

God knows, no one would want to belittle a neighboring farmer and his family. The more so when there's been a chair for you at their kitchen fire every night for a score or more years. But not to put a tooth in it and to make due allowance for bitter tongues, the Bennetts are known throughout the length and breadth of the parish as notorious bloody land-grabbers. They've gobbled up every small holding in the town-land that went on the market for years past. Even where it was a forced sale. A halt was put to their gallop a while back when James—the old man—took to the bed. Still by that time they had gathered together a few hundred acres of the best land hereabouts. With a world of cattle and sheep to keep it stocked up.

But if they are big farmers itself, they are bloody wee in their ways. They may grant you the heat of the fire, but you'll not be left long enough sitting idle to scorch the knees of your pants. From the time you cross the threshold till you say good night, it's constant litany.

"There's turf wanted. Take the big creel. It'll save the double journey."

"Put another few sods on the fire, will you."

"The heifer's roaring. Better go out to the byre and make sure she's all right."

"Bring in a couple of buckets of water."

"The morrow's Sunday. The shoes could do with a lick of polish."

The rest of the time you're hunched up beside the bellows wheel keeping the fire going or shifting the kettle up and down on the arm of the crane or poking around with the tongs gathering up the scattered embers.

So it's easy to tell there's something wrong when for once you're let take your seat by the fire without being called to order. Susie, the mother, is not around herself. Only the two young fellows.

"A brave class of a night, lads."

A civil enough remark, you'd think. But for all the heed paid to it, you might have been talking to two dummies.

"Good growthy weather, wouldn't you say?"

Not a mute out of either of them.

"That sup of rain this morning'll do no harm."

No reply.

The thick ignorant whelps. Sitting there crouched over the fire. Without a word to throw to a dog.

"Is your father improving any?"

John, the eldest buck, turns his head, a stupid look on his face.

"Henh?" says he.

"What form is the old fellow in the day?"

"The Boss-man is it?" says he. "He got a bad turn around teatime. Didn't he, Martin?"

"Aye."

Not very forthcoming, you'd be at liberty to say.

"He's had the priest and the doctor. He's in a poor way. Isn't he, Martin?"

"Aye."

"His breathing's a class of choked. It's a fret to listen to it."

No word of a lie in that statement. You could hear the wheezing through the closed door of the bedroom upstairs.

"He'll not last the night. Isn't that what the doctor said, Martin?"

The young chap gives him a look that would sour your stomach.

"Damned well you know what the doctor said. Weren't you there at the time?"

"I was only asking a civil question."

"Weren't you right beside me when I was talking to the doctor?"

"I was only asking—"

"You ask too many bucking questions, if you ask me. And you know the answers to them all before you start."

And Martin into him with the castigating and the casting up. Allowing for John being a class of an idiot and Martin himself maybe having enough on his plate, it's still a bit bloody thick. There's a time and a place for everything. It's a disgrace to be chawing the fat with your poor father dying above in the room.

"You blabber too much," says Martin.

"Only for you're a big-mouthed slob," says he, "there'd have been no need for either priest or doctor."

"How do you mean?"

"What need was there to tell the Boss about the malicious antics of the neighbors?"

"Malicious antics?"

"Aye. Leaking out to him that Gormley is running up an extension to the haggard. You must have known that would put him frothing at the mouth."

In the name of God, what's this? The river field again. For years past, the source of contention and doggery. It is a scraggy strip of land that wouldn't graze a goat, but it mears on the Bennett property, blocking them off from watering their stock in the river. Old James has been trying these many years to buy it from the owner, Peter Gormley, a half-baked sheep farmer who has as much regard for the Bennett family as he has for sheep dip. The river field lies on the far side of the road from the Gormley farmstead, so he describes it as the Out Farm. It is littered with rusting, secondhand farm machinery that Gormley trucks in as a sideline. There is an old timber shed on it used for storing what is described in the local paper as "SPECIAL OFFERS, FOR ONE WEEK ONLY." A man in his right mind wouldn't take a gift of the whole rickmatick—shed, machinery, and land. But Gormley won't sell. At any price. Claims the shed has become a class of a bloody emporium. With farmers coming from all arts and parts to buy top-grade farm equipment. And Bennett grinding his teeth with rage every time he sees a harrow or a binder or a potato digger towed into the river field. To say nothing but the truth, for the last while back the poor man can think of nothing else but "Gormley's haggard." No wonder, in his present state of health, he gets a bad turn when he hears your man is running up an addition to it.

"There's no use in you trying to make excuses." Martin is still giving out the pay. "You put your two big ignorant feet in it, as usual."

"Aw jay, Martin, have a heart. You're always larding into me."

"Haven't I every right to? The Lord knows what manner of misfortune you're after bringing about with your tattling tongue. There could be a poor enough way on us if the Boss doesn't pull out of his turn."

Now what's all this about? You'd think to listen to him that they haven't a shilling to their name. Instead of being the wealthiest ranchers in the whole barony. Begod, some people don't know when they're well off.

John is digging the wax out of one ear, his forefinger working like the plunger of a churn.

"Och, things can't be as bad as that," says he.

"We could well be walking the road," says Martin, "without a roof over our heads if the ould fellow hasn't put his affairs in order."

"Henh?"

Finger still jammed in his ear, John gapes at the brother. Properly flummoxed. And no wonder. A statement the like of yon would put the hair standing on your head. Walking the roads, no less. The arse out of their breeches. And sleeping at the back of a ditch with the winds of the world for company. Fat chance of that happening to greedy corbies the like of the Bennetts. Unless—? Hold on now!

"Have you no savvy, man?" says Martin. "Don't you know that if the Boss hasn't made a will, that bloody brother of ours will fall in for his share of the property? We'll be ruined paying him out his portion."

"Francis, is it?" John is frowning at the wax on his fingernail. "Sure, he's abroad in Tasmania, the last we heard of him."

"Wherever he is, it won't be long till he finds out that he can get something for nothing."

Ho-ho! So that's it! Old James hasn't settled his affairs. Loth, like many another, to quit the jockey seat. Well, it looks as if it's too late now. If the old fellow snuffs it, Francis can claim his share of the kitty—house, lands, stock, and the nest egg that's surely in the bank. You can hardly fault Martin for being worried. After all, when Francis was hunted out of the country twenty years ago, the Bennetts were small farmers like the rest of us. And now that they're wealthy ranchers, the black sheep of the family can levy a toll on all those years of sweat and skulduggery.

Martin is on his feet, prowling about the kitchen, every so often stopping at the foot of the stairs to cock an ear towards the room above.

"Bad enough," says he, "if we have to cripple ourselves for life paying him out his share, as long as he stays away from us. In Australia or Tasmania or wherever the hell he's supposed to be. But," says he, with a look of horror on his face, the like of what you'd see on a Redemptorist when he's describing the fate of the damned, "what will we do if he takes it into his head to come home and squat here, drinking the piece out till he has us ruined and disgraced with his blackguardly behavior?"

It's a queer thing about young bucks the like of Martin. They're all the time beefing off to other people. Laying down the law as though they are the only ones who know the answers. But if you listen closely, you find they are really talking to themselves. Especially if they are worried or excited. It would seem as if they build up such a head of steam that they must let it off. No matter who is listening. So here is Martin giving out the pay like a hoor at a christening.

"That Francie fellow," says he, "was a proper affliction. No wonder the Boss gave him the run. If he had been let fly his kite for much longer, the whole bloody farm would have come under the hammer. He was nothing but a drunken bum."

You could say a lot more than that about Francie without repeating yourself. He would drink the cross off an ass. For the price of a pint, he'd perform any manner of villainy, let it be grand larceny itself. And when he was drunk—which was every night of the week—he was a notorious ruffian. Singing and shouting, arguing the point, spilling drinks, breaking glasses, puking up his guts, before he wrecked the jakes. He would latch on to you at the bar counter. Never let up till he had you milked dry. Then you'd be lucky if he didn't mill you with a bottle for refusing to buy him a drink. A barbarous bloody savage, that's what he was. And yet he could get any woman he wanted. Whatever they saw in him.

"Sure you're maybe worrying your head about nothing," says John. "The Boss-man would never overlook a thing like making a will."

"Well, you're wrong there. He has no will made. I'm positive of that."

"Isn't it a wonder now you never tackled him about it long since?"

"Tackled him about it?" Martin, neck outstretched, hisses like an angry goose. "Haven't I been harping at him since he took to the bed six months ago. But it's no use. He keeps on saying that he can't put his affairs in order till he has the river field got. He can think of nothing else but that bloody field. And the wretched haggard. He has himself convinced that Gormley put up yon ould shed just to annoy him. Between the pair of them, I'm bloody near demented."

And God knows, the sight of him striding up and down, waving his arms and spitting out maledictions against his poor dying father would put you wondering. After all, the Bennetts were a queer broody class of a connection. You would never know where you were with them. There was Uncle Dan, a godless heathen if ever there was one, always giving off about relics and statues and religion in general, who had a framed picture of the Sacred Heart, almost as big as himself, tied round his bare chest with a hay rope. And Rosie, the aunt, a withered up old maid, who used to go out to the fields every morning at daybreak and roll herself stark naked in the dew so as to keep her skin young. And the grandfather, who would wear you down with talk of temperance, the while he was lapping up the booze in the security of his bedroom until at the latter end, overcome by the horrors of drink, he would parade the village in the small hours of the morning clad in nothing but his shirt and pledge-pin, a lighted candle in each hand and him roaring: "Sprinkle me for fear of God!" Not to speak of the present company, for John was never considered to be more than a half-wit. If the truth be told, there was a want in the whole seed, breed, and generation of them.

"So help me Jaysus, I'd be better off—" Martin is just getting properly into his stride when Susie comes out of the bedroom, the finger to her lips.

"Ssh!" says she. "He's just dozed off."

She's at the foot of the stairs before she says:

"Oh *you're* here!"

There's barely time to mutter: "Sorry to hear poor James was taken bad," before she starts giving off.

"My God!" she says. "What's come over you? Sitting there with the fire dying out before your eyes. No! No! Gather up the embers first. Get a few sods of turf. Small dry ones. Put them at the back where they'll light quicker. Not that way! On their ends. Now give a spin to the bellows wheel. Take it easy! Don't you see you're scattering sparks?"

She's a professional cribber, the Susie one. Satisfied with nothing. If the old fellow above in the room were to croak, she would be grumbling about how inconsiderate it was of him to die and him knowing full well how expensive it would be, what with feeding the mourners and stuffing them with drink and cigarettes and keeping fires going day and night in every room and folk trampling about everywhere, ruining the floors with their dirty boots and the cost of a funeral with hearse, mourning cars, and a coffin, more than likely of unseasoned timber that would buckle and warp before it's rightly underground and what in God's holy name will a High Mass run to, with priests to no end loafing around inside the altar rails mak-

ing no effort to earn their money and gravediggers that get
better paid than County Council workers for digging a bit of a
hole in the ground and then filling it up again.

"How is he, Ma?" says John, who, dim-witted as he is, has
still more savvy than to get up off his arse and help with the
fire.

"I've seen him worse," says she. "He'll maybe pull out of it."
She draws up a chair to the fire and squats down straddle-
legged, toasting her thighs.

"The doctor says he won't last till morning," says Martin.
And you would know by the whine in his voice what class of a
worry is on him.

"Och, I suppose if it's laid down," says she, "it'll come to
pass."

She starts swaying back and forth, massaging her legs with
the flat of her hands. Says she:

"Father Bourke was talking to me after he gave your poor
father the last rites. 'Don't worry, Mrs. Bennett,' says he. 'I
never saw a man better prepared for death. Completely resigned,' says he. 'It was a most edifying sight. There is no
doubt in my mind,' says he, 'that God will forgive him his
trespasses as James himself,' says he, 'has forgiven those of his
neighbors.' And what's more—"

Before she can say any more, Martin reins her back on her
haunches.

"What about Gormley?" says he.

"Gormley?" says she.

"Aye. If there's trespasses to be forgiven, wouldn't it be as
well, before it's too late, for himself and the Boss to make the
peace?"

Could you beat that for sheer effrontery? Proposing a deathbed reconciliation so that he can lay hands on the loot. He has
the neck of a giraffe, that young fellow.

Susie gapes at him, goggle-eyed.

"Are you gone out of your mind," says she. "Allow that ruf-

fian into the house to rant and rave at your poor father's bed-
side? Dragging up old scandals that are best forgotten? Sure
there's no sense to the man. Nothing will convince him but
that our Francie was responsible for—"

"Ma!" says Martin. You'd think he's checking a dog that's
after lifting a leg against the dresser.

And no wonder. Susie's chapfallen expression tells its own
story. She has let the cat out of the bag. A disreputable tomcat
by the name of Francie. Very liable to commit scandal when on
the prowl. And in this parish, scandal means only the one
thing—poling a woman. So very likely that's why Francie decamped. And wait now! A short while after the flitting didn't
Gormley's daughter, Helen, get herself what her father described as "a grand job" in England? A notorious kittling-
ground for colleens in disgrace. Bejeezus, that's it! She sneaked
off to that immoral country to have her ba. And . . . Hold on!
Hold on! Wasn't that the same year that Robert, Helen's
brother, left the seminary in his last term. Just before he was
due for ordination. They were bloody strict in those days. One
rattle from the closet where your family skeleton was stored
and you were out the window. Nothing for it but to creep
home in the guise of a spoiled priest, giving out to all and sun-
dry that you had the misfortune to lose your vocation. After
all, if it became known that you were turfed out of the college
because your sister was a manifest trollop, your family could
never hold up their heads in the village again.

So Robert is shipped off to the States where if he opens his
mouth too wide over a few pints, it'll not give rise to local
gossip. And everybody sympathizes with his poor father in his
sad bereavement, for spoiled priests are a rare enough commodity in this part of the country.

Can you beat it? Over all these years Mister Slippy-tit has
been codding the natives with his bragging and boasting that
no one can point the finger of scorn at one of the Gormleys.
But the cost of keeping his halo intact has been high. There he

is, clocking in a big barn of a house, with nothing but the walls for company. Small blame to him if he hates the guts of the Bennett family and holds them to ransom for a patch of ground and a rickety shed.

Susie has recovered herself and is holding forth once more as though nothing has happened.

"He was a good man, your father," says she. "None better. In the front seat at Mass every Sunday. Year in, year out. Always attended to his Easter duty. Headed the list in every church collection. Father Burke claims there wasn't a pick of malice in his bones. It's a great comfort to hear the like of that from a priest."

Over by the fireplace, John wags his poll in agreement.

"Aye, indeed," says he. "A great comfort."

Martin is gritting his teeth like he's chewing granite. But before he can get a word in edgeways, the uproar breaks out in the room above. It is a cross between a howl and a moan. The sort of a bellow a person lets out of him when he is struggling out of a nightmare.

Susie throws up her hands in holy horror.

"Mother of God!" she says. "He's done for!"

There's a rush for the stairs with everyone stumbling and tripping over each other and muttering pious ejaculations and getting wedged in the bedroom door.

Now you'll always discover in upstarts the like of the Bennetts that no matter how much land or coin they muster together, never can they shake off the mean streak that was their driving force from the beginning. Stingy they were reared and they'll give up the ghost in the same condition. Still you'd think they'd throw a strip of lino on the bare boards of a sickroom or have something better than an army blanket on the bed or stretch a curtain itself across the window.

The old fellow is propped up on the pillow, hands clawing at the blanket, eyes squeezed shut. His jaw is hanging and there's a shocking wheeze to his breathing. You can see by the look of him he's a done duck. So it's down on your knees and into the prayers for the dying, with Susie reading out the litany at the rate of no man's business from a battered old prayer book. It's maybe as well the poor bugger perishing in the bed is panting too loud to hear the words, for it would be cold comfort to him to hear his wife rattling off the blood and thunder invocations, with their talk of damnation and eternal night, punishment with darkness, chastisement with flames, and condemnation to torments. She is going full blast when his breathing eases a little and he opens his eyes. As he glowers at her, she keeps babbling on, one eye on the book, the other on the bed.

"Deliver, O Lord," she says, "the soul of Thy servant from all danger of hell, from all pain and tribulation."

"What's all this commotion about?" says he, in a hoarse whisper.

They scramble to their feet. Not a cheep out of one of them. Their hands hanging the one length with embarrassment.

"You'll not get shut of me before my time," says he.

He's badly out in that statement, but a cranky little weasel he always was and you can hardly expect him to change at the latter end of his days.

Martin clears his throat and starts rummaging in the inner pocket of his jacket.

"What else could we do?" says he, "And you getting another attack just after you were anointed."

The old fellow is puffing through his pursed lips like a goods train laboring on a hill.

"There's men," says he, "got the last rites . . . years ago . . . and they're still . . . walking the roads."

"What did the doctor tell you?" says he.

Martin pays no heed. He is studying the rumpled paper he has pulled from his pocket.

"What did the doctor say?" says the old fellow.

Martin looks up. Casual like.

"He said you're dying," says he.

Christ, that's sinking the boot into the uppers with a vengeance. Jeffreys, the hanging judge, could hardly have made a better job of passing sentence at the Bloody Assizes.

"My Jesus, mercy!" says Susie. And you wouldn't know whether it was pity or piety was moving her.

"Amen," says John.

"Dying?" says the old fellow.

"Aye." Martin spreads the paper out on the blanket and takes a pen from his pocket. "Wouldn't this be a good time to settle your affairs?"

Well, you'd have to hand it to that young thick. He never takes his eye off the ball. Not till it's in the back of the net. He must have been carrying that paper around with him for months. Only waiting for the chance to get it signed. And what better time than when the party concerned is stretched on the bed with nothing between himself and the Day of Judgment but the last few gasps. What harm if it is your own old fellow. He's a Bennett like yourself and there'll be no hard feelings.

Old James is staring down at the paper spread out on the blanket. The breathing is coming hard on him again and there's a class of a whistle to it that you'd find in a horse with the heaves.

"The doctor," says he, wheezing out the words. "Was he . . . positive?"

"He was," says Martin. "He said 'tis beyond dispute." He is crouched over the bed, tapping the paper with his pen.

"You sign your name down here," says he.

The old fellow goes into a fit of coughing and spluttering.

"Beyond . . . dispute," says he. "That's . . . a good one."

The next thing his head is back on the pillow and he's quaking and quivering and jerking till the bed is clattering under him like a rattley-box. The eyes are squinting out of his head. He's slobbering at the mouth. His jaws are gaping open with the teeth showing to the roots. And there are queer clucking noises coming out of the back of his throat that you'd hear nowhere barring a fowl house. To say nothing but the truth, the sight and sound of him would scare the living daylights out of you.

Susie is wringing her hands.

"He's done for this time," says she. "It's the last agony."

"He's gone into convulsions," says she.

"Convulsions, begor," says John, the eyebrows up in his hair.

"Convulsions, me arse!" says Martin. "He's making a mock of us all."

And sure enough, the old fellow is cackling away to himself. Laughing his head off as though he hadn't a care in the world.

Martin is fit to be tied. There's a scowl on his face that would scare rats and he's muttering away under his breath. You can be full sure it's not the praying he's at, but laying maledictions on his silly old fool of a father for making a buck idiot of himself on his deathbed when he'd be better employed regulating his testamentary obligations.

The old man has cackled himself to a standstill. He is stretched out on the bed, groaning and gasping, his chest going like a bellows. If the sweat pouring out of him is any indication, he is well and truly invoiced.

"Martin," says he, and you'd hardly hear him, the voice is so weak. "Come here, son."

Martin is like a man that's after getting a glimpse of the Promised Land. You can see the glory of this vision shining out of his greedy little eyes. Land and cattle and coin to be had for the scribbling of a couple of words. He wastes no time moving in for the kill.

"Now," says he, proddling the old man's fingers with the pen. "Down here you sign."

Not so much as a "by your leave" or "after you, MacNaughton." It's a case of disgorge the loot and away you go to Kingdom Come.

But James has no notion of signing wills or the like. He pushes the pen aside.

"Martin," says he. "What do you think yourself? Will I last till morning?" says he.

Martin is still stooped over the bed, trying to get the unwilling fingers to grasp the pen.

"Not a hope," says he, without looking up.

The old fellow gathers himself together, lips working, eyebrows drawn down in concentration. You can see by the queer gleam in his eye that he has something important to say. Something that'll not let him die easy till he's got it off his chest. Perhaps he's worried about what'll happen to Susie after he's gone. Or it could be the question about where he wants to be buried. Or maybe 'tis some old debt that's still outstanding.

He levers himself up in the bed, knocking pen and paper flying.

"Listen, son," says he. "This would be the blessed night to burn down Gormley's haggard."

Samuel Beckett (1906–1989)

Samuel Beckett was born in Foxrock, near Dublin, in 1906. He came from an upper-middle class Protestant family and was educated at some of Ireland's best schools. An excellent athlete, he was captain of his school's cricket team. He entered Trinity College, Dublin, in 1923, specializing in French. After graduation, he taught at the Ecole Normale Supérieure in Paris. Beckett returned briefly to Ireland but lived mainly in France. He settled in Paris in 1937. In Paris he met James Joyce, then completing Finnegans Wake, *and was one of a small group hand-picked by Joyce to explain* Finnegans Wake *to the world. Beckett remained in France during World War II, claiming, legend has it, that "France at war is better than Ireland at peace." Beckett is best known for his plays, including* Waiting For Godot (1952), End Game (1956), Krapp's Last Tape (1960), *and* Happy Days (1961), *but his prose is equally, if not more, important. His first published work of fiction was the collection of short stories* More Pricks Than Kicks (1934), *set in Dublin, and whose central character is an Irish student, Belacqua Shulah. Beckett wrote two novels in English,* Murphy (1938) *and* Watt (1953), *but almost all his fiction after World War II has been written and published first in French, then translated into English, usually by Beckett himself. Among Beckett's other works of fiction are* Molloy (1955), Malone Dies (1956), The Unnamable (1958), How It Is (1964), No's Knife (1967), The Lost Ones (1973) *with* Mercier and Camier (1974), *and* Company (1980). *Beckett was awarded the Nobel Prize for literature in 1969. "Dante and the Lobster" is taken from* More Pricks Than Kicks.

Dante and the Lobster

It was morning and Belacqua was stuck in the first of the canti in the moon. He was so bogged that he could move neither backward nor forward. Blissful Beatrice was there, Dante also, and she explained the spots on the moon to him. She showed him in the first place where he was at fault, then she put up her own explanation. She had it from God, therefore he could rely on its being accurate in every particular. All he had to do was to follow her step by step. Part one, the refutation, was plain sailing. She made her point clearly, she said what she had to say without fuss or loss of time. But part two, the demonstration, was so dense that Belacqua could not make head or tail of it. The disproof, the reproof, that was patent. But then came the proof, a rapid shorthand of the real facts, and Belacqua was bogged indeed. Bored also, impatient to get on to Piccarda. Still he pored over the enigma, he would not concede himself conquered, he would understand at least the meanings of the words, the order in which they were spoken, and the nature of the satisfaction that they conferred on the misinformed poet, so that when they were ended he was refreshed and could raise his heavy head, intending to return thanks and make formal retraction of his old opinion.

He was still running his brain against this impenetrable passage when he heard midday strike. At once he switched his mind off its task. He scooped his fingers under the book and shoveled it back till it lay wholly on his palms. The *Divine Comedy* face upward on the lectern of his palms. Thus disposed he raised it under his nose and there he slammed it shut. He held it aloft for a time, squinting at it angrily, pressing the boards inwards with the heels of his hands. Then he laid it aside.

He leaned back in his chair to feel his mind subside and the itch of this mean quodlibet die down. Nothing could be done until his mind got better and was still, which gradually it did and was. Then he ventured to consider what he had to do next.

There was always something that one had to do next. Three large obligations presented themselves. First lunch, then the lobster, then the Italian lesson. That would do to be going on with. After the Italian lesson he had no very clear idea. No doubt some niggling curriculum had been drawn up by someone for the late afternoon and evening, but he did not know what. In any case it did not matter. What did matter was: one, lunch; two, the lobster; three, the Italian lesson. That was more than enough to be going on with.

Lunch, to come off at all, was a very nice affair. If his lunch was to be enjoyable, and it could be very enjoyable indeed, he must be left in absolute tranquillity to prepare it. But if he were disturbed now, if some brisk tattler were to come bouncing in now with a big idea or a petition, he might just as well not eat at all, for the food would turn to bitterness on his palate or, worse again, taste of nothing. He must be left strictly alone, he must have complete quiet and privacy, to prepare the food for his lunch.

The first thing to do was to lock the door. Now nobody could come at him. He deployed an old *Herald* and smoothed it out on the table. The rather handsome face of McCabe the assassin stared up at him. Then he lit the gas ring and unhooked the square flat toaster, asbestos grill, from its nail and set it precisely on the flame. He found he had to lower the flame. Toast must not on any account be done too rapidly. For bread to be toasted as it ought, through and through, it must be done on a mild steady flame. Otherwise you only charred the outside and left the pith as sodden as before. If there was one thing he abominated more than another it was to feel his teeth meet in a bathos of pith and dough. And it was so easy to do the thing properly. So, he thought, having regulated the flow and adjusted the grill, by the time I have the bread cut that will be just right. Now the long barrel loaf came out of its biscuit tin and had its end evened off on the face of McCabe. Two inexorable drives with the bread saw and a pair of neat

rounds of raw bread, the main elements of his meal, lay before
him, awaiting his pleasure. The stump of the loaf went back
into prison, the crumbs, as though there were no such thing as
a sparrow in the wide world, were swept in a fever away, and
the slices snatched up and carried to the grill. All these prelim-
inaries were very hasty and impersonal.

It was now that real skill began to be required, it was at this
point that the average person began to make a hash of the entire proceedings. He laid his cheek against the soft of the bread,
it was spongy and warm, alive. But he would very soon take
that plush feel off it, by God but he would very quickly take
that fat white look off its face. He lowered the gas a suspicion
and plaqued one flabby slab plump down on the glowing fab-
ric, but very pat and precise, so that the whole resembled the
Japanese flag. Then on top, there not being room for the two
to do evenly side by side, and if you did not do them evenly
you might just as well save yourself the trouble of doing them
at all, the other round was set to warm. When the first candi-
date was done, which was only when it was black through and
through, it changed places with its comrade, so that now it in
its turn lay on top, done to a dead end, black and smoking,
waiting till as much could be said of the other.

For the tiller of the field the thing was simple, he had it from
his mother. The spots were Cain with his truss of thorns, dis-
possessed, cursed from the earth, fugitive and vagabond. The
moon was that countenance fallen and branded, seared with
the first stigma of God's pity, that an outcast might not die
quickly. It was a mix-up in the mind of the tiller, but that did
not matter. It had been good enough for his mother, it was
good enough for him.

Belacqua on his knees before the flame, poring over the grill,
controlled every phase of the broiling. It took time, but if a
thing was worth doing at all it was worth doing well, that was
a true saying. Long before the end the room was full of smoke
and the reek of burning. He switched off the gas, when all that

human care and skill could do had been done, and restored the toaster to its nail. This was an act of dilapidation, for it seared a great weal in the paper. This was hooliganism pure and simple. What the hell did he care? Was it his wall? The same hopeless paper had been there fifty years. It was livid with age. It could not be disimproved.

Next a thick paste of Savora, salt, and cayenne on each round, well worked in while the pores were still open with the heat. No butter, God forbid, just a good foment of mustard and salt and pepper on each round. Butter was a blunder, it made the toast soggy. Buttered toast was all right for Senior Fellows and Salvationists, for such as had nothing but false teeth in their heads. It was no good at all to a fairly strong young rose like Belacqua. This meal that he was at such pains to make ready, he would devour it with a sense of rapture and victory, it would be like smiting the sledded Polacks on the ice. He would snap at it with closed eyes, he would gnash it into a pulp, he would vanquish it utterly with his fangs. Then the anguish of pungency, the pang of the spices, as each mouthful died, scorching his palate, bringing tears.

But he was not yet all set, there was yet much to be done. He had burnt his offering, he had not fully dressed it. Yes, he had put the horse behind the tumbrel.

He clapped the toasted rounds together, he brought them smartly together like cymbals, they clave the one to the other on the viscid salve of Savora. Then he wrapped them up for the time being in any old sheet of paper. Then he made himself ready for the road.

Now the great thing was to avoid being accosted. To be stopped at this stage and have conversational nuisance committed all over him would be a disaster. His whole being was straining forward towards the joy in store. If he were accosted now he might just as well fling his lunch into the gutter and walk straight back home. Sometimes his hunger, more of mind, I need scarcely say, than of body, for this meal amounted to such a frenzy that he would not have hesitated to strike any man rash enough to buttonhole and baulk him, he would have shouldered him out of his path without ceremony. Woe betide the meddler who crossed him when his mind was really set on this meal.

He threaded his way rapidly, his head bowed, through a familiar labyrinth of lanes and suddenly dived into a little family grocery. In the shop they were not surprised. Most days, about this hour, he shot in off the street in this way.

The slab of cheese was prepared. Separated since morning from the piece, it was only waiting for Belacqua to call and take it. Gorgonzola cheese. He knew a man who came from Gorgonzola, his name was Angelo. He had been born in Nice but all his youth had been spent in Gorgonzola. He knew where to look for it. Every day it was there, in the same corner, waiting to be called for. They were very decent obliging people.

He looked sceptically at the cut of cheese. He turned it over on its back to see was the other side any better. The other side was worse. They had laid it better side up, they had practiced that little deception. Who shall blame them? He rubbed it. It was sweating. That was something. He stooped and smelt it. A faint fragrance of corruption. What good was that? He didn't want fragrance, he wasn't a bloody gourmet, he wanted a good stench. What he wanted was a good green stenching rotten lump of Gorgonzola cheese, alive, and by God he would have it.

He looked fiercely at the grocer.

"What's that?" he demanded.

The grocer writhed.

"Well?" demanded Belacqua, he was without fear when roused, "is that the best you can do?"

"In the length and breadth of Dublin" said the grocer "you won't find a rottener bit this minute."

Belacqua was furious. The impudent dogsbody, for two pins he would assault him.

"It won't do" he cried, "do you hear me, it won't do at all. I won't have it." He ground his teeth.

The grocer, instead of simply washing his hands like Pilate, flung out his arms in a wild crucified gesture of supplication. Sullenly Belacqua undid his packet and slipped the cadaverous tablet of cheese between the hard cold black boards of the toast. He stumped to the door where he whirled round however.

"You heard me?" he cried.

"Sir" said the grocer. This was not a question, nor yet an expression of acquiescence. The tone in which it was let fall made it quite impossible to know what was in the man's mind. It was a most ingenious riposte.

"I tell you" said Belacqua with great heat "this won't do at all. If you can't do better than this" he raised the hand that held the packet "I shall be obliged to go for my cheese elsewhere. Do you mark me?"

"Sir" said the grocer.

He came to the threshold of his store and watched the indignant customer hobble away. Belacqua had a spavined gait, his feet were in ruins, he suffered with them almost continuously. Even in the night they took no rest, or next to none. For then the cramps took over from the corns and hammer toes, and carried on. So that he would press the fringes of his feet desperately against the end-rail of the bed or better again, reach down with his hand and drag them up and back towards the instep. Skill and patience could disperse the pain, but there it was, complicating his night's rest.

The grocer, without closing his eyes or taking them off the receding figure, blew his nose in the skirt of his apron. Being a warmhearted human man he felt sympathy and pity for this queer customer who always looked ill and dejected. But at the same time he was a small tradesman, don't forget that, with a small tradesman's sense of personal dignity and what was what. Thruppence, he cast it up, thruppence worth of cheese per day, one and a tanner per week. No, he would fawn on no man for that, no, not on the best in the land. He had his pride.

Stumbling along by devious ways towards the lowly public where he was expected, in the sense that the entry of his grotesque person would provoke no comment or laughter, Belacqua gradually got the upper hand of his choler. Now that lunch was as good as a *fait accompli*, because the incontinent bosthoons of his own class, itching to pass on a big idea or inflict an appointment, were seldom at large in this shabby quarter of the city, he was free to consider items two and three, the lobster and the lesson, in closer detail.

At a quarter to three he was due at the school. Say five to three. The public closed, the fishmonger reopened, at half past two. Assuming then that his lousy old bitch of an aunt had given her order in good time that morning, with strict injunctions that it should be ready and waiting so that her blackguard boy should on no account be delayed when he called for it first thing in the afternoon, it would be time enough if he left the public as it closed, he could remain on till the last moment. Benissimo. He had half a crown. That was two pints of draft anyway and perhaps a bottle to wind up with. Their bottled stout was particularly excellent and well up. And he would still be left with enough coppers to buy a *Herald* and take a tram if he felt tired or was pinched for time. Always assuming, of course, that the lobster was all ready to be handed over. God damn these tradesmen, he thought, you can never rely on them. He had not done an exercise but that did not matter. His Professoressa was so charming and remarkable. Signorina Adriana Ottolenghi! He did not believe it possible for a woman to be more intelligent or better informed than the little Ottolenghi. So he had set her on a pedestal in his mind, apart from other women. She had said last day that they would read

Il Cinque Maggio together. But she would not mind if he told her, as he proposed to, in Italian, he would frame a shining phrase on his way from the public, that he would prefer to postpone the *Cinque Maggio* to another occasion. Manzoni was an old woman, Napoleon was another. Napoleone di mezza calzetta, fa l'amore a Giacominetta. Why did he think of Manzoni as an old woman? Why did he do him that injustice? Pellico was another. They were all old maids, suffragettes. He must ask his Signorina where he could have received that impression, that the nineteenth century in Italy was full of old hens trying to cluck like Pindar. Carducci was another. Also about the spots on the moon. If she could not tell him there and then she would make it up, only too gladly, against the next time. Everything was all set now and in order. Bating, of course, the lobster, which had to remain an incalculable factor. He must just hope for the best. And expect the worst, he thought gaily, diving into the public, as usual.

Belacqua drew near to the school, quite happy, for all had gone swimmingly. The lunch had been a notable success, it would abide as a standard in his mind. Indeed he could not imagine its ever being superseded. And such a pale soapy piece of cheese to prove so strong! He must only conclude that he had been abusing himself all these years in relating the strength of cheese directly to its greenness. We live and learn, that was a true saying. Also his teeth and jaws had been in heaven, splinters of vanquished toast spraying forth at each gnash. It was like eating glass. His mouth burned and ached with the exploit. Then the food had been further spiced by the intelligence, transmitted in a low tragic voice across the counter by Oliver the improver, that the Malahide murderer's petition for mercy, signed by half the land, having been rejected, the man must swing at dawn in Mountjoy and nothing could save him. Ellis the hangman was even now on his way. Belacqua, tearing

at the sandwich and swilling the precious stout, pondered on
McCabe in his cell.

The lobster was ready after all, the man handed it over in-
stanter, and with such a pleasant smile. Really a little bit of
courtesy and goodwill went a long way in this world. A smile
and a cheerful word from a common workingman and the face
of the world was brightened. And it was so easy, a mere question of muscular control.

"Lepping" he said cheerfully, handing it over.

"Lepping?" said Belacqua. What on earth was that?

"Lepping fresh, sir" said the man, "fresh in this morning."

Now Belacqua, on the analogy of mackerel and other fish
that he had heard described as lepping fresh when they had
been taken but an hour or two previously, supposed the man
to mean that the lobster had very recently been killed.

Signorina Adriana Ottolenghi was waiting in the little front
room off the hall, which Belacqua was naturally inclined to
think of rather as the vestibule. That was her room, the Italian
room. On the same side, but at the back, was the French room.
God knows where the German room was. Who cared about
the German room anyway?

He hung up his coat and hat, laid the long knobby brown-
paper parcel on the hall table, and went prestly in to the Ottolenghi.

After about half an hour of this and that obiter, she compli-
mented him on his grasp of the language.

"You make rapid progress" she said in her ruined voice.

There subsisted as much of the Ottolenghi as might be expected to of the person of a lady of a certain age who had
found being young and beautiful and pure more of a bore than
anything else.

Belacqua, dissembling his great pleasure, laid open the moon
enigma.

"Yes" she said "I know the passage. It is a famous teaser.

Offhand I cannot tell you, but I will look it up when I get home."

The sweet creature! She would look it up in her big Dante when she got home. What a woman!

"It occurred to me" she said "apropos of I don't know what, that you might do worse than make up Dante's rare movements of compassion in Hell. That used to be" her past tenses were always sorrowful "a favorite question."

He assumed an expression of profundity.

"In that connection" he said "I recall one superb pun anyway: '*qui vive la pietà quando è ben morta . . .*' "

She said nothing.

"Is it not a great phrase?" he gushed.

She said nothing.

"Now" he said like a fool "I wonder how you could translate that?"

Still she said nothing. Then:

"Do you think" she murmured "it is absolutely necessary to translate it?"

Sounds as of conflict were borne in from the hall. Then silence. A knuckle tambourined on the door, it flew open and lo it was Mlle. Glain, the French instructress, clutching her cat, her eyes out on stalks, in a state of the greatest agitation.

"Oh" she gasped "forgive me. I intrude, but what was in the bag?"

"The bag?" said the Ottolenghi.

Mlle. Glain took a French step forward.

"The parcel" she buried her face in the cat "the parcel in the hall."

Belacqua spoke up composedly.

"Mine" he said, "a fish."

He did not know the French for lobster. Fish would do very well. Fish had been good enough for Jesus Christ, Son of God, Saviour. It was good enough for Mlle. Glain.

"Oh" said Mlle. Glain, inexpressibly relieved, "I caught him in the nick of time." She administered a tap to the cat. "He would have tore it to flitters."

Belacqua began to feel a little anxious.

"Did he actually get at it?" he said.

"No no" said Mlle. Glain "I caught him just in time. But I did not know" with a bluestocking snigger "what it might be, so I thought I had better come and ask."

Base prying bitch.

The Ottolenghi was faintly amused.

"Puisqu'il n'y a pas de mal . . ." she said with great fatigue and elegance.

"Heureusement" it was clear at once that Mlle. Glain was devout "heureusement."

Chastening the cat with little skelps she took herself off. The grey hairs of her maidenhead screamed at Belacqua. A devout, virginal bluestocking, honing after a penny's worth of scandal.

"Where were we?" said Belacqua.

But Neapolitan patience has its limits.

"Where are we ever?" cried the Ottolenghi, "where we were, as we were."

Belacqua drew near to the house of his aunt. Let us call it Winter, that dusk may fall now and a moon rise. At the corner of the street a horse was down and a man sat on its head. I know, thought Belacqua, that that is considered the right thing to do. But why? A lamplighter flew by on his bike, tilting with his pole at the standards, jousting a little yellow light into the evening. A poorly dressed couple stood in the bay of a pretentious gateway, she sagging against the railings, her head lowered, he standing facing her. He stood up close to her, his hands dangled by his sides. Where we were, thought Belacqua, as we were. He walked on gripping his parcel. Why not piety and pity both, even down below? Why not mercy and Godliness together? A little mercy in the stress of sacrifice, a little mercy to rejoice against judgment. He thought of Jonah and

the gourd and the pity of a jealous God on Nineveh. And poor
McCabe, he would get it in the neck at dawn. What was he
doing now, how was he feeling? He would relish one more
meal, one more night.

His aunt was in the garden, tending whatever flowers die at
that time of year. She embraced him and together they went
down into the bowels of the earth, into the kitchen in the basement. She took the parcel and undid it and abruptly the lobster
was on the table, on the oilcloth, discovered.

"They assured me it was fresh" said Belacqua.

Suddenly he saw the creature move, this neuter creature.
Definitely it changed its position. His hand flew to his mouth.

"Christ!" he said "it's alive."

His aunt looked at the lobster. It moved again. It made a
faint nervous act of life on the oilcloth. They stood above it,
looking down on it, exposed cruciform on the oilcloth. It
shuddered again. Belacqua felt he would be sick.

"My God" he whined "it's alive, what'll we do?"

The aunt simply had to laugh. She bustled off to the pantry
to fetch her smart apron, leaving him goggling down at the
lobster, and came back with it on and her sleeves rolled up, all
business.

"Well" she said "it is to be hoped so, indeed."

"All this time" muttered Belacqua. Then, suddenly aware of
her hideous equipment: "What are you going to do?" he cried.

"Boil the beast" she said, "what else?"

"But it's not dead" protested Belacqua "you can't boil it like
that."

She looked at him in astonishment. Had he taken leave of
his senses.

"Have sense" she said sharply, "lobsters are always boiled
alive. They must be." She caught up the lobster and laid it on
its back. It trembled. "They feel nothing" she said.

In the depths of the sea it had crept into the cruel pot. For
hours, in the midst of its enemies, it had breathed secretly. It

had survived the Frenchwoman's cat and his witless clutch. Now it was going alive into scalding water. It had to. Take into the air my quiet breath.

Belacqua looked at the old parchment of her face, gray in the dim kitchen.

"You make a fuss" she said angrily "and upset me and then lash into it for your dinner."

She lifted the lobster clear of the table. It had about thirty seconds to live.

Well, thought Belacqua, it's a quick death, God help us all.

It is not.

Michael McLaverty (1907–1992)

Michael McLaverty was born in Carrickmacrass, County Monaghan, in 1907, but as a small child he moved with his parents to Belfast. He was educated at Saint Malachy's College, and at Queen's University in Belfast where he graduated with a Master of Science degree in 1933. He then turned to a full-time career as a schoolteacher. He has published eight novels, including Call My Brother Back *(1939),* The Three Brothers *(1948), and* The Choice *(1958). His best-known collection of short stories is* The Game Cock and Other Stories *(1947). "Six Weeks On and Two Ashore" was first published in 1948 in the magazine* Irish Writing, *edited by David Marcus, and is now included in a selection of McLaverty stories entitled* The Road to the Shore *(1976). Poolbeg Press in Dublin published McLaverty's* Collected Stories *in 1978.*

Six Weeks On
and Two Ashore

In the early hours of the night it had rained and the iron gate that led to the lightkeepers' houses had rattled loose in the wind, and as it cringed and banged it disturbed Mrs. O'Brien's spaniel where he lay on a mat in the dark, drafty hallway. Time and again he gave a muffled growl, padded about the hall, and scratched at the door. His uneasiness and the noise of the wind had wakened Mrs. O'Brien in the room above him, and she lay in bed wondering if she should go down and let him into the warm comfort of the kitchen. Beside her her husband was asleep, snoring loudly, unaware of her wakefulness or of the windows shaking in their heavy frames. The rain rattled like hailstones against the panes and raced in a flood into the zinc tank at the side of the house. God in Heaven, how anybody could sleep through that, she said—it was enough to waken the dead and there he was deep asleep as if it were a calm summer night. What kind of a man was he at all! You'd think he'd be worrying about his journey to the Rock in the morning and his long six weeks away from her. He was getting old—there was no mistake about that. She touched his feet—they were cold, as cold as a stone you'd find on a wintry beach.

The dog growled again, and throwing back the bedclothes she got up and groped on the table for the matchbox. She struck one match but it was a dead one, and she clicked her tongue in disapproval. She was never done telling Tom not to be putting his spent matches back into the box but he never heeded her. It was tidy he told her; it was exasperating if she knew anything. She struck three before coming upon a good one, and in the spurt of flame she glanced at the alarm clock and saw that it was two hours after midnight. She slipped downstairs, lit the lamp, and let the dog into the kitchen. She patted his head and he jumped on the sofa, thumped it loudly with his tail and curled up on a cushion. On the floor Tom's hampers lay ready for the morning when the boatmen would come to row him out to the lighthouse to relieve young Frank Coady. She looked at the hampers with sharp calculation, wondering if she had packed everything he needed. She was always sure to forget something—boot polish or a pullover or a corkscrew or soap—and he was always sure to cast it up to her as soon as he stepped ashore for his two-weeks leave. She could never remember a time when he arrived back without some complaint or other. But this time she was sure she had forgotten nothing for she had made a list and ticked each item off as she packed them into the cases. Yes, he wouldn't be able to launch any of his ill humor on her this time!

She quenched the lamp, and returning to her room she stood at the window for a moment and saw the lighthouse beam shine on the clouds and sweep through the fine wire of falling rain. Tom was still asleep, heedless of his coming sojourn on that windy stub of rock. But maybe if the wind would hold during the night the boatmen would be unable to row him out in the morning. But even that would be no comfort—waiting, and waiting, and watching the boatmen sheltering all day in the lee of the boathouse expecting the sea to settle. It'd be better, after all, that they'd be able to take him. She got into bed and turned her back to him, and as she listened to the rain she thought of how it would wash the muddy paw marks from the cement paths and save her the trouble of getting down on her hands and knees in the morning.

She awoke without aid of the alarm clock, and from her bed she saw the washed blue of the sky, and in the stillness heard the hollow tumult of the distracted sea. He'd have to go out this morning—there was no doubt about that! But God grant he'd return to her in better form! She got up quietly, and buttoning her frock at the window she gazed down at the Coadys' house. The door was open to the cold sun and Delia Coady was on her knees freshly whitening the doorstep that had been streaked in the night's rain. All her windows were open, the curtains bulging in the uneasy draft. Delia raised her head and looked round but Mrs. O'Brien withdrew to the edge of the window and continued to watch her. Delia was singing now and going to the zinc tank at the side of the house for a bucket of water.

Tom stirred in his bed and threw one arm across the pillow.

"Do you hear her?" his wife said.

"Hear who?" he mumbled crossly and pulled the clothes up round his chest.

"Delia Coady is singing like a lark."

"Well, let her sing. Isn't it a free country?"

The alarm clock buzzed on the table and she let it whirl out to the end of its spring.

Tom raised his head from the pillow and stared at her.

"Isn't it a great wonder you didn't switch that damned thing off and you up before it?"

"You'd better get up, Tom. Delia will think you're in no hurry to take her Frank off the Rock."

"I'll go when it suits me—not a second faster. When young Coady's as long on the lights as I am he'll not hurry much. The way to get on in my job is to go slow, slow, slow—dead slow, snail slow, and always slow. Do you remember what one of the commissioners said to me on the East Light in Rathlin? 'Mister O'Brien,' he said, 'there's not as much dust in the whole place as would fill a matchbox.' And the secret is—slow."

"No commissioner would use such a word as 'matchbox.' "

"And do you think, woman, that I'm making up that story? What would you have him say?" and he affected a mincing, feminine accent: " 'Lightkeeper O'Brien, there is not as much elemental dust in the hallowed precincts of this lighthouse as would fill a silver snuffbox.' Is that what you would have him say?" he added crossly.

"I don't think he'd pass any remark about dust or dirt."

"You don't think! You don't think! It's a wonder you didn't think of switching off the damned alarm clock and you knowing I hate the sound of it."

She said nothing. All their quarrels seemed to arise out of the simplest remarks—one remark following another, spreading out and involving them, before they were aware, in a quarrel of cold cruelty. She, herself, was to blame for many of them. She should have let him have his little story of "the matchbox." What on earth possessed her to turn a word on him and this the last day she'd be speaking to him for six long weeks? She checked a long sigh, tidied the things in the room quietly, and all the time tried to find something to say that would soften her last words to him. She crossed to the window and put her hand to the snib to lower it. Delia was still singing and standing out from the door the better to see the freshly whitened windowsills and doorstep.

"She has a blue frock on," she said over her shoulder. "I never saw her in that before; it fairly becomes her."

"Didn't I tell you she was married in blue! It'll be the same frock."

"She has a nice voice."

"I think you're jealous of her."

"Hm, I used to be able to sing very well myself."

"I must say I heard precious little of it."

"Maybe you didn't! Maybe you'd be interested to know I gave that up shortly after we were married—some twelve years ago."

"And whose fault was that?"

"Oh, I don't know," she said, controlling herself.

He pulled the clothes over his shoulder and she pleaded with him to get up and not be the sort that'd deprive another man of even one hour of his leave on shore.

"Is it Frank Coady I'd hurry for! Not me! I'll take my time. I'm over thirty years on the lights and he's a bare half dozen. He doesn't rush much if he's coming out to relieve me."

"You can't blame him and he not long married," she said, scarcely knowing what she was saying as she spoke into the mirror and brushed her hair.

"Last time he came out to relieve me I was waiting for the boat all morning and it didn't come to the afternoon. And what did he say as he stepped ashore? 'God, Tom, I'm sorry the boat's late. I took a hellish pain in my stomach and had to lie down for a couple of hours.' That's what the scamp said to me instead of offering to give me an extra day on account of his hellish pains. Well, I feel tired this morning and I'm not stirring hand or foot for another hour at least!"

She turned round in her chair from the mirror: "I'm beginning to get tired of that word 'tired' of yours. You were tired last night, tired the night before—always tired. You've said nothing else since you stepped ashore two weeks ago. Tired!—it's not out of any consideration you show me. Going off to the pub of an evening and waiting there till somebody gives you a lift home."

"And what do you want me to do? What do you want off me?"

"Oh, nothing," she almost cried, "nothing! I'm used to loneliness now! I'm used to my married widowhood!—in my marriage! You won't come for a game of bridge of an evening. You're tired—you always say. And if I go you won't wait up till I come back. You lower the lamp and go to your bed. Oh, it's no wonder my hair is beginning to turn gray at the temples."

"My own is white!"

"What do you expect and you nearing sixty?"

"You're lovely company!"

"Company! Only for the companionship of the old dog I'd go out of my mind."

"If you'd go out of this room I might think of getting up."

"Oh, if I thought I was keeping you back I'd have gone long ago," and she lifted the alarm clock, the box of matches, and hastened from the room.

He stretched his arms and looked at the glass of water on the table. He'd not drink that! The stale taste of it would upset him—and what with his stomach upset and his mind upset he'd be in a nice fix for a journey on the sea. He'd smoke a cigarette—and stretching out to the chair for his coat, he lit one, and lay back on the pillows, frowning now and then at the cold air that blew through the open window. He could hear Delia singing and he wondered if Mag sang when she was expecting him home. He doubted it! She was more attached to that damned old dog, and she thought nothing of walking five miles of an evening for a game of cards and bringing the old dog with her. If she were on the Rock for a while it'd soon tether her, soon take the skip out of her step. Ah, he should have married somebody less flighty, somebody a bit older and settled, somebody that'd enjoy a glass of stout with you of an evening and not be wanting to drag you over the whole blasted country in search of a game of bridge.

Downstairs he heard Mag opening the front door and letting out the dog for a run, and he heard her speak across to Delia and say how glad she was that it had cleared up in time for Frank's homecoming. Hm, he thought, she's greatly concerned about the neighbors. He looked at the cigarette in his hand, and from the bed he tried to throw it through the open window but it struck the pane and fell on the floor, and he had to get up and stamp on the lighted end.

His clothes were folded neatly for him on the edge of the table: a clean white shirt, his trousers creased, and the brass buttons on his jacket brightly polished. He pulled on the cold, starched shirt and gave a snort of contempt. He wished she'd be less particular—ye'd think he was expecting a visit from the commissioners on the Rock. Damn the thing you ever saw out there except an exhausted pigeon or a dead cormorant that you'd have to kick into the sea to keep the blowfly from stalking around it. It's remarkable the nose a blowfly has for decaying flesh—flying two or three miles out to sea to lay its eggs on a dead seabird. Nature's remarkable when you come to think about it—very remarkable.

Mag tapped the stairs with her knuckles and called out that his breakfast was ready, and when he came down, she glanced at him furtively, trying to read from his face the effect of her remark to him about his white hair. If only she could tell him that she was sorry. But it was better not to—it was better to let it pass and speak to him as if nothing had happened.

"Oh, Tom," she said brightly, "Delia was over to see what time you expected to go."

"And how the hell do I know at what time I'm expected to

go? I'll wait till the boatmen call—and to my own slow and unhurried time."

"She has plenty of paint on, this morning," she added to restore ease.

"Who has?"

"The old boat, I mean," she flashed back.

There it was again: they were back to where they started from—chilling one another with silent hostility or with words that would spurt in bitter fury. Oh, she thought, if only he had shown some of his old love for her during the past two weeks they would not now be snapping at one another, and there would be ease and satisfaction and longing in this leave-taking.

She brought a hot plate of rashers and eggs from the range and poured out tea for him.

"Maybe, Tom, I should run over and tell Delia you'll be ready as soon as the boatmen arrive. I'd like to take the full of my eyes of her place as she does of ours. I always think there's a heavy smell of paraffin in her kitchen. Do you ever find it, Tom?"

"That smell's been in my nose ever since I joined the Lights. Do you know what I'm going to tell you?" and he raised the fork in his hand as she sat down opposite him. "There's nothing as penetrating and as permanent as the smell of paraffin. It's remarkable. It seeps into the walls and it would ooze out again through two coats of new paint. It's in my nose and I wouldn't know the differs between it and the smell of a flower."

She smiled, for she at that moment caught sight of two cases of Guinness's stout on the floor and she yearned to tell him jokingly that he had a fine perfume for something else. But she repressed that desire and turned to the dog as he laid his nose on her lap. She threw him a few scraps from the table and he snapped at them greedily. She fondled his head and toyed with one of his ears, turning it inside out.

"It's a great wonder you wouldn't put out that dog and let

me get my breakfast in some sort of Christian decency. There's a bad smell from him."

"And you said a moment ago that you could smell nothing only paraffin."

"Well, I get the smell of him—and that's saying something."

At that moment the dog walked under the table to his side and he made a kick at it and it yelped and ran under the sofa.

"Come here, Brian," she called coaxingly, and the dog came out and walked timorously towards her.

"Either he goes out of this or I don't finish my breakfast!"

Without a word she got up and let the dog out.

"Maybe that'll please you," she said, coming back to the table. "Anything I love, you despise."

"That's a damned lie!"

"It's true—and because you thought I was jealous of Delia you praised her."

"That's another infernal lie!"

"It's too true, Tom. Nothing pleases you—and you used to be so different. You used to be so jolly—one could joke and laugh with you. But of late you've changed."

"It's you that's changed!"

She took her handkerchief and blew her nose. She felt the tears rising to her eyes and she held her head, trying to regain her self-control.

A shadow passed the window. There was a knock at the door and she opened it to admit three of the boatmen.

"We'd like to catch the tide, Mister O'Brien," they said, and lifting the hampers they shuffled out of the house.

Tom finished his breakfast slowly and went upstairs. He came down after a short time, dressed, and ready for the road. In a glance she saw that he hadn't a breast-pocket handkerchief, and telling him to wait for a minute she ran upstairs to get one, and coming down again she found he was gone. She hurried after him and overtook him at the iron gate.

"Don't keep me back," he said, "didn't you hear as well as I did that we've to catch the tide!" But she held him, and as he tried to wrench himself free she folded the handkerchief into his pocket.

"Tom, don't go away from me like that!" and she looked up at him with an anxious, pleading face.

"You're making a fine laughingstock of me!" he said, and pushing the handkerchief out of sight into his pocket he walked off.

She stood at the gate waiting for him to turn and wave his hand to her but he went on stolidly, erect, along the loose sandy road to the shore. He smoked his pipe, the road sloping before him, its sand white in places from the feet of the boatmen and dark with rain where it was untrodden.

The men were already in the boat, baling out the night's rainwater, and as Tom picked his steps over the piles of slabby wrack on the shore they kept calling out to him to be careful. They assisted him into the boat and he sat in the stern, his legs apart, and his arms dangling between his knees. The boatmen spat on their hands, gripped the oars, and in a few minutes were out from the shelter of the cove and saw ahead of them the black rock with its stub of a lighthouse like a brooding seabird. The men rowed with quick, confident strokes, and the boat rose and fell, cutting white swathes on the green sward of the sea.

"Take your time," Tom said, "take your time. You're not paid for sweating yourselves. We'll be there soon enough."

They said nothing, and as they came nearer to the rock they saw the white path curving from the top to the water's edge and saw the waves jabbing and shouldering one another in mad confusion. They dipped their oars now with short, snappy strokes, their eyes on the three lightkeepers who awaited them.

"Ye'll have to jump for it, Mister O'Brien, when we give the word. We'll get the cases landed first," and while one held off the boat with a boathook, two stood at the stern with a case waiting their chance to hoist it onto the outstretched hands of those on shore. When the cases were roped and landed Frank Coady jumped and alighting on the gunwale he balanced himself on one leg as lightly as a ballet dancer. "The fairy godmother!" he said, and folding his arms he spun round on his toe with emphatic daintiness, and then bowing he kissed his fingers to those on shore.

Tom O'Brien lumbered up to him, putting his pipe in his pocket.

"Now, Tom, my lad, let me give you a hand," said Coady, stretching out his hand to him.

"Get away from me, you bloody fool!" said O'Brien, steadying one foot on the gunwale.

"Be careful now, Mister O'Brien, be careful!" the boatmen shouted. "Wait till that big fellow passes. Take him on the rise!"

But O'Brien wasn't listening to them. He took his leap on the descent of the wave, missed the path, and was all but disappearing into the sea when the lightkeepers gripped him and hauled him ashore.

"I'm all right! I'm all right!" he said, as they laughed at his soaked trousers, the kneecap cut and the blood oozing out of it.

"Are you O.K., Tom?" shouted Coady from the boat.

"Ah, go to hell, you!" said O'Brien.

"He's a cranky oul divil," Coady said to the boatmen as he took off his coat and lifted an oar. "Now, my hearties, let us see how you can make her leap!" He pulled on his oar with all his strength: "Up, my hearty fellows! Up she jumps! That's the way to make her skip! I'll leave a pint for all hands in the pub! A pint from Frank Coady!"

Near the shore he turned his head and saw his wife awaiting him.

"There she is, my hearty men! Knitting and waiting for her darling Frank!" He threw down his oar and perched himself on the bow ready to jump ashore.

"Take care you don't go like O'Brien," they laughed.

"O'Brien's as stiff as a man on stilts! Here she goes!" and he jumped lightly onto the rock and spinning round he warded off the boat with his foot.

In a minute he was in his wife's arms, and linked together they went off slowly along the sandy road, and for a long time the boatmen could hear him laughing and they knew he was laughing at O'Brien.

Through the iron gate they went arm in arm. Mag O'Brien was outside her house with the dog and as Frank drew near he told her with much joyous relish how Tom had cut the knee of his trousers.

"He wasn't hurt?" she said.

"Hurt—not a bit! He strode up the path after it like a man in training for the half mile. The only thing you need to worry about is to get a nice patch." And taking Delia by the hand they swung across to their own house, stood for a minute admiring the whitened doorstep, and going inside they closed the door.

Mag withdrew and sat for a minute at her own window that overlooked their house. Her head ached, and she thought how careless she was in forgetting to pack a bandage or a taste of iodine that he could daub on his bruised knee. One can't think of everything, she said, and she laid her hands on her lap and gazed across at Coady's house that was now silent and still. With an effort she got to her feet and withdrew from the window, and taking a stick she called her dog and set off through the iron gate and away to the shore that was nearest to the Rock.

She scanned the Rock and the white path down to the sea. If only he saw her and came out on the parapet as he used to do and signal to her she'd be content—her mind would be eased.

She sat down on a green slope and waited. There was no stir about the rock, only a gull or two tilting and gliding above the sea. She got up and waved her hand. The dog scratched at the ground, leapt sideways, impatient to be off. She waved again— still there was no sign that she was being seen. She turned and felt the soft wind—it was light and tired: exhausted after its rampage. She stretched herself and stood facing it but it was too weak even to shake her hair. If only it were strong, blowing against her with force she would delight in it. But there was no strength in it—it was indolent and inert, as tired as an old man. She looked once more at the Rock, and seeing a black whorl of smoke rising from it she knew that it was Tom putting on a good fire. He would take a book now, or a bottle of Guinness and his pipe, and after that he would close his eyes and sleep.

The dog barked and ran up the slope after a rabbit. She followed after him and looking to the right she saw the iron gate and the clump of houses she had just left. There was nothing there but silence and sunlight, and behind her the stir of the cold sea.

Bryan MacMahon (1909–   )

Bryan MacMahon was born in County Kerry in 1909. He has lived most of his life in his small native town, Listowel, where he has been a schoolteacher and, from 1941 to 1975, principal of its national school. During the 1940s he published a number of stories in Sean O'Faolain's magazine The Bell. *Since then he has published three collections of stories,* The Lion Tamer *(1948),* The Red Petticoat *(1955), and* The Sound of Hooves *(1985); two novels,* Children of the Rainbow *(1952) and* The Honey Spike *(1967); and several plays, including* The Bugle in the Blood *(1949) and* The Song of the Anvil *(1960). "Exile's Return" is taken from* The Red Petticoat. *Poolbeg Press has published a good selection of his stories in* The End of the World and Other Stories *(1976).*

Exile's Return

Far away the train whistled. The sound moved in rings through the rain falling on the dark fields. On hearing the whistle the little man standing on the railway bridge gave a quick glance into the up-line darkness and then began to hurry downwards towards the station. Above the metal footbridge the lights came on weak and dim as he hurried onwards. The train beat him to the station; all rattle and squeak and bright playing cards placed in line, it drew in beneath the bridge. At the station's end the engine lurched uneasily: then it puffed and huffed, blackened and whitened, and eventually, after a loud release of steam, stood chained.

One passenger descended—a large man with the appearance of a heavyweight boxer. He was dressed in a new cheap suit and overcoat. A black stubble of beard littered his scowling jowls. The eyes under the cap were black and daft. In his hand he carried a battered attaché case tied with a scrap of rope. Dourly slamming the carriage door behind him, he stood glaring up and down the platform.

A passing porter looked at him, abandoned him as being of little interest, then as on remembrance glanced at him a second time. As he walked away the porter's eyes still lingered on the passenger. A hackney driver, viewing with disgust the serried unprofitable door handles, smiled grimly to himself at the sight of the big fellow. Barefooted boys grabbing cylinders of magazines that came hurtling out of the luggage van took no notice whatsoever of the man standing alone. The rain's falling was visible in the pocking of the cut limestone on the platform's edge.

Just then the little man hurried in by the gateway of the station. His trouser ends were tied over clay-daubed boots above which he wore a cast-off green Army greatcoat. A sweat-soiled hat sat askew on his poll. After a moment of hesitation he hurried forward to meet the swaying newcomer.

"There you are, Paddy!" the small man wheezed brightly, yet not coming too close to the big fellow.

The big fellow did not answer. He began to walk heavily out of the station. The little man moved hoppingly at his side, pelting questions to which he received no reply.

"Had you a good crossing, Paddy?" "Is it true that the Irish Sea is as wicked as May Eve?" "There's a fair share of Irish in Birmingham, I suppose?" Finally, in a tone that indicated that this question was closer to the bone than its fellows: "How long are you away now, Paddy? Over six year, eh?"

Paddy plowed ahead without replying. When they had reached the first of the houses of the county town, he glowered over his shoulder at the humpy bridge that led over the railway line to the open country: after a moment or two he dragged his gaze away and looked at the street that led downhill from the station.

"We'll have a drink, Timothy!" the big man said dourly.

"A drink, Paddy!" the other agreed.

The pub glittered in the old-fashioned way. The embossed wallpaper between the shelving had been painted lime green. As they entered the bar, the publican was in the act of turning with a full pint-glass in his hand. His eyes hardened on seeing Paddy: he delayed the fraction of a second before placing the glass on the high counter in front of a customer.

Wiping his hands in a blue apron, his face working overtime, "Back again, eh, Paddy?" the publican asked, with false cheer. A limp handshake followed.

Paddy grunted, then lurched towards the far corner of the bar. There, sitting on a high stool, he crouched against the counter. Timothy took his seat beside him, seating himself sideways to the counter as if protecting the big fellow from the gaze of the other customers. Paddy called for two pints of porter: he paid for his call from an old-fashioned purse bulky with English treasury notes. Timothy raised his full glass—its size tended to dwarf him—and ventured: "Good health!" Paddy growled a reply. Both men tilted the glasses on their heads and gulped three-quarters of the contents. Paddy set down his glass and looked moodily in front of him. Timothy carefully replaced his glass on the counter, then placed his face closer to the other's ear.

"Yeh got my letter, Paddy?"

"Ay!"

"You're not mad with me?"

"Mad with *you?*" The big man's guffaw startled the bar. There was a long silence.

"I got yer letter!" Paddy said abruptly. He turned and for the first time looked his small companion squarely in the face. Deliberately he set the big, battered index finger of his right hand inside the other's collar stud. As, slowly, he began to twist his finger, the collarband tightened. When it was taut Paddy drew the other's face close to his own. So intimately were the two men seated that the others in the bar did not know what was going on. Timothy's face changed color, yet he did not raise his hands to try to release himself.

"Yer swearin' 'tis true?" Paddy growled.

Gaspingly: "God's gospel, it's true!"

"Swear it!"

"That I may be struck down dead if I'm tellin' you a word of a lie! Every mortal word I wrote you is true!"

"Why didn't you send me word afore now?"

"I couldn't rightly make out where you were, Paddy. Only for Danny Greaney comin' home I'd never have got your address. An' you know I'm not handy with the pen."

"Why didn't you let me as I was—not knowin' at all?"

"We to be butties always, Paddy. I thought it a shame you to keep sendin' her lashin's o' money an' she to be like that! You're chokin' me, Paddy!"

As Paddy tightened still more, the buttonhole broke and the stud came away in the crook of his index finger. He looked at it stupidly. Timothy quietly put the Y of his hand to his chafed neck. Paddy threw the stud behind him. It struck the timbered encasement of the stairway.

"*Ach!*" he said harshly. He drained his glass and with its heel tapped on the counter. The publican came up to refill the glasses.

Timothy, whispering: "What'll you do, Paddy?"

"What'll I do?" Paddy laughed. "I'll drink my pint," he said. He took a gulp. "Then, as likely as not, I'll swing for her!"

"Sssh!" Timothy counseled.

Timothy glanced into an advertising mirror; behind the picture of little men loading little barrels onto a little lorry he saw the publican with his eyes fast on the pair of them. Timothy warned him off with a sharp look. He looked swiftly around: the backs of the other customers were a shade too tense for his liking. Then suddenly the publican was in under Timothy's guard.

Swabbing the counter: "What way are things over, Paddy?"

"Fair enough!"

"I'm hearin' great accounts of you from Danny Greaney. We were all certain you'd never again come home, you were doin' so well. How'll you content yourself with a small place like this, after what you've seen? But then, after all, home is home!"

The publican ignored Timothy's threatening stare. Paddy raised his daft eyes and looked directly at the man behind the bar. The swabbing moved swiftly away.

"Swing for her, I will!" Paddy said again. He raised his voice. "The very minute I turn my back . . ."

"Sssh!" Timothy intervened. He smelled his almost empty glass, then said in a loud whisper: "The bloody stout is casky. Let's get away out o' this!"

The word *casky* succeeded in moving Paddy. It also nicked the publican's pride. After they had gone the publican, on the pretense of closing the door, looked after them. He turned and threw a joke to his customers. A roar of laughter was his reward.

Paddy and Timothy were now wandering towards the humpy bridge that led to the country. Timothy was carrying the battered case: Paddy had his arm around his companion's shoulder. The raw air was testing the sobriety of the big fellow's legs.

"Nothin' hasty!" Timothy was advising. "First of all we'll pass out the cottage an' go on to my house. You'll sleep with me tonight. Remember, Paddy, that I wrote that letter out o' pure friendship!"

Paddy lifted his cap and let the rain strike his forehead. "I'll walk the gallows high for her!" he said.

"Calm an' collected, that's my advice!"

"When these two hands are on her throat, you'll hear her squealin' in the eastern world!"

"Nothin' hasty, Paddy: nothin' hasty at all!"

Paddy pinned his friend against the parapet of the railway bridge. "Is six years hasty?" he roared.

"For God's sake, let go o' me, Paddy! I'm the only friend you have left! Let go o' me!"

The pair lurched with the incline. The whitethorns were now on each side of them releasing their raindrops from thorn to thorn in the darkness. Far away across the ridge of the barony a fan of light from a lighthouse swung its arc on shore and sea and sky. Wherever there was a break in the hedges a bout of wind mustered its forces and vainly set about capsizing them.

Paddy began to growl a song with no air at all to it.

"Hush, man, or the whole world'll know you're home," Timothy said.

"As if to sweet hell I cared!" Paddy stopped and swayed. After a pause he muttered: "Th' other fellah—is he long gone?"

Timothy whinnied. "One night only it was, like Duffy's Circus." He set his hat farther back on his poll and then, his solemn face tilted to the scud of the moon, said: "You want my firm opinion, Paddy? 'Twas nothin' but a chance fall. The mood an' the man meetin' her. 'Twould mebbe never again happen in a million years. A chance fall, that's all it was, in my considered opinion."

Loudly: "Did you ever know me to break my word?"

"Never, Paddy!"

"Then I'll swing for her! You have my permission to walk into the witness box and swear that Paddy Kinsella said he'd swing for her!"

He resumed his singing.

"We're right beside the house, Paddy. You don't want to wake your own children, do you? Your own fine, lawful-got sons! Eh, Paddy? Do you want to waken them up?"

Paddy paused: "Lawful-got is right!—you've said it there!"

"Tomorrow is another day. We'll face her tomorrow and see how she brazens it out. I knew well you wouldn't want to disturb your own sons."

They lurched on through the darkness. As they drew near the low thatched cottage that was slightly below the level of the road, Timothy kept urging Paddy forward. Paddy's boots were more rebellious than heretofore. Timothy grew anxious at the poor progress they were making. He kept saying: "Tomorrow is the day, Paddy! I'll put the rope around her neck for you. Don't wake the lads tonight."

Directly outside the cottage, Paddy came to a halt. He swayed and glowered at the small house with its tiny windows. He drew himself up to his full height.

"She in bed?" he growled.

"She's up at McSweeney's. She goes there for the sake of company. Half an hour at night when the kids are in bed— you'll not begrudge her that, Paddy?"

"I'll not begrudge her that!" Paddy yielded a single step, then planted his shoes still more firmly on the roadway. He swayed.

"The . . . ?" he queried.

"A girl, Paddy, a girl!"

A growl, followed by the surrender of another step.

"Goin' on six year, is it?"

"That's it, Paddy, six year."

Another step. "Like the ma, or . . . the da?"

"The ma, Paddy. Mostly all the ma. Come on now, an' you'll have a fine sleep tonight under my roof."

Paddy eyed the cottage. Growled his contempt of it, then spat on the roadway. He gave minor indications of his inten-

tion of moving forward. Then unpredictably he pounded off
the restraining hand of Timothy, pulled violently away and
went swaying towards the passage that led down to the cottage.

After a fearful glance uproad, Timothy wailed: "She'll be
back in a minute!"

"I'll see my lawful-got sons!" Paddy growled.

When Timothy caught up with him the big fellow was
fumbling with the padlock on the door. As on a thought he
lurched aside and groped in vain in the corner of the window
sill.

"She takes the key with her," Timothy said. "For God's sake
leave it till mornin'."

But Paddy was already blundering on the cobbled pathway
that led around by the gable of the cottage. Finding the back
door bolted, he stood back from it angrily. He was about to
smash it in when Timothy discovered that the hinged window
of the kitchen was slightly open. As Timothy swung the window open the smell of turf smoke emerged. Paddy put his boot
on an imaginary niche in the wall and dug in the plaster until
he gained purchase of a sort. "Gimme a leg!" he ordered
harshly.

Timothy began clawing Paddy's leg upwards. Belaboring the
small man's shoulders with boot and hand, the big fellow
floundered through the open window. Spread-eagled on the
kitchen table he remained breathing harshly for a full minute,
then laboriously he grunted his way via a *sugan* chair to the
floor.

"You all right, Paddy?"

A grunt.

"Draw the bolt of the back door, Paddy."

A long pause followed. At last the bolt was drawn. "Where
the hell's the lamp?" Paddy asked as he floundered in the darkness.

"She has it changed. It's at the right of the window now."

Paddy's match came erratically alight. He held it aloft. Then he slewed forward and removed the lamp chimney and placed it on the table. " 'Sall right!" he said, placing a match to the wick and replacing the chimney. Awkwardly he raised the wick. He began to look here and there about the kitchen.

The fire was raked in its own red ashes. Two *sugan* chairs stood one on each side of the hearthstone. Delph glowed red, white, and green on the wide dresser. The timber of the chairs and the deal table were white from repeated scrubbings. Paddy scowled his recognition of each object. Timothy stood watching him narrowly.

"See my own lads!" Paddy said, focusing his gaze on the bedroom door at the rear of the cottage.

"Aisy!" Timothy counseled.

Lighting match held aloft, they viewed the boys. Four lads sleeping in pairs in iron-headed double beds. Each of the boys had a mop of black hair and a pair of heavy eyebrows. The eldest slept with the youngest and the two middle-aged lads slept together. They sprawled anyhow in various postures.

Paddy had turned surprisingly sober. " 'Clare to God!" he said. "I'd pass 'em on the road without knowin' 'em!"

"There's a flamin' lad!" Timothy caught one of the middle-aged boys by the hair and pivoted the sleep-loaded head. Transferring his attention to the other of this pair: "There's your livin' spit, Paddy!" Indicating the eldest: "There's your own ould fellah born into the world a second time, devil's black temper an' all!" At the youngest: "Here's Bren—he was crawlin' on the floor the last time you saw him. Ay! Bully pups all!"

"Bully pups all!" Paddy echoed loudly. The match embered in his fingers. When there was darkness: "My lawful-got sons!" he said bitterly.

Timothy was in the room doorway. "We'll be off now, Paddy!" he said. After a growl, Paddy joined him.

Timothy said: "One of us'll have to go out by the window. Else she'll spot the bolt drawn."

Paddy said nothing.

"You'll never manage the window twice."

"I'll be after you," Paddy said.

Timothy turned reluctantly away.

"Where's the . . . ?" Paddy asked. He was standing at the kitchen's end.

"The . . . ?"

"Yeh!"

"She's in the front room. You're not goin' to . . . ?" Paddy was already at the door of the other room.

"She sleeps like a cat!" Timothy warned urgently. "If she tells the mother about me, the fat'll be in the fire!"

Paddy opened the door of the front room. Breathing heavily he again began fumbling with the matchbox. Across the window moved the scudding night life of the sky. The matchlight came up and showed a quilt patterned with candlewick. Then abruptly where the bedclothes had been a taut ball there was no longer a ball. As if playing a merry game, the little girl, like Jill-in-the-box, flax-curled and blue-eyed, sprang up.

"Who is it?" she asked fearlessly.

The matchlight was high above her. Paddy did not reply.

The girl laughed ringingly. "You're in the kitchen, Timothy Hannigan," she called out. "I know your snuffle."

"Holy God!" Timothy breathed.

"I heard you talking too, boyo," she said gleefully as the matchlight died in Paddy's fingers.

" 'Tis me all right, Maag," said Timmy, coming apologetically to the doorway of the room. "Come on away!" he said in a whisper to Paddy.

"Didn't I know right well 'twas you, boyo!" Maag laughed. She drew up her knees and locked her hands around them in a mature fashion.

Another match sprang alive in Paddy's fingers.

"Who's this fellah?" Maag enquired of Timothy.

Timothy put his head inside the room. "He's your . . . your uncle!"

"My uncle what?"

"You uncle . . . Paddy!"

Paddy and Maag looked fully at one another.

Timothy quavered: "You won't tell your mother I was here?"

"I won't so!" the girl laughed. "Wait until she comes home!"

Timothy groaned. "C'm'on away to hell outa this!" he said, showing a spark of spirit. Surprisingly enough, Paddy came. They closed the room door behind them.

"Out the back door with you," Timothy said. "I'll manage the lamp and the bolt."

"Out, you!" Paddy growled. He stood stolidly like an ox. Dubiously: "Very well!"

Timothy went out. From outside the back door he called: "Shoot the bolt quick, Paddy. She'll be back any minute."

Paddy shot the bolt.

"Blow out the lamp, Paddy!" Timothy's head and shoulders were framed in the window.

After a pause Paddy blew out the lamp.

"Hurry, Paddy! Lift your leg!"

No reply.

"Hurry, Paddy, I tell you. What's wrong with you, man?"

Paddy gave a deep growl. "I'm sorry now I didn't throttle you."

"Throttle me! Is that my bloody thanks?"

"It was never in my breed to respect an informer."

"Your breed!" Timothy shouted. "You, with a cuckoo in your nest."

"If my hands were on your throat . . ."

"Yehoo! You, with the nest robbed."

"Go, while you're all of a piece. The drink has me lazy. I'll give you while I'm countin' five. One, two . . ."

Timothy was gone.

Paddy sat on the rough chair at the left of the hearth. He began to grope for the tongs. Eventually he found it. He drew the red coals of turf out of the ashes and set them together in a kind of pyramid. The flames came up.

The door of the front bedroom creaked open. Maag was there, dressed in a long white nightdress.

"Were you scoldin' him?"

"Ay!" Paddy answered.

"He wants scoldin' badly. He's always spyin' on my Mom."

After a pause, the girl came to mid-kitchen.

"Honest," she asked, "are you my uncle?"

"In a class of a way!"

"What class of a way?" she echoed. She took a step closer.

"Are you cold, girlie?" Paddy asked.

"I am an' I am not. What class of a way are you my uncle?"

There was no reply.

"Mebbe you're my ould fellah back from England?" she stabbed suddenly.

"Mebbe!"

The girl's voice was shaken with delight. "I knew you'd be back! They all said no, but I said yes—that you'd be back for sure." A pause. A step nearer. "What did you bring me?"

Dourly he put his hand into his pocket. His fingers encountered a pipe, a half-quarter of tobacco, a six-inch nail, a clotted handkerchief, and the crumpled letter from Timothy.

"I left it after me in the carriage," he said limply.

Her recovery from disappointment was swift. "Can't you get it in town o' Saturday?" she said, drawing still closer.

"That's right!" he agreed. There was a short pause. Then: "Come hether to the fire," he said.

She came and stood between his knees. The several hoops of her curls were between him and the firelight. She smelled of soap. His fingers touched her arms. The mother was in her surely. He knew it by the manner in which her flesh was sure and unafraid.

They remained there without speaking until the light step on the road sent her prickling alive. "Mom'll kill me for bein' out of bed," she said. Paddy's body stiffened. As the girl struggled to be free, he held her fast. Of a sudden she went limp, and laughed: "I forgot!" she whispered. "She'll not touch me on account of you comin' home." She rippled with secret laughter. "Wasn't I the fooleen to forget?"

The key was in the padlock. The door moved open. The woman came in, her shawl down from her shoulders. "Maag!" she breathed. The girl and the man were between her and the firelight.

Without speaking the woman stood directly inside the door. The child said nothing but looked from one to the other. The woman waited for a while. Slowly she took off her shawl, then closed the door behind her. She walked carefully across the kitchen. A matchbox noised. She lighted the warm lamp. As the lamplight came up Paddy was seen to be looking steadfastly into the fire.

"You're back, Paddy?"

"Ay!"

"Had you a good crossin'?"

"Middlin'!"

"You hungry?"

"I'll see . . . soon!"

There was a long silence. Her fingers restless, the woman stood in mid-kitchen.

She raised her voice: "If you've anything to do or say to me, Paddy Kinsella, you'd best get it over. I'm not a one for waitin'!"

He said nothing. He held his gaze on the fire.

"You hear me, Paddy? I'll not live cat and dog with you. I

know what I am. Small good your brandin' me when the countryside has me well branded before you."

He held his silence.

"Sayin' nothin' won't get you far. I left you down, Paddy. Be
a man an' say it to my face!"

Paddy turned: "You left me well down," he said clearly. He
turned to the fire and added, in a mutter: "I was no angel myself!"

Her trembling lips were unbelieving. "We're quits, so?" she
ventured at last.

"Quits!"

"You'll not keep firin' it in my face?"

"I'll not!"

"Before God?"

"Before God!"

The woman crossed herself and knelt on the floor. "In the
presence of my God," she said, "because you were fair to me,
Paddy Kinsella, I'll be better than three wives to you. I broke
my marriage-mornin' promise, but I'll make up for it. There's
my word, given before my Maker!"

Maag kept watching with gravity. The mother crossed herself and rose.

Paddy was dourly rummaging in his coat pocket. At last his
fingers found what he was seeking. "I knew I had it somewhere!" he said. He held up a crumpled toffee-sweet. "I got it
from a kid on the boat."

Maag's face broke in pleasure: " 'Twill do—till Saturday!"
she said.

The girl's mouth came down upon the striped toffee. Then,
the sweet in her cheek, she broke away and ran across the
kitchen. She flung open the door of the boys' bedroom.

"Get up outa that!" she cried out. "The ould fellah is
home!"

Flann O'Brien (1911–1966)

Flann O'Brien was born Brian O'Nolan in Strabane, County Tyrone, in 1911. After his graduation from University College, Dublin, in 1935, he entered the Irish Civil Service and became a permanent citizen of Dublin. He published his first novel, At Swim-Two-Birds, *in 1939. It was praised by James Joyce, but otherwise received little attention until 1960 when it was republished and became an underground classic. In 1941 he published a novel in Gaelic,* An Beal Bocht, *translated into English as* The Poor Mouth *in 1973. During his career in Dublin, he was best known as a brilliant journalist with his regular column "Cruiskeen Lawn" in* The Irish Times. *As a journalist he used another pseudonym, Myles na gCopaleen. O'Brien's other novels are* The Hard Life *(1961),* The Dalkey Archive *(1964), and* The Third Policeman, *published in 1967 but first written in the 1940s. He has also written a play,* Faustus Kelly, *performed at the Abbey Theatre in 1943. There have been several collections of his journalistic pieces, the most complete of which is* The Best of Myles *(1968). "The Martyr's Crown" is taken from* Stories and Plays *(1973).*

The Martyr's Crown

Mr. Toole and Mr. O'Hickey walked down the street together in the morning.

Mr. Toole had a peculiarity. He had the habit, when accompanied by another person, of saluting total strangers; but only if these strangers were of important air and costly raiment. He meant thus to make it known that he had friends in high places, and that he himself, though poor, was a person of quality fallen on evil days through some undisclosed sacrifice made in the interest of immutable principle early in life. Most of the strangers, startled out of their private thoughts, stammered a salutation in return. And Mr. Toole was shrewd. He stopped at that. He said no more to his companion, but by some little private gesture, a chuckle, a shake of the head, a smothered imprecation, he nearly always extracted the one question most melodious to his ear: *"Who was that?"*

Mr. Toole was shabby, and so was Mr. O'Hickey, but Mr. O'Hickey had a neat and careful shabbiness. He was an older and a wiser man, and was well up to Mr. Toole's tricks. Mr. Toole at his best, he thought, was better than a play. And he now knew that Mr. Toole was appraising the street with beady eye.

"Gorawars!" Mr. Toole said suddenly.

We are off, Mr. O'Hickey thought.

"Do you see this hop-off-my-thumb with the stick and the hat?" Mr. Toole said.

Mr. O'Hickey did. A young man of surpassing elegance was approaching; tall, fair, darkly dressed; even at fifty yards his hauteur seemed to chill Mr. O'Hickey's part of the street.

"Ten to one he cuts me dead," Mr. Toole said. "This is one of the most extraordinary pieces of work in the whole world."

Mr. O'Hickey braced himself for a more than ordinary impact. The adversaries neared each other.

"How are we at all, Sean a chara?" Mr. Toole called out.

The young man's control was superb. There was no glare, no glance of scorn, no sign at all. He was gone, but had left in his wake so complete an impression of his contempt that even Mr. Toole paled momentarily. The experience frightened Mr. O'Hickey.

"Who . . . who was *that?*" he asked at last.

"I knew the mother well," Mr. Toole said musingly. "The woman was a saint." Then he was silent.

Mr. O'Hickey thought: there is nothing for it but bribery—again. He led the way into a public house and ordered two bottles of stout.

"As you know," Mr. Toole began, "I was Bart Conlon's right-hand man. Bart, of course, went the other way in 'twenty-two."

Mr. O'Hickey nodded and said nothing. He knew that Mr. Toole had never rendered military service to his country.

"In any case," Mr. Toole continued, "there was a certain day early in 'twenty-one and orders come through that there was to be a raid on the Sinn Fein office above in Harcourt Street. There happened to be a certain gawskogue of a cattle jobber from the County Meath had an office on the other side of the street. And he was well in with a certain character be the name of Mick Collins. I think you get me drift?"

"I do," Mr. O'Hickey said.

"There was six of us," Mr. Toole said, "with meself and Bart Conlon in charge. Me man the cattle jobber gets an urgent call to be out of his office accidentally on purpose at four o'clock, and at half-four the six of us is parked inside there with two machine guns, the rifles, and a class of a homemade bomb that Bart used to make in his own kitchen. The military arrived in two lurries on the other side of the street at five o'clock. That was the hour in the orders that come. I believe that man Mick Collins had lads working for him over in the War Office across in London. He was a great stickler for the British being punctual on the dot."

"He was a wonderful organizer," Mr. O'Hickey said.

"Well, we stood with our backs to the far wall and let them have it through the open window and them getting down off the lurries. Sacred godfathers! I never seen such murder in me life. Your men didn't know where it was coming from, and a

lot of them wasn't worried very much when it was all over, because there was no heads left on some of them. Bart then gives
the order for retreat down the back stairs; in no time we're in
the lane, and five minutes more the six of us upstairs in Martin
Fulham's pub in Camden Street. Poor Martin is dead since."

"I knew that man well," Mr. O'Hickey remarked.

"Certainly you knew him well," Mr. Toole said, warmly.
"The six of us was marked men, of course. In any case, fresh
orders come at six o'clock. All hands was to proceed in military
formation, singly, be different routes to the house of a great
skin in the Cumann na mBan, a widow be the name of
Clougherty that lived on the south side. We were all to lie low,
do you understand, till there was fresh orders to come out and
fight again. Sacred wars, they were very rough days them days;
will I ever forget Mrs. Clougherty! She was certainly a marvelous figure of a woman. I never seen a woman like her to bake
bread."

Mr. O'Hickey looked up.

"Was she," he said, "was she . . . all right?"

"She was certainly nothing of the sort," Mr. Toole said
loudly and sharply. "By God, we were all thinking of other
things in them days. Here was this unfortunate woman in a
three-story house on her own, with some quare fellow in the
middle flat, herself on the ground floor, and six bloodthirsty
pultogues hiding above on the top floor, every manjack ready
to shoot his way out if there was trouble. We got feeds there I
never seen before or since, and the *Independent* every morning.
Outrage in Harcourt Street. The armed men then decamped
and made good their excape. I'm damn bloody sure we made
good our excape. There was one snag. We couldn't budge out.
No exercise at all—and that means only one thing . . ."

"Constipation?" Mr. O'Hickey suggested.

"The very man," said Mr. Toole.

Mr. O'Hickey shook his head.

"We were there a week. Smoking and playing cards, but

when nine o'clock struck, Mrs. Clougherty come up, and, Protestant, Catholic, or Jewman, all hands had to go down on the
knees. A very good . . . strict . . . woman, if you understand me,
a true daughter of Ireland. And now I'll tell you a damn good
one. About five o'clock one evening I heard a noise below
and peeped out of the window. Sanctified and holy godfathers!"

"What was it—the noise?" Mr. O'Hickey asked.

"What do you think, only two lurries packed with military,
with my nabs of an officer hopping out and running up the
steps to hammer at the door, and all the Tommies sitting back
with their guns at the ready. Trapped! That's a nice word—
trapped! If there was ever rats in a cage, it was me unfortunate
brave men from the battle of Harcourt Street. God!"

"They had you at what we call a disadvantage," Mr.
O'Hickey conceded.

"She was in the room herself with the teapot. She had a big
silver satteen blouse on her; I can see it yet. She turned on us
and gave us all one look that said: *Shut up, ye nervous lousers.*
Then she foostered about a bit at the glass and walks out of the
room with bang-bang-bang to shake the house going on
downstairs. And I seen a thing . . ."

"What?" asked Mr. O'Hickey.

"She was a fine—now you'll understand me, Mr. O'Hickey,"
Mr. Toole said carefully; "I seen her fingers on the buttons of
the satteen, if you follow me, and she leaving the room."

Mr. O'Hickey, discreet, nodded thoughtfully.

"I listened at the stairs. Jakers I never got such a drop in me
life. She clatters down and flings open the hall door. This
young pup is outside, and asks—awsks—in the law-de-daw
voice, "Is there any men in this house?" The answer took me
to the fair altogether. She puts on the guttiest voice I ever
heard outside Moor Street and says, "Sairtintly not at this hour
of the night; I wish to God there was. Sure, how could the
poor unfortunate women get on without them, officer?" Well

lookat. I nearly fell down the stairs on top of the two of them. The next thing I hear is, "Madam this and madam that" and "Sorry to disturb and I beg your pardon," "I trust this and I trust that," and then the whispering starts, and at the windup the hall door is closed and into the room off the hall with the pair of them. This young bucko out of the Borderers in a room off the hall with a headquarters captain of the Cumann na mBan! *Give us two more stouts there, Mick!*"

"That is a very queer one, as the man said," Mr. O'Hickey said.

"I went back to the room and sat down. Bart had his gun out, and we were all looking at one another. After ten minutes we heard another noise."

Mr. Toole poured out his stout with unnecessary care.

"It was the noise of the lurries driving away," he said at last. "She'd saved our lives, and when she come up a while later she said 'We'll go to bed a bit earlier tonight, boys; kneel down all.' That was Mrs. Clougherty the saint."

Mr. O'Hickey, also careful, was working at his own bottle, his wise head bent at the task.

"What I meant to ask you was this," Mr. O'Hickey said, "that's an extraordinary affair altogether, but what has that to do with that stuck-up young man we met in the street, the lad with all the airs?"

"Do you not see it, man?" Mr. Toole said in surprise. "For seven hundred year, thousands—no, I'll make it millions—of Irish men and women have died for Ireland. We never rared jibbers; they were glad to do it, and will again. But that young man was *born* for Ireland. There was never anybody else like him. Why wouldn't he be proud?"

"The Lord save us!" Mr. O'Hickey cried.

"A saint I called her," Mr. Toole said, hotly. "What am I talking about—she's a martyr and wears the martyr's crown today!"

Mary Lavin (1912-   )

Mary Lavin was born in East Walpole, Massachusetts, of Irish parents, in 1912. She moved to Ireland at the age of ten, settling for a brief time on the estate of Bective House, County Meath, where her father was manager. She was educated at Loreto Convent, Dublin, and at University College, Dublin, where she earned an M.A. in English. She began writing while at the university, and has divided her time between writing and farming. When her first husband died, she and her three daughters continued to work their farm in County Meath. She has since remarried. Lavin has published two novels, The House in Clewe Street *(1945) and* Mary O'Grady *(1950), but her main work has been in the short story. Frank O'Connor has written, "She fascinates me more than any other of the writers of my generation." She has published numerous collections, including* Tales From Bective Ridge *(1942),* The Long Ago *(1944),* The Becker Wives *(1946),* A Single Lady *(1951),* Happiness *(1969),* A Memory *(1972), and* A Family Likeness *(1985). "Happiness" is the title story of her collection* Happiness.

Happiness

Mother had a lot to say. This does not mean she was always talking but that we children felt the wells she drew upon were deep, deep, deep. Her theme was happiness: what it was, what it was not; where we might find it, where not; and how, if found, it must be guarded. Never must we confound it with pleasure. Nor think sorrow its exact opposite.

"Take Father Hugh," Mother's eyes flashed as she looked at him. "According to him, sorrow is an ingredient of happiness—a *necessary* ingredient, if you please!" And when he tried to protest she put up her hand. "There may be a freakish truth in the theory—for some people. But not for me. And not, I hope, for my children." She looked severely at us three girls. We laughed. None of us had had much experience with sorrow. Bea and I were children and Linda only a year old when our father died suddenly after a short illness that had not at first seemed serious. "I've known people to make sorrow a *substitute* for happiness," Mother said.

Father Hugh protested again. "You're not putting me in that class, I hope?"

Father Hugh, ever since our father died, had been the closest of anyone to us as a family, without being close to any one of us in particular—even to Mother. He lived in a monastery near our farm in County Meath, and he had been one of the celebrants at the Requiem High Mass our father's political importance had demanded. He met us that day for the first time, but he took to dropping in to see us, with the idea of filling the crater of loneliness left at our center. He did not know that there was a cavity in his own life, much less that we would fill it. He and Mother were both young in those days, and perhaps it gave scandal to some that he was so often in our house, staying till late into the night and, indeed, thinking nothing of stopping all night if there was any special reason, such as one of us being sick. He had even on occasion slept there if the night was too wet for tramping home across the fields.

When we girls were young, we were so used to having Father Hugh around that we never stood on ceremony with him but in his presence dried our hair and pared our nails and never minded what garments were strewn about. As for Mother—she thought nothing of running out of the bathroom in her slip, brushing her teeth or combing her hair, if she wanted to tell him something she might otherwise forget. And she brooked no criticism of her behavior. "Celibacy was never meant to take all the warmth and homeliness out of their lives," she said.

On this point, too, Bea was adamant. Bea, the middle sister, was our oracle. "I'm so glad he *has* Mother," she said, "as well as her having him, because it must be awful the way most women treat them—priests, I mean—as if they were pariahs. Mother treats him like a human being—that's all!"

And when it came to Mother's ears that there had been gossip about her making free with Father Hugh, she opened her eyes wide in astonishment. "But he's only a priest!" she said.

Bea giggled. "It's a good job he didn't hear *that,*" she said to me afterwards. "It would undo the good she's done him. You'd think he was a eunuch."

"Bea!" I said. "Do you think he's in love with her?"

"If so, he doesn't know it," Bea said firmly. "It's her soul he's after! Maybe he wants to make sure of her in the next world!"

But thoughts of the world to come never troubled Mother. "If anything ever happens to me, children," she said, "suddenly, I mean, or when you are not near me, or I cannot speak to you, I want you to promise you won't feel bad. There's no need! Just remember that I had a happy life—and that if I had to choose my kind of heaven I'd take it on this earth with you again, no matter how much you might annoy me!"

You see, annoyance and fatigue, according to Mother, and even illness and pain, could coexist with happiness. She had a habit of asking people if they were happy at times and in places that—to say the least of it—seemed to us inappropriate. "But are you happy?" she'd probe as one lay sick and bathed in sweat, or in the throes of a jumping toothache. And once in our presence she made the inquiry of an old friend as he lay upon his deathbed.

"Why not?" she said when we took her to task for it later.

"Isn't it more important than ever to be happy when you're dying? Take my own father! You know what he said in his last moments? On his deathbed, he defied me to name a man who had enjoyed a better life. In spite of dreadful pain, his face *radiated* happiness!" Mother nodded her head comfortably. "Happiness drives out pain, as fire burns out fire."

Having no knowledge of our own to pit against hers, we thirstily drank in her rhetoric. Only Bea was sceptical. "Perhaps you *got* it from him, like spots, or fever," she said. "Or something that could at least be slipped from hand to hand."

"Do you think I'd have taken it if that were the case!" Mother cried. "Then, when he needed it most?"

"Not there and then!" Bea said stubbornly. "I meant as a sort of legacy."

"Don't you think in *that* case," Mother said, exasperated, "he would have felt obliged to leave it to your grandmother?"

Certainly we knew that in spite of his lavish heart our grandfather had failed to provide our grandmother with enduring happiness. He had passed that job on to Mother. And Mother had not made too good a fist of it, even when Father was living and she had him—and, later, us children—to help.

As for Father Hugh, he had given our grandmother up early in the game. "God Almighty couldn't make that woman happy," he said one day, seeing Mother's face, drawn and pale with fatigue, preparing for the nightly run over to her own mother's flat that would exhaust her utterly.

There were evenings after she came home from the library where she worked when we saw her stand with the car keys in her hand, trying to think which would be worse—to slog over there on foot, or take out the car again. And yet the distance was short. It was Mother's day that had been too long.

"Weren't you over to see her this morning?" Father Hugh demanded.

"No matter!" said Mother. She was no doubt thinking of the forlorn face our grandmother always put on when she was leaving. ("Don't say good night, Vera," Grandmother would plead. "It makes me feel too lonely. And you never can tell— you might slip over again before you go to bed!")

"Do you know the time?" Bea would say impatiently, if she happened to be with Mother. Not indeed that the lateness of the hour counted for anything, because in all likelihood Mother *would* go back, if only to pass by under the window and see that the lights were out, or stand and listen and make sure that as far as she could tell all was well.

"I wouldn't mind if she was happy," Mother said.

"And how do you know she's not?" we'd ask.

"When people are happy, I can feel it. Can't you?"

We were not sure. Most people thought our grandmother was a gay creature, a small birdy being who even at a great age laughed like a girl, and—more remarkably—sang like one, as she went about her day. But beak and claw were of steel. She'd think nothing of sending Mother back to a shop three times if her errands were not exactly right. "Not sugar like that—that's *too* fine; it's not castor sugar I want. But *not* as coarse as *that,* either. I want an in-between kind."

Provoked one day, my youngest sister, Linda, turned and gave battle. "You're mean!" she cried. "You love ordering people about!"

Grandmother preened, as if Linda had acclaimed an attribute. "I was always hard to please," she said. "As a girl, I used to be called Miss Imperious."

And Miss Imperious she remained as long as she lived, even when she was a great age. Her orders were then given a wry twist by the fact that as she advanced in age she took to calling her daughter Mother, as we did.

There was one great phrase with which our grandmother opened every sentence: "if only." "If only," she'd say, when we came to visit her—"if only you'd come earlier, before I was worn out expecting you!" Or if we were early, then if only it was later, after she'd had a rest and could enjoy us, be *able* for us. And if we brought her flowers, she'd sigh to think that if only we'd brought them the previous day she'd have had a visitor to appreciate them, or say it was a pity the stems weren't longer. If only we'd picked a few green leaves, or included some buds, because, she said disparagingly, the poor flowers we'd brought were already wilting. We might just as well not have brought them! As the years went on, Grandmother had a new bead to add to her rosary: if only her friends were not all dead! By their absence, they reduced to nil all *real* enjoyment in anything. Our own father—her son-in-law—was the one person who had ever gone close to pleasing her. But even here there had been a snag. "If only he was my real son!" she used to say, with a sigh.

Mother's mother lived on through our childhood and into our early maturity (though she outlived the money our grandfather left her), and in our minds she was a complicated mixture of valiance and defeat. Courageous and generous within the limits of her own life, her simplest demand was yet enormous in the larger frame of Mother's life, and so we never could see her with the same clarity of vision with which we saw our grandfather, or our own father. Them we saw only through Mother's eyes.

"Take your grandfather!" she'd cry, and instantly we'd see him, his eyes burning upon us—yes, upon *us,* although in his day only one of us had been born: me. At another time, Mother would cry, "Take your own father!" and instantly we'd see *him*—tall, handsome, young, and much more suited to marry one of us than poor bedraggled Mother.

Most fascinating of all were the times Mother would say "Take me!" By magic then, staring down the years, we'd see blazingly clear a small girl with black hair and buttoned boots, who, though plain and pouting, burned bright, like a star. "I was happy, you see," Mother said. And we'd strain hard to try and understand the mystery of the light that still radiated from her. "I used to lean along a tree that grew out over the river," she said, "and look down through the gray leaves at the water flowing past below, and I used to think it was not the stream that flowed but me, spread-eagled over it, who flew through the air! Like a bird! That I'd found the secret!" She made it seem there might *be* such a secret, just waiting to be found. Another time she'd dream that she'd be a great singer.

"We didn't know you sang, Mother!"

She had to laugh. "Like a crow," she said.

Sometimes she used to think she'd swim the Channel.

"Did you swim *that* well, Mother?"

"Oh, not really—just the breaststroke," she said. "And then only by the aid of two pig bladders blown up by my father and tied around my middle. But I used to throb—yes, throb—with happiness."

Behind Mother's back, Bea raised her eyebrows.

What was it, we used to ask ourselves—that quality that she, we felt sure, misnamed? Was it courage? Was it strength, health, or high spirits? Something you could not give or take—a conundrum? A game of catch-as-catch-can?

"I know," cried Bea. "A sham!"

Whatever it was, we knew that Mother would let no wind of violence from within or without tear it from her. Although, one evening when Father Hugh was with us, our astonished ears heard her proclaim that there might be a time when one had to slacken hold on it—let go—to catch at it again with a surer hand. In the way, we supposed, that the high-wire walker up among the painted stars of his canvas sky must wait to fling himself through the air until the bar he catches at has started to sway perversely from him. Oh no, no! That downward drag at our innards we could not bear, the belly swelling to the shape of a pear. Let happiness go by the board. "After all, lots of people seem to make out without it," Bea cried. It was too tricky a business. And might it not be that one had to be born with a flair for it?

"A flair would not be enough," Mother answered. "Take Fa-

ther Hugh. He, if anyone, had a flair for it—a natural capacity!
You've only to look at him when he's off guard, with you children, or helping me in the garden. But he rejects happiness! He
casts it from him."

"That is simply not true, Vera," cried Father Hugh, over-
hearing her. "It's just that I don't place an inordinate value on
it like you. I don't think it's enough to carry one all the way.
To the end, I mean—and after."

"Oh, don't talk about the end when we're only in the middle," cried Mother. And, indeed, at that moment her own face
shone with such happiness it was hard to believe that her earth
was not her heaven. Certainly it was her constant contention
that of happiness she had had a lion's share. This, however, we,
in private, doubted. Perhaps there were times when she had
had a surplus of it—when she was young, say, with her re-
doubtable father, whose love blazed circles around her, making
winter into summer and ice into fire. Perhaps she did have a
brimming measure in her early married years. By straining
hard, we could find traces left in our minds from those days of
milk and honey. Our father, while he lived, had cast a magic
over everything, for us as well as for her. He held his love up
over us like an umbrella and kept off the troubles that afterwards came down on us, pouring cats and dogs!

But if she did have more than the common lot of happiness
in those early days, what use was that when we could remember so clearly how our father's death had ravaged her? And how
could we forget the distress it brought on us when, afraid to let
her out of our sight, Bea and I stumbled after her everywhere,
through the woods and along the bank of the river, where, in
the weeks that followed, she tried vainly to find peace.

The summer after Father died, we were invited to France to
stay with friends, and when she went walking on the cliffs at
Fécamp our fears for her grew frenzied, so that we hung on to
her arm and dragged at her skirt, hoping that like leaded
weights we'd pin her down if she went too near to the edge.

But at night we had to abandon our watch, being forced to follow the conventions of a family still whole—a home still intact—and go to bed at the same time as the other children. It was at that hour, when the coast guard was gone from his rowing boat offshore and the sand was as cold and gray as the sea, that Mother liked to swim. And when she had washed, kissed, and left us, our hearts almost died inside us and we'd creep out of bed again to stand in our bare feet at the mansard and watch as she ran down the shingle, striking out when she reached the water where, far out, wave and sky and mist were one, and the grayness closed over her. If we took our eyes off her for an instant, it was impossible to find her again.

"Oh, make her turn back, God, please!" I prayed out loud one night.

Startled, Bea turned away from the window. "She'll *have* to turn back sometime, won't she? Unless. . . ?"

Locking our damp hands together, we stared out again. "She wouldn't!" I whispered. "It would be a sin!"

Secure in the deterring power of sin, we let out our breath. Then Bea's breath caught again. "What if she went out so far she used up all her strength? She couldn't swim back! It wouldn't be a sin then!"

"It's the intention that counts," I whispered.

A second later, we could see an arm lift heavily up and wearily cleave down, and at last Mother was in the shallows, wading back to shore.

"Don't let her see us!" cried Bea. As if our chattering teeth would not give us away when she looked in at us before she went to her own room on the other side of the corridor, where, later in the night, sometimes the sound of crying would reach us.

What was it worth—a happiness bought that dearly.

Mother had never questioned it. And once she told us, "On a wintry day, I brought my own mother a snowdrop. It was the first one of the year—a bleak bud that had come up stunted before its time—and I meant it for a sign. But do you know what your grandmother said? 'What good are snowdrops to me now?' Such a thing to say! What good is a snowdrop at all if it doesn't hold its value always, and never lose it! Isn't that the whole point of a snowdrop? And that is the whole point of happiness, too! What good would it be if it could be erased without trace? Take me and those daffodils!" Stooping, she buried her face in a bunch that lay on the table waiting to be put in vases. "If they didn't hold their beauty absolute and inviolable, do you think I could bear the sight of them after what happened when your father was in hospital?"

It was a fair question. When Father went to hospital, Mother went with him and stayed in a small hotel across the street so she could be with him all day from early to late. "Because it was so awful for him—being in Dublin!" she said. "You have no idea how he hated it."

That he was dying neither of them realized. How could they know, as it rushed through the sky, that their star was a falling star! But one evening when she'd left him asleep Mother came home for a few hours to see how we were faring, and it broke her heart to see the daffodils out all over the place—in the woods, under the trees, and along the sides of the avenue. There had never been so many, and she thought how awful it was that Father was missing them. "You sent up little bunches to him, you poor dears!" she said. "Sweet little bunches, too— squeezed tight as posies by your little fists! But stuffed into vases they couldn't really make up to him for not being able to see them growing!"

So on the way back to the hospital she stopped her car and pulled a great bunch—the full of her arms. "They took up the whole back seat," she said, "and I was so excited at the thought of walking into his room and dumping them on his bed—you know—just plomping them down so he could smell them, and feel them, and look and look! I didn't mean them to be put in vases, or anything ridiculous like that—it would have taken a rainwater barrel to hold them. Why, I could hardly see over them as I came up the steps; I kept tripping. But when I came into the hall, that nun—I told you about her—that nun came up to me, sprang out of nowhere it seemed, although I know now that she was waiting for me, knowing that somebody had to bring me to my senses. But the way she did it! Reached out and grabbed the flowers, letting lots of them fall—I remember them getting stood on. "Where are you going with those foolish flowers, you foolish woman?" she said. "Don't you know your husband is dying? Your prayers are all you can give him now!"

"She was right. I *was* foolish. But I wasn't cured. Afterwards, it was nothing but foolishness the way I dragged you children after me all over Europe. As if any one place was going to be different from another, any better, any less desolate. But there was great satisfaction in bringing you places your father and I had planned to bring you—although in fairness to him I must say that he would not perhaps have brought you so young. And he would not have had an ulterior motive. But above all, he would not have attempted those trips in such a dilapidated car."

Oh, that car! It was a battered and dilapidated red sports car, so depleted of accessories that when, eventually, we got a new car Mother still stuck out her hand on bends, and in wet weather jumped out to wipe the windscreen with her sleeve. And if fussed, she'd let down the window and shout at people, forgetting she now had a horn. How we had ever fitted into it with all our luggage was a miracle.

"You were never lumpish—any of you!" Mother said proudly. "But you were very healthy and very strong." She turned to me. "Think of how you got that car up the hill in Switzerland!"

"The Alps are not hills, Mother!" I pointed out coldly, as I

had done at the time, when, as actually happened, the car failed
to make it on one of the inclines. Mother let it run back until
it wedged against the rock face, and I had to get out and push
till she got going again in first gear. But when it got started it
couldn't be stopped to pick me up until it got to the top,
where they had to wait for me, and for a very long time.

"Ah, well," she said, sighing wistfully at the thought of
those trips. "You got something out of them, I hope. All that
traveling must have helped you with your geography and your
history."

We looked at each other and smiled, and then Mother herself laughed. "Remember the time," she said, "when we were
in Italy, and it was Easter, and all the shops were chock-full of
food? The butchers' shops had poultry and game hanging up
outside the doors, fully feathered, and with their poor heads
dripping blood, and in the windows they had poor little lambs
and suckling pigs and young goats, all skinned and hanging by
their hind feet." Mother shuddered. "They think so much
about food. I found it revolting. I had to hurry past. But
Linda, who must have been only four then, dragged at me and
stared and stared. You know how children are at that age; they
have a morbid fascination for what is cruel and bloody. Her
face was flushed and her eyes were wide. I hurried her back to
the hotel. But next morning she crept into my room. She crept
up to me and pressed against me. 'Can't we go back, just once,
and look again at that shop?' she whispered. 'The shop where
they have the little children hanging up for Easter!' It was the
young goats, of course, but I'd said 'kids,' I suppose. How we
laughed." But her face was grave. "You were *so* good on those
trips, all of you," she said. "You were really very good children
in general. Otherwise I would never have put so much effort
into rearing you, because I wasn't a bit maternal. You brought
out the best in me! I put an unnatural effort into you, of
course, because I was taking my standards from your father,

forgetting that his might not have remained so inflexible if he had lived to middle age and was beset by life, like other parents."

"Well, the job is nearly over now, Vera," said Father Hugh. "And you didn't do so badly."

"That's right, Hugh," said Mother, and she straightened up, and put her hand to her back the way she sometimes did in the garden when she got up from her knees after weeding. "I didn't go over to the enemy anyway! We survived!" Then a flash of defiance came into her eyes. "And we were happy. That's the main thing!"

Father Hugh frowned. "There you go again!" he said.

Mother turned on him. "I don't think you realize the on-slaughts that were made upon our happiness! The minute Robert died, they came down on me—cohorts of relatives, friends, even strangers, all draped in black, opening their arms like bats to let me pass into their company. 'Life is a vale of tears,' they said. 'You are privileged to find it out so young!' Ugh! After I staggered onto my feet and began to take hold of life once more, they fell back defeated. And the first day I gave a laugh—pouff, they were blown out like candles. They weren't living in a real world at all; they belonged to a ghostly world where life was easy; all one had to do was sit and weep. It takes effort to push back the stone from the mouth of the tomb and walk out."

Effort. Effort. Ah, but that strange-sounding word could in-voke little sympathy from those who had not learned yet what it meant. Life must have been hardest for Mother in those years when we older ones were at college—no longer children, and still dependent on her. Indeed, we made more demands on her than ever then, having moved into new areas of activity and emotion. And our friends! Our friends came and went as freely as we did ourselves, so that the house was often like a café—and one where pets were not prohibited but took their places on our chairs and beds, as regardless as the people. And anyway it was hard to have sympathy for someone who got things into such a state as Mother. All over the house there was clutter. Her study was like the returned-letter department of a post office, with stacks of paper everywhere, bills paid and unpaid, letters answered and unanswered, tax returns, pamphlets, leaflets. If by mistake we left the door open on a windy day, we came back to find papers flapping through the air like frightened birds. Efficient only in that she managed eventually to conclude every task she began, it never seemed possible to outsiders that by Mother's methods anything whatever could be accomplished. In an attempt to keep order elsewhere, she made her own room the clearinghouse into which the rest of us put everything: things to be given away, things to be mended, things to be stored, things to be treasured, things to be returned—even things to be thrown out! By the end of the year, the room resembled an obsolescence dump. And no one could help her; the chaos of her life was as personal as an act of creation—one might as well try to finish another person's poem.

As the years passed, Mother rushed around more hectically. And although Bea and I had married and were not at home anymore, except at holiday time and for occasional weekends, Linda was noisier than the two of us put together had been, and for every follower we had brought home she brought twenty. The house was never still. Now that we were reduced to being visitors, we watched Mother's tension mount to vertigo, knowing that, like a spinning top, she could not rest till she fell. But now at the smallest pretext Father Hugh would call in the doctor and Mother would be put on the mail boat and dispatched for London. For it was essential that she get far enough away to make phoning home every night prohibitively costly.

Unfortunately, the thought of departure often drove a spur into her and she redoubled her effort to achieve order in her affairs. She would be up until the early hours ransacking her

desk. To her, as always, the shortest parting entailed a preparation as for death. And as if it were her end that was at hand, we
would all be summoned, although she had no time to speak a
word to us, because five minutes before departure she would
still be attempting to reply to letters that were the acquisition
of weeks and would have taken whole days to dispatch.

"Don't you know the taxi is at the door, Vera?" Father
Hugh would say, running his hand through his gray hair and
looking very disheveled himself. She had him at times as distracted as herself. "You can't do any more. You'll have to leave
the rest till you come back."

"I can't, I can't!" Mother would cry. "I'll have to cancel my
plans."

One day, Father Hugh opened the lid of her case, which was
strapped up in the hall, and with a swipe of his arm he cleared
all the papers on the top of the desk pell-mell into the suitcase.
"You can sort them on the boat," he said, "or the train to
London!"

Thereafter, Mother's luggage always included an empty case
to hold the unfinished papers on her desk. And years afterwards
a steward on the Irish Mail told us she was a familiar figure,
working away at letters and bills nearly all the way from Holy-
head to Euston. "She gave it up about Rugby or Crewe," he
said. "She'd get talking to someone in the compartment." He
smiled. "There was one time coming down the train I was just
in time to see her close up the window with a guilty look. I
didn't say anything, but I think she'd emptied those papers of
hers out the window!"

Quite likely. When we were children, even a few hours away
from us gave her composure. And in two weeks or less, when
she'd come home, the well of her spirit would be freshened.
We'd hardly know her—her step so light, her eye so bright,
and her love and patience once more freely flowing. But in no
time at all the house would fill up once more with the noise
and confusion of too many people and too many animals, and

again we'd be fighting our corner with cats and dogs, bats, mice, bees, and even wasps. "Don't kill it!" Mother would cry if we raised a hand to an angry wasp. "Just catch it, dear, and put it outside. Open the window and let it fly away!" But even this treatment could at times be deemed too harsh. "Wait a minute. Close the window!" she'd cry. "It's too cold outside. It will die. That's why it came in, I suppose! Oh dear, what will we do?" Life would be going full blast again.

There was only one place Mother found rest. When she was at breaking point and fit to fall, she'd go out into the garden— not to sit or stroll around but to dig, to drag up weeds, to move great clumps of corms or rhizomes, or indeed quite frequently to haul huge rocks from one place to another. She was always laying down a path, building a dry wall, or making compost heaps as high as hills. However jaded she might be going out, when dark forced her in at last her step had the spring of a daisy. So if she did not succeed in defining happiness to our understanding, we could see that whatever it was, she possessed it to the full when she was in her garden.

One of us said as much one Sunday when Bea and I had dropped round for the afternoon. Father Hugh was with us again. "It's an unthinking happiness, though," he caviled. We were standing at the drawing-room window, looking out to where in the fading light we could see Mother on her knees weeding, in the long border that stretched from the house right down to the woods. "I wonder how she'd take it if she were stricken down and had to give up that heavy work!" he said. Was he perhaps a little jealous of how she could stoop and bend? He himself had begun to use a stick. I was often a little jealous of her myself, because although I was married and had children of my own, I had married young and felt the weight of living as heavy as a weight of years. "She doesn't take enough care of herself," Father Hugh said sadly. "Look at her out there with nothing under her knees to protect her from the damp ground." It was almost too dim for us to see her, but even in the drawing room it was chilly. "She should not be let stay out there after the sun goes down."

"Just you try to get her in then!" said Linda, who had come into the room in time to hear him. "Don't you know by now anyway that what would kill another person only seems to make Mother thrive?"

Father Hugh shook his head again. "You seem to forget it's not younger she's getting!" He fidgeted and fussed, and several times went to the window to stare out apprehensively. He was really getting quite elderly.

"Come and sit down, Father Hugh," Bea said, and to take his mind off Mother she turned on the light and blotted out the garden. Instead of seeing through the window, we saw into it as into a mirror, and there between the flower-laden tables and the lamps it was ourselves we saw moving vaguely. Like Father Hugh, we, too, were waiting for her to come in before we called an end to the day.

"Oh, this is ridiculous!" Father Hugh cried at last. "She'll have to listen to reason." And going back to the window he threw it open. "Vera!" he called. "Vera!"—sternly, so sternly that, more intimate than an endearment, his tone shocked us. "She didn't hear me," he said, turning back blinking at us in the lighted room. "I'm going out to get her." And in a minute he was gone from the room. As he ran down the garden path, we stared at each other, astonished; his step, like his voice, was the step of a lover. "I'm coming, Vera!" he cried.

Although she was never stubborn except in things that mattered, Mother had not moved. In the wholehearted way she did everything, she was bent down close to the ground. It wasn't the light only that was dimming; her eyesight also was failing, I thought, as instinctively I followed Father Hugh.

But halfway down the path I stopped. I had seen something he had not: Mother's hand that appeared to support itself in a forked branch of an old tree peony she had planted as a bride was not in fact gripping it but impaled upon it. And the hand that appeared to be grubbing in the clay in fact was sunk into the soft mold. "Mother!" I screamed, and I ran forward, but when I reached her I covered my face with my hands. "Oh Father Hugh!" I cried. "Is she dead?"

It was Bea who answered, hysterical. "She is! She is!" she cried, and she began to pound Father Hugh on the back with her fists, as if his pessimistic words had made this happen.

But Mother was not dead. And at first the doctor even offered hope of her pulling through. But from the moment Father Hugh lifted her up to carry her into the house we ourselves had no hope, seeing how effortlessly he, who was not strong, could carry her. When he put her down on her bed, her head hardly creased the pillow. Mother lived for four more hours.

Like the days of her life, those four hours that Mother lived were packed tight with concern and anxiety. Partly conscious, partly delirious, she seemed to think the counterpane was her desk, and she scrabbled her fingers upon it as if trying to sort out a muddle of bills and correspondence. No longer indifferent now, we listened, anguished, to the distracted cries that had for all our lifetime been so familiar to us. "Oh, where is it? Where is it? I had it a minute ago! Where on earth did I put it?"

"Vera, Vera, stop worrying," Father Hugh pleaded, but she waved him away and went on sifting through the sheets as if they were sheets of paper. "Oh, Vera!" he begged. "Listen to me. Do you not know—"

Bea pushed between them. "You're not to tell her!" she commanded. "Why frighten her?"

"But it ought not to frighten her," said Father Hugh. "This is what I was always afraid would happen—that she'd be frightened when it came to the end."

At that moment, as if to vindicate him, Mother's hands fell

idle on the coverlet, palm upward and empty. And turning her head she stared at each of us in turn, beseechingly. "I cannot face it," she whispered. "I can't! I can't! I can't!"

"Oh, my God!" Bea said, and she started to cry.

"Vera. For God's sake listen to me," Father Hugh cried, and pressing his face to hers, as close as a kiss, he kept whispering to her, trying to cast into the dark tunnel before her the light of his own faith.

But it seemed to us that Mother must already be looking into God's exigent eyes. "I can't!" she cried. "I can't!"

Then her mind came back from the stark world of the spirit to the world where her body was still detained, but even that world was now a whirling kaleidoscope of things which only she could see. Suddenly her eyes focused, and, catching at Father Hugh, she pulled herself up a little and pointed to something we could not see. "What will be done with them?" Her voice was anxious. "They ought to be put in water anyway," she said, and, leaning over the edge of the bed, she pointed to the floor. "Don't step on that one!" she said sharply. Then, more sharply still, she addressed us all. "Have them sent to the public ward," she said peremptorily. "Don't let that nun take them; she'll only put them on the altar. And God doesn't want them! He made them for *us*—not for Himself!"

It was the familiar rhetoric that all her life had characterized her utterances. For a moment we were mystified. Then Bea gasped. "The daffodils!" she cried. "The day Father died!" And over her face came the light that had so often blazed over Mother's. Leaning across the bed, she pushed Father Hugh aside. And, putting out her hands, she held Mother's face between her palms as tenderly as if it were the face of a child. "It's all right, Mother. You don't *have* to face it! It's over!" Then she who had so fiercely forbade Father Hugh to do so blurted out the truth. "You've finished with this world, Mother," she said, and, confident that her tidings were joyous, her voice was strong.

Mother made the last effort of her life and grasped at Bea's meaning. She let out a sigh, and, closing her eyes, she sank back, and this time her head sank so deep into the pillow that it would have been dented had it been a pillow of stone.

Benedict Kiely (1919-   )

Benedict Kiely was born in Dromore, County Tyrone, in 1919, and grew up in neighboring Omagh. He was educated at the Christian Brothers' schools, Omagh, and at University College, Dublin. For many years he was a literary, drama, and film critic for Dublin newspapers, and he served for fourteen years as the literary editor of The Irish Press. *He has traveled widely, especially as a guest lecturer in American universities, and he now lives in Dublin where he frequently appears on Irish television. Among his novels are* Land Without Stars *(1946),* Honey Seems Bitter *(1952),* The Captain With the Whiskers *(1960),* Dogs Enjoy the Morning *(1968),* Proxopera *(1977), and* Nothing Happens in Carmincross *(1985). He has also published a study of William Carleton and a survey of modern Irish fiction. The first volume,* Drink to the Bird, *of a projected two-volume autobiography, appeared in 1992. Kiely's four collections of short stories are* A Journey to the Seven Streams *(1963),* A Ball of Malt and Madame Butterfly *(1973),* A Cow in the House *(1978), and* A Letter to Peachtree *(1987). "A Ball of Malt and Madame Butterfly" is the title story from the collection of the same name.*

A Ball of Malt and Madame Butterfly

On a warm but not sunny June afternoon on a crowded Dublin street, by no means one of the city's most elegant streets, a small hotel, a sort of bed-and-breakfast place, went on fire.

There was pandemonium at first, more panic than curiosity in the crowd. It was a street of decayed Georgian houses, high and narrow, with steep wooden staircases, and cluttered small shops on the ground floors: all great nourishment for flames. The fire, though, didn't turn out to be serious. The brigade easily contained and controlled it. The panic passed, gave way to curiosity, then to indignation and finally, alas, to laughter about the odd thing that happened when the alarm was at its worst.

This was it.

From a window on the topmost floor a woman, scantily clad, puts her head out and waves a patchwork bed coverlet, and screams for help. The stairway, she cries, is thick with smoke, herself and her husband are afraid to face it. On what would seem to be prompting from inside the room, she calls down that they are a honeymoon couple up from the country. That would account fairly enough for their still being abed on a warm June afternoon.

The customary ullagone and ullalu goes up from the crowd. The fire-engine ladder is aimed up to the window. A fireman begins to run up the ladder. Then suddenly the groom appears in shirt and trousers, and barefooted. For, to the horror of the beholders, he makes his bare feet visible by pushing the bride back into the room, clambering first out of the window, down the ladder like a monkey although he is a fairly corpulent man; with monkey-like agility dodging round the ascending fireman, then disappearing through the crowd. The people, indignant enough to trounce him, are still too concerned with the plight of the bride, and too astounded to seize him. The fireman ascends to the nuptial casement, helps the lady through the window and down the ladder, gallantly offering his jacket which covers some of her. Then when they are halfways down, the fireman, to the amazement of all, is seen to be laughing right merrily, the bride vituperating. But before they reach the ground she is also laughing. She is brunette, tall, but almost Japanese in appearance, and very handsome. A voice says: If she's a bride I can see no confetti in her hair.

She has fine legs which the fireman's jacket does nothing to conceal and which she takes pride, clearly, in displaying. She is a young woman of questionable virginity and well known to the firemen. She is the toast of a certain section of the town to whom she is affectionately known as Madame Butterfly, although unlike her more famous namesake she has never been married, nor cursed by an uncle bonze for violating the laws of the gods of her ancestors. She has another, registered, name: her mother's name. What she is her mother was before her, and proud of it.

The barefooted fugitive was not, of course, a bridegroom, but a long-established married man with his wife and family and a prosperous business in Longford, the meanest town in Ireland. For the fun of it the firemen made certain that the news of his escapade in the June afternoon got back to Longford. They were fond of, even proud of, Butterfly as were many other men who had nothing at all to do with the quenching of fire.

But one man loved the pilgrim soul in her and his name was Pike Hunter.

Like Borgnefesse, the buccaneer of Saint Malo on the Rance, who had a buttock shot or sliced off in action on the Spanish Main, Pike Hunter had a lopsided appearance when sitting down. Standing up he was as straight and well-balanced as a man could be: a higher civil servant approaching the age of forty, a shy bachelor, reared, nourished, and guarded all his life by a trinity of upper-middle-class aunts. He was pink-faced, with a little fair hair left to emphasize early baldness, mild in his ways, with a slight stutter, somewhat afraid of women. He wore always dark-brown suits with a faint red stripe, dark-brown hats, rimless spectacles, shiny square-toed brown handmade shoes with a wide welt. In summer, even on the hottest day, he carried a raincoat folded over his arm, and a rolled umbrella. When it rained he unfolded and wore the raincoat and opened and raised the umbrella. He suffered mildly from hay fever. In winter he belted himself into a heavy brown overcoat and wore galoshes. Nobody ever had such stiff white shirts. He favored brown neckties distinguished with a pearl-headed pin. Why he sagged to one side, just a little to the left, when he sat down, I never knew. He had never been sliced or shot on the Spanish Main.

But the chance of a sunny still Sunday afternoon in Stephen's Green and Grafton Street, the select heart or soul of the city's south side, made a changed man out of him.

He had walked at his ease through the Green, taking the sun gratefully, blushing when he walked between the rows of young ladies lying back in deck chairs. He blushed for two reasons: they were reclining, he was walking; they were as gracefully at rest as the swans on the lake, he was awkwardly in motion, conscious that his knees rose too high, that his sparse hair—because of the warmth he had his hat in his hand—danced long and ludicrously in the little wind, that his shoes squeaked. He was fearful that his right toe might kick his left heel, or vice versa, and that he would fall down and be laughed at in laughter like the sound of silver bells. He was also alarmingly aware of the bronze knees, and more than knees, that the young ladies exposed as they leaned back and relaxed in their light summer frocks. He would honestly have liked to stop and enumerate those knees, make an inventory—he was in the Department of Statistics; perhaps pat a few here and there. But the fearful regimen of that trinity of aunts forbade him even to glance sideways, and he stumbled on like a winkered horse, demented by the flashing to right and to left of bursting globes of bronze light.

Then on the park pathway before him, walking towards the main gate and the top of Grafton Street, he saw the poet. He had seen him before, but only in the Abbey Theatre and never on the street. Indeed it seemed hardly credible to Pike Hunter that such a man would walk on the common street where all ordinary or lesser men were free to place their feet. In the Abbey Theatre the poet had all the strut and style of a man who could walk with the gods, the Greek gods that is, not the gods in the theater's cheapest seats. His custom was to enter by a small stairway, at the front of the house and in full view of the audience, a few moments before the lights dimmed and the famous gong sounded and the curtain rose. He walked slowly, hands clasped behind his back, definitely balancing the prone brow oppressive with its mind, the eagle head aloft and crested with foaming white hair. He would stand, his back to the curtain and facing the house. The chatter would cease, the fiddlers in the orchestra would saw with diminished fury. Some of the city wits said that what the poet really did at those times was to count the empty seats in the house and make a rapid reckoning of the night's takings. But their gibe could not diminish the majesty of those entrances, the majesty of the stance of the man. And there he was now, hands behind back, noble head high, pacing slowly, beginning the course of Grafton Street. Pike Hunter walked behind him, suiting his pace to the poet's, to the easy deliberate rhythms of the early love poetry: I would that we were, my beloved, white birds on the foam of the sea. There is a queen in China or, maybe, it's in Spain.

They walked between the opulent windows of elegant glittering shops, doors closed for Sunday. The sunshine had drawn the people from the streets: to the park, to the lush green country, to the seaside. Of the few people they did meet, not all of them seemed to know who the poet was, but those who did know saluted quietly, with a modest and unaffected reverence, and one young man with a pretty girl on his arm stepped off the pavement, looked after the poet, and clearly whispered to the maiden who it was that had just passed by the way. Stepping behind him at a respectful distance Pike felt like an aco-

lyte behind a celebrant and regretted that there was no cope or
cloak of cloth of gold of which he could humbly carry the
train.

So they sailed north towards the Liffey, leaving Trinity College, with Burke standing haughty-headed and Goldsmith sipping at his honeypot of a book, to the right, and the Bank and
Grattan orating Esto Perpetua, to the left, and Thomas Moore
of the Melodies, brown, stooped, and shabby, to the right; and
came into Westmoreland Street where the wonder happened.
For there approaching them came the woman Homer sung: old
and gray and, perhaps, full of sleep, a face much and deeply
lined and haggard, eyes sunken, yet still the face of the queen
she had been when she and the poet were young and they had
stood on the cliffs on Howth Head, high above the promon-
tory that bears the Bailey Lighthouse as a warning torch and
looks like the end of the world; and they had watched the
soaring of the gulls and he had wished that he and she were
only white birds, my beloved, buoyed out on the foam of the
sea. She was very tall. She was not white, but all black in
widow's weeds for the man she had married when she wouldn't
marry the poet. Her black hat had a wide brim and, from the
brim, an old-fashioned veil hung down before her face. The
pilgrim soul in you, and loved the sorrows of your changing
face.

Pike stood still, fearing that in a dream he had intruded on
some holy place. The poet and the woman moved dreamlike towards each other, then stood still, not speaking, not saluting,
at opposite street corners where Fleet Street comes narrowly
from the east to join Westmoreland Street. Then still not
speaking, not saluting, they turned into Fleet Street. When
Pike tiptoed to the corner and peered around he saw that they
had walked on opposite sides of the street for, perhaps, thirty
paces, then turned at right angles, moved towards each other,
stopped to talk in the middle of the street where a shaft of
sunlight had defied the tall overshadowing buildings. Apart

from themselves and Pike that portion of the town seemed to
be awesomely empty; and there Pike left them and walked in a
daze by the side of the Liffey to a pub called the Dark Cow.
Something odd had happened to him: poetry, a vision of love?

It so happened that on that day Butterfly was in the Dark
Cow, as, indeed, she often was: just Butterfly and Pike, and
Jody with the red carbuncled face who owned the place and
was genuinely kind to the girls of the town, and a few honest
dockers who didn't count because they had money only for
their own porter and were moral men, loyal to wives or sweet-
hearts. It wasn't the sort of place Pike frequented. He had
never seen Butterfly before: those odd slanting eyes, the glistening high-piled black hair, the well-defined bud of a mouth,
the crossed legs, the knees that outclassed to the point of
mockery all the bronze globes in Stephen's Green. Coming on
top of his vision of the poet and the woman, all this was too
much for him, driving him to a reckless courage that would
have flabbergasted the three aunts. He leaned on the counter.
She sat in an alcove that was a sort of throne for her, where on
busier days she sat surrounded by her sorority. So he says to
Jody whom he did not yet know as Jody: May I have the favor
of buying the lady in the corner a drink?
    —That you may, and more besides.
    —Please ask her permission. We must do these things prop-
erly.
    —Oh there's a proper way of doing everything, even screw-
ing a goose.
    But Jody, messenger of love, walks to the alcove and for-
mally asks the lady would she drink if the gentleman at the
counter sends it over. She will. She will also allow him to join
her. She whispers: Has he any money?
    —Loaded, says Jody.
    —Send him over so. Sunday's a dull day.
    Pike sits down stiffly, leaning a little away from her, which

seems to her quite right for him as she has already decided that he's a shy sort of man, upper class, but shy, not like some. He excuses himself from intruding. She says: You're not inthrudin'.

He says he hasn't the privilege of knowing her name.

Talks like a book, she decides, or a play in the Gaiety.

—Buttherfly, she says.

—Butterfly, he says, is a lovely name.

—Me mother's name was Trixie, she volunteers.

—Was she dark like you?

—Oh, a natural blonde and very busty, well developed, you know. She danced in the old Tivoli where the newspaper office is now. I'm neat, not busty.

To his confusion she indicates, with hands moving in small curves, the parts of her that she considers are neat. But he notices that she has shapely long-fingered hands and he remembers that the poet had admitted that the small hands of his beloved were not, in fact, beautiful. He is very perturbed.

—Neat, she says, and well made. Austin McDonnell, the fire-brigade chief, says that he read in a book that the best sizes and shapes would fit into champagne glasses.

He did wonder a little that a fire-brigade chief should be a quotable authority on female sizes and shapes, and on champagne glasses. But then and there he decided to buy her champagne, the only drink fit for such a queen who seemed as if she came, if not from China, at any rate from Japan.

—Champagne, he said.

—Bubbly, she said. I love bubbly.

Jody dusted the shoulders of the bottle that on his shelves had waited a long time for a customer. He unwired the cork. The cork and the fizz shot up to the ceiling.

—This, she said, is my lucky day.

—The divine Bernhardt, said Pike, had a bath in champagne presented to her by a group of gentlemen who admired her.

—Water, she said, is better for washing.

But she told him that her mother who knew everything about actresses had told her that story, and told her that when, afterwards, the gentlemen bottled the contents of the bath and drank it, they had one bottleful too many. He was too far gone in fizz and love's frenzy to feel embarrassed. She was his discovery, his oriental queen.

He said: You're very oriental in appearance. You could be from Japan.

She said: My father was, they say. A sailor. Sailors come and go.

She giggled. She said: That's a joke. Come and go. Do you see it?

Pike saw it. He giggled with her. He was a doomed man.

She said: Austin McDonnell says that if I was in Japan I could be a geisha girl if I wasn't so tall. That's why they call me Buttherfly. It's the saddest story. Poor Madame Buttherfly died that her child could be happy across the sea. She married a sailor, too, an American lieutenant. They come and go. The priest, her uncle, cursed her for marrying a Yank.

—The priests are good at that, said Pike who, because of his reading allowed himself, outside office hours, a soupçon of anticlericalism.

Touched by Puccini they were silent for a while, sipping champagne. With every sip Pike realized more clearly that he had found what the poet, another poet, an English one, had called the long-awaited long-expected Spring, he knew his heart had found a time to sing, the strength to soar was in his spirit's wing, that life was full of a triumphant sound and death could only be a little thing. She was good on the nose, too. She was wise in the ways of perfume. The skin of her neck had a pearly glow. The three guardian aunts were as far away as the moon. Then one of the pub's two doors—it was a corner house—opened with a crash and a big man came in, well drunk, very jovial. He wore a wide-brimmed gray hat. He walked to the counter. He said: Jody, old bootlegger, old friend of mine, old friend of Al Capone, serve me a drink to sober me up.

—Austin, said Jody, what will it be?

—A ball of malt, the big man said, and Madame Butterfly.

—That's my friend, Austin, she said, he always says that for a joke.

Pike whose face, with love or champagne or indignation, was taut and hot all over, said that he didn't think it was much of a joke.

—Oh, for Janey's sake, Pike, be your age.

She used his first name for the first time. His eyes were moist.

—For Janey's sake, it's a joke. He's a father to me. He knew my mother.

—He's not Japanese.

—Mind your manners. He's a fireman.

—Austin, she called. Champagne. Pike Hunter's buying champagne.

Pike bought another bottle, while Austin towered above them, swept the wide-brimmed hat from his head in a cavalier half-circle, dropped it on the head of Jody whose red carbuncled face was thus half-extinguished. Butterfly giggled. She said: Austin, you're a scream. He knew Trixie, Pike. He knew Trixie when she was the queen of the boards in the old Tivoli.

Sitting down, the big man sang in a ringing tenor: For I knew Trixie when Trixie was a child.

He sipped at his ball of malt. He sipped at a glass of Pike's champagne. He said: It's a great day for the Irish. It's a great day to break a fiver. Butterfly, dear girl, we fixed the Longford lout. He'll never leave Longford again. The wife has him tethered and spanceled in the haggard. We wrote poison-pen letters to half the town, including the parish priest.

—I never doubted ye, she said. Leave it to the firemen, I said.

—The Dublin Fire Brigade, Austin said, has as long an arm as the Irish Republican Army.

—Austin, she told Pike, died for Ireland.

He sipped champagne. He sipped whiskey. He said: Not once, but several times. When it was neither popular nor profitable. By the living God, we was there when we was wanted. Volunteer McDonnell, at your service.

His bald head shone and showed freckles. His startlingly blue eyes were brightened and dilated by booze. He said: Did I know Trixie, light on her feet as the foam on the fountain? Come in and see the horses. That's what we used to say to the girls when I was a young fireman. Genuine horsepower the fire engines ran on then, and the harness hung on hooks ready to drop on the horses as the firemen descended the greasy pole. And where the horses were, the hay and the straw were plentiful enough to make couches for Cleopatra. That was why we asked the girls in to see the horses. The sailors from the ships, homeless men all, had no such comforts and conveniences. They used to envy us. Butterfly, my geisha girl, you should have been alive then. We'd have shown you the jumps.

Pike was affronted. He was almost prepared to say so and take the consequences. But Butterfly stole his thunder. She stood up, kissed the jovial big man smack on the bald head, and then, as light on her feet as her mother ever could have been, danced up and down the floor, tight hips bouncing, fingers clicking, singing: I'm the smartest little geisha in Japan, in Japan. And the people call me Rolee Polee Nan, Polee Nan.

Drowning in desire, Pike forgot his indignation and found that he was liking the man who could provoke such an exhibition. Breathless, she sat down again, suddenly kissed Pike on the cheek, said: I love you too. I love champagne. Let's have another bottle.

They had.

—Rolee Polee Nan, she sang as the cork and the fizz ascended.

—A great writer, a Russian, Pike said, wrote that his ideal was to be idle and to make love to a plump girl.

—The cheek of him. I'm not plump. Turkeys are plump. I love being tall, with long legs.

Displaying the agility of a trained high-kicker with hinges in her hips she, still sitting, raised her shapely right leg, up and up as if her toes would touch the ceiling, up and up until stocking top, suspender, bare thigh, and a frill of pink panties showed. Something happened to Pike that had nothing at all to do with poetry or Jody's champagne. He held Butterfly's hand. She made a cat's cradle with their fingers and swung the locked hands pendulum-wise. She sang: Janey Mac, the child's a black, what will we do on Sunday? Put him to bed and cover his head and don't let him up until Monday.

Austin had momentarily absented himself for gentlemanly reasons. From the basement jakes his voice singing rose above the soft inland murmur of falling water: Oh my boat can lightly float in the heel of wind and weather, and outrace the smartest hooker between Galway and Kinsale.

The dockers methodically drank their pints of black porter and paid no attention. Jody said: Time's money. Why don't the two of you slip upstairs. Your heads would make a lovely pair on a pillow.

Austin was singing: Oh she's neat, oh she's sweet, she's a beauty every line, the Queen of Connemara is that bounding barque of mine.

He was so shy, Butterfly said afterwards, that he might have been a Christian Brother and a young one at that, although where or how she ever got the experience to enable her to make the comparison, or why she should think an old Christian Brother less cuthallacht than a young one, she didn't say. He told her all about the aunts and the odd way he had been reared and she, naturally, told Austin and Jody and all her sorority. But they were a kind people and no mockers, and Pike never knew, Austin told me, that Jody's clientele listened with such absorbed interest to the story of his life, and of his heart and his lovemaking. He was something new in their experience, and Jody's stable of girls had experienced a lot, and Austin a lot more, and Jody more than the whole shebang, and all the fire brigade, put together.

For Jody, Austin told me, had made the price of the Dark Cow in a basement in Chicago. During the prohibition, as they called it, although what they prohibited it would be hard to say. He was one of five brothers from the bogs of Manulla in the middle of nowhere in the County of Mayo. The five of them emigrated to Chicago. When Al Capone and his merry men discovered that Jody and his brothers had the real true secret about how to make booze, and to make it good, down they went into the cellar and didn't see daylight nor breathe fresh air, except to surface to go to Mass on Sundays, until they left the U.S.A. They made a fair fortune. At least four of them did. The fifth was murdered.

Jody was a bachelor man and he was good to the girls. He took his pleasures with them as a gentleman might, with the natural result that he was poxed to the eyebrows. But he was worth more to them than the money he quite generously paid after every turn or trick on the rumpled, always unmade bed in the two-storied apartment above the pub. He was a kind uncle to them. He gave them a friendly welcome, a place to sit down, free drink and smokes and loans, or advances for services yet to be rendered, when they were down on their luck. He had the ear of the civic guards and could help a girl when she was in trouble. He paid fines when they were unavoidable, and bills when they could no longer be postponed, and had an aunt who was reverend mother in a home for unmarried mothers and who was, like her nephew, a kindly person. Now and again, like the Madame made immortal by Maupassant, he took a bevy or flock of the girls for a day at the seaside or in the country. A friend of mine and myself, traveling into the granite mountains south of the city, to the old stonecutters' villages of Lackan and Ballyknockan where there were aged people who had never seen Dublin, thirty miles away, and never wanted to, came upon a most delightful scene in the old country pub in Lackan. All around the bench around the walls sat the mountainy men, the stonecutters, drinking their pints. But the floor was in the possession of a score of wild girls, all dancing together, resting off and on for more drink, laughing, happy, their gaiety inspired and directed by one man in the middle of the floor: red-faced, carbuncled, oily black hair sleeked down and parted up the middle in the style of Dixie Dean, the famous soccer center-forward, whom Jody so much admired. All the drinks were on generous Jody.

So in Jody's friendly house Pike had, as he came close to forty years, what he never had in the cold abode of the three aunts: a home with a father, Austin, and a brother, Jody, and any God's amount of sisters; and Butterfly who, to judge by the tales she told afterwards, was a motherly sort of lover to him and, for a while, a sympathetic listener. For a while, only: because nothing in her birth, background, rearing, or education had equipped her to listen to so much poetry and talk about poetry.

—Poor Pike, she'd say, he'd puke you with poethry. Poethry's all very well, but.

She had never worked out what came after that qualifying: But.

—Give us a bar of a song, Austin. There's some sense to singing. But poethry. My heart leaps up when I behold a rainbow in the sky. On Linden when the sun was low. The lady of Shalott left the room to go to the pot. Janey preserve us from poethry.

He has eyes, Jody told Austin and myself, for no girl except Butterfly. Reckon, in one way, we can't blame him for that. She sure is the smartest filly showing in this paddock. But there must be moderation in all things. Big Anne, now, isn't bad, nor her sister, both well-built Sligo girls and very cooperative, nor Joany Maher from Waterford, nor Patty Daley from

Castleisland in the County Kerry who married the Limey in Brum but left him when she found he was as queer as a three-dollar bill. And what about little Red Annie Byrne from Kilkenny City, very attractive if it just wasn't for the teeth she lost when the cattleman that claimed he caught gonorrhea from her gave her an unmerciful hammering in Cumberland Street. We got him before he left town. We cured more than his gonorrhea.

—But, Austin said, when following your advice, Jody, and against my own better judgment, I tried to explain all that to Pike, what does he do but quote to me what the playboy of the Abbey Theatre, John M. Synge, wrote in a love poem about counting queens in Glenmacnass in the Wicklow mountains.

—In the Wicklow mountains, said Jody. Queens? With the smell of the bog and the peat smoke off them.

Austin, a great man, ever, to sing at the top of his tenor voice about Dark Rosaleen and the Queen of Connemara and the County of Mayo, was a literary class of fireman. That was one reason why Pike and himself got on so well together, in spite of that initial momentary misunderstanding about the ball of malt and Madame Butterfly.

—Seven dog days, Austin said, the playboy said he let pass, he and his girl, counting queens in Glenmacnass. The queens he mentions, Jody, you never saw, even in Chicago.

—Never saw daylight in Chicago.

—The Queen of Sheba, Austin said, and Helen, and Maeve the warrior queen of Connacht, and Deirdre of the Sorrows and Gloriana that was the great Elizabeth of England and Judith out of the Bible that chopped the block of Holofernes.

—All, said Jody, in a wet glen in Wicklow. A likely bloody story.

—There was one queen in the poem that had an amber belly.

—Jaundice, said Jody. Or Butterfly herself that's as sallow as any Jap. Austin, you're a worse lunatic than Pike.

—But in the end, Jody, his own girl was the queen of all queens. They were dead and rotten. She was alive.

—Not much of a compliment to her, Jody said, to prefer her to a cartload of corpses.

—Love's love, Jody. Even the girls admit that. They've no grudge against him for seeing nobody but Butterfly.

—They give him a fool's pardon. But no doll in the hustling game, Austin, can afford to spend all her time listening to poetry. Besides, girls like a variety of pricks. Butterfly's no better or worse than the next. When Pike finds that out he'll go crazy. If he isn't crazy already.

That was the day, as I recall, that Butterfly came in wearing the fancy fur coat—just a little out of season. Jody had, for some reason or other, given her a five-pound note. Pike knew nothing about that. And Jody told her to venture the five pounds on a horse that was running at the Curragh of Kildare, that a man in Kilcullen on the edge of the Curragh had told him that the jockey's wife had already bought her ball dress for the victory celebration. The Kilcullen man knew his onions, and his jockeys, and shared his wisdom only with a select few so as to keep the odds at a good twenty to one.

—She's gone out to the bookie's, said Jody, to pick up her winnings. We'll have a party tonight.

Jody had a tenner on the beast.

—She could invest it, said Austin, if she was wise. The day will come when her looks will go.

—Pike might propose to her, said Jody. He's mad enough for anything.

—The aunts would devour him. And her.

—Here she comes, Jody said. She invested her winnings on her fancy back.

She had too, and well she carried them in the shape of pale or silver musquash, and three of her sorority walked behind her like ladies-in-waiting behind the Queen of England. There was a party in which even the dockers joined, but not Pike, for that evening and night one of his aunts was at death's door in a nursing home, and Pike and the other two aunts were by her side. He wasn't to see the musquash until he took Butterfly on an outing to the romantic hill of Howth where the poet and the woman had seen the white birds. That was the last day Pike ever took Butterfly anywhere. The aunt recovered. They were a thrawn hardy trio.

Pike had become a devotee. Every day except Sunday he lunched in Jody's, on a sandwich of stale bread and leathery ham and a glass of beer, just on the off-chance that Butterfly might be out of the doss and abroad, and in Jody's, at that, to her, unseasonable hour of the day. She seldom was, except when she was deplorably short of money. In the better eating places on Grafton Street and Stephen's Green, his colleagues absorbed the meals that enabled higher civil servants to face up to the afternoon and the responsibilities of State: statistics, land commission, local government, posts and telegraphs, internal revenue. He had never, among his own kind, been much of a mixer: so that few of his peers even noticed the speed with which, when at five in the evening the official day was done, he took himself, and his hat and coat and umbrella, and legged it off to Jody's: in the hope that Butterfly might be there, bathed and perfumed and ready for wine and love. Sometimes she was. Sometimes she wasn't. She liked Pike. She didn't deny it. She was always an honest girl, as her mother, Trixie, had been before her—so Austin said when he remembered Trixie who had died in a hurry, of peritonitis. But, Janey Mac, Butterfly couldn't have Pike Hunter for breakfast, dinner, tea, and supper, and nibblers as well, all the livelong day and night. She still, as Jody said, had her first million to make, and Pike's inordinate attachment was coming between her and the real big business, as when, say, the country cattlemen were in town for the market. They were the men who knew how to get rid of the money.

—There is this big cattleman, she tells Austin once, big he is in every way, who never knows or cares what he's spending. He's a gift and a godsend to the girls. He gets so drunk that all you have to do to humor him is play with him a little in the taxi going from pub to pub and see that he gets safely to his hotel. The taximen are on to the game and get their divvy out of the loot.

One wet and windy night, it seems, Butterfly and this phil-anthropist are flying high together, he on brandy, she on champagne, for which that first encounter with Pike has given her a ferocious drouth. In the back of the taxi touring from pub to pub, the five-pound notes are flowing out of your man like water out of a pressed sponge. Butterfly is picking them up and stuffing them into her handbag, but not all of them. For this is too good and too big for any taximan on a fair percent-age basis. So for every one note she puts into her handbag she stuffs two or three down into the calf-length boots she is wear-ing against the wet weather. She knows, you see, that she is too far gone in bubbly to walk up the stairs to her own room, that the taximan, decent fellow, will help her up and then, fair enough, go through her bag and take his cut. Which, indeed, in due time he does. When she wakes up, fully clothed, in the morning on her own bed, and pulls off her boots, her ankles, what with the rain that had dribbled down into her boots, are poulticed and plastered with notes of the banks of Ireland and of England, and one moreover of the Bank of Bonnie Scotland.

—Rings on my fingers, she says, and bells on my toes.

That was the gallant life that Pike's constant attendance was cutting her off from. She also hated being owned. She hated other people thinking she was owned. She hated like hell when Pike would enter the Dark Cow and one of the other girls or, worse still, another man, a bit of variety, would move away from her side to let Pike take the throne. They weren't married, for Janey's sake. She could have hated Pike, except that she was as tenderhearted as Trixie had been, and she liked champagne. She certainly felt at liberty to hate the three aunts who made a mollycoddle out of him. She also hated, with a hatred that grew and grew, the way that Pike puked her with poethry. And all this time poor Pike walked in a dream that he never defined for us, perhaps not even for himself, but that certainly must have looked higher than the occasional trick on Jody's rumpled bed. So dreaming, sleepwalking, he persuaded Butterfly to go to Howth Head with him one dull hot day when the town was empty and she had nothing better to do. No place could have been more fatally poetic than Howth. She wore her musquash. Not even the heat could part her from it.

—He never let up, she said, not once from the moment we boarded the bus on the quays. Poethry. I had my bellyful.

—Sure thing, said Jody.

—Any man, she said, that won't pay every time he performs is a man to keep a cautious eye on. Not that he's not generous. But at the wrong times. Money down or no play's my motto.

—Well I know that, Jody said.

—But Pike Hunter says that would make our love mercenary, whatever that is.

—You're a great girl, said Austin, to be able to pronounce it.

—Your middle name, said Jody, is mercenary.

—My middle name, thank you, is Imelda. And the cheek of Pike Hunter suggesting to me to go to a doctor because he noticed something wrong with himself, a kidney disorder, he said. He must wet the bed.

—Butterfly, said Austin, he might have been giving you good advice.

—Nevertheless. It's not for him to say.

When they saw from the bus the Bull Wall holding the northern sand back from clogging up the harbor, and the Bull Island, three miles long, with dunes, bent grass, golfers, bath-

ers, and skylarks, Pike told her about some fellow called
Joyce—there was a Joyce in the Civic Guards, a Galwayman
who played county football, but no relation—who had gone
walking on the island one fine day and laid eyes on a young
one, wading in a pool, with her skirts well pulled up; and let a
roar out of him. By all accounts this Joyce was no addition to
the family for, as Pike told the story, Butterfly worked out that
the young one was well under age.

Pike and Butterfly had lunch by the edge of the sea, in the
Claremont Hotel, and that was all right. Then they walked in
the grounds of Howth Castle, Pike had a special pass, and the
flowers and shrubs were a sight to see if only Pike had kept his
mouth shut about some limey by the name of Spenser who
landed there in the year of God, and wrote a poem as long as
from here to Killarney about a fairy queen and a gentle knight
who was pricking on the plain like the members of the Harp
Cycling Club, Junior Branch, up above there in the Phoenix
Park. He didn't get time to finish the poem, the poet that is,
not Pike, for the Cork people burned him out of house and
home and, as far as Butterfly was concerned, that was the only
good deed she ever heard attributed to the Cork people.

The Phoenix Park and the Harp Club reminded her that one
day Jody had said, meaning no harm, about the way Pike
moped around the Dark Cow when Butterfly wasn't there, that
Pike was the victim of a semihorn and should go up to the Fifteen Acres in the Park and put it in the grass for a while and
run around it. But when, for fun, she told this to Pike he got
so huffed he didn't speak for half an hour, and they walked
Howth Head until her feet were blistered and the heel of her
right shoe broke, and the sweat, with the weight of the musquash and the heat of the day, was running between her shoulder blades like a cloudburst down the gutter. Then the row and
the ructions, as the song says, soon began. He said she should
have worn flat-heeled shoes. She said that if she had known
that he was conscripting her for a forced march over a moun-

tain she'd have borrowed a pair of boots from the last soldier
she gave it to at cut price, for the soldiers, God help them,
didn't have much money but they were more openhanded with
what they had than some people who had plenty, and soldiers
didn't waste time and breath on poetry: Be you fat or be you
lean there is no soap like Preservene.

So she sat on the summit of Howth and looked at the lighthouse and the seagulls, while Pike walked back to the village to
have the broken heel mended, and the sweat dried cold on her,
and she was perished. Then when he came back, off he was
again about how that white-headed old character that you'd see
across the river there at the Abbey Theatre, and Madame Gone
Mad McBride that was the age of ninety and looked it, and
known to all as a roaring rebel, worse than Austin, had stood
there on that very spot, and how the poet wrote a poem wishing for himself and herself to be turned into seagulls, the big
dirty brutes that you'd see along the docks robbing the pigeons
of their food. Butterfly would have laughed at him, except that
her teeth by this time were tap-dancing with the cold like the
twinkling feet of Fred Astaire. So she pulled her coat around
her and said: Pike, I'm no seagull. For Janey's sake take me
back to civilization and Jody's where I know someone.

But, God sees, you never knew anybody, for at that moment
the caveman came out in Pike Hunter, he that was always so
backward on Jody's bed and, there and then, he tried to flatten
her in the heather in full view of all Dublin and the coast of
Ireland as far south as Wicklow Head and as far north as where
the Mountains of Mourne sweep down to the sea.

—Oh none of that, Pike Hunter, she says, my good musquash will be crucified. There's a time and a place and a price
for everything.

You and your musquash, he tells her.

They were wrestling like Man Mountain Dean and Jack
Doyle, the Gorgeous Gael.

—You've neither sense nor taste, says he, to be wearing a fur coat on a day like this.

—Bloody well for you to talk, says she, with your rolled umbrella and your woollen combinations and your wobbly ass that won't keep you straight in the chair, and your three witches of maiden aunts never touched, tasted, or handled by mortal man, and plenty of money, and everything your own way. This is my only coat that's decent, in case you haven't noticed, and I earned it hard and honest with Jody, a generous man but a monster on the bed. I bled after him.

That put a stop to the wrestling. He brought her back to the Dark Cow and left her at the door and went his way.

He never came back to the Dark Cow but once, and Butterfly wasn't on her throne that night. It was the night before the cattle market. He was so lugubrious and woebegone that Jody and Austin and a few merry newspaper men, including myself, tried to jolly him up, take him out of himself, by making jokes at his expense that would force him to come alive and answer back. Our efforts failed. He looked at us sadly and said: Boys, Beethoven, when he was dying, said: Clap now, good friends, the comedy is done.

He was more than a little drunk and, for the first time, seemed lopsided when standing up; and untidy.

—Clap now indeed, said Jody.

Pike departed and never returned. He took to steady drinking in places like the Shelbourne Hotel or the Buttery in the Hibernian where it was most unlikely, even with Dublin being the democratic sort of town that it is, that he would ever encounter Madame Butterfly. He became a great problem for his colleagues and his superior officers in the civil service, and for his three aunts. After careful consultation they, all together, persuaded him to rest up in Saint Patrick's Hospital where, as you all may remember, Dean Swift died roaring. Which was, I feel sure, why Pike wasn't there to pay the last respects to the dead when Jody dropped from a heart attack and was waked in the bedroom above the Dark Cow. The girls were there in force to say an eternal farewell to a good friend. Since the drink was plentiful and the fun and the mourning intense, somebody, not even Austin knew who, suggested that the part of the corpse that the girls knew best should be tastefully decorated with black crepe ribbon. The honor of tying on the ribbon naturally went to Madame Butterfly but it was Big Anne who burst into tears and cried out: Jody's dead and gone forever.

Austin met her, Butterfly not Big Anne, a few days afterwards at the foot of the Nelson Pillar. Jody's successor had routed the girls from the Dark Cow. Austin told her about Pike and where he was. She brooded a bit. She said it was a pity, but nobody could do nothing for him, that those three aunts had spoiled him forever and, anyway, didn't Austin think that he was a bit astray in the head.

—Who knows, Butterfly? Who's sound or who's silly? Consider yourself for a moment.

—What about me, Austin?

—A lovely girl like you, a vision from the romantic East, and think of the life you lead. It can have no good ending. Let me tell you a story, Butterfly. There was a girl once in London, a slavey, a poor domestic servant. I knew a redcoat here in the old British days who said he preferred slaveys to anything else because they were clean, free, and flattering.

—Austin, I was never a slavey.

—No Butterfly, you have your proper pride. But listen: this slavey is out one morning scrubbing the stone steps in front of the big house she works in, bucket and brush, carbolic soap and all that, in one of the great squares in one of the more classy parts of London Town. There she is on her bended knees when a gentleman walks past, a British army major in the Coldstream Guards or the Black Watch or something.

—I've heard of them, Austin.

—So this British major looks at her, and he sees the naked backs of her legs, thighs you know, and taps her on the shoulder or somewhere and he says: Oh rise up, lovely maiden and come along with me, there's a better life in store for you somewhere else. She left the bucket and the brush, and the stone steps half-scrubbed, and walked off with him and became his girl. But there were even greater things in store for her. For, Butterfly, that slavey became Lady Emma Hamilton, the beloved of Lord Nelson, the greatest British sailor that ever sailed, and the victor of the renowned battle of Trafalgar. There he is up on the top of the Pillar.

—You wouldn't think to look at him, Austin, that he had much love in him.

—But, Butterfly, meditate on that story, and rise up and get yourself out of the gutter. You're handsome enough to be the second Lady Hamilton.

After that remark, Austin brought her into Lloyd's, a famous house of worship in North Earl Street under the shadow of Lord Nelson and his pillar. In Lloyd's he bought her a drink and out of the kindness of his great singing heart, gave her some money. She shook his hand and said: Austin, you're the nicest man I ever met.

Austin had, we may suppose, given her an image, an ideal. She may have been wearied by Pike and his sad attachment to poetry, but she rose to the glimmering vision of herself as a great lady beloved by a great and valiant lord. A year later she married a docker, a decent quiet hardworking fellow who had slowly sipped his pints of black porter and watched and waited all the time.

—Oddly enough, Austin told me when the dignity of old age had gathered around him like the glow of corn stubble in the afterwards of harvest.

He could still sing. His voice never grew old.

—Oddly enough, I never had anything to do with her. That

way, I mean. Well you know me. Fine wife, splendid sons, no-body like them in the world. Fine daughters, too. But a cousin of mine, a ship's wireless operator who had been all round the world from Yokohama to the Belgian Congo and back again, and had had a ship burned under him in Bermuda and, for good value, another ship burned under him in Belfast, said she was the meanest whore he ever met. When he had paid her the stated price, there were some coppers left in his hand and she grabbed them and said: give us these for the gas meter.

But he said, also, that at the high moments she had a curious and diverting way of raising and bending and extending her left leg—not her right leg which she kept as flat as a plumb level. He had never encountered the like before, in any color or in any country.

James Plunkett (1920–   )

James Plunkett was born James Plunkett Kelly in Sandymount, Dublin, in 1920. He was educated at Christian Brothers' schools, and studied violin and viola at the Dublin Municipal School of Music. For a time, he worked for the Dublin Gas Company, and in 1945 he became an official of the Worker's Union of Ireland, directed by Jim Larkin. Plunkett later wrote a radio play about Larkin entitled Big Jim *(1954), and Larkin also appears as a character in Plunkett's first novel,* Strumpet City *(1969). His second novel,* Farewell Companions, *was published in 1977. He has also written a nonfiction work,* The Gems She Wore: A Book of Irish Places *(1972) and numerous short stories. "A Walk Through the Summer" is taken from the English edition of his first collection of stories,* The Trusting and the Maimed *(1959).*

A Walk Through the Summer

I

At intervals while he walked, the man, who was old, allowed his stick to touch the railings which bounded the plot about the ivy-covered church. It was not a very well cared plot. The grasses had grown high with summer and there were tall dandelions about the notice board. The notice itself had loosened with heat. Already one corner folded limply away from the wood. The loose end made no stir, the grasses stood perfectly still under the glowing sky. The notice read, "I Am The Way The Truth And The Life." It was the end of a summer evening.

Almost opposite the board, the print on which was large and aggressive, the old man stood still and listened. He was blind. He was also lost. He stood at the edge of the path and would have crossed if he had known for certain that some light still remained. But the silence, the heavy feel of the air about his face, the motionlessness and warmth suggested summer darkness. He allowed his stick to rest against the path's edge until a distant door dragged on its weatherboard. Then the blind man began to make tapping noises without moving from his position.

Casey stepped out into the summer evening. The quietness made him hesitate before descending the steps. He acknowledged the sky with its remote streaks of color behind long rolling furrows of black cloud. For Casey it was a pregnant evening, an hour of decision. He thought uneasily of Barbara, who had probably spent the day at the sea with John and the children. His own evening had gone on some exercises in counterpoint, several dreary and unrewarding hours spent in the overfurnished room which Mrs. O'Keeffe provided in addition to his meals for the all-in sum of three pounds per week. It was reasonable, Casey knew. Yet he found it expensive. The weekend trip to Galway was likely to prove expensive too. After a moment he dropped his cigarette over the railings, dug one hand deep into his pocket, and took the steps slowly.

In a house some miles away Barbara shook sand from a towel and heard John leaving the bathroom upstairs. He always bathed immediately on their return from the sea. She shouted up to him:

"Who's coming tonight? Will there be a crowd?"

"Only the Manpowers. He wants to discuss the Cork trip. I put all the rest off as best I could."

"My God—why didn't you say. Did you ask them for dinner?"

"No. I can take the Manpowers in small doses only."

"Did you put Tom off?"

"Who?"

"Tom Casey."

"Why?"

"Because I think I asked him. It could be embarrassing. I didn't know about the ghastly Manpowers."

She listened carefully for his answer.

"Don't worry. We'll have some music anyway." She folded the brightly colored towel before resuming.

"What shall we play?"

"Darling, let's not gossip. I'm mother naked."

"Sorry."

"We'll put on the new issues from the Haydn Society. Do you think?"

"Chamber music. The Manpowers will be furious."

"Damn the Manpowers," John shouted back. "Just give them plenty to drink."

She heard him scampering towards the bedroom.

They met at the notice board. The aggressive letters were familiar to Casey.

"Can I help you?"

"I was looking for Ravensdale Avenue."

"It's certainly not around here."

"A road with houses only just built."

"There are no new houses around here. A little further on there's the river. Then Ballsbridge."

"Them railings behind me?"

"They surround the church."

The blind man misunderstood and crossed himself. Casey smiled. "It's not that kind of church," he said gently.

The blind man cursed at his mistake.

"I've a little time to spare. I'll help you to try some of the back roads."

The blind man allowed him to take his arm and shuffled along beside him, muttering angrily to himself. Casey, without minding very much, noticed he had not been thanked.

The girl who looked after the children for Barbara got them to bed. They were overtired and cross. They emptied little mounds of fine sand from their sandals and quarreled with each other. There were three of them, two boys and a girl. Then she made tea in Russian fashion for Barbara who liked it that way after a day on the sands. She would sit for an hour perhaps, being lazy, hardly talking, until it seemed time to ask John to pour a drink while she changed and prepared for her guests.

The girl sat down dutifully opposite to her. She was a Pole, a refugee Barbara had offered to take care of. A couple of years before she had come from a world of devastated homes, a chaos of maimed people and orphaned children, so remote from the untouched safety of Dublin that few who met her realized that it had had any real existence. But they treated her with kindness. She was almost, but not quite, one of the family. Barbara sipped the tea and studied the young, grave face which seemed absorbed in the piece of knitting she had automatically picked up. It was not a pretty face, but foreign and strange and therefore different enough, Barbara knew, to prove attractive. Barbara herself was very pretty, in a well-groomed very feminine way. Her hands were particularly beautiful and delicate; her face, at thirty-four, quite unlined and untouched, perhaps because whatever she thought or felt never seemed quite to reach it. Nature had shaped her to go with the rich, warm room, the novels, the records, the Russian tea. And Barbara, for her part, encouraged nature.

"You had a dreadfully boring afternoon, I'm sure." Her voice, too, was very beautiful.

The head above the knitting shook emphatically.

"Oh, no."

"It's such a nuisance not having room. John and I were wishing you were with us."

"That was kind."

"If I'd known John was going to Cork tomorrow I could have got out of weekending with the Burkes. But he never tells me these things. You'll have the children to manage all on your own."

"I do not mind."

"It's only for the weekend of course. I'll get back on Monday afternoon."

"I hope you have a lovely time."

"Not in Galway, dear. Lough Corrib is such a bore. Festooned with fishermen."

The brows puckered for a moment at the unfamiliar phrase, the eyes lifted enquiringly, then returned to the knitting. Barbara sipped her tea. Everything was working out nicely.

II

"If I could only get the feel of the streets," the blind man complained. He hurried his step. There was no purpose in doing so, Casey knew, but he quickened also. It was quite a hopeless quest. Two or three times, when asked what road they were on, Casey was unable to say.

"Can't you ask someone?"

"There's no one about."

"You live near at hand. It seems queer you don't know."

"There are no nameplates," Casey patiently explained.

"You can't read nameplates in the dark, anyway."

"It's not altogether dark."

"The dark leaves you just as helpless as I am. You don't have to make excuses. I'm not a fool."

Casey, his arm linked in that of the blind man, grew tired and noticed that his companion smelled. It was a faint smell, a pitiable smell really because it sprang, in all probability, from helplessness and infirmity. It was also, of course, the result of poverty. Poverty nearly always smelled. Casey, for all he himself knew, might possess his own peculiar odor. It would be fainter though, because he was a little more capable and a little less poor. It was all very natural. Clothes worn for too long often caused it. Also a condition of the health. Casey was aware always of living on the fringe of such a world, saved only from its indignity by youth and a touch of fastidiousness.

They emerged from the leafy quietude of an elegant backwater onto the main road. Traffic passed on its way down the coast. Neon signs flashed in various colors, though not brilliantly, for the sky was not as yet dark. The clock of the Royal Dublin Society chimed.

"Where are we now?" the old man enquired.

"Ballsbridge," Casey told him. He found himself saying it with a touch of triumph, as though it had been necessary to prove it by demonstration. That brought both of them to a standstill.

"Look," Casey said, "it's ten o'clock."

The blind man screwed up his face unpleasantly.

"I mightn't be able to see," he said, "but I can hear a clock as well as the next."

"You might let me finish," Casey objected. "It's ten o'clock and I want a drink before they close at half past. Would you like one?"

"Is it far?"

"Across the road."

"I've no money."

"I'll stand you one."

"All right so," the blind man said, "but watch the traffic."

"I think you can trust me."

"Damn the thing I'll trust for many a long day after this." As they crossed the road the blind man explained himself.

"I'll have nothing but the height of bad luck this night," he predicted, "and me after saluting a bloody Protestant church."

*   *   *

The bar was pretty crowded. They moved down towards the end. As people were clearing a passage for the blind man a familiar voice rang out. It was Ellis.

Ellis, like Casey, knew the loneliness of furnished rooms and moved in a world of small salaries. In return for such respectabilities as a post office savings account and the renunciation of alcohol and tobacco it offered a tenuous measure of security—even the possibility, ultimately, of marriage to a respectable girl. These were ideals which Ellis had deliberately pondered and then contemptuously rejected.

As they came over he lowered his paper and there was a pint of stout on the counter in front of him.

"What'll you have?"

"A pint," Casey said.

"And your friend?"

"I'll leave it to yourself," the blind man answered.

"That's what the jarvey said. I suppose it means whiskey." He called for a pint and a small Jameson.

"Not Jameson," the blind man said. "Jameson's is a Protestant crowd. Get me Powers."

Ellis raised his eyebrows at Casey. Casey smiled tolerantly. Ellis shrugged and amended the order. Then he tapped the racing page with the back of his hand and said:

"There's where I should have gone today. The Curragh. I'd have had the first two favorites. Then I'd have backed Canty's mount—I'd reliable information and it came in at tens."

Casey, his mind on Barbara and the fact that he was on the eve of arranging an adulterous weekend, found it hard to concentrate. But he managed to say:

"What put you off?"

"Oul Pringle had a liver on in the office and I didn't want to ask for the time off. So instead I went to the dogs after tea and lost a bloody stack. Here's health."

The drinks had arrived. Ellis put the whiskey glass in the blind man's hand and poured some water into it.

"There's a drop of holy water to go with it," he said. The blind man's hand shook with anger.

"Don't mock at God, young man," he said, "don't try to be smart about God." He raised the glass unexpectedly and emptied it at a swallow. Then he put it down with a bang which very nearly shattered it. Ellis waited for some time for the customary salutation. None came.

Motioning him not to mind, Casey said, "Good luck."

Ellis acknowledged and said, "I suppose you spent the day in virtuous pursuits."

"At harmony and counterpoint exercises."

"Ah. Messrs. Bach and Beethoven. How are they keeping?"

Casey smiled and said, "Deceased—I fear."

"For God's sake," Ellis exclaimed, as though the news was unexpected. "That was very sudden."

"It's the way of us all," Casey said, falling in with his mood. "Here today and gone tomorrow."

"It's Mrs. Bach I pity most. All them children. Twenty— isn't it?"

"Twenty-seven," Casey corrected.

Ellis made a slow, clicking noise with his tongue.

"Have you two gentlemen lost someone," the blind man asked. He had gathered little of the conversation.

"Bach and Beethoven," Ellis explained. "It's a great shock."

The blind man's face grimaced unpleasantly once again. He said, "Death comes for all." There was a belligerent note in his voice. The thought seemed to satisfy some need in him. Perhaps it was the fact that all infirmity fell away in that one universal infirmity. Ultimately all men would be equal.

"You're right," Casey agreed. "That's a day we'll all see."

"If God spares us," Ellis added without a smile.

It was Ellis who posed the question at closing time. They had drunk rather fast, partly because the blind man kept emptying everything immediately it was placed in front of him. He knocked each drink back and then stared ahead of him, his jaws champing most of the time and his lips dribbling now and then from one side. At times some inner anger showed in his face, at other times greed. Near closing time Ellis asked:

"Are you going out to John's?"

"What put that into your head?"

"It's Friday. Don't you want to hear some music?"

"I've had my bellyful of music today," Casey evaded. He had hoped Ellis would not be going.

"Then—the divine Barbara ... ?" Ellis had said similar things in the past. Casey found it hard to assess just how much he guessed. He decided not to comment.

"What about our friend?"

"Shunt him off."

"We can't do that. He's still lost."

"We'd better bring him with us so. We haven't time to go messing round."

"What about John?"

"John is a philanthropist."

Casey doubtfully supposed it would be all right. It was an unexpected complication.

"You'll get a meal," Ellis said to the blind man. "And we'll get you home."

The blind man hesitantly accepted. He appeared to be suspicious.

They took a bus. Ellis deliberately deposited the blind man in a seat apart and led Casey to the back.

"That's not a very appealing specimen of afflicted humanity," he explained.

"What can we do. If we left him home we'd miss our last bus."

Ellis said: "I know. Duty before everything. I hope you have the fare."

"Barely."

"That's why I'm going to John's, if you want to know. I'm going to knock him for a tenner."

"Everybody knocks John for money. It's a bit thick, in a way."

"Better than knocking him for his wife."

Casey stiffened. Ellis only meant it as a joke.

"I don't think that's funny."

"Don't mind me," Ellis said, "I like saying things like that. As a matter of fact, she has an eye for you. You could nearly have a go there."

"I don't want to discuss it."

But Ellis kept on. He pushed his hat back and produced two packets of potato crisps from his pocket.

"Have a chew," he offered.

Casey refused. Ellis put back the second packet and tore his own open. He stuffed a wad of crisps into his mouth.

"I'm not offering jembo over there any. He drank enough free whiskey to satisfy a bishop. That's another good reason for going to John's. We'll get something to eat. I'd nothing for tea except a sandwich I managed to lift in the canteen today. It fell off one of the trays onto the floor."

"What did you do—put your foot on it?"

"Dropped my napkin over it. A bloody lovely sandwich. You should have seen your woman when she came back to pick it up and throw it out. She didn't know Ellis had it safe in his arse pocket."

Casey smiled again and looked out the window. The bus had swung onto a looping road which skirted the bay. Tall street-lamps spread long orange streaks on the full waters and the stream of air which raked through the open glass panel smelled of the sea. Ellis crumpled the empty crisp bag with a sigh and flung it on the floor.

"That'd be a pleasurable night's work," he observed.

"What?"

"The fair Barbara."

Casey once again controlled the anger which in the eyes of Ellis would betray him, if he allowed it to show. Ellis, he felt, was pumping for information.

"I want happiness—not pleasure."

"Happiness is not without pleasure."

"But pleasure can be without happiness."

Ellis looked astounded. He opened the second packet of crisps.

"I'll need a bit of nourishment to sort that one out," he said.

"Happiness is the object—pleasure merely the accident. The object is legitimate, but the accident may operate in conflict with the object."

"Illustration required," Ellis invited, his mouth full of crisps.

"All right. Drink too much and you get a head. Result—unhappiness. Eat too much and you get sick. Result—ditto."

"Mysterioso Profoundo."

"You should read Aquinas."

"Ah. Aquinas. How's he keeping?"

"Deceased also," Casey said, to draw the subject further away from its beginnings.

"It's terrible," Ellis said, "all the old crowd dropping off one by one." He shook out the bag and three small crisps fell into his hand. He gazed at them sadly, then showed them to Casey.

"There you are," he said, "there's only a few of us left."

III

"I think that's about all," Mr. Manpower said. "The main thing is to keep the American end interested."

When he spoke of business he spoke with authority.

"Bloody dreary," John said, and Mrs. Manpower, a refined, spinsterish woman, looked startled. Mr. Manpower used such expressions frequently. But a well-bred person, who had been to university. And before the ladies.

"Why can't Wallace come to Dublin?" John complained.

"He never does. He never flies from New York. Always comes by boat. And he won't trust any form of Irish transport." Mr. Manpower paused. "You keep a good drop, John," he added, eyeing his glass with great friendliness.

"Have some more," John invited.

"Henry," Mrs. Manpower warned.

"Do me good," Mr. Manpower said easily.

A gentle snore drew their attention to a presence they had almost forgotten. A long, thin, aristocratic form lay sleeping in an easy chair.

"Poor Haddington," Barbara apologized. She gently relieved the long fingers of a glass which dangled perilously from them and placed it on a shelf.

"How did he get here. He couldn't have driven out."

"The bus," John explained. "He comes now and then. He was a dear friend of my father's."

"One doesn't expect it really," Mrs. Manpower suggested carefully, "certainly not from a professor."

"That's what you call scholarly drinking," Mr. Manpower enthused.

"I think it most unbecoming," Mrs. Manpower reproved, making it clear that she was going to stick to her guns.

Mr. Manpower winked vulgarly at John. "Good thing for her," he said jovially, indicating his infuriated spouse, "that I'm only half educated."

John pretended to be amused, and Barbara, because Mr. Manpower was of considerable financial importance, managed a thin smile. Then she said sweetly:

"Don't you think, darling, a little music would be amusing."

IV

The bus left them at its lonely terminus, a point of the bay marked by a few shops and a road which ran steeply uphill between tall hedges. As they climbed, the blind man linked between them, they saw it reverse and make its way back along the road below, a small smear of light pursued at water level by its own reflection. The blind man, who was puffing with exertion, stopped and suddenly lost his temper.

"What sort of a fool am I to be led on a wild goose chase like this?" he demanded. "What class of a heathen hideout are youse heading for at this unholy hour of the night?"

"We're heading for records and novelties," Ellis assured him, "long hair and sturdy bank balances. You'll find it eminently respectable."

After a while they turned into the tree-lined avenue. At the end stood the house, well lit, self-assured, master of its own well-kept grounds.

"How do you think they'll take it," Ellis asked, meaning the blind man.

"You're the one who said it was going to be all right."

"That was approximately an hour ago."

"So you've changed your mind?"

"That is what distinguishes man from the brute. The cow chews the cud. But does it get any nearer inventing the milking machine? When man ruminates he moves from idea to idea. I have been ruminating."

"I'll say this for your friend," the blind man confessed to Casey, "he's an eloquent young blade."

"You mean you've developed cold feet," Casey grumbled. "You'd better go to the front door with our friend. I'll slip round the back and explain matters."

The French windows at the back stood open to the night. A piano trio of Haydn grew louder as Casey approached, his feet crunching on the gravel. The occupants of the room sat around in various attitudes of attention. Each had a drink. Though he had sat in it so many times the soft lighting and the warm luxury of the room affected Casey pleasantly. Money and graciousness did not always go together as they did so flawlessly here. Barbara, who was facing the windows sat up and said:

"Tom."

"My dear Tom," John greeted, rising.

"I'm interrupting," Casey apologized. Then he explained quickly about the blind man.

"Delighted," John said. "Is he a musician?"

"No. An ignorant and rather aggressive old man who smells."

"Oh, no," Barbara said.

The Manpowers detached themselves from contemplation of the music in order to look surprised.

"This is delightful," John said. "Bring him in."

"Good evening, everybody," Casey said generally. The Manpowers switched on automatic smiles and went back with alacrity to the music. Casey went through to the hall door where Ellis was waiting with the blind man. Between them they brought him into the room and seated him down. John asked him if he would have a drink but Barabara said, "Please, John." John smiled at everybody and said sorry. When the music had finished the guests expressed their opinions.

"Damn good," Mr. Manpower applauded. "You're a powerful man for the music." His wife made a great show of pleasure and said rapturously, "I adore Haydn."

Haddington, who was half awake, murmured approvingly but incoherently. Casey recognized him as the author of a number of difficult philosophical books.

"Mr. and Mrs. Manpower," John introduced. "Meet Mr. Casey . . . Mr. Ellis."

"Glad to know you," Manpower responded heartily.

"Delighted," Mrs. Manpower confirmed, but coolly. She had noted that they were rather shabbily dressed.

"And of couse, Professor Haddington."

Haddington mumbled unintelligibly but with great courtesy and politeness. Casey remembered that he was said to rise at six o'clock every morning and work until noon. At noon, but never before, he opened his first bottle of whiskey. The professor had the reputation of being a man of unshakable habit. No

one had ever known him to utter anything intelligible after
five o'clock.

"And your friend?" John asked.

There was a noticeable pause.

"They never asked me, mister," the blind man said triumphantly. "It's Moore . . . Tom Moore."

"Our national poet," Mrs. Manpower said sweetly, but to
John and Barbara only.

"A shoneen, ma'am," the blind man contradicted, "who
aped the English gentry because he took them to be his bet-
ters."

There was a pause. John decided to offer drinks. Sara, who
was still smiling a little at the Rondo which had just con-
cluded, rose to get glasses.

"Don't fuss, dear," Barbara said, "I'll get them." When she
had gone a little while she called out to Casey. He joined her in
the dining room.

"Well?" he questioned.

"Everything is beautiful."

"John is definitely going?"

"Tomorrow, by train. He made no fuss at all about leaving
the car when I told him I'd like to spend the weekend with the
Burkes. That was the only thing which worried me."

"What?"

"I thought he might bitch about leaving the car." She
paused.

"Aren't you going to say it's wonderful?"

"Of course," Casey said. He kissed her. It was all that was
required to spark off his desire. But he regretted just a little
that such things had to be planned. It would be so much easier
if they just happened. They remained in each other's arms for
some moments. Barbara said:

"Don't let John delay you tonight by offering you the car.
Leave with the Manpowers. They'll drop you home."

"But why?"

"I don't want you to take the car. I must have it fairly early tomorrow morning."

"What on earth for?"

"Don't ask so many questions, darling."

"The Manpowers don't look very musical to me."

"They're ghastly. Business friends of John. At least he is. She's just a drip. And poor, dear, befuddled Haddington. What a collection."

"Wait till the blind man gets going."

"Why on earth did you bring him along?"

Casey held her closer, pressing his face against her hair and reflected why. Love? Because you just could not meet a blind man who was lost without putting him right? Superstition? For some dark primitive reason his infirmity gave him the right to your service? Incompetence? Why not get a policeman to look after everything.

"Love," Casey said.

"Little Sir Christopher," Barbara murmured. Casey, knowing she had probably meant to say Saint Christopher, disengaged himself without pointing out the mistake. She handed him glasses.

"Take these in while I get Sara to give you something to eat."

V

John filled out whiskey and put on another trio. John's measures were liberal. This time it took the blind man two gulps to finish it. When John noticed he filled the glass again. An empty glass in the hands of a guest made him feel restless. His generosity was misguided. The blind man threw it back. Some minutes later, cutting across the music and the reverent silence, he said loudly, "You're a gentleman."

Mrs. Manpower shot upright. Her husband showed a moment's surprise, then grinned happily.

"Thank you," John said with a smile. The blind man wiped his lips noisily.

"Don't think I'm trying to scratch your back."

"Not at all."

"I'm not that class. There's a lot of our people and when they get thrown in with moneyed people they lose themselves in embarrassment. But I'm an Irish Catholic and I'm not ashamed to be what I am whether I'm in the company of Protestants or Communists."

Nobody answered, in the hope that in that way their desire to listen to the music might register most forcibly. It worked for some minutes. Then the blind man groped for his stick and made a fumbling attempt to rise.

"I can see I'm not wanted."

John jumped up and went across. "Please," he said, pushing him back gently into the chair.

"Then why does nobody talk to me?"

"We were listening to the music."

"Can't you listen and talk."

"Really," Mrs. Manpower observed. "What a peculiar way to behave."

"Don't you think because I'm blind that I lack for education. I'd the school of the blind to go to when I was young. And the nuns still come to read to me once a week."

John, with a grimace of resignation, went over and touched the reject button. The music gave up.

"What a shame," Mrs. Manpower whispered. Mr. Manpower looked relieved. Casey felt responsible and consequently embarrassed. He was also a little surprised that anything stupid could happen on a night of such importance to Barbara and himself. In the silence Haddington, registering that something was missing but unable to give it a name, began a vague and incompetent search of his pockets.

"Do have a drink or something," John invited. He began to

fill the glasses and gave an extra large helping to the blind man. Barbara and Sara reappeared with sandwiches. They placed a plate between Ellis and Casey and one on a special table beside the blind man. Barbara arranged herself gracefully and asked for some music. Casey, contemplating her with tenderness, was startled by a half-choked exclamation from the blind man.

"Holy God," he spluttered.

"Is something wrong?"

"Meat," the blind man said. "Meat of a Friday. And I swallowed some of it."

"Is it meat?" John asked wearily.

"Of course it's meat," Barbara snapped, "how was I to know."

Ellis guffawed, sending a shower of crumbs about the carpet.

"Do you find it so amusing?" Barbara shot at him.

"Gas," Ellis confirmed. He winked at Mrs. Manpower, who glared. Barbara asked Sara to get some cheese and tomato sandwiches and when they arrived Barbara put them beside the blind man and said, "Now for goodness' sake let's have some music."

"I'd like this one from the beginning if nobody minds," John said to the rest.

Everyone appeared to approve.

While John adjusted the record player the blind man began to eat. He attacked his sandwiches ravenously and not by any means quietly. The task of satisfying his appetite absorbed him. Casey saw Barbara turn away her eyes in disgust, but in a remarkably short time the blind man disposed of the sandwiches and brushed the crumbs from his lap. Then he became abstracted. It was possible at last to attend to the music. Barbara, no longer irritated, smiled at Casey and bowed her head to listen. There was a grace about everything she did, an appositeness of word and gesture which, though studied, was nevertheless quite charming. It had been so a year before, when

Casey met her on a road some miles beyond the town of Galway. She had been marooned in her car in the middle of a flock of sheep then, unable to go forwards or backwards. The air was full of the smell of animals and their bleating calls; the sun drew waves of heat from the long stretches of moor and rock. Casey, who was on foot, picked his way slowly through the woolly mass and as he passed her she threw him a grimace of humorous resignation which had the effect of fixing her image pleasantly in his mind for some considerable time. About half an hour later her car drew in beside him.

"You look so dusty," she invited. "Hop in."

He eased the rucksack from his shoulder and accepted. The car, which was roomy and luxurious, smelled in the heat. It was a comfortably expensive smell.

"Clifden any use?"

"That's where I'm going," he said.

"On foot?"

She sounded surprised.

"It's a hobby of mine."

"Have you been fishing or shooting somewhere?"

"No. Collecting folk music."

"Oh. Is that another hobby?"

"No. I'm doing that for a thesis."

"Any luck?"

"No. In fact I've spent most of my time teaching the people their own folk tunes. I must say they found them quaint and interesting."

"Too bad for the thesis."

"Not if you're inventive enough. After all, it isn't difficult to make up a folk tune or two."

He offered a cigarette.

"Don't the examiners know the difference?"

"Either they don't, or they don't examine them very closely."

She remained smiling for some time.

Lakes came up to the edge of the road at times and then were left behind, the sheer and desolate mountains lifting steeply on their right accompanied them mile by mile.

"What beautiful country," she remarked.

They stayed at the same hotel. They went about together for some days. There were the beach and dancing and quiet walks. Some lovemaking too which she made no effort to discourage. One evening when they were sitting in the lounge she was called to the telephone to take a trunk call and when she returned she remained silent for so long that he asked her if it had been bad news.

"No," she said, "it was just about my ring."

"Your ring?"

"My wedding ring. I left it on the dressing table at the Burkes' place. They phoned to tell me it was safe." Casey found it impossible to say anything. He waited. After a while she said, "Well . . . now you know."

Casey noted that for a moment she seemed to have lost her studied elegance. She was hunched, even miserable. This proved an even greater shock than the first, until it occurred to him that this too fitted perfectly. It was both touching and disarming. Next morning she was her sophisticated self and before she left asked him to visit them when he got back to the city. John, she said, adored music.

VI

The look on the blind man's face held Casey's uneasy attention for some time before he realized that anything was going to happen. At first it was unusually pale, with saliva showing at the side of his mouth. His head began to nod from side to side, as though in rhythm with the music. Then his fingers tightened on the arms of his chair as he heaved himself to his feet. He was halfway across the floor before the others realized what was happening, and before Casey could reach him he got violently sick. Mrs. Manpower gave a little scream and gazed in horror at the carpet.

"Good God!" Barbara exclaimed.

The blind man, whom Casey had gripped and helped back to his chair, shuddered all over. When he had recovered he said: "It was the food. Tomatoes and cheese is far too rich for me. You shouldn't have given them to me."

"Sorry," John said.

"It's all right," the blind man said, "it can't be helped now."

"I like that," Barbara exploded, "what the hell did you eat it for if it wasn't going to agree with you?"

"Why does anybody eat anything that doesn't agree with him," the blind man snarled back.

"The pleasure principle," Ellis contributed, addressing Casey exclusively. "The man is a philosopher."

"I hear the fellow with the smart talk," the blind man said.

"Can't you shut up, Ellis," Casey complained, "you always manage to make things a good deal worse."

Sara, who had left the room immediately the incident happened, returned now with a bucket and some cloths.

"Poor Sara," Barbara sympathized. The rest withdrew, including Haddington, who made his way after them. It required remarkable concentration, but he managed it unaided. The Manpowers, once on their feet, gently declined the invitation to move into another room. They had had a most interesting evening, Mrs. Manpower said, but it was quite late and time to go home.

Mr. Manpower agreed. He offered lifts. "We'll take Professor Haddington."

"Of course," Mrs. Manpower said.

Haddington acknowledged courteously, waved a vague leave-taking, and shuffled out into the night.

"The back seat, Professor," Mrs. Manpower called out after

him, with great sweetness. Haddington's unintelligible reply made her smile at the others.

"Such a curious man," she said, "but, after all, so brilliant."

Mr. Manpower extended the offer to Casey, Ellis, and the blind man.

"But we'd hardly have room, dear."

"We've managed six before," Mr. Manpower said hospitably.

But the blind man was found to be very unsteady and upset still.

"I think you'd better leave us," Casey said regretfully.

"Yes, do," John urged. "Tom here can take our car. We won't need it."

"But we do, dear. I wanted it tomorrow morning."

"Tom can bring it back early."

Barbara said, "Never in history has Tom been known to bring back a car early."

She appealed to Casey, "Couldn't you manage him?" She looked at him in a way which conveyed the very special nature of her appeal.

"He's not well enough at the moment," Casey resisted. "Put him in a car now and he'll be sick all over again."

"We mustn't keep the professor waiting," Mrs. Manpower said, failing to hide her alarm.

Everybody accompanied them to their car, the gravel crunching under their feet and the night warm about them.

"Hello," Mr. Manpower exclaimed when he had opened the door, "where's Haddington?"

There was no one in the back seat and no one to be seen anywhere near. A search proved fruitless. They called out several times but got no answer. The night had swallowed Haddington.

"Let's spread out and search the grounds," John said. It was obvious that he was finding it difficult to remain calm.

VII

In the now silent house Sara bent over her unpleasant task.
There was a shadow of suffering on her face but her voice betrayed no note of complaint.

"Who are you?" the blind man asked.

"I am Sara," she said.

"A foreigner?"

"Yes—a refugee."

"One of the crowd that gets everything while the poor of
Ireland gets nothing. I wonder if you know how lucky you
are."

"I think I do."

She was mopping the floor, her task half completed.

"From where?"

"I beg your pardon?"

"Where do you come from?"

"From Poland."

"You're a Catholic so?"

"Yes. I am a Catholic."

"What do you think of them giving me meat of a Friday.
What would you do if it happened to you?"

"Probably I would eat it."

That brought him to a standstill. But only for a moment. He
took it up again.

"No doubt," he said. "Foreign Catholics is notorious luke-
warmers. They're not a patch on Irish Catholics. The Pope
himself said that."

The girl squeezed the cloth into the bucket and the water
slopped about.

"Is there a cigarette handy?"

"Please . . . in one moment."

"Don't hurry yourself. Irish Catholics didn't get it soft like
you. They suffered for the Faith."

"Please . . . ?"

"Never mind. You're a foreign Catholic. Brought up in indifference. Then taken into good homes where you get the height of good feeding. You never suffered."

"I think we suffered."

"No. You've a loose way of living, you foreign Catholics. Not like Irish Catholics. What about that cigarette?"

The girl went out to empty the bucket, washed her hands, and returned with a cigarette. She lit it for him and he rattled on. He talked about the great faith of the Irish and about all they suffered. Some people didn't appreciate how lucky they were, living free in comfortable Irish homes. As she tidied up he asked her questions. She made no answers. For some reason she had begun to weep. But quietly. She did not want him to know.

VIII

The rest failed to find Haddington and after half an hour the Manpowers gave up and drove off. As the wheels crunched on the gravel Barbara waved for a moment and then linked Casey's arm. They moved together towards the house. John and Ellis were still searching. They saw Sara going across to join them.

"We'll search the house," Barbara shouted.

"He couldn't possibly be in the house," John shouted back.

"No harm trying," she answered. "He must be somewhere."

Barbara and Casey went from room to room. In the children's room he was about to switch on the light when she stopped him. It would waken them, she said. They passed through into Sara's room, leaving the door open. A small, illuminated cross glowed red in a covering of glass. The air in the room was warm still from the earlier sunshine. It was a small room. On a bed at one side the pillow and sheets looked extraordinarily white.

"You let the Manpowers go," she accused.

With a shrug he said, "What could I do?"

"You'll have to take the car now, of course. But you must promise to bring it back early in the morning. It's quite important."

"Won't it do in the afternoon. We'll have the whole day driving down."

"The shops close. There are things I want which can't be got just anywhere."

"Such as?"

She moved into his arms.

"Don't be such a dumb idiot," she said in a small embarrassed voice.

He realized then what she meant. There were certain preparations; there were the necessary womanly precautions.

"I'm sorry," he said. "Put it down to my peasant stupidity."

After that Casey was silent. He had made a humiliating discovery. He was not as sophisticated as he had believed.

IX

The rest of the night was hardly more successful. They had some more drinks and listened to some more records. But for some reason there was no point of contact between them. The blind man lay back in his chair, looking very pale and breathing heavily. Ellis was unusually subdued. Sara kept her head bowed, her natural gravity emphasized by the lack of communication between the others. Casey looked from Barbara to John and felt the situation keenly. He knew that John had his own infidelities from time to time. He felt, however, that it was not quite the same thing; or rather, that in matters of the kind he himself was not made of quite the same clay. The prospect of the long trip, the excuses, the lies which would inevitably be necessary, began to suggest themselves in a new light. The situation would pass and give way to new situations, but for the moment he saw clearly that it would require a betrayal of his personality which he would have to sustain for many months, perhaps even for life. He felt about such matters at a far deeper level than either Barbara or John, for whom money and well-trained manners had rounded the edges of reality. He saw beyond the situation to its effects. He was not himself pure and he was far from being a prude. But he could not help seeing impurity as a state and not simply as a word. So palpable was it that in a moment of alarming comprehension it had stood before him. It was a brown shroud stiff with the remains which stuck to it, sticky to touch—if one dared. He had seen it a moment before, when the reason why Barbara wanted the car had suddenly become clear to him.

Between his mood and the innocent good humor of the Haydn trio there was a gap which no effort of concentration could close. Once or twice he smiled across at John, who liked to share their mutual appreciation in that way. He was much relieved when the trio finished and he could rise to take his leave. John gave him the keys of the car.

"What are we to do about Haddington?" he said.

"We've done all we can about Haddington," Barbara decided. She had had her fill of upsets.

"We really ought to phone the police or something," John said.

"Perhaps he walked," Casey offered.

"Or climbed a tree," Ellis suggested. His effort was not appreciated.

The blind man had to be assisted. When they reached the car they decided to prop him up between them on the front seat. It was difficult in the darkness, but at last they got him fixed. Casey found the switch for the headlights and the half circle of gravel glared back at him suddenly. John waved good-bye. Barbara warned:

"Tomorrow morning early. For God's sake don't oversleep."

"Don't worry," Casey shouted, "you'll have it back."

*   *   *

The bordering trees spun in a gleaming half circle and they were off. Casey drove. Ellis held the blind man upright. It was a tight squeeze with the three of them in front.

"Not a very successful evening," Casey said, when they had been driving for some time.

"I got my ten pounds. I wouldn't complain."

Ellis lit a contented cigarette and looked out of the window to his left, where at regular intervals the beam of a lighthouse traced a golden passage across the calm waters of the bay. The night was heavy and still.

"Light me one of those," Casey asked. Ellis lit another cigarette and when he had handed it to him he said:

"I met Sara in the garden tonight and she was crying. Something his nibs here said to her."

"What was it about?"

"She wouldn't say."

Some minutes later Ellis took up the theme again. He sounded sleepy. But it was obvious that he had been turning it over in his mind.

"I don't think a woman has cried in front of me like that ever before. She's quite an alluring piece of stuff, the fair Sara."

"Remember your bachelor vows."

"Ellis will remain single. But not necessarily celibate."

"Hardchaw," Casey said.

He knew something of Sara's background, things Barbara had mentioned to him from time to time. It was a topic he did not wish to pursue. They made the circuit in silence and swung away from the coast road, encountering a long, hedge-lined suburban avenue and then, quite suddenly it seemed, a wide street, closed and shuttered shops, the first traffic lights.

"You're very subdued," Casey remarked.

"I'm trying to keep Father Rabelais here from falling off the bloody seat. He has me half strangled."

"How is he?"

"Still breathing—I think."

"We didn't ask him where he lived."

"No."

"I suppose you wouldn't have room . . ."

"No."

"That's what I thought. No harm asking."

"Divil the bit. You're welcome."

That was that. Casey took responsibility for furnishing accommodation for the blind man. They had a job wakening him when Ellis was being dropped, but after a good deal of rough treatment he opened his eyes.

"Where am I?" he asked.

"Back in the city," Ellis said. "You'd better lean on your own shoulder from now on. I'm getting out."

        x

There was a hint of grayness in the air when Casey got home. He brought the blind man up the steps and into his bedroom. He led him over to the bed.

"Where are you going to sleep yourself?" the blind man asked.

"In the car."

"That'll be cold enough."

"I'll take a blanket."

The blind man removed his boots and began to undress.

"Where do you keep the yoke?" he asked.

Casey was puzzled. The blind man got annoyed.

"Don't tell me you don't use a yoke. Everyone has a yoke in the bedroom."

Light dawned on Casey. "I use the toilet in the bathroom," he said.

"You can't expect me to be able to find that."

It was, Casey supposed, a reasonable point of view. He looked around. In an ornamental bowl by the window Mrs. O'Keeffe kept a depressing geranium. Casey removed the plant and handed the bowl to the blind man. It was a fancy bowl with teethed edges which were meant to represent the opening bud of a flower. The blind man ran his hands around it and began to criticize it.

"This is a highly dangerous contraption . . ." he began.

Casey cut him short.

"It's the only yoke available," he said. "You'll have to do your best with it."

He closed the hall door softly and realized that morning had come. He could see the houses opposite and below him the car, its shape misty with dew, black-skinned and moist like a large slug. He walked down past it and up the road, past the railings of the church, past the notice board with its aggressive message and its unkept plot of graves and dandelions. They smelled sweetly and damply now in the early morning air. Then he turned back and as he did so he arrived at a decision. He was not going to Galway with Barbara. She would feel badly about it, he knew, but in the long run it would be better. It had been more than exciting, the whole prospect. She was beautiful, she was rich, so much so that her interest in him had always been something of a mystery to Casey. He was humble enough most of the time to wonder what she could see in him. She would suffer, of course. How much Casey could not venture to guess. Not very much he thought. In her world there were plenty of distractions. Besides, it would do her no harm. Out of some nightmare background of suffering, at some awakened memory of a family scattered and murdered, Sara had wept in front of Ellis. He had been touched to the extent that he desired to seduce her. And that was all. As for himself, he would retire once again to Mrs. O'Keeffe's room and the companionship of her favorite geranium, thinking now and then of the indignity to which circumstances had subjected its fancy container; thinking now and then also of a sunlit road, animal cries, and the huddled, white gleaming of fleece.

*   *   *

Casey opened the door of the car and froze. Someone was sitting on the back seat.

"You," he exclaimed.

"You took a devilish long time," Haddington complained. "What on earth kept you?"

"How did you get here?" Casey asked.

"Come, come," Haddington said. "I was told to sit in the back seat."

Quite suddenly Casey saw that there was a simple explanation.

"My God!" he said. "You got into the wrong car."

"I waited quite a long time, then fell asleep. I appear to have slipped off the seat at some stage. When I woke up a while ago I was lying on the floor."

"We searched for you for hours."

"You mustn't blame me. After all, you knew there were two cars. I didn't."

"It never occurred to us."

"I have noticed myself," Haddington observed, "that the simple and obvious never really does. However, what are we going to do?"

"I don't know what you intend to do," Casey said, "but I'm going to sleep."

"Here in the car?"

"Yes, I have a blanket."

Haddington considered the matter while Casey settled down. Then he said:

"Could you spare me a corner of the blanket?"

"Certainly," Casey said. He rearranged it so that it covered both of them. He felt Haddington's head on his shoulder, a bony casket, which housed a rich store of erudition, a mind capable of fine distinctions which, in its time too, had probably differentiated between happiness and pleasure.

"I had a drink or two last night," Haddington confessed.

Casey smiled quietly. Along the garden of the house outside a line of sunshine had appeared, the first thin manifestation.

"The sun has risen," Casey said.

Haddington gave careful thought to this latest intelligence.

"Alleluia," he murmured at last. Then they both slept— more or less.

Aidan Higgins (1927–   )

Aidan Higgins was born in County Kildare in 1927. As a young man, Higgins traveled widely, working in England, Germany, and South Africa. His first book, a collection of short stories entitled Felo de se, *was published in 1960. Since then, he has published five novels,* Langrishe Go Down *(1966),* Balcony of Europe *(1972),* Scenes from a Receding Past *(1977),* Bornholm Night-Ferry *(1983), and* Lions of the Grunewald *(1993); a notebook,* Images of Africa *(1971); a collection of travel pieces,* Ronda Gorge and Other Precipices *(1989); and a collection of short stories,* Helsinger Station and Other Departures *(1989). He now lives in Dublin and frequently contributes articles and reviews to Irish journals. "Killachter Meadow" is taken from* Felo de Se, *recently republished in a slightly revised edition entitled* Asylum and Other Stories *(1978).*

Killachter Meadow

The remains of Miss Emily Norton Kervick were committed to the grave one cold day in March of 1927. On that morning—the third—a Mass for the Dead had been offered for the repose of her soul, and she was buried without delay in Griffenwrath cemetery.

The day previously the body had been laid out on its high bed in a room too full of the stupefying odor of arum lilies. It had been her bedroom. The furnishings were not remarkable. A fierce wallpaper design of bamboo and prodigal shoots appeared to contract the walls on two sides. Within that area and

resting on the bare boards, white and sedate, decked with flowers, stood the deathbed. This bed, notwithstanding its panoply,
notwithstanding its character of unmistakable intent, or its oc-
cupant, seemed to move on its castors at a slow, almost imper-
ceptible rate of its own—as small craft in a difficult roadstead
will creep from their moorings.

Then the room shook under the tread of mourners. They
came unsolicited on the first day, a mixed bag of male and
female gentry come to pay what they described as "their last
respects." Wearing the appropriate expression they took up a
position by the bed head. They were not relatives but locals.
And every so often they so far forgot themselves as to make
that hurried, somewhat cupidinous gesture of piety—blessed
themselves. Emily-May's forbidding manner had repulsed them
in life and now, destitute of sense, it finally routed them.

This corpse, so exact and still, was impervious to all human
compassion; their presence seemed superfluous or worse—as
though uninvited they had arrived at the wrong funeral. In the
hot-press her linen lay stored and ready; her cases stood packed
in the next room. It did not seem that she had died and
escaped them; on the contrary, dead, she had come to stay.

She offered no help herself, being content to lie there, grey
and heavy, dressed in a monk's dark habit which even covered
her upturned toes, clutching rosary beads cumbersome as man-
acles. The head was thrust back into the folds of the cowl, out
of which an arrogant warrior's nose and pronounced cheek-
bones appeared in a scarred and discolored face. On her chest,
in addition, was balanced a phenomenally heavy crucifix. In
posture she resembled a Crusader in a tomb, seemingly just on
the point of rising up violently and dashing the Cross to the
ground: the general effect being more military than strictly religious.

Warily the survivors circled this ambiguous deathbed, half
conscious of the permutations it had already undergone, hoping it had gone through them all. Now boatlike on no high

seas; now solid and as though cast in rock like a tomb; now
shrunken to the dimensions of a litter. So they could make
nothing of it and had to retire baffled. A day later the bed itself
lay stripped and empty. Death had borne the last disquieting
image of Emily Norton Kervick down with it into the grave.

I

Forty-five years before, in the hopeful 1880s, a couple by the
name of Kervick bought Springfield House outright from the
Land Commission for the purpose of farming and raising a
family. Springfield House was a freehold premises in the barony
of old Killachter, situated one mile from Celbridge village and
the ramparts of Marley Abbey, whilom home of Hester Van-
homrigh.

Two decades later this couple had passed away, unmourned
and almost forgotten in their own time, leaving behind as a
legacy for four unprepossessing and unmarriageable daughters
a seventy-two-acre estate so fallen into neglect that it had to be
parceled out as grazing land. Over the years the rockery and
vegetable gardens had merged to become a common wilder-
ness. In the orchard the untrimmed branches sank until lost in
the dense uprising of grass. Four spinsters grew up there. They
were christened, in order of appearance: Emily Norton (known
as Emily-May), Tess, Helen, Imogen.

Imogen Kervick had the nondescript face of a plaster Ma-
donna, pallor and all. Her small opportunist mouth daubed
with dark lipstick recalled the 1920s, and she favored also the
trenchcoats and the hats of that period. Her movements were
at once prosaic and portentous; she conjured up lascivious
dreamy knees for herself, and a heart full of vicissitudes, the
morals of a rhesus monkey. From her a declaration of love
would have to be as detailed as a death sentence; fortunately
the occasion never arose. Imprisoned in her own particular
folly, she refused to behave as if there were any such condition

as *âge dangereuse* or any such policy as relenting. She preferred to represent herself as if lodged within a ring of persecution— making considered motions with the hand, waiting only for the faggots to be lit under her. Sometimes, laying down her knife and fork, she wept at table, her eyes wide open and no tears falling.

It was into this unlikely subject that Cupid had discharged his bolts. Some years previously she had created a modest stir by indulging her fancy with a pallid youth named Klaefisch. No one had ever looked at him before, least of all a woman, least of all with favor. He came from Bavaria. He had one good lung, and resembled a gawky version of Constantine Guys. It was she who persuaded him to live with them, but outside, like a dog, in a clapboard and tar edifice that stood on raised ground. Here Otto Klaefisch came for peace and quiet, for free board or a little love—if that was to be part of the price; but mainly in order to complete his three-year-old thesis, *Das Soziale Schicksal in den Novellen Theodor Storms*.

Throughout that summer the swallows went shrieking over- head, and Imogen came and went from the house with tray after tray of food. She walked boldly into the pavilion and came out later carrying pages for typing scored with a bold Gothic script. Did he make attempts on her virtue in there? Nobody knew. From the frameless window the face of the nine day's wonder peered, the sun glinting on bifocals and the cor- ners of his mouth drawn down.

Gliding past of an evening they heard his nasal drone punc- tuating the dark. It was Otto reciting Schiller to himself. (*"Der Mensch muss hinaus in's feindliche Leben,"* muttered Otto darkly, *"muss wirken und streben!"*). Indifferent to them, he was traveled, well-read, uncommunicative, loose-living, free. But this idyll of late-flowering love was of short duration.

For one short summer only Otto tolerated her ardors. For one season only were they treated to the unedifying spectacle of a spinster-virgin in rut, their shameless sister. Then one day she found herself alone again with the three resident she-devils. Otto had departed with his thesis, finished and bound in dark blue leather.

The weeks and the years passed almost unnoticed. The weeds grew upwards, rotted, passed away. The wheel of the seasons spun round; quite soon she had forgotten him. Like her sisters she was lost in a career of unblemished idleness. She had some sort of an understanding with Helen. Sometimes they talked to each other for hours at a stretch. When she and Helen came to speak together, each had to rise to the surface in order to say what they had to say, after which they sank again to their respective depths.

Tess was the eldest-but-one. Of her let it be said, she played Demon Patience for her nerves, liked to work in the garden for her health, drank gin for preference, enjoyed outside contacts, was Joseph's employer. She had red hair, buck teeth, and a child's high voice. Tess was a Patroness of Adversity, and a pawn to the other's Kings and Queens. She is not in this story.

The third daughter was Helen.

Helen Kervick was a collector of dead things, right from the start. She discarded dolls (capable of modestly lowering their eyes) in favor of rabbits strangled in the snares and overrun with lice and fleas, and these she disentangled and buried with her own hands. It was they, dumb disfigured creatures, who got all her compassion, as she grew up. She went her own way, inventing games for herself alone that required no partners. All her life that tendency would continue—the game that required neither the presence nor the assistance of a second party.

—I just live for the day, she said, —and I try not to think of anything much. . . .

She sat often in the window seat in the sun, sometimes manufacturing dark rings under her eyes with a typewriter brush.

II

Emily-May was the fourth, the firstborn, the heaviest by far. In her distant youth she had been a holy terror on the tennis court, performing in a headband and one of papa's discarded cricket shirts, worn moody and loose, panting about the court, perspiring under her armpits. Languidly she moved to serve. Heavily she served, elaborate and inaccurate, recalling to mind the high action of obsolete fieldpieces. She toed the baseline, measured Tess's ground with a merciless eye, served. Into the net went the ball. Again. She threw the service ball high into the air, squared at it, refused the strike, recaught it! At a third or even fourth attempt she might be induced, with much caracoling, to make a stroke—the sun flashing on the racket and the ball once again crashing into the net.

All through summer endless games of singles were contested with the patient Tess. Rallies were infrequent. Some of the high returns had to be retrieved from the beech hedge with a long stepladder. Tess kept the score.

—Thirty-fiff! she cried in her intolerable tennis voice. *Thirty-fiff!*

Missel thrushes came floating down from the great trees into the evergreens. Dusk crept around Springfield. The sun descended into the wood. Tess served again. Emily-May, model of rectitude, crouched in the Helen Wills Moody position. Dim figures stirred again. It had all happened in the long ago.

Otherwise Emily-May's gestures betrayed few emotions. Her gestures and progress, reduced to a minimum, were as uniformly dull as her clothes. Her face, a full pod of flesh, was bulky and uneasy; her manner was so abashed that it could only be seen or thought of by degrees. For there are such faces. Her entire corporal presence had the unknown quality of things stared at so often that they are no longer seen. Her condition was one of constant and virtually unrelieved embarrassment. Here was a person who had run out of enthusiasms early on in life, and in the halls of her spirit, so to speak, toadstools grew. Imogen, who detested her, had appointed herself Emily-May's biographer and amanuensis. But all the thin slanders assembled by her bounced harmlessly off the sebaceous elder, whom few cared to address directly. Emily-May took ridiculously small steps for a person of her bulk and moved rapidly, pigeon-toed, from thickset hips with a repressed fury that was painful to see. Physically she belonged to what Kretschmer called the pyknic type (all arse and occiput). Add to this a disagreeable set of countenance and an uncommon air, for a lady, of suffering from hypertrophy of the prostate. The creature had commenced to put on flesh at an early age, and as well as that found herself prematurely bald before the age of thirty. Those unhappy people who speak of being "thrown back" upon themselves, in the sense of being confounded, would perhaps have understood her best. For she was a throwback, stem and corolla risen to new heights, bound to please no one; one single forbidding link, alive and growing into itself, casting a brave shadow in a world loathsome beyond words, from root to flower.

Poultry abounded in the backyard, a hundred yards away from the house. Everything from fidgety bantams to turkeys, spurred and fierce, savagely disposed towards all, were allowed their freedom there.

Helen was greatly attached to the hens and their little ways and liked nothing better than to spend hours observing them. This she did with the aid of a collapsible campstool, moving about from point to point in their wake, and then sitting stock-still in her battered old hat, not knowing her mind between one beat of her heart and the next. Endlessly patient she sat there, Crusoe with his beginnings. The hens themselves seemed to live in a lifelong coma, disturbed only by the rats who sought to catch them on the ground at night; or by Joseph, ready to lay violent hands on them by day—for though

Helen herself was a vegetarian both Tess and Emily-May were gluttons for spring chicken served with new potatoes.

While they lived the hens collected grubs, flies, took dust baths, waited for the cock to rush upon them and have his way; sometimes they ventured far afield into the meadows. The evening was their time. They seemed happier then, a little surer of themselves. They sang in a cracked unhinged key that rose, more lament than song, hesitated (they were sure of nothing), broke off before the phrase ended. Up the ramp at dusk they stumbled after the white cock, and one by one they dropped inside.

They were early astir in the morning in the dock- and pollen-infested yard, scratching and rooting about, emitting sad droning cries, *Key-key-kee-kee-keeeeee,* that then trickled off into silence. One of their number would sometimes take fright, call out three or four times, then stand petrified as all the other red hens froze about the yard. A dog was moving behind the wall; a hawk was hovering above, preparing to fall out of the sky and rend one of them. Then that danger too seemed to pass. The first one would move again, dipping its head and clucking. Then one by one all would resume their activities as before. They seemed pleased with the filthiest surroundings—the lime-fouled henhouse or the pig troughs. Imogen it was who fed them. They got into the mush the better to enjoy it.

Helen spent whole days among them, listening to their talk; in it there was neither statement, question, nor reply; and this characteristic greatly pleased her.

Helen sat indoors, uncomfortably on her raised seat in the upper cabin, lost in *The Anatomy of Melancholy.* The last daylight swam in the clouded pockets of the little window, as from a bathysphere, before her eyes. Evening clouds were moving across that portion of the sky visible to her. She was thinking of Emily-May, about whom she was attempting to write something (closing her Burton and shutting her eyes). Her eldest sister, who from the tenderest age onwards could be seen lurking in the background in a succession of family snapshots, invariably surprised in a slovenly pose, off guard, her weight resting on one hip—effacing herself, so that she became more distant than a distant relative. But she did this so well it had become almost indelicate to notice it. Well, she had been foundering in some such confusion all her life—a life lonely and shy, subjected to a process of erosion that had reduced her in some irreparable way. Until at last she came to resemble that other person trapped in the snapshot, a version of herself perpetuated in some anxious pose and unable to walk forward out of that paralysis.

The cabin was flooded with a white afterlight, an emulsion reflected from a nonexistent sea. The sun was setting. Evening benediction had begun. Helen stared through the glass and never saw the dogs moving cautiously about the yard, for her mind's eye was fixed on other things.

In the hot summers and sometimes even in winter, Emily-May went bathing more or less every day, naked into the river. Grotesque in modesty as in everything else, she crept down to the water, both chubby hands shielding her various allurements, overpowering as the Goddess Frigga at the bath. Avoiding the main current (for she could not swim) she floated awkwardly downriver in the shallows, using one fat leg as a keel, touching bottom, floating on. At such times she was happy, no longer caring that she might be seen and find herself in the Court of Assizes on a charge of indecent exposure, and she no longer feared that she might drown. The noises of the river delighted her, the sensation of floating also, the nakedness too. Her nerves relented, she let go, she was calm, she felt free.

Thus did Emily-May indulge herself all day long in the summer. After these excursions she had the whetted appetite of a female Cyclops. Shoulders of beef, haunches of lamb, fish and poultry and game, washed down with soup and beer, all these and many more condiments disappeared into that voracious crop. She lived in indescribable squalor among the scattered remains of Scotch shortbread, preserves, chewed ends of anchovy toast, boxes of *glacé* fruit, rounds of digestive biscuits lurid with greengage jam. Indoors and out she ate, day and night, winter and summer, odds and ends in the pantry, lettuce and bananas with cold rabbit by the river. But little of what her mouth contained was by her ferocious stomach received, no, but from rapidly champing jaws did fall and by the passing current was carried away, *secundum carnem.*

In her lair, safe from intrusion, Helen wrote into her day-book: *As a person may mime from a distance "I-have-been-unavoidably delayed" by a subtle displacement of dignity, such as the wry face, the hapless gesture of the hand, etc., etc., so Emily-May's manner of walking has become the equivalent of the shrug of the shoulders. The fear of becoming the extreme sort of person she might, in other circumstances, have become has thrown her far back. The pattern of a final retreat runs through her like a grain in rough delf.*
None of this high-flown Della-Cruscan pleasing her, Helen broke off, closing her book and putting aside her pencil. She looked out. The yard gates stood wide apart. Great dogs were lifting their hind legs and wetting the doors of outhouses—acts mannered and ceremonial as in a Votive Mass. Peace reigned in Griffenwrath. Then far away in the fields someone called. Helen threw open the window. Amazed, the dogs took to their heels. Helen drew in her head and went quietly downstairs.

III
Joseph the gardener sat drinking stout under a prunus tree out of the heat of the day. The shambles of his awkward feet lay before him, side by side and abject in their thick woolen socks. He had removed his boots and laid them aside. A smell of cap-

tive sweat pervaded his person and something else too, the stench of something in an advanced state of decay.

Joseph killed silently and with the minimum of effort. His victims the hens had scarcely time to cry out before they were disemboweled. Fowl and vermin were dispatched with equal impartiality, for he was their slaughterman. He was a great punter too. His speculating on the turf met with an almost unqualified lack of success, but this did not deter him in the least. His drab waistcoat blazed with insignia—half were seed catalogues and half rejected betting slips.

A passive and indolent man by nature, he spent his working day among the moss roses and privets, or kneeling among the azaleas—weeding, praying, farting, no one knew. He spent much time in such poses, and it required quite a feat of imagination to see him upright and on the move. Yet move he did—a crab but recently trodden on who must struggle back to find first its legs, torn off by an aggressor, and then its element. His balance was only restored to him when in position, in servitude, behind a wheelbarrow, say, or a rake. He knew his place, and kept himself to himself.

Laboring in the garden, on which his labors made so little impression, he kept his Wild Woodbines out of harm's way under his hat, with the lunch. He was their gardener, he was indispensable, he knew it. Joseph the mock father lay sleeping under the prunus tree, pandering to a chronic ataraxy.

He was the person who saw most of Helen, all that there was to be seen of Helen. She spent most of her time indoors, drawn up like a bat in daylight behind the window curtains on the first floor. Groping in the earth sometimes he felt her eyes fixed upon him. Turning to see, framed in the darkness of the window where the progress of the creeper was broken, the white face of the recluse staring at him. Half risen he then attempted a salute (as if taking aim with a gun) from which she turned away. The gesture could not be repeated. She was reading.

The other three women seldom saw her, lacking either the

energy or the interest to raise their tired eyes. They passed to and fro below, plucking at themselves and mumbling, exercising soberly about the various levels of the garden, fond of the tangled grottos, trailing through shade like insane persons or nuns of a silent order.

A great impressive hedge, a beech, eighteen feet high, ran the length of the garden; beyond it lay the orchard. Alongside this hedge Emily-May had worn a path hard and smooth in her regular patrols, tramping down the pretty things, a veritable Juggernaut, the coltsfoot, the valerian, the dock. It bore her onward, at night shining under her like a stream. Her shadow moved below like a ship's hull.

At long intervals Helen too appeared in the garden. After winter rain she liked to walk in the orchard. Joseph spied on her, marveling as the gray engaged figure urged itself on among the stunted trees, appearing and disappearing again, like something recorded.

At other times she left the window open and gramophone music started above his head. She sang foreign songs in a melancholy drawn-out fashion, more chant than song, and not pleasant either way. She sang:

> *Es brennt mir unter beiden Sohlen,*
> *Tret' ich auch schon auf Eis und SCHNEEEE!*

Joseph covered his ears; this was too much. Night once more was falling on this graceless Mary, on her fondest aspirations as on her darkest fears—the confusion of one day terminating in the confusion of the next. Joseph, in his simplicity, believed that she had been something in vaudeville, in another country.

Urge, urge, urge; dogs gnawing.

IV

The apartment was cluttered with an assortment of casual tables on which stood divers bottles and jars. A submarine light filtered through the angled slots of the venetian blinds, dust swirling upwards in its wake, passing slowly through sunlight and on up out of sight. A frieze could be distinguished, depicting a seaside scene, presented as a flat statement in color as though for children (the room had formerly been a nursery), beneath which at calculated intervals hung a line of heavily built ancestors in gilt frames, forbidding in aspect as a rogues' gallery, leaning into the room as from the boxes of a theater.

Out of the depths of a tattered armchair Helen's pale features began to emerge, as Imogen went towards her, to the sound of defunct springs. A miscellaneous collection of fur and feathered life moved as she moved, flitting into obscure hiding places. High above their strong but unnamable smell rose the fetid reek of old newspapers. In one corner a great pile had mounted until jammed between floor and ceiling, like clenched teeth. An unknown number of chiming clocks kept up a morose-sounding chorus, announcing the hours with subdued imprecision. Even in high summer the place gave off a succession of offensive cold-surface smells: an unforgettable blend of rotting newspaper, iodine, mackintosh, cat.

Here on this day and at this hour was Helen Jeanne Kervick, spinster and potential authoress, at home and receiving. In the gloom her voice came faint as from another person in a distant room—a weak and obstinate old voice:

—And our dead ones (she was saying), our parents, do you think of them? When we were young they were old already. And when we in turn were no longer young, why they seemed hardly to have changed. They went past us in the end, crackling like parchment.

She stirred in her antique chair. After a while she went on:

—Do you suppose they intercede for us now, in Heaven, before the throne of Almighty God? Now that they have become what they themselves always spoke so feelingly of—"The Dear

Departed"—when they were alive? Oh my God, she said with feeling, what will become of us all, and how will it end?

Imogen said nothing, watching Helen's long unringed fingers stroking the upholstery of her chair. The friction produced a fine dust that rose like smoke. Beyond it, in it, Helen's voice continued:

—Ah, how can we be expected to behave in a manner that befits a lady? How can we? Everything is moving (a motion of the hand), and I don't move quickly enough. Yes, yes, we envy the thing we cannot be. So, we're alive, yes, that's certain. It's certain that we're old women. At least we stink as old women should.

It was the beginning of a long rambling tirade.

Like all Helen's tirades, it had the inconclusive character of a preamble. As she spoke, pausing for a word here, losing track of the argument there, the captive wildlife began to grow increasingly restive.

—We take everything into account, everything except the baseness of God's little images. What a monster he must be! We've set ourselves up here like scarecrows and only frighten the life out of one another when we come up against ourselves in the wrong light. And in winter the damned sky comes down until it's hanging over our ears, and all we can think about are the mundane things of the world and its rottenness. And then there's that bald glutton Emily-May having seizures in her bottomless pit, and we can't even distinguish her screams from the noises in our heads.

She stopped, and sat silent for a long time. Then she said:

—When one lives in the country long enough, one begins to see the cities as old and queer. It's like looking back centuries.

She went on:

—Listen, have you ever considered this: that Crusoe's life could only cease to be intolerable when he stopped looking for a sail and resigned himself to living with his dependents under a mountain—have you ever thought of that? No. Trust in providence, my dear, and remember, no roc is going to sit on its eggs until they are hatched out of all proportions; or if there ever was such a bird, I haven't heard of her.

From by the door Imogen's voice called something. Drawing closer then and pointing a finger, she said in a child's high voice:

—Dust hath closed Helen's eyes.

Something hard struck Helen's forehead and she allowed herself to fall back without another word. She heard feet lagging on the stairs and after that silence again. Pressing fingers to her brow like electrodes she bent forward until she was almost stifling. A heady smell of dust, undisturbed by time, and the parochial odor of her own person entered her throat and filled her eyes with unshed tears. Something began to ring, blow upon blow, in her head. She straightened up again with a hand to her heart and listened.

A distant sound of wild ringing in the air.

It was the workmen's bell in Killadoon that was tolling. Faint and drifting, carried hither, finally ceasing. Almost, for there was the aftertone. There it was again, the last of it. She felt relieved. The men had finished another day of labor and were departing on their bicycles. From the shelter of the trees she had watched them go. That heavy and toilsome lift of the leg, and then away, slowly home under the walnut trees, past the lodge gate, down the long back drive of Colonel Clement's estate, home to their sausages and tea.

Blood was groping and fumbling in her, pounding through her, greedy lungs and mean heart. "Bleed no more, Helen Kervick, bleed no more!" the blood said. No more the thin girl child, no more the anemic spinster; no more of it. She rose and dusted her person. Where now?

She crossed to the window and peered through the blinds at what remained of the day. High-scudding cloud, the wood, sky on the move, feeling of desolation. Already she regretted everything she had said to Imogen. Yes, every word. It was all vanity and foolishness. And herself just a bit of time pushed to the side. That was all. She heaved a sigh, allowed the slat to fall back into place, and stepped back.

The door stood open. Dusk was everywhere in the room. The landing lay below her, bathed in a spectral light. She stepped down onto its faded surface. Her mind was still disturbed; she was thinking of the departing men. They dug in the earth; they knew it, through and through; it was their element; things grew for them. One day they too would be put down into it themselves, parting the sods and clay easily, going down like expert divers.

—The faith, they said, have you not the faith? She had not. It was something they carried about with them, not to be balked, heavy and reliable, like themselves. She felt at peace in their company. They were solid men; but their faith was repugnant to her. Their stiff genuflecting, as if on sufferance, and their laborers' hands locked in prayer (for she had gone to Mass to be among them)—their contrite hearts. Out of all this, which in her heart she detested, she was locked. And yet they offered her peace. How did that come about?

Here Tess, tired of waiting for the evening cock-pheasant to put in an appearance, strolled out from behind a tree in the field below and began to move along the plantation edge, as though she had intended something else.

v

Members of the Kervick family, too old now to have any sense, strolled vaguely about the house and along the landings, appearing suddenly in rooms sealed off since the death of their parents. Sometimes their heads showed in the currant bushes; at other periods they stood under the plum tree with their mouths half open. They began to collect loganberries industriously in a bowl by the loganberry wall. They cut wasps out of the last apples and worms out of the last pears in the fall.

There was a time when Helen could scarcely walk into the garden without flushing out one of them—such was their patience—collapsed onto a rustic seat and lost in some wretched reverie or dolor. For the combined misery of the Kervick *Lebensgefühl* was oppressive enough to turn the Garden of Eden into another Gethsemane overnight.

Plucking up courage, they would set off for unknown destinations on high antiquated bicycles, pedaling solemnly down the wrong drives and out of sight for the day. Dressed in her Louis XV green, Tess was bound for the back road and Lady Ismay's gin. Emily-May herself was off again to paint in Castletown demesne. In the course of a long career over four hundred versions of the house and reaches of the river, drawn from the life, had been accumulated, most of them duplicates.

At a bend in the front drive, where the paling interfered with Helen's line of sight, watching from the window, the cyclist (it was Emily-May, gross and splendid with a hamper strapped onto the rear carrier) jerked forward out of perspective as if sliced in two—the upper section traveling on, astonished and alone, with augmented rapidity. It was not unknown for one or both of the cyclists to return in a suspicious condition; but unsober or not they never returned together.

Alone and safe from intrusion now, Helen crouched in her sky cabin. Alternating between it and the window seat, she relied on her mood and on the waning light to inform her where to go. Indeed at any time of the day or night the curtains might part and Helen Kervick palely emerge, clad from head to toe in *bouclé* tweed, clutching her Burton or translations from the Latin masters, making her way to the bright convenience on the upper landing. Her head was sometimes seen suspended from that window with hair swinging in her eyes. After dark she closed the curtains carefully behind her, extinguished the oil lamp, passed down the main stairs to the hall, ignoring the dim print of Lady Elizabeth Butler's *Scotland for Ever!*, arriving on the gravel dressed for walking. In the window seat in

winter she bore patiently the cold and the affront of contin-
uous rain, sighing down her life for the last time again—on the
garden, on laboring Joseph, on the parallels, on the flying rain.
Stay Time a while thy flying.

Air!

VI

Towards midday, the weather being fine and bright, early
March weather, Joseph appeared with a tremendous rake and
began to scuffle the gravel before the house, but without much
heart and not for long. Somewhere a window went up and a
sharp voice called his name.

He did not appear to hear: an image dark and laboring in the
weak sun with a halo of light above his head, outside the world
of tears and recrimination, his gloom cast for all time. But
there was no escaping.

—TEA! the voice screamed.

Joseph came to a halt and removed his hat.

—Oh come along now, Joseph! the high bright voice invited
mellifluously.

Emily-May freewheeled by Paisley's corner for the last time
and soon had passed Marley Abbey on her right hand. Van-
essa's old home. Swift had gone there on horseback, jig, jig,
long ago. Emily-May went coasting on into the village. She ordered half a dozen Guinness from Dan Breen and began, on
account of the gradient, to walk her bicycle uphill towards the
great demesne gates. She passed the convent where with the
other little girls of First Infants she had studied her Catechism.
Later, in First Communion veils, models of rectitude, they sang
in childish trebles, *O Salutaris Hostia* and *Tantum Ergo.* Bowing
her head she passed in silence through Castletown gates—the
skeleton branches rigid above her, Emily-May descended into
her nether world.

Core, Hart, Hole, Keegan, Kervick, Coyle. Damp forgotten

life; passing, passing. Some had lived at Temple Mill, some at Great Tarpots, and some at Shatover. Molly North lived at St. Helen's Court: she had long black hair and was beautiful, unlike Emily-May who had tow hair and was considered hideous.

She passed through. Beyond March's bare trees she saw the sun hammering on the river: the water flowed by like a muscle, the summer returned, something turned over in Emily-May and she became young and voluptuous once more (she had never been either). A few minutes later she had reached her secret place behind a clump of pampas grass. She spared herself nothing. Trembling she began to undo her buttons and release her powerful elastic girdle. She, a stout Christian who could not swim a stroke to save her life, pulled off her remaining drawers, charged into the piercing water and struck out at a dog crawl. The damp morning was like so much sugar in her blood. The bitterly cold water ate into her spine as the main current began to draw her downstream. Under wet hanging branches she was carried, dropping her keel, touching nothing but water. By fields, by grazing cattle, by calm estate walls, Emily Odysseus Kervick drifted, the last of her line, without issue, distinction, or hope. She could not cry out; frozen to the bone now, steered by no passing bell, she floated weirwards towards extinction and forgetting. The river carried her on, the clay banks rearing up on either side, and there she seemed to see her little sisters, grown minute as dolls, playing their old games. She saw Tess clearly and behind, holding her hand, the infant Imogen. She screamed once, but they neither heard nor answered and after a while they ran away. Suddenly, directly overhead, Helen's crafty face appeared. She looked straight down, holding in her hands the fishing lines. As a child Emily-May had a passion for writing her name and address on sheets of paper, plugging them into bottles and dropping them in the river below the mill. She imagined now that Helen had remembered this too, and that Helen alone could retrieve or save her. But when she looked again Helen had become a child. Innocence had bestowed on her sister another nature, an ideal nature outside corruption and change, watched over by herself—drowned, grown more ugly and more remote—so that the decades and decades of her own life, past now, seemed a series of mechanical devices arranged at intervals like the joints of a telescope held inverted to the eye—to distort everything she inspected and to separate her from life and from whatever happiness life had to offer. Brought sharply into focus, it became clear that Helen had not escaped to a later innocence, not at all, but in growing up had merely adopted a series of disguises, each one more elaborate and more perfect, leaving her essential nature unchanged. As they stared hopelessly into each other's faces something altered in Helen's. For an instant the child's face was overlaid by the adult face known to Emily-May—this one a mask, long and perverted. It stared down unmoved on her wretchedness—naked, "presumed lost"—itself empty of expression, disfigured now, as though beyond participation. (Here Helen herself closed her Burton and rose up sighing. As her foot touched the floor she drew down the chain with a nervous disengaged hand.)

But the dark gulf was already opening for her sister. Swept towards it by an unbearable wind, courage and endurance (she never had either) ceased to matter. Emily-May saw that and closed her eyes on the roaring, the ROARING. The rockery and roaring gardens were together under the weeds, the untrimmed branches in the orchard were lost; lost until all, prostrate and rank, sank from human sight.

William Trevor (1928–   )

William Trevor was born in Mitchelstown, County Cork, in 1928. He spent his childhood in provincial Ireland, and attended Irish secondary schools before entering Trinity College, Dublin. He has published several prize-winning collections of short stories, including The Ballroom of Romance *(1972);* Angels at the Ritz *(1975), a book Graham Greene described as "surely one of the best collections, if not the best, since Joyce's* Dubliners"; Lovers of Their Time *(1978);* Beyond the Pale *(1981); and* News from Ireland *(1986). His* Collected Stories *first appeared in 1983; an expanded edition was published in 1992. Among his novels are* The Old Boys *(1964),* The Boarding House *(1965),* Mrs. Eckdorf in O'Neill's Hotel *(1969),* The Children of Dynmouth *(1976),* Fools of Fortune *(1983), and* Felicia's Journey *(1995). Trevor now lives in Devon with his family. "The Ballroom of Romance" is the title story from the collection* The Ballroom of Romance and Other Stories.

The Ballroom of Romance

On Sundays, or on Mondays if he couldn't make it and often he couldn't, Sunday being his busy day, Canon O'Connell arrived at the farm in order to hold a private service with Bridie's father, who couldn't get about anymore, having had a leg amputated after gangrene had set in. They'd had a pony and cart then and Bridie's mother had been alive: it hadn't been difficult for the two of them to help her father onto the cart in order to make the journey to Mass. But two years later the pony had gone lame and eventually had to be destroyed; not long after that her mother had died. "Don't worry about it at all," Canon O'Connell had said, referring to the difficulty of transporting her father to Mass. "I'll slip up by the week, Bridie."

The milk lorry called daily for the single churn of milk, Mr. Driscoll delivered groceries and meal in his van, and took away the eggs that Bridie had collected during the week. Since Canon O'Connell had made his offer, in 1953, Bridie's father hadn't left the farm.

As well as Mass on Sundays and her weekly visits to a wayside dance hall Bridie went shopping once every month, cycling to the town early on a Friday afternoon. She bought things for herself, material for a dress, knitting wool, stockings, a newspaper, and paper-backed Wild West novels for her father. She talked in the shops to some of the girls she'd been at school with, girls who had married shop assistants or shopkeepers, or had become assistants themselves. Most of them had families of their own by now. "You're lucky to be peaceful in the hills," they said to Bridie, "instead of stuck in a hole like this." They had a tired look, most of them, from pregnancies and their efforts to organize and control their large families.

As she cycled back to the hills on a Friday Bridie often felt that they truly envied her her life, and she found it surprising that they should do so. If it hadn't been for her father she'd have wanted to work in the town also, in the tinned meat factory maybe, or in a shop. The town had a cinema called the Electric, and a fish-and-chip shop where people met at night, eating chips out of newspaper on the pavement outside. In the evenings, sitting in the farmhouse with her father, she often thought about the town, imagining the shop windows lit up to display their goods and the sweetshops still open so that people could purchase chocolates or fruit to take with them to the Electric cinema. But the town was eleven miles away, which was too far to cycle, there and back, for an evening's entertainment.

"It's a terrible thing for you, girl," her father used to say, genuinely troubled, "tied up to a one-legged man." He would sigh heavily, hobbling back from the fields, where he managed as best he could. "If your mother hadn't died," he'd say, not finishing the sentence.

If her mother hadn't died her mother could have looked after him and the scant acres he owned, her mother could somehow have lifted the milk churn onto the collection platform and attended to the few hens and the cows. "I'd be dead without the girl to assist me," she'd heard her father saying to Canon O'Connell, and Canon O'Connell replied that he was certainly lucky to have her.

"Amn't I as happy here as anywhere?" she'd say herself, but her father knew she was pretending and was saddened because the weight of circumstances had so harshly interfered with her life.

Although her father still called her a girl, Bridie was thirty-six. She was tall and strong: the skin of her fingers and her palms were stained, and harsh to touch. The labor they'd experienced had found its way into them, as though juices had come out of vegetation and pigment out of soil: since childhood she'd torn away the rough scotch grass that grew each spring among her father's mangolds and sugar beet; since childhood she'd harvested potatoes in August, her hands daily rooting in the ground she loosened and turned. Wind had toughened the flesh of her face, sun had browned it; her neck and nose were lean, her lips touched with early wrinkles.

But on Saturday nights Bridie forgot the scotch grass and the soil. In different dresses she cycled to the dance hall, encouraged to make the journey by her father. "Doesn't it do you good, girl?" he'd say, as though he imagined she begrudged herself the pleasure. "Why wouldn't you enjoy yourself?"

She'd cook him his tea and then he'd settle down with the wireless, or maybe a Wild West novel. In time, while still she danced, he'd stoke the fire up and hobble his way upstairs to bed.

The dance hall, owned by Mr. Justin Dwyer, was miles from anywhere, a lone building by the roadside with treeless boglands all around and a gravel expanse in front of it. On pink pebbled cement its title was painted in an azure blue that matched the depth of the background shade yet stood out well, unfussily proclaiming *The Ballroom of Romance.* Above these letters four colored bulbs—in red, green, orange, and mauve— were lit at appropriate times, an indication that the evening rendezvous was open for business. Only the façade of the building was pink, the other walls being a more ordinary gray. And inside, except for pink swing doors, everything was blue.

On Saturday nights Mr. Justin Dwyer, a small, thin man, unlocked the metal grid that protected his property and drew it back, creating an open mouth from which music would later pour. He helped his wife to carry crates of lemonade and packets of biscuits from their car, and then took up a position in the tiny vestibule between the drawn-back grid and the pink swing doors. He sat at a card table, with money and tickets spread out before him. He'd made a fortune, people said: he owned other ballrooms also.

People came on bicycles or in old motorcars, country people like Bridie from remote hill farms and villages. People who did not often see other people met there, girls and boys, men and women. They paid Mr. Dwyer and passed into his dance hall, where shadows were cast on pale blue walls and light from a crystal bowl was dim. The band, known as the Romantic Jazz Band, was composed of clarinet, drums, and piano. The drummer sometimes sang.

Bridie had been going to the dance hall since first she left the Presentation Nuns, before her mother's death. She didn't mind the journey, which was seven miles there and seven miles back: she'd traveled as far every day to the Presentation Nuns on the same bicycle, which had once been the property of her mother, an old Rudge purchased originally in 1936. On Sundays she cycled six miles to Mass, but she never minded either: she'd grown quite used to all that.

"How're you, Bridie?" inquired Mr. Justin Dwyer when she arrived in a new scarlet dress one autumn evening in 1971. She said she was all right and in reply to Mr. Dwyer's second query she said that her father was all right also. "I'll go up one of these days," promised Mr. Dwyer, which was a promise he'd been making for twenty years.

She paid the entrance fee and passed through the pink swing doors. The Romantic Jazz Band was playing a familiar melody of the past, "The Destiny Waltz." In spite of the band's title, jazz was not ever played in the ballroom: Mr. Dwyer did not personally care for that kind of music, nor had he cared for various dance movements that had come and gone over the years. Jiving, rock and roll, twisting, and other such variations had all been resisted by Mr. Dwyer, who believed that a ballroom should be, as much as possible, a dignified place. The Romantic Jazz Band consisted of Mr. Maloney, Mr. Swanton, and Dano Ryan on drums. They were three middle-aged men who drove out from the town in Mr. Maloney's car, amateur performers who were employed otherwise by the tinned-meat factory, the Electricity Supply Board, and the County Council.

"How're you, Bridie?" inquired Dano Ryan as she passed him on her way to the cloakroom. He was idle for a moment with his drums, "The Destiny Waltz" not calling for much attention from him.

"I'm all right, Dano," she said. "Are you fit yourself? Are the eyes better?" The week before he'd told her that he'd developed a watering of the eyes that must have been some kind of cold or other. He'd woken up with it in the morning and it had persisted until the afternoon: it was a new experience, he'd told her, adding that he'd never had a day's illness or discomfort in his life.

"I think I need glasses," he said now, and as she passed into the cloakroom she imagined him in glasses, repairing the roads, as he was employed to do by the County Council. You hardly ever saw a road mender with glasses, she reflected, and she wondered if all the dust that was inherent in his work had perhaps affected his eyes.

"How're you, Bridie?" a girl called Eenie Mackie said in the cloakroom, a girl who'd left the Presentation Nuns only a year ago.

"That's a lovely dress, Eenie," Bridie said. "Is it nylon, that?"

"Tricel actually. Drip-dry."

Bridie took off her coat and hung it on a hook. There was a small washbasin in the cloakroom above which hung a discolored oval mirror. Used tissues and pieces of cotton wool, cigarette butts, and matches covered the concrete floor. Lengths of green-painted timber partitioned off a lavatory in a corner.

"Jeez, you're looking great, Bridie," Madge Dowding remarked, waiting for her turn at the mirror. She moved towards it as she spoke, taking off a pair of spectacles before endeavoring to apply makeup to the lashes of her eye. She stared myopically into the oval mirror, humming while the other girls became restive.

"Will you hurry up, for God's sake!" shouted Eenie Mackie. "We're standing here all night, Madge."

Madge Dowding was the only one who was older than Bridie. She was thirty-nine, although often she said she was younger. The girls sniggered about that, saying that Madge Dowding should accept her condition—her age and her squint and her poor complexion—and not make herself ridiculous going out after men. What man would be bothered with the like of her anyway? Madge Dowding would do better to give herself over to do Saturday night work for the Legion of Mary: wasn't Canon O'Connell always looking for aid?

"Is that fellow there?" she asked now, moving away from the mirror. "The guy with the long arms. Did anyone see him outside?"

"He's dancing with Cat Bolger," one of the girls replied. "She has herself glued to him."

"Lover boy," remarked Patty Byrne, and everyone laughed because the person referred to was hardly a boy any more, being over fifty it was said, a bachelor who came only occasionally to the dance hall.

Madge Dowding left the cloakroom rapidly, not bothering to pretend she was not anxious about the conjunction of Cat Bolger and the man with the long arms. Two sharp spots of red had come into her cheeks, and when she stumbled in her haste the girls in the cloakroom laughed. A younger girl would have pretended to be casual.

Bridie chatted, waiting for the mirror. Some girls, not wishing to be delayed, used the mirrors of their compacts. Then in twos and threes, occasionally singly, they left the cloakroom and took their places on upright wooden chairs at one end of the dance hall, waiting to be asked to dance. Mr. Maloney, Mr. Swanton, and Dano Ryan played "Harvest Moon" and "I Wonder Who's Kissing Her Now" and "I'll Be Around."

Bridie danced. Her father would be falling asleep by the fire; the wireless, tuned in to Radio Eireann, would be murmuring in the background. Already he'd have listened to *Faith and Order* and *Spot the Talent*. His Wild West novel, *Three Rode Fast* by Jake Matall, would have dropped from his single knee on to the flagged floor. He would wake with a jerk as he did every night and, forgetting what night it was, might be surprised not to see her, for usually she was sitting there at the table, mending clothes or washing eggs. "Is it time for the news?" he'd automatically say.

Dust and cigarette smoke formed a haze beneath the crystal bowl, feet thudded, girls shrieked and laughed, some of them dancing together for want of a male partner. The music was loud, the musicians had taken off their jackets. Vigorously they played a number of tunes from *State Fair* and then, more romantically, "Just One of Those Things." The tempo increased for a Paul Jones, after which Bridie found herself with a youth who told her he was saving up to emigrate, the nation in his opinion being finished. "I'm up in the hills with the uncle," he said, "laboring fourteen hours a day. Is it any life for a young fellow?" She knew his uncle, a hill farmer whose stony acres were separated from her father's by one other farm only. "He has me gutted with work," the youth told her. "Is there sense in it at all, Bridie?"

At ten o'clock there was a stir, occasioned by the arrival of three middle-aged bachelors who'd cycled over from Carey's public house. They shouted and whistled, greeting other people across the dancing area. They smelt of stout and sweat and whiskey.

Every Saturday at just this time they arrived, and, having sold them their tickets, Mr. Dwyer folded up his card table and locked the tin box that held the evening's takings: his ballroom was complete.

"How're you, Bridie?" one of the bachelors, known as Bowser Egan, inquired. Another one, Tim Daly, asked Patty Byrne how she was. "Will we take the floor?" Eyes Horgan suggested to Madge Dowding, already pressing the front of his navy blue suit against the net of her dress. Bridie danced with Bowser Egan, who said she was looking great.

The bachelors would never marry, the girls of the dance hall considered: they were wedded already, to stout and whiskey and laziness, to three old mothers somewhere up in the hills. The man with the long arms didn't drink but he was the same in all other ways: he had the same look of a bachelor, a quality in his face.

"Great," Bowser Egan said, feather-stepping in an inaccurate and inebriated manner. "You're a great little dancer, Bridie."

"Will you lay off that!" cried Madge Dowding, her voice

shrill above the sound of the music. Eyes Horgan had slipped two fingers into the back of her dress and was now pretending they'd got there by accident. He smiled blearily, his huge red face streaming with perspiration, the eyes which gave him his nickname protuberant and bloodshot.

"Watch your step with that one," Bowser Egan called out, laughing so that spittle sprayed on to Bridie's face. Eenie Mackie, who was also dancing near the incident, laughed also and winked at Bridie. Dano Ryan left his drums and sang. "Oh, how I miss your gentle kiss," he crooned, "and long to hold you tight."

Nobody knew the name of the man with the long arms. The only words he'd ever been known to speak in the Ballroom of Romance were the words that formed his invitation to dance. He was a shy man who stood alone when he wasn't performing on the dance floor. He rode away on his bicycle afterwards, not saying good night to anyone.

"Cat has your man leppin' tonight," Tim Daly remarked to Patty Byrne, for the liveliness that Cat Bolger had introduced into foxtrot and waltz was noticeable.

"I think of you only," sang Dano Ryan. "Only wishing, wishing you were by my side."

Dano Ryan would have done, Bridie often thought, because he was a different kind of bachelor: he had a lonely look about him, as if he'd become tired of being on his own. Every week she thought he would have done, and during the week her mind regularly returned to that thought. Dano Ryan would have done because she felt he wouldn't mind coming to live in the farmhouse while her one-legged father was still about the place. Three could live as cheaply as two where Dano Ryan was concerned because giving up the wages he earned as a road worker would be balanced by the saving made on what he paid for lodgings. Once, at the end of an evening, she'd pretended that there was a puncture in the back wheel of her bicycle and he'd concerned himself with it while Mr. Maloney and Mr. Swanton waited for him in Mr. Maloney's car. He'd blown the tire up with the car pump and had said he thought it would hold.

It was well known in the dance hall that she fancied her chances with Dano Ryan. But it was well known also that Dano Ryan had got into a set way of life and had remained in it for quite some years. He lodged with a widow called Mrs. Griffin and Mrs. Griffin's mentally affected son, in a cottage on the outskirts of the town. He was said to be good to the affected child, buying him sweets and taking him out for rides on the crossbar of his bicycle. He gave an hour or two of his time every week to the Church of Our Lady Queen of Heaven, and he was loyal to Mr. Dwyer. He performed in the two other rural dance halls that Mr. Dwyer owned, rejecting advances from the town's more sophisticated dance hall, even though it was more conveniently situated for him and the fee was more substantial than that paid by Mr. Dwyer. But Mr. Dwyer had discovered Dano Ryan and Dano had not forgotten it, just as Mr. Maloney and Mr. Swanton had not forgotten their discovery by Mr. Dwyer either.

"Would we take a lemonade?" Bowser Egan suggested. "And a packet of biscuits, Bridie?"

No alcoholic liquor was ever served in the Ballroom of Romance, the premises not being licensed for this added stimulant. Mr. Dwyer in fact had never sought a licence for any of his premises, knowing that romance and alcohol were difficult commodities to mix, especially in a dignified ballroom. Behind where the girls sat on the wooden chairs Mr. Dwyer's wife, a small stout woman, served the bottles of lemonade, with straws, and the biscuits and the crisps. She talked busily while doing so, mainly about the turkeys she kept. She'd once told Bridie that she thought of them as children.

"Thanks," Bridie said, and Bowser Egan led her to the trestle table. Soon it would be the intermission: soon the three members of the band would cross the floor also for refreshment. She thought up questions to ask Dano Ryan.

When first she'd danced in the Ballroom of Romance, when she was just sixteen, Dano Ryan had been there also, four years older than she was, playing the drums for Mr. Maloney as he played them now. She'd hardly noticed him then because of his not being one of the dancers: he was part of the ballroom's scenery, like the trestle table and the lemonade bottles, and Mrs. Dwyer and Mr. Dwyer. The youths who'd danced with her then in their Saturday-night blue suits had later disappeared into the town, or to Dublin or Britain, leaving behind them those who became the middle-aged bachelors of the hills. There'd been a boy called Patrick Grady whom she had loved in those days. Week after week she'd ridden away from the Ballroom of Romance with the image of his face in her mind, a thin face, pale beneath black hair. It had been different, dancing with Patrick Grady, and she'd felt that he found it different dancing with her, although he'd never said so. At night she'd dreamed of him and in the daytime too, while she helped her mother in the kitchen or her father with the cows. Week by week she'd returned to the ballroom, smiling on its pink façade and dancing then in the arms of Patrick Grady. Often they'd stood together drinking lemonade, not saying anything, not knowing what to say. She knew he loved her, and she believed then that he would lead her one day from the dim, romantic ballroom, from its blueness and its pinkness and its crystal bowl of light and its music. She believed he would lead her into sunshine, to the town and the Church of Our Lady Queen of Heaven, to marriage and smiling faces. But someone else had got Patrick Grady, a girl from the town who'd never danced in the wayside ballroom. She'd scooped up Patrick Grady when he didn't have a chance.

Bridie had wept, hearing that. By night she'd lain in her bed in the farmhouse, quietly crying, the tears rolling into her hair and making the pillow damp. When she woke in the early morning the thought was still naggingly with her and it remained with her by day, replacing her daytime dreams of happiness. Someone told her later on that he'd crossed to Britain, to Wolverhampton, with the girl he'd married, and she imagined him there, in a place she wasn't able properly to visualize, laboring in a factory, his children being born and acquiring the accent of the area. The Ballroom of Romance wasn't the same without him, and when no one else stood out for her particularly over the years and when no one offered her marriage, she found herself wondering about Dano Ryan. If you couldn't have love, the next best thing was surely a decent man.

Bowser Egan hardly fell into that category, nor did Tim Daly. And it was plain to everyone that Cat Bolger and Madge Dowding were wasting their time over the man with the long arms. Madge Dowding was already a figure of fun in the ballroom, the way she ran after the bachelors; Cat Bolger would end up the same if she wasn't careful. One way or another it wasn't difficult to be a figure of fun in the ballroom, and you didn't have to be as old as Madge Dowding: a girl who'd just left the Presentation Nuns had once asked Eyes Horgan what he had in his trouser pocket and he told her it was a penknife. She'd repeated this afterwards in the cloakroom, how she'd requested Eyes Horgan not to dance so close to her because his penknife was sticking into her. "Jeez, aren't you the right baby!" Patty Byrne had shouted delightedly: everyone had laughed, knowing that Eyes Horgan only came to the ballroom for stuff like that. He was no use to any girl.

"Two lemonades, Mrs. Dwyer," Bowser Egan said, "and two packets of Kerry Creams. Is Kerry Creams all right, Bridie?"

She nodded, smiling. Kerry Creams would be fine, she said.

"Well, Bridie, isn't that the great outfit you have!" Mrs. Dwyer remarked. "Doesn't the red suit her, Bowser?"

By the swing doors stood Mr. Dwyer, smoking a cigarette that he held cupped in his left hand. His small eyes noted all developments. He had been aware of Madge Dowding's anxiety when Eyes Horgan had inserted two fingers into the back opening of her dress. He had looked away, not caring for the incident, but had it developed further he would have spoken to Eyes Horgan, as he had on other occasions. Some of the younger lads didn't know any better and would dance very close to their partners, who generally were too embarrassed to do anything about it, being young themselves. But that, in Mr. Dwyer's opinion, was a different kettle of fish altogether because they were decent young lads who'd in no time at all be doing a steady line with a girl and would end up as he had himself with Mrs. Dwyer, in the same house with her, sleeping in a bed with her, firmly married. It was the middle-aged bachelors who required the watching: they came down from the hills like mountain goats, released from their mammies and from the smell of animals and soil. Mr. Dwyer continued to watch Eyes Horgan, wondering how drunk he was.

Dano Ryan's song came to an end, Mr. Swanton laid down his clarinet, Mr. Maloney rose from the piano. Dano Ryan wiped sweat from his face and the three men slowly moved towards Mrs. Dwyer's trestle table.

"Jeez, you have powerful legs," Eyes Horgan whispered to Madge Dowding, but Madge Dowding's attention was on the man with the long arms, who had left Cat Bolger's side and was proceeding in the direction of the men's lavatory. He never took refreshments. She moved, herself, towards the men's lavatory, to take up a position outside it, but Eyes Horgan followed her. "Would you take a lemonade, Madge?" he asked. He had a small bottle of whiskey on him: if they went into a corner they could add a drop of it to the lemonade. She didn't drink spirits, she reminded him, and he went away.

"Excuse me a minute," Bowser Egan said, putting down his bottle of lemonade. He crossed the floor to the lavatory. He too, Bridie knew, would have a small bottle of whiskey on him.

She watched while Dano Ryan, listening to a story Mr. Maloney was telling, paused in the center of the ballroom, his head bent to hear what was being said. He was a big man, heavily made, with black hair that was slightly touched with grey, and big hands. He laughed when Mr. Maloney came to the end of his story and then bent his head again, in order to listen to a story told by Mr. Swanton.

"Are you on your own, Bridie?" Cat Bolger asked, and Bridie said she was waiting for Bowser Egan. "I think I'll have a lemonade," Cat Bolger said.

Younger boys and girls stood with their arms still around one another, queueing up for refreshments. Boys who hadn't danced at all, being nervous because they didn't know any steps, stood in groups, smoking and making jokes. Girls who hadn't been danced with yet talked to one another, their eyes wandering. Some of them sucked at straws in lemonade bottles.

Bridie, still watching Dano Ryan, imagined him wearing the glasses he'd referred to, sitting in the farmhouse kitchen, reading one of her father's Wild West novels. She imagined the three of them eating a meal she'd prepared, fried eggs and rashers and fried potato cakes and tea and bread and butter and jam, brown bread and soda and shop bread. She imagined Dano Ryan leaving the kitchen in the morning to go out to the fields in order to weed the mangolds, and her father hobbling off behind him, and the two men working together. She saw hay being cut, Dano Ryan with the scythe that she'd learned to use herself, her father using a rake as best he could. She saw herself, because of the extra help, being able to attend to things in the farmhouse, things she'd never had time for because of the cows and the hens and the fields. There were bedroom curtains that needed repairing where the net had ripped, and wallpaper that had become loose and needed to be stuck up with flour paste. The scullery required whitewashing.

The night he'd blown up the tire of her bicycle she'd thought he was going to kiss her. He'd crouched on the ground in the darkness with his ear to the tire, listening for escaping air. When he could hear none he'd straightened up and said he thought she'd be all right on the bicycle. His face had been quite close to hers and she'd smiled at him. At that moment, unfortunately, Mr. Maloney had blown an impatient blast on the horn of his motorcar.

Often she'd been kissed by Bowser Egan, on the nights when he insisted on riding part of the way home with her. They had to dismount in order to push their bicycles up a hill and the first time he'd accompanied her he'd contrived to fall against her, steadying himself by putting a hand on her shoulder. The next thing she was aware of was the moist quality of his lips and the sound of his bicycle as it clattered noisily on the road. He'd suggested then, regaining his breath, that they should go into a field.

That was nine years ago. In the intervening passage of time she'd been kissed as well, in similar circumstances, by Eyes Horgan and Tim Daly. She'd gone into fields with them and permitted them to put their arms about her while heavily they breathed. At one time or another she had imagined marriage with one or other of them, seeing them in the farmhouse with her father, even though the fantasies were unlikely.

Bridie stood with Cat Bolger, knowing that it would be some time before Bowser Egan came out of the lavatory. Mr. Maloney, Mr. Swanton, and Dano Ryan approached, Mr. Maloney insisting that he would fetch three bottles of lemonade from the trestle table.

"You sang the last one beautifully," Bridie said to Dano Ryan. "Isn't it a beautiful song?"

Mr. Swanton said it was the finest song ever written, and Cat Bolger said she preferred "Danny Boy," which in her opinion was the finest song ever written.

"Take a suck of that," said Mr. Maloney, handing Dano

Ryan and Mr. Swanton bottles of lemonade. "How's Bridie tonight? Is your father well, Bridie?"

Her father was all right, she said.

"I hear they're starting a cement factory," said Mr. Maloney.
"Did anyone hear talk of that? They're after striking some
commodity in the earth that makes good cement. Ten feet
down, over at Kilmalough."

"It'll bring employment," said Mr. Swanton. "It's employment that's necessary in this area."

"Canon O'Connell was on about it," Mr. Maloney said.
"There's Yankee money involved."

"Will the Yanks come over?" inquired Cat Bolger. "Will
they run it themselves, Mr. Maloney?"

Mr. Maloney, intent on his lemonade, didn't hear the questions and Cat Bolger didn't repeat them.

"There's stuff called Optrex," Bridie said quietly to Dano
Ryan, "that my father took the time he had a cold in his eyes.
Maybe Optrex would settle the watering, Dano."

"Ah sure, it doesn't worry me that much—"

"It's terrible, anything wrong with the eyes. You wouldn't
want to take a chance. You'd get Optrex in a chemist, Dano,
and a little bowl with it so that you can bathe the eyes."

Her father's eyes had become red-rimmed and unsightly to
look at. She'd gone into Riordan's Medical Hall in the town
and had explained what the trouble was, and Mr. Riordan had
recommended Optrex. She told this to Dano Ryan, adding
that her father had had no trouble with his eyes since. Dano
Ryan nodded.

"Did you hear that, Mrs. Dwyer?" Mr. Maloney called out.
"A cement factory for Kilmalough."

Mrs. Dwyer wagged her head, placing empty bottles in a
crate. She'd heard references to the cement factory, she said: it
was the best news for a long time.

"Kilmalough'll never know itself," her husband commented,
joining her in her task with the empty lemonade bottles.

" 'Twill bring prosperity certainly," said Mr. Swanton. "I was saying just there, Justin, that employment's what's necessary."

"Sure, won't the Yanks—" began Cat Bolger, but Mr. Maloney interrupted her.

"The Yanks'll be in at the top, Cat, or maybe not here at all—maybe only inserting money into it. It'll be local labor entirely."

"You'll not marry a Yank, Cat," said Mr. Swanton, loudly laughing. "You can't catch those fellows."

"Haven't you plenty of homemade bachelors?" suggested Mr. Maloney. He laughed also, throwing away the straw he was sucking through and tipping the bottle into his mouth. Cat Bolger told him to get on with himself. She moved towards the men's lavatory and took up a position outside it, not speaking to Madge Dowding, who was still standing there.

"Keep a watch on Eyes Horgan," Mrs. Dwyer warned her husband, which was advice she gave him at this time every Saturday night, knowing that Eyes Horgan was drinking in the lavatory. When he was drunk Eyes Horgan was the most difficult of the bachelors.

"I have a drop of it left, Dano," Bridie said quietly. "I could bring it over on Saturday. The eye stuff."

"Ah, don't worry yourself, Bridie—"

"No trouble at all. Honestly now—"

"Mrs. Griffin has me fixed up for a test with Dr. Cready. The old eyes are no worry, only when I'm reading the paper or at the pictures. Mrs. Griffin says I'm only straining them due to lack of glasses."

He looked away while he said that, and she knew at once that Mrs. Griffin was arranging to marry him. She felt it instinctively: Mrs. Griffin was going to marry him because she was afraid that if he moved away from her cottage, to get married to someone else, she'd find it hard to replace him with another lodger who'd be good to her affected son. He'd become a father to Mrs. Griffin's affected son, to whom already he was kind. It was a natural outcome, for Mrs. Griffin had all the chances, seeing him every night and morning and not having to make do with weekly encounters in a ballroom.

She thought of Patrick Grady, seeing in her mind his pale, thin face. She might be the mother of four of his children now, or seven or eight maybe. She might be living in Wolverhampton, going out to the pictures in the evenings, instead of looking after a one-legged man. If the weight of circumstances hadn't intervened she wouldn't be standing in a wayside ballroom, mourning the marriage of a road mender she didn't love. For a moment she thought she might cry, standing there thinking of Patrick Grady in Wolverhampton. In her life, on the farm and in the house, there was no place for tears. Tears were a luxury, like flowers would be in the fields where the mangolds grew, or fresh whitewash in the scullery. It wouldn't have been fair ever to have wept in the kitchen while her father sat listening to *Spot the Talent:* her father had more right to weep, having lost a leg. He suffered in a greater way, yet he remained kind and concerned for her.

In the Ballroom of Romance she felt behind her eyes the tears that it would have been improper to release in the presence of her father. She wanted to let them go, to feel them streaming on her cheeks, to receive the sympathy of Dano Ryan and of everyone else. She wanted them all to listen to her while she told them about Patrick Grady who was now in Wolverhampton and about the death of her mother and her own life since. She wanted Dano Ryan to put his arm around her so that she could lean her head against it. She wanted him to look at her in his decent way and to stroke with his road mender's fingers the backs of her hands. She might wake in a bed with him and imagine for a moment that he was Patrick Grady. She might bathe his eyes and pretend.

"Back to business," said Mr. Maloney, leading his band across the floor to their instruments.

"Tell your father I was asking for him," Dano Ryan said. She smiled and she promised, as though nothing had happened, that she would tell her father that.

She danced with Tim Daly and then again with the youth who'd said he intended to emigrate. She saw Madge Dowding moving swiftly towards the man with the long arms as he came out of the lavatory, moving faster than Cat Bolger. Eyes Horgan approached Cat Bolger. Dancing with her, he spoke earnestly, attempting to persuade her to permit him to ride part of the way home with her. He was unaware of the jealousy that was coming from her as she watched Madge Dowding holding close to her the man with the long arms while they performed a quickstep. Cat Bolger was in her thirties too.

"Get away out of that," said Bowser Egan, cutting in on the youth who was dancing with Bridie. "Go home to your mammy, boy." He took her into his arms, saying again that she was looking great tonight. "Did you hear about the cement factory?" he said. "Isn't it great for Kilmalough?"

She agreed. She said what Mr. Swanton and Mr. Maloney had said: that the cement factory would bring employment to the neighborhood.

"Will I ride home with you a bit, Bridie?" Bowser Egan suggested, and she pretended not to hear him. "Aren't you my girl, Bridie, and always have been?" he said, a statement that made no sense at all.

His voice went on whispering at her, saying he would marry her tomorrow only his mother wouldn't permit another woman in the house. She knew what it was like herself, he reminded her, having a parent to look after: you couldn't leave them to rot, you had to honor your father and your mother.

She danced to "The Bells Are Ringing," moving her legs in time with Bowser Egan's while over his shoulder she watched Dano Ryan softly striking one of his smaller drums. Mrs. Griffin had got him even though she was nearly fifty, with no looks at all, a lumpish woman with lumpish legs and arms. Mrs. Griffin had got him just as the girl had got Patrick Grady.

The music ceased, Bowser Egan held her hard against him, trying to touch her face with his. Around them, people whistled and clapped: the evening had come to an end. She walked away from Bowser Egan, knowing that not ever again would she dance in the Ballroom of Romance. She'd been a figure of fun, trying to promote a relationship with a middle-aged County Council laborer, as ridiculous as Madge Dowding dancing on beyond her time.

"I'm waiting outside for you, Cat," Eyes Horgan called out, lighting a cigarette as he made for the swing doors.

Already the man with the long arms—made long, so they said, from carrying rocks off his land—had left the ballroom. Others were moving briskly. Mr. Dwyer was tidying the chairs.

In the cloakroom the girls put on their coats and said they'd see one another at Mass the next day. Madge Dowding hurried. "Are you O.K., Bridie?" Patty Byrne asked and Bridie said she was. She smiled at little Patty Byrne, wondering if a day would come for the younger girl also, if one day she'd decide that she was a figure of fun in a wayside ballroom.

"Good night so," Bridie said, leaving the cloakroom, and the girls who were still chatting there wished her good night. Outside the cloakroom she paused for a moment. Mr. Dwyer was still tidying the chairs, picking up empty lemonade bottles from the floor, setting the chairs in a neat row. His wife was sweeping the floor. "Good night, Bridie," Mr. Dwyer said. "Good night, Bridie," his wife said.

Extra lights had been switched on so that the Dwyers could see what they were doing. In the glare the blue walls of the ballroom seemed tatty, marked with hair oil where men had leaned against them, inscribed with names and initials and hearts with arrows through them. The crystal bowl gave out a light that was ineffective in the glare; the bowl was broken here and there, which wasn't noticeable when the other lights weren't on.

"Good night so," Bridie said to the Dwyers. She passed through the swing doors and descended the three concrete steps on the gravel expanse in front of the ballroom. People were gathered on the gravel, talking in groups, standing with their bicycles. She saw Madge Dowding going off with Tim Daly. A youth rode away with a girl on the crossbar of his bicycle. The engines of motorcars started.

"Good night, Bridie," Dano Ryan said.

"Good night, Dano," she said.

She walked across the gravel towards her bicycle, hearing Mr. Maloney, somewhere behind her, repeating that no matter how you looked at it the cement factory would be a great thing for Kilmalough. She heard the bang of a car door and knew it was Mr. Swanton banging the door of Mr. Maloney's car because he always gave it the same loud bang. Two other doors banged as she reached her bicycle and then the engine started up and the headlights went on. She touched the two tires of the bicycle to make certain she hadn't a puncture. The wheels of Mr. Maloney's car traversed the gravel and were silent when they reached the road.

"Good night, Bridie," someone called, and she replied, pushing her bicycle towards the road.

"Will I ride a little way with you?" Bowser Egan asked.

They rode together and when they arrived at the hill for which it was necessary to dismount she looked back and saw in the distance the four colored bulbs that decorated the façade of the Ballroom of Romance. As she watched the lights went out, and she imagined Mr. Dwyer pulling the metal grid across the front of his property and locking the two padlocks that secured it. His wife would be waiting with the evening's takings, sitting in the front of their car.

"D'you know what it is, Bridie," said Bowser Egan, "you were never looking better than tonight." He took from a

pocket of his suit the small bottle of whiskey he had. He un-
corked it and drank some and then handed it to her. She took
it and drank. "Sure, why wouldn't you?" he said, surprised to
see her drinking because she never had in his company before.
It was an unpleasant taste, she considered, a taste she'd experienced only twice before, when she'd taken whiskey as a remedy
for toothache. "What harm would it do you?" Bowser Egan
said as she raised the bottle again to her lips. He reached out a
hand for it, though, suddenly concerned lest she should con-
sume a greater share than he wished her to.

She watched him drinking more expertly than she had. He
would always be drinking, she thought. He'd be lazy and useless, sitting in the kitchen with the *Irish Press*. He'd waste
money buying a secondhand motorcar in order to drive into
the town to go to the public houses on fair days.

"She's shook these days," he said, referring to his mother.
"She'll hardly last two years, I'm thinking." He threw the
empty whiskey bottle into the ditch and lit a cigarette. They
pushed their bicycles. He said:

"When she goes, Bridie, I'll sell the bloody place up. I'll sell
the pigs and the whole damn one and twopence worth." He
paused in order to raise the cigarette to his lips. He drew in
smoke and exhaled it. "With the cash that I'll get I could improve some place else, Bridie."

They reached a gate on the left-hand side of the road and automatically they pushed their bicycles towards it and leaned
them against it. He climbed over the gate into the field and she
climbed after him. "Will we sit down here, Bridie?" he said,
offering the suggestion as one that had just occurred to him, as
though they'd entered the field for some other purpose.

"We could improve a place like your own one," he said,
putting his right arm around her shoulders. "Have you a kiss
in you, Bridie?" He kissed her, exerting pressure with his teeth.
When his mother died he would sell his farm and spend the
money in the town. After that he would think of getting mar-

ried because he'd have nowhere to go, because he'd want a fire to sit at and a woman to cook food for him. He kissed her again, his lips hot, the sweat on his cheeks sticking to her. "God, you're great at kissing," he said.

She rose, saying it was time to go, and they climbed over the gate again. "There's nothing like a Saturday," he said. "Good night to you so, Bridie."

He mounted his bicycle and rode down the hill, and she pushed hers to the top and then mounted it also. She rode through the night as on Saturday nights for years she had ridden and never would ride again because she'd reached a certain age. She would wait now and in time Bowser Egan would seek her out because his mother would have died. Her father would probably have died also by then. She would marry Bowser Egan because it would be lonesome being by herself in the farmhouse.

Edna O'Brien (1930-   )

Edna O'Brien was born in County Clare in 1930. She became an overnight sensation with her first novel, The County Girls, *in 1960. Among her other novels are* The Lonely Girl *(1962),* Girls in Their Married Bliss *(1964),* August Is a Wicked Month *(1965),* Casualties of Peace *(1966),* A Pagan Place *(1970), and, most recently,* Time and Tide *(1992). Her collections of short stories include* The Love Object *(1968),* A Scandalous Woman *(1974),* Mrs. Reinhardt and Other Stories *(1978), and* Lantern Slides *(1990). A choice of old and new stories,* A Fanatic Heart, *was published in 1984. She has also written an autobiographical account of Ireland,* Mother Ireland *(1976), with photographs by Fergus Bourke. "The Creature" is taken from her collection* A Scandalous Woman.

The Creature

She was always referred to as The Creature by the townspeople, the dressmaker for whom she did buttonholing, the sacristan, who used to search for her in the pews on the dark winter evenings before locking up, and even the little girl Sally, for whom she wrote out the words of a famine song. Life had treated her rottenly, yet she never complained but always had a ready smile, so that her face with its round rosy cheeks was more like something you could eat or lick; she reminded me of nothing so much as an apple fritter.

I used to encounter her on her way from devotions or from

Mass, or having a stroll, and when we passed she smiled, but she never spoke, probably for fear of intruding. I was doing a temporary teaching job in a little town in the west of Ireland and soon came to know that she lived in a tiny house facing a garage that was also the town's undertaker. The first time I visited her, we sat in the parlor and looked out on the crooked lettering on the door. There seemed to be no one in attendance at the station. A man helped himself to petrol. Nor was there any little muslin curtain to obscure the world, because, as she kept repeating, she had washed it that very day and what a shame. She gave me a glass of rhubarb wine, and we shared the same chair, which was really a wooden seat with a latticed wooden back, that she had got from a rubbish heap and had varnished herself. After varnishing, she had dragged a nail over the wood to give a sort of mottled effect, and you could see where her hand had shaken, because the lines were wavery.

I had come from another part of the country; in fact, I had come to get over a love affair, and since I must have emanated some sort of sadness she was very much at home with me and called me "dearest" when we met and when we were taking leave of one another. After correcting the exercises from school, filling in my diary, and going for a walk, I would knock on her door and then sit with her in the little room almost devoid of furniture—devoid even of a plant or a picture—and oftener than not I would be given a glass of rhubarb wine and sometimes a slice of porter cake. She lived alone and had done so for seventeen years. She was a widow and had two children. Her daughter was in Canada; the son lived about four miles away. She had not set eyes on him for the seventeen years—not since his wife had slung her out—and the children that she had seen as babies were big now, and, as she heard, marvelously handsome. She had a pension and once a year made a journey to the southern end of the country, where her relatives lived in a cottage looking out over the Atlantic.

Her husband had been killed two years after their marriage,

shot in the back of a lorry, in an incident that was later described by the British Forces as regrettable. She had had to conceal the fact of his death and the manner of his death from her own mother, since her mother had lost a son about the same time, also in combat, and on the very day of her husband's funeral, when the chapel bells were ringing and reringing, she had to pretend it was for a traveling man, a tinker, who had died suddenly. She got to the funeral at the very last minute on the pretext that she was going to see the priest.

She and her husband had lived with her mother. She reared her children in the old farmhouse, eventually told her mother that she, too, was a widow, and as women together they worked and toiled and looked after the stock and milked and churned and kept a sow to whom she gave the name of Bessie. Each year the bonhams would become pets of hers and follow her along the road to Mass or wherever, and to them, too, she gave pretty names. A migrant workman helped in the summer months, and in the autumn he would kill the pig for their winter meat. The killing of the pig always made her sad, and she reckoned she could hear those roars—each successive roar—over the years, and she would dwell on that, and then tell how a particular naughty pig stole into the house one time and lapped up the bowls of cream and then lay down on the floor, snoring and belching like a drunken man. The workman slept downstairs on the settle bed, got drunk on Saturdays, and was the cause of an accident; when he was teaching her son to shoot at targets, the boy shot off three of his own fingers. Otherwise, her life had passed without incident.

When her children came home from school, she cleared half the table for them to do their exercises—she was an untidy woman—then every night she made blancmange for them, before sending them to bed. She used to color it red or brown or green as the case may be, and she marveled at these coloring essences almost as much as the children themselves did. She knitted two sweaters each year for them—two identical sweaters of bowneen wool—and she was indeed the proud mother when her son was allowed to serve at Mass.

Her finances suffered a dreadful setback when her entire stock contracted foot-and-mouth disease, and to add to her grief she had to see the animals that she so loved die and be buried around the farm, wherever they happened to stagger down. Her lands were disinfected and empty for over a year, and yet she scraped enough to send her son to boarding school and felt lucky in that she got a reduction of the fees because of her reduced circumstances. The parish priest had intervened on her behalf. He admired her and used to joke her on account of the novelettes she so cravenly read. Her children left, her mother died, and she went through a phase of not wanting to see anyone—not even a neighbor—and she reckoned that was her Garden of Gethsemane. She contracted shingles, and one night, dipping into the well for a bucket of water, she looked first at the stars then down at the water and thought how much simpler it would be if she were to drown. Then she remembered being put into the well for sport one time by her brother, and another time having a bucket of water douched over her by a jealous sister, and the memory of the shock of these two experiences and a plea to God made her draw back from the well and hurry up through the nettle garden to the kitchen, where the dog and the fire, at least, awaited her. She went down on her knees and prayed for the strength to press on.

Imagine her joy when, after years of wandering, her son returned from the city, announced that he would become a farmer, and that he was getting engaged to a local girl who worked in the city as a chiropodist. Her gift to them was a patchwork quilt and a special border of cornflowers she planted outside the window, because the bride-to-be was more than proud of her violet-blue eyes and referred to them in one way or another whenever she got the chance. The Creature thought how nice it would be to have a border of complementary flow-

ers outside the window, and how fitting, even though *she* preferred wallflowers, both for their smell and their softness.
When the young couple came home from the honeymoon, she
was down on her knees weeding the bed of flowers, and, looking up at the young bride in her veiled hat, she thought, an oil
painting was no lovelier or no more sumptuous. In secret, she
hoped that her daughter-in-law might pare her corns after they
had become intimate friends.

Soon, she took to going out to the cow shed to let the
young couple be alone, because even by going upstairs she
could overhear. It was a small house, and the bedrooms were
directly above the kitchen. They quarreled constantly. The first
time she heard angry words she prayed that it be just a lovers'
quarrel, but such spiteful things were said that she shuddered
and remembered her own dead partner and how they had never
exchanged a cross word between them. That night she dreamed
she was looking for him, and though others knew of his where-
abouts they would not guide her. It was not long before she
realized that her daughter-in-law was cursed with a sour and
grudging nature. A woman who automatically bickered over
everything—the price of eggs, the best potato plants to put
down, even the fields that should be pasture and those that
should be reserved for tillage. The women got on well enough
during the day, but rows were inevitable at night when the son
came in and, as always, The Creature went out to the cow shed
or down the road while things transpired. Up in her bedroom,
she put little swabs of cotton wool in her ears to hide whatever
sounds might be forthcoming. The birth of their first child did
everything to exacerbate the young woman's nerves, and after
three days the milk went dry in her breasts. The son called his
mother out to the shed, lit a cigarette for himself, and told her
that unless she signed the farm and the house over to him he
would have no peace from his young barging wife.

This The Creature did soon after, and within three months
she was packing her few belongings and walking away from

the house where she had lived for fifty-eight of her sixty years. All she took was her clothing, her Aladdin lamp, and a tapestry denoting ships on a hemp-colored sea. It was an heirloom. She found lodgings in the town and was the subject of much curiosity, then ridicule, because of having given her farm over to her son and daughter-in-law. Her son defected on the weekly payments he was supposed to make, but though she took the matter to her solicitor, on the appointed day she did not appear in court and as it happened spent the entire night in the chapel, hiding in the confessional.

Hearing the tale over the months, and how The Creature had settled down and made a soup most days, was saving for an electric blanket, and much preferred winter to summer, I decided to make the acquaintance of her son, unbeknownst to his wife. One evening I followed him to the field where he was driving a tractor. I found a sullen, middle-aged man, who did not condescend to look at me but proceeded to roll his own cigarette. I recognized him chiefly by the three missing fingers and wondered pointlessly what they had done with them on that dreadful day. He was in the long field where she used to go twice daily with buckets of separated milk, to feed the suckling calves. The house was to be seen behind some trees, and either because of secrecy or nervousness he got off the tractor, crossed over and stood beneath a tree, his back balanced against the knobbled trunk. It was a little hawthorn and, somewhat superstitious, I hesitated to stand under it. Its flowers gave a certain dreaminess to that otherwise forlorn place. There is something gruesome about plowed earth, maybe because it suggests the grave.

He seemed to know me and he looked, I thought, distastefully at my patent boots and my tweed cape. He said there was nothing he could do, that the past was the past, and that his mother had made her own life in the town. You would think she had prospered or remarried, his tone was so caustic when he spoke of "her own life." Perhaps he had relied on her to die.

I said how dearly she still held him in her thoughts, and he said that she always had a soft heart and if there was one thing in life he hated it was the sodden handkerchief.

With much hedging, he agreed to visit her, and we arranged an afternoon at the end of that week. He called after me to keep it to myself, and I realized that he did not want his wife to know. All I knew about his wife was that she had grown withdrawn, that she had had improvements made on the place—larger windows and a bathroom installed—and that they were never seen together, not even on Christmas morning at chapel.

By the time I called on The Creature that eventful day, it was long after school, and, as usual, she had left the key in the front door for me. I found her dozing in the armchair, very near the stove, her book still in one hand and the fingers of the other hand fidgeting as if she were engaged in some work. Her beautiful embroidered shawl was in a heap on the floor, and the first thing she did when she wakened was to retrieve it and dust it down. I could see that she had come out in some sort of heat rash, and her face resembled nothing so much as a frog's, with her little raisin eyes submerged between pink swollen lids.

At first she was speechless; she just kept shaking her head. But eventually she said that life was a crucible, life was a crucible. I tried consoling her, not knowing what exactly I had to console her about. She pointed to the back door and said things were kiboshed from the very moment he stepped over that threshold. It seems he came up the back garden and found her putting the finishing touches to her hair. Taken by surprise, she reverted to her long-lost state of excitement and could say nothing that made sense. "I thought it was a thief," she said to me, still staring at the back door, with her cane hanging from a nail there.

When she realized who he was, without giving him time to catch breath, she plied both food and the drink on him, and I could see that he had eaten nothing, because the ox tongue in its mold of jelly was still on the table, untouched. A little whiskey bottle lay on its side, empty. She told me how he'd aged and that when she put her hand up to his gray hairs he backed away from her as if she'd given him an electric shock. He who hated the soft heart and the sodden handkerchief must have hated that touch. She asked for photos of his family, but he had brought none. All he told her was that his daughter was learning to be a mannequin, and she put her foot in it further by saying there was no need to gild the lily. He had newspapers in the soles of his shoes to keep out the damp, and she took off those damp shoes and tried polishing them. I could see how it all had been, with her jumping up and down trying to please him but in fact just making him edgy. "They were drying on the range," she said, "when he picked them up and put them on." He was gone before she could put a shine on them, and the worst thing was that he had made no promise concerning the future. When she asked, "Will I see you?" he had said, "Perhaps," and she told me that if there was one word in the English vocabulary that scalded her, it was the word "perhaps."

"I did the wrong thing," I said, and, though she didn't nod, I knew that she also was thinking it—that secretly she would consider me from then on a meddler. All at once I remembered the little hawthorn tree, the bare plowed field, his heart as black and unawakened as the man I had come away to forget, and there was released in me, too, a gigantic and useless sorrow. Whereas for twenty years she had lived on that last high tightrope of hope, it had been taken away from her, leaving her without anyone, without anything, and I wished that I had never punished myself by applying to be a sub in that stagnant, godforsaken little place.

Eugene McCabe (1930–   )

Eugene McCabe was born in Glasgow in 1930. He is a graduate of University College, Cork, and began his literary career by publishing a short story in David Marcus's magazine, Irish Writing. *He subsequently turned to drama, and made his name as a playwright with* King of the Castle, *which was first performed at the Dublin Theatre Festival in 1964. His subsequent work includes a number of plays for the stage and for television; two collections of short stories,* Heritage (1978) and Christ in the Fields (1993); and the historical novel, Death and Nightingales (1992).

Cancer

Today there was an old Anglia and five bicycles outside the cottage. Boyle parked near the bridge. As he locked the car Dinny came through a gap in the ditch: "Busy?"

"From the back of Carn Rock and beyont: it's like a wake inside."

For a living corpse Boyle thought.

"How is he?"

"Never better."

"No pain?"

"Not a twitch . . . ates rings round me and snores the night long." Boyle imagined Joady on the low stool by the hearth in the hot, crowded kitchen, his face like turf ash. Everyone knew he was dying. Women from townlands about had offered to cook and wash. Both brothers had refused. "Odd wee men," the women said. "Course they'd have no sheets, and the blankets must be black." "And why not," another said, "no woman body ever stood in aither room this forty years." At which another giggled and said "or lay." And they all laughed because Dinny and Joady were undersized. And then they were ashamed of laughing and said "poor Joady cratur" and "poor Dinny he'll be left: that's worse." And people kept bringing things: bacon and chicken, whiskey and stout, seed cake, fresh-laid eggs, whole-meal bread; Christmas in February.

In all his years Joady had never slept away from the cottage, so that when people called now he talked about the hospital, the operation, the men who died in the ward. In particular he talked about the shattered bodies brought to the hospital morgue from the explosion near Trillick. When he went on about this, Protestant neighbors kept silent. Joady noticed and said: "A bad doin', Albert, surely, there could be no luck after thon." To Catholic neighbors he said: "Done it their selves to throw blame on us" and spat in the fire.

It was growing dark at the bridge, crows winging over from Annahullion to roost in the fibrous trees about the disused Spade Mill.

"A week to the day we went up to Enniskillen," Dinny said. "That long."

"A week to the day, you might say to the hour. Do you mind the helicopter?" He pointed up. "It near sat on that tree."

Boyle remembered very clearly. It had seemed to come from a quarry of whins dropping as it crossed Gawley's flat. Like today he had driven across this Border bridge and stopped at McMahon's iron-roofed cottage. Without looking up, he could sense the machine chopping its way up from the Spade Mill. He left the car engine running. Dinny came out clutching a bottle of something. The helicopter hung directly over a dead alder in a scrub of egg bushes between the cottage and the river. Dinny turned and flourished the bottle upwards shouting above the noise: "I hope to Jasus yis are blown to shit." He grinned and waved the bottle again. Boyle looked up. Behind the curved, bulletproof shield two pale urban faces stared down, impassive.

"Come on, Dinny, get in."

He waved again: a bottle of Lucozade.

Boyle put the car in gear and drove North. They could hear the machine overhead. Dinny kept twisting about in the front seat trying to see up.

"The whores," he screeched, "they're trackin' us."

On a long stretch of road the helicopter swooped ahead and dropped to within a yard of the road. It turned slowly and moved towards them, a gigantic insect with revolving swords. Five yards from the car it stopped. The two faces were now very clear: guns, uniform, apparatus, one man had earphones. He seemed to be reading in a notebook. He looked at the registration number of Boyle's car and said something. The helicopter tilted sharply and rose clapping its way towards Armagh across the sour divide of fields and crooked ditches. Boyle remained parked in the middle of the road, until he could hear nothing. His heart was pumping strongly: "What the hell was all that?"

"They could see we had Catholic faces," Dinny said and winked. There was a twist in his left eye. "The mouth" McMahon neighbors called him, pike lips set in a bulbous face, a cap glued to his skull. Boyle opened a window. The fumes of porter were just stronger than the hum of turf smoke and a strong personal pong.

"It's on account of Trillick," Boyle said, "they'll be very active for a day or two."

"You'll get the news now."

Boyle switched on the car radio and a voice was saying:

"—five men in a Land-Rover on a track leading to a television transmitter station on Brougher Mountain near Trillick between Enniskillen and Omagh. Two B.B.C. officials and three workers lost their lives. An Army spokesman said that the booby trap blew a six-foot-deep crater in the mountainside and lifted the Land-Rover twenty yards into a bog. The bodies of the five men were scattered over an area of 400 square yards. The area has been sealed off."

Boyle switched off the radio and said: "Dear God."

They passed a barnlike church set in four acres of graveyard. Dinny tipped his cap to the dead: McCaffreys, Boyles, Grues, Gunns, McMahons, Courtneys, Mulligans; names and bones from a hundred townlands.

"I cut a bit out of the *Anglo-Celt* once," Dinny said, "about our crowd, the McMahons."

"Yes?"

"Kings about Monaghan for near a thousand years, butchered, and driv' north to these bitter hills, that's what it said, and the scholar that wrote it up maintained you'll get better-bred men in the cabins of Fermanagh than you'll find in many's a big house."

Boyle thumbed up at the graveyard: "One thing we're sure of, Dinny, we'll add our bit."

"Blood tells," Dinny said, "it tells in the end."

A few miles on they passed a waterworks. There was a soldier pacing the floodlit jetty.

"Wouldn't care for his job, he'll go up with it some night."

"Unless there's changes," Boyle said.

"Changes! What changes. Look in your neighbor's face; damn little change you'll see there. I wrought four days with Gilbert Wilson before Christmas, baggin' turf beyont Doon, and when the job was done we dropped into Corranny pub, and talked land, and benty turf, and the forestry takin' over and the way people are leavin' for factories, the pension scheme for hill farmers and a dose of things: no side in any of it, not one word of politics or religion, and then all of a shot he leans over to me and says: 'Fact is, Dinny, the time I like you best, I could cut your throat.' A quare slap in the mouth, but I didn't rise to it; I just said: 'I'd as lief not hear the like, Gilbert.' 'You,' says he, 'and all your kind, it must be said.' 'It's a mistake, Gilbert, to say the like, or think it.' 'Truth,' he said, 'and you mind it, Dinny.' "

He looked at Boyle: "What do you think of that for a spake?"

They came to the main road and Moorlough: "Are them geese or swans," Dinny was pointing. He wound down his window and stared out. On the Loughside field there seemed to be fifty or sixty swans, very white against the black water. Boyle slowed for the trunk road, put on his headlights.

"Hard to say."

"Swans," Dinny said.

"Your sure?"

"Certain sure."

"So far from water?"

"I seen it before on this very lake in the twenties, bad sign."

"Of what?"

"Trouble."

The lake was half a mile long and at the far end of it there was a military checkpoint. An officer came over with a boy soldier and said "Out, please." Two other soldiers began searching the car.

"Name?"

"Boyle, James."

"Occupation?"

"Teacher."

"Address?"

"Tiernahinch, Kilrooskey, Fermanagh."

"And this gentleman?"

Boyle looked away. Dinny said nothing. The officer said again: "Name?"

"Denis McMahon, Gawley's Bridge, Fermanagh."

"Occupation?"

"I'm on the national health."

The boy beside the officer was writing in a notebook. A cold wind blowing from the lake chopped at the water, churning up angry flecks. The officer had no expression in his face. His voice seemed bored and flat.

"Going where?"

"Enniskillen," Boyle said.

"Purpose?"

"To visit this man's brother, he's had an operation."

"He's lying under a surgeont," Dinny said.

The officer nodded.

"And your brother's name?"

"Joady, Joseph, I'm next-of-kin."

The boy with the notebook went over to a radio Jeep. The officer walked away a few paces. They watched. Boyle thought he should say aloud what they were all thinking, then decided not to; then heard himself say: "Awful business at Trillick."

The officer turned, looked at him steadily for a moment and nodded. There was another silence until Dinny said: "Trillick is claner nor a man kicked to death by savages fornent his childer."

The officer did not look round. The boy soldier came back from the Jeep and said everything was correct, sir. The officer nodded again, walked away and stood looking at the lake.

Dinny dryspat towards the military back as they drove off. " 'And this gentleman!' Smart bugger, see the way he looked at me like I was sprung from a cage."

"His job, Dinny!"

"To make you feel like an animal! 'Occupation' is right!"

Near Lisnaskea Dinny said: "Cancer, that's what we're all

afeerd of, one touch of it and you're a dead man. My ould fella
died from a rare breed of it. If he went out in the light, the
skin would rot from his face and hands, so he put in the latter
end of his life in a dark room, or walkin' about the roads at
night. In the end it killed him. He hadn't seen the sun for
years."

He lit a cigarette butt.

"A doctor tould me once it could be in the blood fifty years,
and then all of a shot it boils up and you're a goner."

For miles after this they said nothing, then Dinny said: "Lis-
bellaw for wappin' straw,/Maguiresbridge for brandy./Linaskea
for drinkin' tay,/But Clones town is dandy. . . . that's a quare
ould one?"

He winked with his good eye.

"You want a jigger, Dinny?"

"I'll not say no."

Smoke, coughing, the reek of a diesel stove and porter met
them with silence and watching. Dinny whispered: "U.D.R.,
wrong shop."

Twenty or more, a clutch of uniformed farmers, faces hardened by wind, rutted from bog, rock, and rain, all staring, in-
vincible, suspicious.

"Wrong shop," Dinny whispered again.

"I know," Boyle said, "we can't leave now."

Near a partition there was a space beside a big man. As Boyle
moved towards it a woman bartender said: "Yes?"

"Two halfs, please."

"What kind?"

"Irish."

"What kind of Irish?"

"Any kind."

Big enough to pull a bullock from a shuck on his own Boyle
thought as the big man spat at the doosy floor and turned
away. Dinny nudged Boyle and winked up at a notice pinned
to a pillar. Boyle read:

LINASKEA AND DISTRICT DEVELOPMENT ASSOCIATION
EXTERMINATION OF VERMIN
1/- for each magpie killed.
2/- for each gray crow killed.
10/- for each gray squirrel killed.
£1 for each fox killed.

Underneath someone had printed with a biro:

For every Fenian Fucker: one old penny.

As the woman measured the whiskeys a glass smashed in the
snug at the counter end. A voice jumped the frosted glass:
"Wilson was a fly boy, and this Heath man's a bum boy, all
them Tories is tricky whores, dale with Micks and Papes and
lave us here to rot. Well, by Christ, they'll come no Pope to
the townland of Invercloon, I'll not be blown up or burned
out, I'll fight to the last ditch."

All listening in the outer bar, faces, secret and serious, un-
comfortable now as other voices joined: "You're right,
George."

"Sit down, man, you'll toss the table."

"Let him say out what's in his head."

"They'll not blow me across no bog; if it's blood they want
then, by Jasus, they'll get it, all they want, gallons of it,
wagons, shiploads."

"Now you're talking, George."

The big man looked at the woman. She went to the hatch,
pushed it, and said something into the snug. The loudness
stopped. A red-ax face stared out, no focus in the eyes. Someone snapped the hatch shut. Silence. The big man spat again
and Dinny said: "I'd as lief drink with pigs."

He held his glass of whiskey across the counter, poured it
into the bar sink and walked out. Boyle finished his whiskey
and followed.

In the car again the words came jerking from Dinny's mouth: "Choke and gut their own childer. Feed them to rats." He held up a black-rimmed nail to the windscreen.

"Before they'd give us *that!*"

"It's very sad," Boyle said, "I see no answer."

"I know the answer, cut the bastards down, every last one of them and it'll come to that, them or us. They got it with guns, kep' it with guns, and guns'll put them from it."

"Blood's not the way," Boyle said.

"There's no other."

At Enniskillen they went by the low end of the town, passed armored cars, and the shattered Crown buildings. Outside the hospital there were four rows of cars, two police cars and a military lorry. Joady's ward was on the ground floor. He was in a corner near a window facing an old man with bad color and a caved-in mouth. In over thirty years Boyle had never seen Joady without his cap. Sitting up now in bed like an old woman, with a white domed head and drained face, he looked like Dinny's ghost shaved and shrunk in regulation pajamas. He shook hands with Boyle and pointed at Dinny's bottle: "What's in that?"

"Lucozade," Dinny said.

"Poison."

"It's recommended for a sick body."

"Rots the insides; you can drop it out the windy."

"I'll keep it," Dinny said, "I can use it."

Boyle could see that Dinny was offended, and remembered his aunt's anger one Christmas long ago. She had knit a pair of wool socks for Joady and asked him about them.

"Bad wool, Miss," he said, "out through the heel in a week, I dropped them in the fire."

She was near tears as she told his mother: "Ungrateful, lazy, spiteful little men, small wonder Protestants despise them and us, and the smell in that house . . . you'd think with nothing else to do but draw the dole and sit by the fire the least they could do is wash themselves: as for religion, no Mass, no altar, nothing ever, they'll burn, they really will, and someone should tell them. God knows you don't want thanks, but to have it flung back in your teeth like that it's . . ."

"It's very trying, Annie," his mother said.

And Boyle wanted to say to his aunt: "No light, no water, no work, no money, nothing all their days but the dole, fire poking, neighbor baiting, and the odd skite on porter, retched off that night in a ditch."

"Communists," his aunt mocked Joady, "I know what real Communists would do with those boyos, what Hitler did with the Jews."

"Annie, that's an awful thing to say."

There was a silence and then his aunt said: "God forgive me, it is, but . . ." and then she wept.

"Because she never married, and the age she's at," his mother said afterwards.

Joady was pointing across a square of winter lawn to the hospital entrance: "Fornent them cars," he said, "the morgue." His eyes swiveled round the ward, "I heard nurses talk about it in the corridor, brought them here in plastic bags from Trillick, laid them out on slabs in a go of sawdust on account of the blood. That's what they're at now, Army doctors tryin' to put the bits together, so's their people can recognize them, and box them proper."

The old man opposite groaned and shifted. Joady's voice dropped still lower: "They say one man's head couldn't be got high or low, they're still tramping the mountain with searchlights."

"Dear God," Boyle said.

"A fox could nip off with a man's head handy enough."

"If it came down from a height it could bury itself in that ould spongy heather and they'd never find it or less they tripped over it."

"Bloodhound dogs could smell it out."

"They wouldn't use bloodhound dogs on a job like that, wouldn't be proper."

"Better nor lavin' it to rot in a bog, course they'd use dogs, they'd have to."

"Stop!"

Across the ward the old man was trying to elbow himself up. The air was wheezing in and out of his lungs, he seemed to be choking: "Stop! Oh God, God, please, I must go . . . I must . . ."

Boyle stood up and pressed the bell near Joady's bed. Visitors round other beds stopped talking. The wheezing got louder, more irregular, and a voice said: "Someone do something."

Another said: "Get a doctor."

Boyle said: "I've rung."

A male nurse came and pulled a curtain round the bed. When a doctor came the man was dead. He was pushed away on a trolley covered with a white sheet. Gradually people round other beds began to talk. A young girl looking sick was led out by a woman.

"That's the third carted off since I come down here."

"Who was he?" Boyle asked.

"John Willie Foster, a bread server from beyont Five-mile town, started in to wet the bed like a child over a year back, they couldn't care for him at home, so they put him to 'Silver Springs,' the ould people's home, but he got worse there so they packed him off here."

"Age," Dinny said, "the heart gave up."

"The heart broke," Joady said, "no one come to see him, bar one neighbor man. He was towld he could get home for a day or two at Christmas, no one come, he wouldn't spake with no one, couldn't quit' cryin'; the man's heart was broke."

"Them Probsbyterians is a hard bunch, cauld, no nature."

There was a silence.

"Did he say what about you Joady? . . . the surgeont?"

"No."

"You asked?"

" 'A deep operation,' he said, 'very deep, an obstruction,' so I said 'Is there somethin' rotten, sir, I want to know, I want to be ready?' 'Ready for what,' says he and smiles, but you can't tell what's at the back of a smile like that. 'Just ready,' I said.

" 'You could live longer nor me,' says he.

"He hasn't come next nor near me since I've come down here to the ground . . . did he tell yous anythin?"

"Dam' to the thing," Dinny said.

And Boyle noticed that Joady's eyes were glassy.

There was a newspaper open on the bed. It showed the Duke of Kent beside an armored car at a shattered customs post. On the top of the photograph the name of the post read "Kilclean." Boyle picked up the newspaper, opened it, and saw headlines: "Significance of bank raids"; "Arms for Bogsiders"; "Failure to track murderer"; "Arms role of I.R.A."

He read, skipping half, half listening to the brothers.

"Insofar as ordinary secret service work is concerned, could be relied on and trusted . . . under the control of certain ministers. Reliable personnel . . . cooperation between Army intelligence and civilian intelligence . . . no question of collusion."

"Lies," Joady said to Dinny, "you don't know who to believe." His voice was odd and his hand was trembling on the bedspread. Boyle didn't want to look at his face and thought, probably has it and knows. Dinny was looking at the floor.

"Lies," Joady said again. And this time his voice sounded better. Boyle put down the paper and said: "I hear you got blood, Joady."

"Who towld you that?"

"One of my past pupils, a nurse here."

"Three pints," Joady said.

Boyle winked and said: "Black blood, she told me you got Paisley's blood."

Joady began shaking, his mouth opened and he seemed to be dry-retching. The laughter when it came was pitched and hoarse. He put a hand on his stitches and stopped, his breathing shallow, his head going like a picaninny on a mission box.

"Paisley's blood, she said that?"

"She did."

"That's tarror," he said, but was careful not to laugh again. Boyle stood up and squeezed his arm: "We'll have to go, Joady, next time can we bring you something you need?"

"Nothin'," Joady said, "I need nothin'."

Walking the glass-walled, rubber corridor Boyle said: "I'll wait in the car, Dinny."

Dinny stopped and looked at the bottle of Lucozade: "We could see him together."

"If you want."

The surgeon detached a sheet of paper from a file, he faced them across a steel-framed table: "In your brother's case," he was saying to Dinny, "it's late, much, much, too late." He paused, no one said anything and then the surgeon said: "I'm afraid so."

"Dying?"

"It's terminal."

"He's not in pain," Boyle said.

"And may have none for quite a while, when the stitches come out he'll be much better at home."

"He doesn't know," Dinny said.

"No, I didn't tell him yet."

"He wants to know."

The surgeon nodded and made a note on a sheet of paper. Dinny asked: "How long has he got, sir?"

The surgeon looked at the sheet of paper as though the death date were inscribed: "Sometime this year ... yes, I'm afraid so."

The Anglia and bicycles were gone now. It had grown dark about the bridge and along the river. Boyle was cold sitting on the wall. Dinny had been talking for half an hour: "He was never sick a day, and five times I've been opened, lay a full year with a bad lung above at Killadeas; he doesn't know what it is to be sick."

Raucous crow noise carried up from the trees around the Spade Mill, cawing, cawing, cawing, blindflapping in the dark. They looked down, listening, waiting, it ceased. "He knows about dying," Boyle said.

"That's what I'm comin' at, he's dyin' and sleeps twelve hours of the twenty-four, ates, smokes, walks, and for a man used never talk much, he talks the hind leg off a pot now, make your head light to hear him."

He took out a glass phial: "I take two of them sleeping caps every night since he come home, and never close an eye. I can't keep nothin' on my stomach, and my skin itches all over; I sweat night and day. I'll tell you what I think: livin's worse nor dyin', and that's a fact."

"It's upsetting, Dinny."

It was dark in the kitchen: Joady gave Boyle a stool, accepted a cigarette, and lit it from the paraffin lamp, his face sharp and withered: a frosted crab.

"Where's the other fella gone?"

"I'm not sure," Boyle said, "he went down the river somewhere."

Joady sucked on the cigarette: "McCaffreys, he's gone to McCaffreys, very neighborly these times, he'll be there until twelve or after."

He thrust at a blazing sod with a one-pronged pitchfork: "Same every night since I come home, away from the house every chance he gets."

"All the visitors you have, Joady, and he's worried."

"Dam' the worry, whingin' and whinin' to every slob that passes the road about *me* snorin' the night long, didn't I hear him with my own ears . . ."

He spat, his eyes twisting: "It's *him* that snores not *me*, him:

it's *me* that's dyin', *me,* not him . . . Christ's sake . . . couldn't he take a back sate until I'm buried."

He got up and looked out the small back window at the night, at nothing: "What would you call it, when your own brother goes contrary, and the ground hungry for you . . . eh! Rotten, that's what I'd call it, rotten."

John McGahern (1934–   )

John McGahern was born in Dublin in 1934, though he was raised in the west of Ireland. A schoolteacher until his second novel, The Dark *(1965), was banned and caused him to lose his job, he now earns his living writing and lecturing. With his first novel,* The Barracks *(1963), he showed promise as one of the major writers of his generation, a promise he has largely fulfilled with* The Dark, *and with three other novels,* The Leavetaking *(1974),* The Pornographer *(1979), and* Amongst Women *(1990); and with three collections of short stories,* Nightlines *(1970),* Getting Through *(1978), and* High Ground *(1985). His* Collected Stories *was published in 1992. "All Sorts of Impossible Things" is taken from* Getting Through.

All Sorts of Impossible Things

They were out coursing on Sunday a last time together but they did not know it, the two friends, James Sharkey and Tom Lennon, a teacher and an agricultural instructor. The weak winter sun had thawed the fields soft enough to course the hare on, and though it still hung blood-orange above the hawthorns on the hill the rims of the hoof tracks were already hardening fast against their tread.

The hounds walked beside them on slip leashes: a purebred fawn bitch that had raced under the name of Coolcarra Queen, reaching the Final of the Rockingham Stakes the season before;

and a wire-haired mongrel, no more than half hound, that the schoolmaster, James Sharkey, borrowed from Charlie's bar for these Sundays. They'd been beating up the bottoms for some hours, and odd snipe, exploding out of the rushes before zigzagging away, was all that had risen.

"If we don't rise something before long we'll soon have to throw our hats at it," Tom Lennon said, and it was a careless phrase. No one had seen the teacher without his eternal brown hat for the past twenty years. "I've been noticing the ground harden all right," the dry answer came.

"Anyhow, I'm beginning to feel a bit humped," Tom Lennon looked small and frail in the tightly belted white raincoat.

"There's no use rimming it, then. There'll be other Sundays."

Suddenly a large hare rose ahead, bounded to the edge of the rushes, and then looped high to watch and listen. With a "Hulla, hulla," they slipped the hounds, the hare racing for the side of the hill. The fawn bitch led, moving in one beautiful killing line as she closed with the hare, the head eellike as it struck; but the hare twisted away from the teeth, and her speed carried the fawn past. The hare had to turn again a second time as the mongrel coming up from behind tried to pick it in the turn. The two men below in the rushes watched in silence as the old dance played itself out on the bare side of the hill: race, turn, race again; the hounds hunting well together, the mongrel making up with cunning what he lacked in grace, pacing himself to strike when the hare was most vulnerable—turning back from the fawn. But with every fresh turn the hare gained, the hounds slithering past on the hard ground. They were utterly beaten by the time the hare left them, going away through the hedge of whitethorns.

"They picked a warrior there."

"That's for sure," Tom Lennon answered as quietly.

The beaten hounds came disconsolately down, pausing at the foot of the hill to lap water from a wheelmark and to lick their paws. They came on towards the men. The paws were bleeding and some of the bitch's nails were broken.

"Maybe we shouldn't have raced her on such hard ground," the teacher said by way of apology.

"That's no difference. She'll never run in the Stakes again. They say there's only two kinds to have—a proper dud or a champion. Her kind, the in-between, are the very worst. They'll always run well enough to tempt you into having another go. Anyhow, there's not the money for that anymore," he said with a sad smile of reflection.

Coolcarra Queen was a relic of his bachelor days that he hadn't been able to bear parting with on getting married and first coming to the place as temporary agricultural instructor.

They'd raced her in the Stakes. She'd almost won. They'd trained her together, turn and turn about. And that cold wet evening, the light failing as they ran off the Finals, they'd stood together in the mud beside the net of torn hares and watched this hare escape into the laurels that camouflaged the pen, and the judge gallop towards the rope on the old fat horse, and stop, and lift the white kerchief instead of the red. Coolcarra Queen had lost the Rockingham Silver Cup and twenty-five pounds after winning the four races that had taken her to the Final.

"Still, she gave us a run for our money," the teacher said as they put the limping hounds on the leashes and turned home.

"Well, it's over now," Tom Lennon said. "Especially with the price of steak."

"Your exams can't be far off now?" the teacher said as they walked. The exams he alluded to were to determine whether the instructor should be made permanent or let go.

"In less than five weeks. The week after Easter."

"Are you anxious about it all?"

"Of course," he said sadly. "If they make me permanent I get paid whether I'm sick or well. They can't get rid of me then. Temporary is only all right while you're single."

"Do you foresee any snags?"

"Not in the exams. I know as much as they'll know. It's the medical I'm afraid of."

"Still," the teacher began lamely and couldn't go on. He knew that the instructor had been born with his heart on the wrong side and it was weak.

"Not that they'll pay much heed to instruction round here. Last week I came on a pair of gentlemen during my rounds. They'd roped a horse mower to a brand-new Ferguson. One was driving the Ferguson, the other sitting up behind on the horse machine, lifting and letting down the blade with a piece of wire. They were cutting thistles."

"That's the form all right," the teacher smiled.

They'd left the fields and had come to the stone bridge into the village. Only one goalpost stood upright in the football field. Below them the sluggish Shannon flowed between its wheaten reeds.

"Still, we must have walked a good twelve miles today from one field to the next. While if we'd to walk that distance along a straight line of road it'd seem a terrible journey."

"A bit like life itself," the teacher laughed sarcastically, adjusting the brown hat firmly on his head. "We might never manage it if we had to take it all in the one gasp. We mightn't even manage to finish it."

"Well, it'd be finished for us then," the instructor countered weakly.

"Do you feel like coming to Charlie's for a glass?" he asked as they stood.

"I told her I'd be back for the dinner. If I'm in time for the dinner she might have something even better for me afterwards," Tom Lennon joked defensively.

"She might indeed. Well, I have to take this towser back to Charlie anyhow. Thanks for the day."

"Thanks yourself," Tom Lennon said.

*   *   *

Above the arms of the stone wall the teacher watched the frail little instructor turn up the avenue towards the Bawn, a straggling rectangular building partly visible through the bare trees, where he had rooms in the tower, all that was left of the old hall.

Charlie was on his stool behind the bar with the Sunday paper when the teacher came with the mongrel through the partition. Otherwise the bar and shop were empty.

"Did yous catch anything?" he yawned as he put aside the paper, drawing the back of his hands over his eyes like a child. There was a dark stain of hair oil behind him on the whitewash where sometimes he leaned his head and slept when the bar was empty.

"We roused only one and he slipped them."

"I'm thinking there's only the warriors left by this time of year," he laughed, and when he laughed the tip of his red nose curled up in a way that caused the teacher to smile with affection.

"I suppose I'll let the old towser out the back?"

Charlie nodded. "I'll get one of the children to throw him some food later." When the door was closed again he said in a hushed, solicitous voice, "I suppose, Master, it'll be whiskey?"

"A large one, Charlie," the teacher said.

In a delicious glow of tiredness from the walking, and the sensuous burning of the whiskey as it went down, he was almost mindless in the shuttle back and forth of talk until he saw Charlie go utterly still. He was following each move his wife made at the other end of the house. The face was beautiful in its concentration, reflecting each move or noise she made as clearly as water will the drifting clouds. When he was satisfied that there was no sudden danger of her coming up to the bar he turned to the shelves. Though the teacher could not see past the broad back, he had witnessed the little subterfuge so often that he could follow it in exact detail: the silent unscrewing of the bottle cap, the quick tip of the whiskey into the glass, the

silent putting back of the cap, and the downing of the whiskey
in one gulp, the movements so practiced that it took but seconds. Coughing violently, he turned and ran the water and
drank the glass of water into the coughing. While he waited
for the coughing to die, he rearranged bottles on the shelves.
The teacher was so intimate with the subterfuge that he might
as well have taken part in the act of murder or of love. "If I'm
home in time for the dinner she might have something even
better for me afterwards," he remembered with resentment.

"Tom didn't come with you?" Charlie asked as soon as he
brought the fit of coughing under control.

"No. He was done in with the walking and the wife was expecting him."

"They say he's coming up for permanent soon. Do you think
he will have any trouble?"

"The most thing he's afraid of is the medical."

Charlie was silent for a while, and then he said, "It's a quare
caper that, isn't it, the heart on the wrong side?"

"There's many a quare caper, Charlie," the teacher replied.
"Life itself is a quare caper if you ask me."

"But what'll he do if he doesn't get permanent?"

"What'll we all do, Charlie?" the teacher said inwardly, and
as always when driven in to reflect on his own life, instinctively
fixed the brown hat more firmly on his head.

Once he did not bother to wear a hat or a cap over his thick
curly fair hair even when it was raining. And he was in love
then with Cathleen O'Neill. They'd thought time would wait
for them forever as they went to the sea in his baby Austin or
to dances after spending Sundays on the river. And then, suddenly, his hair began to fall out. Anxiety exasperated desire to a
passion, the passion to secure his life as he felt it all slip away,
to moor it to the woman he loved. Now it was her turn to linger. She would not marry him and she would not let him go.

"Will you marry me or not? I want an answer one way or

the other this evening." He felt his whole life like a stone on the edge of a boat out on water.

"What if I don't want to answer?" They were both proud and iron-willed.

"Then I'll take it as no."

"You'll have to take it whatever way you want, then." Her face was flushed with resentment.

"Good-bye, then." He steeled himself to turn away.

Twice he almost paused but no voice calling him back came. At the open iron gate above the stream he did pause. "If I cross it here it is the end. Anything is better than the anguish of uncertainty. If I cross here I cannot turn back even if she should want." He counted till ten, and looked back, but her back was turned, walking slowly uphill to the house. As she passed through the gate he felt a tearing that broke as an inaudible cry.

No one ever saw him afterwards without his brown hat, and there was great scandal the first Sunday he wore it in the body of the church. The man kneeling next to him nudged him, gestured with his thumb at the hat, but the teacher did not even move. Whispers and titters and one hysterical whinny of laughter that set off a general sneeze ran through the congregation as he unflinchingly wore it through the service.

The priest was up to the school just before hometime the very next day. They let the children home early.

"Have you seen Miss O'Neill recently, Jim?" the priest opened cautiously, for he liked the young teacher, the most intelligent and competent he had.

"No, Father. That business is finished."

"There'd be no point in me putting in a word?"

"There'd be no point, Father."

"I'm sorry to hear that. It's no surprise. Everything gets round these parts in a shape."

"In a shape, certainly, Father." There was dry mockery in the voice.

"When it gets wild it is different, when you hear talk of nothing else—and that's what has brought me up. What's going the rounds now is that you wore your hat all through Mass yesterday."

"They were right for once, Father."

"I'm amazed."

"Why, Father?"

"You're an intelligent man. You know you can't do that, Jim."

"Why not, Father?"

"You don't need me to tell you that it'd appear as an extreme form of disrespect."

"If the church can't include my own old brown hat, it can't include very much, can it, Father?"

"You know that and I know that, but we both know that the outward shows may least belie themselves. It'd not be tolerated."

"It'll have to be tolerated, Father, or . . ."

"You can't be that mad. I know you're the most intelligent man round here."

"Thanks, Father. All votes in that direction count round here. 'They said I was mad and I said they were mad, and confound them they outvoted me,' " he quoted. "That's about it, isn't it, Father?"

"Ah, stop it, Jim. Tell me why. Seriously, tell me why."

"You may have noticed recently, Father," he began slowly, in rueful mockery, "a certain manifestation that my youth is ended. Namely, that I'm almost bald. It had the effect of *timor mortis*. So I decided to cover it up."

"Many lose their hair. Bald or grey, what does it matter? We all go that way."

"So?"

"When I look down from the altar on Sunday half the heads on the men's side are bald."

"The women must cover their crowning glory and the men

must expose their lack of a crown. So that's the old church in her wisdom bringing us all to heel?"

"I can't understand all this fooling, Jim."

"I'm deadly serious. I'll wear my hat in the same way as you wear your collar, Father."

"But that's nonsense. It's completely different."

"Your collar is the sublimation of *timor mortis,* what else is it, in Jesus Christ. All I'm asking is to cover it up."

"But you can't wear it all the time?"

"Maybe not in bed but that's different."

"Listen. This joking has gone far enough. I don't care where you wear your hat. That's your problem. But if you wear it in church you make it my problem."

"Well, you'll have to do something about it then, Father."

The priest went very silent but when he spoke all he said was: "Why don't we lock up the school? We can walk down the road together."

What faced the priest was alarmingly simple: he couldn't have James Sharkey at Mass with his hat on and he couldn't have one of his teachers not at Sunday Mass. Only late that night did a glimmer of what might be done come to him. Every second Sunday the teacher collected coins from the people entering the church at a table just inside the door. If the collection table was moved out to the porch and Sharkey agreed to collect the coins every Sunday, perhaps he could still make his observances while keeping his infernal hat on. The next morning he went to the administrator.

"By luck we seem to have hit on a solution," he was able to explain to the teacher that evening.

"That's fine with me. I never wanted to be awkward," the teacher said.

"You never wanted to be awkward," the priest exploded. "You should have heard me trying to convince the administrator this morning that it was better to move the table out into the porch than to move you out of the school. I've never seen a man so angry in my life. You'd have got short shrift, I'm telling you, if you were in his end of the parish. Tell me, tell me what would you have done if the administrator had got his way and fired you?"

"I'd have got by somehow. Others do," he answered.

And soon people had got so used to the gaunt face under the brown hat behind the collection table every Sunday that they'd be as shocked now to see him without it after all the years as they had been on the first Sunday he wore it.

"That's right, Charlie. What'll we all do?" he repeated as he finished the whiskey beside the oil heater. "Here. Give us another drop before the crowd start to come in and I get caught."

"My brown hat and his heart on the wrong side, and you tippling away secretly when the whole parish including your wife knows it. It's a quare caper indeed, Charlie," he thought as he quickly finished his whiskey to avoid getting caught by the crowd due to come in.

There was no more coursing together again after that Sunday. The doctor's car was parked a long time outside the white gate that led to the Bawn the next day, and when Tom Lennon's old Ford wasn't seen around the roads that day or the next or the next the teacher went to visit him, taking a half bottle of whiskey. Lennon's young wife, a warm soft country girl of few words, let him in.

"How is he?" he asked.

"The doctor'll be out again tomorrow," she answered timidly and led him up the creaky narrow stairs. "He'll be delighted to see you. He gets depressed not being able to be up and about."

From the circular room of the tower that they used as a living room he could hear happy gurgles of the baby as they

climbed the stairs, and as soon as she showed him into the bedroom she left. In the pile of bedclothes Tom Lennon looked
smaller and more frail than he usually did.

"How is the patient?"

"Fed up," he said. "It's great to see a face after staring all day
at the ceiling."

"What is it?"

"The old ticker. As soon as I'd eaten after getting home on
Sunday it started playing me up. Maybe I overdid the walking.
Still, it could be worse. It'd be a damned sight worse if it had
happened in five weeks' time. Then we'd be properly in the
soup."

"You have oodles of time to be fit for the exam," the teacher
said, hiding his dismay by putting the whiskey down on the
dressing table. "I brought this little something." There was, he
felt, a bloom of death in the room.

"You never know," the instructor said some hours later as
the teacher took his leave. "I'm hoping the doctor'll have me
up tomorrow." He'd drunk only a little of the whiskey in a
punch his wife had made, while the hatted man on the chair
slowly finished his own half bottle neat.

The doctor did not allow him up that week or the next, and
the teacher began to come every evening to the house, and two
Sundays later he asked to take the hounds out on his own. He
did not cross the bridge to the Plains as they'd done the Sunday
together but went along the river to Doireen. The sedge of the
long lowlands rested wheaten and dull between two hills of
hazel and briar in the warm day. All winter it had been flooded
but the pale dead grass now crackled under his feet like tinder.
He beat along the edges of the hills, feeling that the hares
might have come out of the scrub to sleep in the sun, and as he
beat he began to feel Tom Lennon's absence like his own
lengthening shadow on the pale sedge.

The first hare didn't get more than halfway from where it

was lying to the cover of the scrub before the fawn's speed caught it, a flash of white belly fur as it rolled over, not being able to turn away from the teeth in the long sedge, and the terror of its crying as both hounds tore it began. He wrested the hare loose and stilled the weird childlike crying with one blow. Soon afterwards a second hare fell in the same way. From several parts of the river lowland he saw hares looping slowly out of the warm sun into the safety of the scrub. He knew they'd all have gone in then, and he turned back for Charlie's. He gave one of the hares to Charlie; the other he skinned and took with him to Tom Lennon's.

"Do you know what I'm thinking?" he said that night. "I'm thinking that I should take the bitch."

He saw sudden fear in the sick man's eyes.

"You know you're always welcome to borrow her any time you want."

"It's not that," he said quickly. "I thought just to take her until you're better. I could feed her. It'd be no trouble. It'd take some of the weight off the wife." And that evening when he left he took the bitch who was excited, thinking that she was going hunting again, though it was dark, and she rose to put paws on his shoulders and to lick his face.

She settled in easily with the teacher. He made a house for her out of a scrapped Ford in the garden but he still let her sleep in the house, and there was a lighter spring in his walk each evening he left school, knowing the excitement with which he would be met as soon as he got home. At night he listened to Tom Lennon's increasingly feverish grumblings as the exam drew closer. And he looked so angry and ill the night after the doctor had told him he could put all thought of the exam out of his mind that the suspicion grew stronger in the teacher's mind that his friend might not after all be just ill.

"What are you going to do?" he asked fearfully.

"Do the exam, of course." There was determination as well as fear in the sunken eyes.

"But you can't do it if the doctor said you weren't fit."

"Let's put it this way," the sick man laughed in harsh triumph, "I can't *not* do it."

The night before the exam he asked the teacher to bring up the clippers. He wanted a haircut. And that night as the teacher wrapped the towel round the instructor's neck and took the bright clippers out of their pale green cardboard box, adjusting the combs, and started to clip, the black hair dribbling down on the towel, he felt for the first time ever a mad desire to remove his hat and stand bareheaded in the room, as if for the first time in years he felt himself in the presence of something sacred.

"That's a great job," Tom Lennon said afterwards. "You know while we're at it, I might as well go the whole hog, and shave as well."

"Do you want me to get you some hot water?"

"That wouldn't be too much trouble?"

"No trouble at all."

Downstairs as they waited for the water to boil, the wife in her quiet voice asked him, "What do you think?"

"He seems determined on it. I tried to talk him out of it but it was no use."

"No. It doesn't seem any use," she said. A starched white shirt and blue suit and tie were draped across a chair one side of the fire.

The teacher sat on the bed's edge and held the bowl of water steady while the instructor shaved. When he finished, he examined himself carefully in the little hand mirror, and joked, "It's as good as for a wedding."

"Maybe it's too risky. Maybe you should send in a certificate. There'll be another chance."

"No. That's finished. I'm going through with it. It's my last chance. There'll be no other chance. If I manage to get made permanent there'd be a weight off my mind and it'd be better than a hundred doctors and tonics."

"Maybe I should give the old car a swing in readiness for the morning, so?"

"That'd be great." The instructor fumbled for his car keys in his trouser pockets on the bed rail.

The engine was cold but started on the sixth or seventh swing. In the cold starlit night he stood and listened to the engine run.

"Good luck, old Tom," he said quietly as he switched it off and took the car keys in.

"Well, good luck tomorrow. I hope all goes well. I'll be up as soon as I see the car back to find out how it went," he said in a singsong voice he used with the children at school in order not to betray his emotion after telling him that the Ford was running like a bird.

Tom Lennon rose the next morning as he said he would, dressed in his best clothes, had tea, told his wife not to worry and that he'd be back about six, somehow got as far as the car, and fell dead over the starting handle the teacher had left in the engine from the previous night.

When word was brought to the school, all the hatted man did was bow his head and murmur, "Thanks." He knew he had been expecting the death for some days. And when he went to the Bawn a last time he felt no terror of the stillness of the brown habit, the folded hands, but only a certain amazement that it was the agricultural instructor who was lying there not he. Two days later his hat stood calmly among the scarved women and bareheaded men about the open grave, and when it was over he went back to Charlie's. The bar was filled with mourners from the funeral-making holiday. A silence seemed to fall as the brown hat came through the partition, but only for a moment. They were arguing about a method of sowing winter wheat that the dead man used to advocate. Some thought it made sense. Others said it would turn out to be a disaster.

"Your old friend won't hunt again," Charlie said as he handed him the whiskey. The voice was hushed. The eyes stared inquiringly but respectfully into the gaunt face beneath the hat. The small red curl of the nose was still.

"No. He'll not hunt again."

"They say herself and the child is going home with her own people this evening. They'll send a van up later for the furniture." His voice was low as a whisper at the corner of the bar.

"That makes sense," the teacher said.

"You have the bitch still?" Charlie asked.

"That's right. I'll be glad to keep her, but the wife may want to take her with her."

"That'll be the least of her troubles. She'll not want."

"Will you have something yourself?" the teacher invited.

"All right then, Master," he paused suddenly. "A quick one then. We all need a little something in the open today," and he smiled an apologetic, rueful smile in his small eyes; but he downed the whiskey, as quickly running a glass of water and drinking it into the coughing as if it hadn't been in the open at all.

The fawn jumped in her excitement on her new master when he finally came home from the funeral. As he petted her down, gripping her neck, bringing his own face down to hers, thinking how he had come by her, he felt the same rush of feeling as he had felt when he watched the locks of hair fall onto the towel round the neck in the room; but instead of prayer he now felt a wild longing to throw his hat away and walk round the world bareheaded, find some girl, not necessarily Cathleen O'Neill, but any young girl, and go to the sea with her as he used to, leave the car at the harbor wall and take the boat for the island, the engine beating like a good heart under the deck boards as the waves rocked it on turning out of the harbor, hold her in one long embrace all night between the hotel sheets; or train the fawn again, feed her the best steak from town, walk her four miles every day for months, stand in the mud and rain again and see her as Coolcarra Queen race through the field in the Rockingham Stakes, see the judge gallop over to the rope on the old fat horse, and this time lift high the red kerchief to give the Silver Cup to Coolcarra Queen.

And until he calmed, and went into the house, his mind raced with desire for all sorts of such impossible things.

FOR THE BEST IN PAPERBACKS, LOOK FOR THE

In every corner of the world, on every subject under the sun, Penguin represents quality and variety—the very best in publishing today.

For complete information about books available from Penguin—including Puffins, Penguin Classics, and Arkana—and how to order them, write to us at the appropriate address below. Please note that for copyright reasons the selection of books varies from country to country.

In the United Kingdom: Please write to *Dept. JC, Penguin Books Ltd, FREEPOST, West Drayton, Middlesex UB7 0BR.*

If you have any difficulty in obtaining a title, please send your order with the correct money, plus ten percent for postage and packaging, to *P.O. Box No. 11, West Drayton, Middlesex UB7 0BR*

In the United States: Please write to *Consumer Sales, Penguin USA, P.O. Box 999, Dept. 17109, Bergenfield, New Jersey 07621-0120.* VISA and MasterCard holders call 1-800-253-6476 to order all Penguin titles

In Canada: Please write to *Penguin Books Canada Ltd, 10 Alcorn Avenue, Suite 300, Toronto, Ontario M4V 3B2*

In Australia: Please write to *Penguin Books Australia Ltd, P.O. Box 257, Ringwood, Victoria 3134*

In New Zealand: Please write to *Penguin Books (NZ) Ltd, Private Bag 102902, North Shore Mail Centre, Auckland 10*

In India: Please write to *Penguin Books India Pvt Ltd, 706 Eros Apartments, 56 Nehru Place, New Delhi 110 019*

In the Netherlands: Please write to *Penguin Books Netherlands bv, Postbus 3507, NL-1001 AH Amsterdam*

In Germany: Please write to *Penguin Books Deutschland GmbH, Metzlerstrasse 26, 60594 Frankfurt am Main*

In Spain: Please write to *Penguin Books S. A., Bravo Murillo 19, 1° B, 28015 Madrid*

In Italy: Please write to *Penguin Italia s.r.l., Via Felice Casati 20, I-20124 Milano*

In France: Please write to *Penguin France S. A., 17 rue Lejeune, F–31000 Toulouse*

In Japan: Please write to *Penguin Books Japan, Ishikiribashi Building, 2–5–4, Suido, Bunkyo-ku, Tokyo 112*

In Greece: Please write to *Penguin Hellas Ltd, Dimocritou 3, GR–106 71 Athens*

In South Africa: Please write to *Longman Penguin Southern Africa (Pty) Ltd, Private Bag X08, Bertsham 2013*